THE STRUGGLE

At Jack's first step, his right knee collapsed, and he noticed for the first time his torn and bloody jeans. Gritting his teeth, he pushed past pain to rise again and lumbered off, now nearly as clumsy as the man he pursued.

A wild, clearly female shriek hastened his footsteps and launched his heart into his throat.

"Reagan!"

He found them struggling on the ground between the boarded house and the near side of a bank of metal storage units. Sergio was on top of her, trying to pin her facedown while Reagan bucked frantically and fought to flip over.

"Get the hell off of her," Jack roared as he lunged forward.

The next moment splintered into shards that impaled themselves in his heart. Sergio's hand darting into the inner pocket of his jacket. The fist emerging with something that gleamed coldly beneath the security light. The distant shrilling of a siren, one Jack sensed could never come in time...

Other books by Colleen Thompson:

FATAL ERROR

FADE the HEAT

COLLEEN THOMPSON

LOVE SPELL

NEW YORK CITY

To the firefighters, EMTs, and paramedics who are there on our worst days, and especially to the crew of the Houston Fire Department, Station 6 "C."

LOVE SPELL®

December 2005

Published by

Dorchester Publishing Co., Inc.
200 Madison Avenue
New York, NY 10016

ISBN 0-505-52648-4

The name "Love Spell" and its logo are trademarks of Dorchester Publishing Co., Inc.

Printed in the United States of America.

Visit us on the web at www.dorchesterpub.com.

ACKNOWLEDGMENTS

I would like to express my heartfelt appreciation to a number of people who helped bring *Fade the Heat* from an idea to a finished novel.

First of all, thanks to my husband, Houston Firefighter Michael Thompson, for sharing the stories, the traditions, and the special bonds that connect the men and women of his department. Special thanks, too, to Acting Paramedic Supervisor Jim Turnbull for answering so many questions and allowing me to tag along throughout a memorable night shift. You'll both be happy to know I left out the part about the rat.

I would also like to express my appreciation to Detective Roben H. Talton of the Harris County Sheriff's Department for sharing her law enforcement expertise and to Bryony Aldous for research assistance. Any factual errors and omissions are my own.

On the writing front, I would like to thank agent Meredith Bernstein, who so ably represented the work, editor Alicia Condon, publicist Brianna Yamashita, and all the wonderful people from Dorchester Publishing.

Last but never least, I want to express my appreciation to the writing friends who never let me down. Thanks to Patricia Kay, Kathleen Y'Barbo, Barbara Taylor Sissel, Betty Joffrion, Linda Helman, and Wanda Dionne for their critiquing and their friendship. I am especially grateful, too, to Jo Anne Banker and the members of Northwest Houston and West Houston RWA for their encouragement and support. And a special thanks to my son, Andrew, for inspiring me to chase my dreams.

FADE the HEAT

Chapter One

"First, you gotta find the perfect bottle," said the Firebug, his voice a rasping whisper that hurt to listen to. "Too hard, and it won't bust when it hits the floor. Too thin, and it explodes on impact with the window, splashing you with fuel mix and burning you to hell."

The visitor leaning over his bed looked down into the noseless face, most of which was mercifully hidden by a thick compression garment. He didn't have to worry that the poor bastard would see him staring because the Firebug's eyelids had been seared off, too, and the burn-unit nurses bandaged whatever had been left behind them. Probably something that looked like a couple of freaking chunks of charcoal anyway.

Suppressing a shudder, the visitor asked, "So once you've found this perfect bottle, what do you put in there, other than the gas?"

When the Firebug tried to answer, the resulting hiss sounded like sand blown across a windshield.

"Water?" the visitor asked. Without waiting for an

answer, he grabbed a cup from the narrow bedside table and held it, though it made him want to puke to watch the man he'd idolized working the bent straw like a baby at a tit.

When he had finished, the Firebug said, "You want it to flare right up, but it don't do any good if it just flashes and goes out. Works best if you make it sticky, so it won't come off of stuff."

Such as flesh and bone . . . For the first time, the visitor noticed the way the Firebug's hands were bandaged, and realized that he must be missing fingers. Maybe all of them.

"And you gotta mix in something else, too," the injured man said. "Somethin' to keep things cooking for a while. Man can burn a tank that way. That's how they did it in the big war."

"What are you, the goddamn History Channel?" The visitor was itching to get the hell out of this place. It stank, for one thing, smelled like medicine and heavy-duty cleaners overlying an undisguisable whiff of human shit. "I just want the recipe, that's all."

"And I gotta have the details. A-all of them." The voice broke like a wave. "What do—what else do I have to live for? You tell me what you're gonna do, I'll help you. Otherwise—"

"You *don't* tell me, I'm gonna—"

"You're gonna do what? Kill me? Go ahead, I'd welcome it. Just tell me how you're gonna use the thing, for *God's* sake. Let me hear the flames speak one more time. Let me smell the smoke. You know you can trust me. You know I'll never say a word, and I'll tell you how to make the best Molotov cocktail this city's ever seen. Maybe the whole damned state of Texas."

The visitor nodded, forgetting the Firebug's blindness for the moment. "All right, then," he said, moving around to block the closed door with a chair. "I can tell you this much, and I swear I'll come back once it's over and give you every detail."

He heard the Firebug's breathing quicken, wouldn't be surprised if the pathetic son of a bitch was getting hard. Presuming his little mishap had left him anything to stiffen.

Swallowing back the thought, the visitor said, "I'm going to burn a man's apartment. And then I'm going to do the man himself. And he's a doctor, can you beat that? I guess I'm moving on up in this world."

Five-year-old Jaime Perez had taken exception to his vaccination shot. So much so that Dr. Jack Montoya's ears rang and his shin ached as he limped out of the exam room.

Gratefully, Jack closed the door on the boy's howls and silently blessed the poor mother, who was struggling to console him with the roll of stickers Jack had left her.

On his way to his next patient, Jack peeked past the reception counter and into the waiting room. There, a pack of tiny, dark-haired children shredded outdated magazines while exhausted-looking women pretended not to notice. Old men hawked into folded handkerchiefs, and a hugely pregnant woman was vomiting into a trash can. Adding to the mayhem, the TV hanging near the water-stained ceiling blared a Spanish-language game show no one watched.

Four-thirty and the crowd hadn't thinned a bit, despite the unseasonably cold October rain rattling against the skylights. Jack cursed the fellow doctor who'd walked out the day before, after he'd been held up at knifepoint in the parking lot at lunch. Jack knew he ought to be more sympathetic, but between the clinic's low pay and the neighborhood of derelict old houses, boarded-up *taquerias*, and rough-and-tumble bars, it could be months before they landed a replacement—if the hospital board didn't nix the position altogether in the latest round of budget cuts.

Hurrying to the next exam room, he grabbed the patient's chart. Before he could read it, the new nurse, Carlota Sanchez, flagged him down.

"Dr. Montoya, it's Mr. Winter—*Darren Winter*—on the line." Carlota's brown eyes were huge, and the hand covering the mouthpiece shook a little. Twenty-two and fresh from nursing school, she had been flashing Jack flirtatious smiles for weeks, which proved she hadn't been in the profession long enough to absorb the male-physicians-are-scum attitude embraced by so many of her fellow nurses.

This afternoon, however, Carlota was obviously flustered by the media frenzy that had focused upon Jack. "Reporters have been calling here all day, and now he's on the air, *live*. Will you talk to him?"

Jack hesitated, thinking maybe he should take the call—and tell Houston talk radio's most overinflated ego where to shove his allegations. Or better yet, Jack could describe for the man's listeners the gut-wrenching horror of watching a child die of a treatable disease. Let them hear the details of the parents' pain, their suffering—and then ask *them* for suggestions on how to tell the next kid, "Sorry, it's against the law for me to help you. Your family came from Mexico illegally."

Jack would love hearing the man reporters were calling the next Schwarzenegger spin *that* to his would-be constituency. It probably wouldn't slow the momentum of Winter's listeners' attempts to help him steal next month's mayoral election with a highly publicized, if unofficial, write-in campaign—but it would feel so good to make the pompous jerk squirm, if only for a moment.

"I'd better not," Jack told Carlota, thinking of the hospital board instead. Since Winter had started his public tirades about the falsified medical records someone had leaked to him, Jack knew his job was on the line. Worse yet, it looked as if the board members might see the incident as the excuse they needed to shut down this chronically underfunded satellite clinic. And leave the kids that he'd been helping completely in the lurch.

Since he didn't have the luxury of venting his frustration, he took the wiser course, the one that led to his next patient. But after closing the exam-room door behind him and taking one look at the fair-skinned blonde who'd been waiting inside, he realized he'd been had. The shrewdness of her gaze all but shouted "Press."

"If Darren Winter or one of the newspapers sent you, you can get the hell out of my office," Jack told his unwelcome visitor, even as he breathed a silent prayer that the papers she held wouldn't prove to be copies of the additional files he'd been praying would stay hidden.

Amusement glinted in her blue eyes, and atop the exam table, she crossed long, jeans-clad legs. "Well, Montoya," she said, stifling a dry, constricted cough. "I'm surprised you're not in some fancy private practice, what with that brilliant bedside manner."

A grin slanted across model-perfect features—not that he could see her prancing down anybody's runway showing off the latest styles. Above the jeans, a faded blue T-shirt peeped out from beneath an unzipped and well-worn leather jacket. Her lace-up boots, too, looked as if she'd had them a long time. But no way did she live around here, not with that short, but feminine, precision haircut or the trio of tiny silver rings that ran along each earlobe.

Still, there was something familiar about her, something that reminded him of . . .

Feeling like an idiot, he glanced down at her chart, something he normally did before entering an exam room. His gaze fastened on the name across the top.

"Reagan Hurley," he read. Despite his troubles, he smiled at the rush of memory that followed. He hadn't seen her in twenty years, since she and her mother had left the city. "I was positive that by now you'd have married some bean counter in the burbs, where the two of you would live with three-point-two blond kiddies and a nice big dog to chase around the yard."

She laughed. "You've got the dog part right, but you're off on everything else, right down to the bit where I'm a reporter or some sort of spy. What's the deal with that?"

Jack shook his head. "Bad assumption. Sorry. There's been a little misunderstanding. People have been after me all week, and—" *And I'm going to answer for it Monday morning.* He pushed aside the thought, which had nagged at him since his supervisor's terse call a few days earlier.

"Forget it," she said before beginning to cough in earnest.

There was a choked quality to the sound Jack didn't like. But before he could ask about it, she handed him the paper she'd been holding.

"I really came to get this signed," she said. "It's a release for work. Just a formality, you know? Some stupid hoop they make you jump through."

Something in him unclenched when he saw the paper was what she claimed. Maybe nothing more *would* surface. Maybe whichever clinic employee had leaked the information had only found the one discrepancy.

Or maybe today's rash of reporter phone calls meant that someone, somewhere, already had the rest. Though needles of panic jabbed his stomach, he examined Reagan's form.

In the blank beside "Employer," he saw *City of Houston*. "Don't you have a regular doctor? Surely your insurance won't cover this clin—"

"Don't sweat it. I'll be paying cash today."

Alarm bells went off in his head, and resentment spiked through him at the thought of all the patients—*real* patients—out there waiting, while he and a single nurse practitioner struggled through an endless afternoon.

"So tell me about your pain," he prompted, because that was what such visits invariably came to. A wrenched back, pinched nerves, and a request for drugs to soothe them. He'd seen it far too often, but for reasons he could not explain, he felt especially disappointed this time.

She shook her head. "I damned well didn't drive over here on a day like this to worm some prescription out of you. I'm not in any pain, and I'm sure as hell no junkie."

Her anger sent a meteor-bright image arcing across his memory: that day near the secluded bayou bend when a girl in pigtails had played David, whacking the meanest Goliath their neighborhood—*this* neighborhood—had to offer between the eyes with a smooth stone. With a lump rising on his forehead and a fist-size rock clutched in his hand, Paulo Rodriguez and his bad-ass brothers might have killed her if Jack hadn't intervened. Still, eight-year-old Reagan hadn't backed down for a second.

Like him, would she carry that terrifying memory forever? Because whether she'd forgotten it or not, he saw that some of that old spirit lingered, no matter what her current problems.

"Then why were you off work?" he asked as he pulled a stethoscope from the pocket of his white coat. "That cough?"

She shrugged. "It's nothing but a cold. I get them— or allergies or something, especially on days like this. But I was sent home because I took a little smoke."

Over the heating system's noisy, if ineffectual, efforts, Jack heard the rasping sound her breathing made. After scanning the vitals recorded by the nurse—all normal—he glanced down at the questionnaire Reagan had filled out. It was the first one he'd seen written on the English side all day.

"You're a firefighter," he noted. "Like your father."

As she nodded, pride and pleasure warmed her features—and took Jack's breath away. He doubted she had any idea of the effect she had on men. Even on one doing his damnedest to remain professional.

"I had to pay a lot of dues first," she said. "Fire science degree, then three years working one of the department's ambulances as an EMT before I made it to a pumper like my dad rode. Only job I ever wanted."

He didn't doubt it one bit, after the way the department had rallied around the Hurleys when Reagan's father died. Jack wondered for a moment how different his life would have been had his family known such support when his own father was murdered in the blazing scrublands of South Texas. Pushing aside the uncomfortable thought, he said, "Let me have a listen to those lungs."

"You don't really need to—" she began, then stopped once he frowned at her. With a sigh, she peeled off her jacket and lifted her T-shirt to make his task easier.

As a physician, it was his job to notice bodies. Hers was lean and well formed. Beautiful, he thought, then shoved aside the unprofessional assessment. Athletic, he amended. Healthy-looking.

Yet, as he'd suspected, the sounds in her bronchial tubes didn't measure up. Now he was certain she'd heard about him on the radio and decided he would be an easy mark.

Scowling, he moved his stethoscope aside. "How many doctors did you go to before you heard about me?"

"I don't know what you mean," she said.

He tried staring her down, but she didn't flinch. He might have known.

"Like I said, I get colds," Reagan added, pulling down her shirt's hem. "And when I came across your name in the phone book, I thought I'd throw some business your way."

That remark sounded so implausible, he chose to ignore it. "Do you wake up nights with trouble breathing?"

She re-crossed her legs. "You can save the screening questions. I'll say no to all of them."

"You'll need a lung-function test," Jack told her. "Though I suspect you've taken one or two before. At least."

She slid off the end of the table. "So you're accusing me of what?"

"Wasting my time, for starters," Jack shot back.

"I spent two hours cooling my heels in your waiting room, so don't talk to me about wasting people's time."

"You've been diagnosed with asthma, right?" he demanded. "And after what you heard about my problems, you figured I'd be sympathetic. Because you need somebody understanding, someone who won't ask too many questions."

"What kind of bullshit—"

But he wasn't finished. "I'm guessing your lungs are bad enough to jeopardize your job. But you don't want to hear you're finished as a firefighter, so you're shopping for a doctor who'll say otherwise."

Pain flashed over her expression before it hardened into fury. "You're completely wrong about me. Again."

He had no idea what she meant, and he was not about to ask her. "Then take the test. But I'll have to send you over to the county hospital to do it. Neighborhood's gone downhill since you left here. We had a break-in last week. Someone made off with our spirometer."

"Forget it. I've had my fill of waiting for one day, and your bedside manner must be an acquired taste." She stuck her hand out. "If you'll just give me back my form . . ."

He held on to it and looked directly into her storm-blue eyes—trying to see past his hurt to the patient who now stood before him, a woman facing fear as well as a disease. "If I'm right about you, there are treatment options," he said, his voice gentler, "specialists to help manage your condition. I'd be happy to refer you to one of the leading pulmonologists in Hou—"

She grabbed her jacket before edging toward the door. "You always were too quick to judge,

Montoya—or at least to judge those of us who check the wrong box on the census form."

It took a moment to sink in that this woman was accusing him—*him*—of prejudice. He'd heard such things before, from black addicts looking for their next fix and even from fellow Hispanics who'd told him he wasn't Mexican enough. But hearing Reagan Hurley say it left him incapable of speech.

Now he was convinced that, just as he did, she remembered every detail of that day near the bayou. Even those he wished he could forget.

Before he could recover, she stepped out of the room. Glancing back over her shoulder, she said, "Keep the damned form. I've got others."

"A whole stack of them, I'll bet," Jack finally managed, but he had to say it to her back.

She was already disappearing from his life.

After a coughing jag triggered by the cold rain, Reagan looked up into the on-rushing steel grill of one damned big green car.

"What the hell?" Whirling out of the way, she threw herself against the spoiler of her beat-up blue Trans Am. Heart thudding against her chest, she called after the fleeing sedan, "Watch where you're going, jerk!"

Its dented hulk squealed around the corner before it disappeared, giving her only a fleeting glimpse of a guy with a black stocking cap pulled down around his ears. She hadn't thought to get the license plate until the car was gone.

On shaking legs, she climbed into the Trans Am, brushed the rain from her face, and cranked the protesting engine until it finally caught. As much as she wanted to tear off to get the moron's plates, her old car refused to cooperate, sputtering and dying no fewer than three times before she finally coaxed it out of the parking lot.

Let him go, she told herself. *Chasing him's not worth the trouble anyway.* The cops, she knew, would pay little heed to anything she told them, since the driver hadn't struck her. Besides, she had too much at stake to spend whatever was left of the day filling out a report that would go nowhere.

"Time to find another doctor," she breathed, her words sounding strange and shaky, as if she'd flung them into a spinning fan. She pulled into an empty spot in front of a long-closed gas station. After glancing around to make sure no one was watching, she removed an inhaler from her pocket.

It took three puffs to get her breath back, puffs she'd sworn to herself this morning she didn't really need. As she waited for the elephant to climb off her chest, she recalled Captain Rozinski—the captain her dad had worked for—telling her, *"I've known you for a lot of years now, kept an eye on you while you grew up. I'm saying this as your friend, not just your captain. Don't keep fighting for a job you can't do."*

Her eyelids burned, and she swallowed past a lump of pain.

"He's right," she said aloud, but the words faded to irrelevance against the images leaping through her brain. She saw herself scrambling onto the ladder truck, still pulling on her gear while lights flashed and the siren wound up; heard fire roaring, breaking above her head as flames flashed over. She soared with the high of hauling in a length of hose, blasting that inverted sea, and smothering the fatal orange waves. But it was so much more than an adrenaline addiction. It was the flood tide of relief she'd felt when an old woman she'd dragged clear of smoke coughed and breathed and lived to hear her grandchildren weeping their relief; the way it felt walking into the station at shift change and knowing she belonged. And it was the sense of connection to the father who had come before her, to Patrick Hurley, the man who had known things as she did. To sever that link, to allow it to ebb away with time, would be like losing him all over again.

Reagan's fingers clutched the wheel so hard they ached. *It can't be finished. I can't.*

"You damned sure are if you give up," she told herself, then flipped through the list of family doctors she'd left lying on the seat. Thirty seconds later, she found a listing for an office located off the next exit down the freeway.

She asked herself why not? But a quick glance at the time gave the reason. It was already 5:06 on Friday. She'd never find a physician in the office now.

Anger blasted past self-pity: anger at the doctors, with their banker's hours and their surreptitious glances at expensive watches as they delivered diagnoses guaranteed to trash a patient's life. And anger at Jack Montoya, who was supposed to be some sort of soft touch but had turned into one of their kind just the same, even if he wore a cheap digital instead.

But the fury that burned hottest was directed at herself, for allowing weakness to snatch away her future . . . and her last connection to a job that had become her life.

Using the back of her leather jacket's sleeve, she wiped away the single tear that had betrayed her. Defeated, she decided to drive home, at least for the time being. But as if it sensed the opportunity to make a bad day worse, the Trans Am stalled again.

She swore anew, hating the thought of taking it back to the shop, where her mechanic would joke that she was sending his three kids through college with the Blue Beast, as he called it. He'd advised her several times to put the old Pontiac out of its misery—or, more precisely, out of hers. But she'd had the car since high school, and Reagan got attached to things.

Besides, she didn't have the money to splurge on a new car—not after she'd used every penny she could scrape together for a down payment on her house, a bungalow in Houston's Heights neighborhood around the corner from a place her grandparents once owned. At the thought of her bank-account balances, she popped the dashboard hard enough to get the wipers slapping. The blow also started up the radio. Unfortunately, the tuner was stuck on the AM station carrying Darren Winter's drive-time show. Though she ought to know better—he usually said something infuriating every eight seconds or so—she turned it up to hear him over the defroster, which was blowing cold air against the steamed-up windshield.

"If we want our borders to mean anything and our economy preserved," an overconfident male voice urged listeners in major-market cities nationwide, *"we have to derail the border runners' gravy train. No access to employment. No education for their kids. And for God's sake, no free healthcare when they come down with the sniffles."*

She rubbed at her still-clouded windshield and wished she could funnel Winter's hot air through her defroster. Even though he wasn't an official candidate—apparently, political commentators weren't allowed to keep their jobs if they ran for office—it scared the hell out of Reagan to imagine his listeners succeeding in getting him elected mayor. She only prayed that once he got control of the city's multi-billion-dollar budget, he wouldn't do anything alarming with the fire department's share.

"Like with this Dr. Jack Montoya I've been telling you about," he began, just as Reagan had been about to cut him off. *"Or I should say* Joaquín *Montoya, the son of a man drowned trying to illegally cross the Rio Grande. No need to guess in which direction this doc's sympathies are skewed."*

"Leave his father out of this, you idiot," Reagan growled. "Or at least get your facts straight."

She'd heard around the old neighborhood that Antonio Montoya had been murdered by *coyotes* on his way to visit his widowed mother in Mexico. For years, Reagan had carried an image of a man savaged by a pack of animals, but as she grew older, she'd learned *coyote* was a name given to criminals who smuggled illegals across the borders. Vicious sons of bitches, they often led their charges to the desert, where they killed them for whatever money and valuables they carried.

"But the fact is," Winter continued, his outrage mounting with each word, *"Dr. Montoya of the East End Clinic doesn't have the luxury of setting policy—or ignoring state law, for that matter. Not when he's working for us, the taxpayers."*

Reagan had heard all this before, including the accusation that Jack had falsified a diagnosis so he could legally treat the child of undocumented workers. For asthma, of all things.

Not that it had made him one bit more sympathetic to Reagan's cause. Sympathetic, nothing—he'd been rude as hell. And to think she'd remembered the guy as a nice kid, the kind of boy who could inspire a younger girl to go squirmy in the stomach and imagine all sorts of stupid things. It just went to show that it didn't take a radio-show platform or political ambition to make a jerk of someone; apparently, having a handsome face and an M.D. tacked onto your name could effect the same result.

The loudmouth's voice grew in volume, as if the mix of ego and indignation had pumped up the wattage on her speakers. *"And I think it's high time this sort of bleeding-heart liberal got the message. Since he won't respond to me, I'd like to put you, my Winter Warriors, into action. I'm not telling anyone what to do, of course, but if several concerned citizens were to, say, visit www-dot-America-for-Americans-dot-com on the Internet, they might find personal contact information for a certain physician who has been—shall we say—'outed' by the fine webmaster, Ernest Rankin, whom many of you know from his frequent guest appearances. To remind Dr. Montoya he is working for you, the taxpayer, and not just any José who can swim a river, why not send him a personal message that we're onto him? Again, that web address is . . ."*

What was that reckless idiot suggesting? Reagan sucked in a startled breath, then exploded in another fit of coughing so hard her eyes teared.

By the time the sound subsided, her speakers bleated the cheesy theme music that let her know the Darren Winter show had just returned from its commercial break. Hammering the dashboard to turn off the radio, she shifted the car through its gears and headed toward her house, where Frank Lee, at least, would wag his tail to see her. Her warm, dry, brick kitchen would be waiting, and even in this weather, her windowsill herb garden would provide enough basil and oregano to throw together a kick-ass pasta dish.

If she could force herself to swallow it. Though she'd had nothing but a chalky-tasting energy bar since breakfast, the thought of cooking—and worse yet, eating—left her nauseated.

She tried to convince herself that things could be worse. Since her friend, rookie firefighter Beau LaRouche, was working, she could at least enjoy an evening free of his nonstop boasting about his paintball prowess or his ruminations about people at the high school both of them had attended years before. Besides, come Monday, she still had a couple hundred other doctors she could hit up for a signature. And unlike Jack Montoya, at least she wasn't going home to an answering machine that would be shorting out under the strain of irate messages from half the country, thanks to Winter and America-for-Americans-dot-com.

But when she ran inside from her detached garage and scooped up the ringing phone, the voice on the other end blew away whatever smugness she'd managed to scrape together.

"Hurley, hoped I'd catch you home." Captain Joe Rozinski's voice hadn't lost that stiff, official manner he'd adopted since she'd transferred to his station. If anything, he sounded more distant than ever.

As Reagan fended off her white greyhound's slobbery kisses, she wished, not for the first time, that she could have back the old captain, the one who had never forgotten her at Christmas or her birthdays, who had become a father to her since the horrible day he'd watched her dad die. But hearing the captain call her "Hurley" reminded Reagan that those days were gone forever—banished by far more than fear that the rest of the crew would accuse him of favoritism.

17

"I just had to pick up a few groceries," she said quickly. Technically, while off sick, a firefighter was required to call the captain for permission to leave home. She'd often enough heard Rozinski complain that he had better things to do than play hall monitor to sick firefighters, but Reagan wondered if, in light of their recent disagreement, he would crack down on her today.

"So you weren't at the doctor's, hunting up a signature?"

"Uh, no. I already got that taken care of," she lied, reasoning that by Thursday, when her crew returned for its next twenty-four-hour shift, she would have the issue covered.

"Really? Then you won't mind dropping by the station with it this evening," he suggested.

Cursing herself, Reagan wracked her brain for a suitable excuse. "I would," she told him, her heart doing a quickstep in her chest, "but I had to take my car in to the shop. I accidentally left the form inside. And besides, I don't have a ride right now."

"So how'd you get your groceries?"

Suddenly sweating, she slipped off her jacket. He knew damned well she was lying. The question was, which of them would blink first?

"Peaches took me after we dropped off the car," Reagan said, hoping the mention of her neighbor's name would convince Rozinski to drop the subject. Though the captain had witnessed scores of gory accidents and gruesome deaths during his thirty-two years in the department, he lost all power of speech when it came to Reagan's fun-loving neighbor.

Reagan supposed she should have warned the guys on her shift that despite her traffic-stopping curves, strawberry-blond bouffant, and world-class flirting skills, Peaches had been born James Paul Tarleton of Amarillo. But only days before Peaches stopped by the station, Reagan's co-workers had amused themselves on a frigid February night by encasing her Trans Am in ice, a mission they'd accomplished by repeatedly sneaking outdoors and misting it with a fire hose. They'd had a good laugh over the gag, but watching them make fools of themselves with Peaches had been worth every minute Reagan spent chipping and thawing her way into the car.

Despite her situation, the memory of their horrified reactions when they learned the truth about Peaches made Reagan grin.

"If you want," she added, "I'll give you Peaches's number. She'll be happy to confirm it, if she's not out shooting pictures." She waited, praying he would not want to risk the razzing he'd get if it got out that he had asked for Peaches's number.

"I'm working a debit day on Monday," Rozinski growled, referring to the extra shift each firefighter worked every three-and-a-half weeks. "Meet me here at the station at 0630—with the form and no excuses. Either that or I'll assume you're at the transfer office putting in for an ambulance position."

He wanted her to return to her old station, where she would spend the better part of her career ferrying headaches, head colds, and head cases to emergency rooms because the patients lacked the insurance—or the good sense—to visit their own doctors. He'd been after her for months about it, since it became apparent that her "colds" were more than that. And last week, when she had coughed so hard she'd been unable to climb a smoke-charged stairwell with her usual seventy pounds of gear, he had finally shouted at her, "*Go home, Hurley. Go home 'til you can do the job, or damn it, don't come back."*

Stung by the demand that she transfer, Reagan lashed out like a wounded animal. "I joined this department to fight fires, like my dad. I've worked for years to get into suppression. I can handle it."

He struck back with the most devastating weapon imaginable. "Your father would never try to hold on like this, wouldn't respect it either. You're not just dragging down yourself here. You're dragging down the crew. You have to stop this, Reagan, for your own good. You have to understand it's over. You're useless to us this way."

She wanted to shout that she would damned well show him who could do the job. Who was it who'd been known from the start for matching male rookies ax-stroke for ax-stroke—despite her slender, five-six frame—and fighting interior fires with a will? And who was it who'd represented the station in the women's boxing division of the annual clash with the cops the past two years? She wasn't finished, not by a long shot.

"If you don't get this problem of yours under control and you refuse to transfer, I'm going to report you as unfit for duty," Rozinski told her. "You and I both know you'll lose your job entirely if it comes to that."

Before she could protest, she heard an alarm go off at the station. She recognized the series of tones even before Rozinski said, "That's for us. I've gotta run."

He hung up, leaving her to imagine the crew—*her* crew—rushing to pull their gear on, climbing on the apparatus . . . and driving off to do the job without her.

Had she even left a hole when she'd gone? Or had they already filled it, with someone whole and strong?

As she set down the receiver, Frank Lee bounded over to the closet where she kept his leash and barked to let her know he'd had enough of waiting. Though she hated going back out into the weather, Reagan responded on autopilot, grabbing an old Astros cap, then leashing up the dog and exiting the front door to take him on his evening walk. She'd better cut it short, she realized as the rain rolled off the cap's brim. Though she'd just used her inhaler, she could feel her damned lungs twitching with the insult of the cold, damp air. But her feet weighed her down like anchors as the captain's words replayed in her head a dozen times.

As she fought the asthma's anaconda grip, she thought of her battle against Rozinski, her illness, and the medical community in general. And how, at 0630 Monday morning, the whole damned mess would come to a head.

She could cave in now or go down swinging, but Reagan Hurley was looking for an Option C . . . some passage through this firestorm that would help her fade the heat.

Chapter Two

Reagan was gone, Jack realized, off to find a quack—and he didn't delude himself into thinking they weren't plentiful—who would sign her damned release. So why, two hours later, was he still remembering her face?

Shivering in a denim jacket that had seemed adequate before this front blew in, he trotted through the rain to his chili-red Explorer, then gaped at what he saw.

A huge dent had caved in the driver's-side door, and the trim was lying mangled on the broken asphalt. Besides that, someone had made angry gouges on the three-year-old SUV's hood, maybe with a screwdriver . . . or a nail file.

"Damn it all," he said aloud, his suspicion settling on the woman who'd been on his mind. As he had followed her to the door to be certain she left without a fuss, hadn't she accused him of not caring that her life was being ruined? And she'd seemed furious enough to do almost anything to get even.

Well, wrecking his truck sure as hell wasn't going to

win him over to her cause. Jack shoved his damp hair from his eyes, surveyed the damage, and tried the crumpled door without success.

Swearing again, he thought of having Reagan Hurley arrested. The green streaks that stood out against the red paint would help identify the car that had hit his. When the cops found that her paint matched and heard his testimony about her behavior, they ought to . . .

He sighed, remembering the little girl who'd had grit enough to hurl rocks at Paulo—who weighed in at one-eighty at the age of thirteen—for his cruelty. Jack could still smell the lighter fluid, could still see the big bastard setting fire to his little brother's GI Joe and hear him hooting with laughter and squealing gleefully, *"I'm melting, Reagan. Save me!"* as if it were hilarious that the girl's dad had died fighting a warehouse blaze a few days before Christmas. Jack remembered, too, how he'd come home, beaten bloody by Paulo after stopping his furious friend from doing God-knows-what to pay her back for the purple knot she'd left on his forehead.

After that day, Jack had never gone back to that wooded bend of the brown bayou, no matter how many times Paulo told him he was over Jack's "betrayal" there. Oh, they'd hung together now and then—in their neighborhood, having Paulo as an ally definitely increased a teenager's chances of survival—but things had never really been the same between them.

And Jack had never again felt quite the same way about the skinny blond pain-in-the-butt who'd followed him—much to his thirteen-year-old horror—to the bayou that windy January day. Even now, he didn't want to hurt Reagan, didn't want trouble over his damaged Explorer to force her out of the job she obviously loved.

Besides, he told himself, if the media whipped up some scandal linking him to a feud with a beautiful blond firefighter, it would heap more fuel on the blaze Winter's accusations had ignited. Fuel enough to see him fired and this desperately needed clinic closed.

So instead of calling the police, he let himself back inside the locked clinic and rummaged through the day's charts until he found Reagan Hurley's. Opening it on a clerk's desk, he found a piece of scratch paper and copied the address and phone number.

As he wrote, the telephone beside his elbow began ringing. Figuring it was probably another reporter, Jack ignored it—until he heard the gruff voice on the answering machine.

"This is Paul Rodriguez calling for Jack Montoya."

Jack stared at the machine, shaken to hear the same Paulo he had thought of only moments earlier. Not that the towering adult, who these days favored sharp suits and expensive haircuts, bore much resemblance to the troublemaking teen . . .

"Jack—you gotta put a stop to this," the speaker barked. "They're trashing the neighborhood's reputation with all this talk about illegals, acting like we're nothing but a bunch of goddamn wetbacks. You call back that fucking Winter and set him straight before he—"

Unable to find the right button to disconnect the call, Jack snatched up the receiver.

"Hey, *'mano*," Jack said, though it had been a lot of years—and a lot of water under the bridge—since the two of them had run the streets together. Even then, Paulo had pounded Jack at least as often as he'd seen fit to help, punishing him for everything from helping his landlord's little girl to suddenly choosing school over *la vida*, the street life.

Fumbling with the answering machine, Jack managed to stop its recording. "What can I do for you?"

"It's what you can do for this neighborhood, not me," Paulo shot back. "That Darren Winter Show—the man is tearing down our people. You gotta stop it now, before we lose all our investors."

Investors. Of course. Jack should have known his old friend's motives weren't completely altruistic. Though Paulo—or Paul, as he now called himself—had turned his rough energies from tormenting little girls and stripping stolen cars to expanding Cheap Wheelz, the small, cut-rate auto rental chain he'd inherited from his grandfather, he was always on the lookout for the next big score.

Rumor had it he was hungrier than ever, thanks to some sort of family medical situation. Jack had never seen Paulo's son, but word was that not long after Paulo's common-law wife ran off, the three-year-old was diagnosed with some serious disorder—Jack thought it might be autism or mental retardation. But sorry as he was about the man's problems, Jack wasn't about to shoulder responsibility for Winter's political agenda.

"What makes you think I have any control over that loudmouth?" asked Jack. "If I did, do you really think I'd let him make me trouble?"

"Tell him you're going to sue," Paulo suggested. "Me and my backers, we'll even foot the bill. We're trying to get federal funds to revitalize the Plaza del Sol center, but we can't do it with him running down the neighborho—"

"I don't have time for this," Jack said, though some

part of him thought of all the jobs and money that would come back to the area if the flood-damaged shopping center were reopened. "Somebody trashed my SUV, and I've got to—"

"Somebody messing with you? 'Cause I still got connections, connections that want to keep good doctors in the neighborhood, want to keep our people healthy. You're one of our own, 'mano. You say the word, we take care of you. You want to use a car, I got it. You need something else, we're up for that, too."

A cold wave detonated in Jack's nervous system, rolling outward to the tips of his fingers and his toes. From the day a hard-ass assistant principal had mocked his goals, Jack had turned himself inside out to show the sorry SOB he would not only graduate, but go to college. In retrospect, the man's scorn had done Jack more good than a whole truckload of softhearted counselors, but none of his friends had a clue that his newfound studiousness was his own brand of rebellion.

Especially not Paulo and his friends, who had stuck with raising hell the old-fashioned way. Though Jack occasionally ran into one or another of his former *compadres*, they rarely acknowledged his existence with more than a tight nod. Yet now, all these years after they'd become men, it seemed he had finally won some measure of their approval.

Now that he couldn't remember why he'd ever wanted such a thing in the first place.

"Thanks," he said carefully, "but I'd rather take care of this myself."

"Just so you *do* take care of it, man—and I was serious about helping you, if you think your old *amigo's* good enough."

"Of course I do," Jack told him, before saying good-bye. Though he had no intention of involving himself with Paulo's business dealings, he'd be a fool to dismiss the offer out of hand. Especially since he hadn't missed the undertone of threat . . .

When someone cleared a throat behind him, he jerked, pulse pounding, and spun toward what he prayed was not some cranked-up thief looking for drugs.

"*Pendejo!* Luz Maria, you scared the liver out of me."

"All that schooling and you give me no better than gutter talk?" His little sister wrinkled her nose and deadpanned an impression of their mother, though no one would have mistaken the twenty-three-year-old social worker, with her dancer's body and her fiery temper, for Candelaria Esmeralda de Vaca Montoya, the reigning queen of suffering. But never, regrettably, of suffering in silence.

"I figured you'd left for the day when I didn't see your car outside," he said. "It hasn't been stolen, has it? Someone did a real number on mine."

Luz Maria sighed. "I wish someone *would* take the thing. It's in the shop again. Piece of trash failed the stupid smog inspection."

"Score one for Houston's air quality index." Luz Maria's ugly orange hatchback had been belching black clouds for months.

"Sure, that's gonna cure the city's problem." Her sarcasm had lost all trace of playfulness. "And *you* don't have to foot the bill on a lowly social worker's salary."

"It's not like my salary's making a huge dent in my student loans—and now I'll have a deductible to pay on my Explorer." Jack's medical school loans loomed like the national debt in his nightmares. But Luz Maria looked so troubled, he couldn't put his heart into their habitual drive-by potshots. "You need a ride? I'll even spring for dinner if you can stand a frozen pizza."

Maybe then she would tell him what, besides her car, was wrong and help take his mind off his own problems.

Shaking her head, she settled into a stained, off-kilter desk chair and rubbed her palms on her jeans. "Frozen pizza, huh? It's no wonder you're not dating."

He'd taken a break from women after his last couple of girlfriends, having figured out what a doctor's life was all about, decided to shoot for oil-company executives instead. "Hey, if you were a real girl instead of just a sister, I'd bite the bullet and call out for delivery."

She didn't even crack a smile, and her gaze slid away from his. "Yeah, well, all I can say is Sergio's gonna have to spring for something better if he knows what's good for him. He's an hour late to pick me up."

No wonder she was brooding. Sergio Cardenas was the latest love of Luz Maria's life. She'd been going on about him for several months now, a marked change from her previous relationships, some of which had lasted only hours. Jack tamped down a comment. Luz Maria often reminded him that he was her older brother, not her papa. Still, he figured that Sergio's standing her up on a Friday evening didn't bode well for their future.

Though he hated to see her hurting, Jack didn't worry much about her love life. She was still too young, in both years and maturity, to get serious about any one man.

Jack perched on the edge of a scuffed and dented metal desk and resigned himself to waiting. No way was he leaving his sister alone in this neighborhood. Even his mother had finally given up on the area, at his and Luz Maria's urging, and moved to a small house in a safer location, nearer to her shop.

"Sure you don't want to come with me?" he asked. "Rockets are on the tube tonight, and there's cold beer in the fridge. If you need a break from Mama, you're welcome to crash on the pull-out tonight."

"No, thanks. Sergio called with some story about being stuck in traffic. He should be here in about ten minutes, and I really need to talk to him." As if her thoughts had wandered somewhere she didn't want her brother following, she abruptly changed the subject. "Did you say somebody messed up your Explorer?"

"Pissed-off patient, I think."

"The *rubia*?" she guessed—the blonde. "I was greeting a client when I saw her storm out. She looked mad enough to stomp kittens. What'd you do to her? Is she a psych case or a druggie or what?"

Jack frowned at the memory of Reagan Hurley, that unsettling combination of guileless beauty and hair-trigger temper. It came as no surprise that his sister didn't recall Reagan, as Luz Maria had been no more than three the year Mrs. Hurley had moved her daughter to the suburbs.

"She needed me to sign a return-to-work release, and I couldn't do it."

"How come?"

Jack shook his head. "Can't discuss it," he said, and she nodded in understanding. Though she'd only worked in social services for eighteen months and inside this clinic for the last three, she had professional confidences of her own she must keep private.

Like a drop of oil on a puddle's surface, a slow smile

spread across Luz Maria's face. She grabbed the slip of paper on top of Reagan's chart. "Well, well. What do we have here? Is Dr. Big Spender planning a personal peace mission? She might have been pissed, but she *was* hot—very *caliente*. Even I could see that."

Before Jack could toss off a denial, Luz Maria suddenly added, "Wait a minute. You didn't hit on her, did you? That wasn't why she was so—"

"What do you take me for? She's a *patient*—and a deranged one, if the damage to my Explorer's any proof."

Yet something inside him whispered that Reagan Hurley was not his patient, that he'd refused her service here today. To his chagrin, it was the same normally penned-up something that had been ogling her body during his examination, so he snapped a mental padlock on its cage.

Luz Maria's good humor shifted into reverse with jarring speed. After thrusting the paper back at him, she threw up her hands, flashing long nails painted a blistering red-orange. "Handle it however you want. There's no need to get snotty."

Once more, Jack was struck by the thought that something serious was bothering her. "What is it, Luz Maria? What's the problem? Don't dare tell me it's nothing, or I'll put Mama on the scent."

"It's this job." Luz Maria's hands darted about like startled birds as she explained. "Not just the job, the system—all of it. You know how we've been talking about all those kids who keep coming in with trouble breathing . . . ?"

Jack shifted uncomfortably at the reminder, wondering for the thousandth time which clinic worker had leaked the copy of little Elena Suarez's charts to Winter, and why someone who saw this suffering every day would do such a thing.

"No one from the health department wants to look into the spike in respiratory ailments or listen to what I have to say about those addresses," Luz Maria said. "And someone there must have complained to my supervisor that I keep calling. Now she's all over my *pompis*, telling me to worry about my own cases and stay off everybody else's."

That didn't much surprise Jack. Since she'd been a tiny child, when Luz Maria zeroed in on something she wanted, she could grind like a belt sander. Besides, she had butted heads with her supervisor almost from day one, when the woman continually mispronounced her name, rhyming it with *buzz* instead of *cruise*.

"I've called, too," he told her. "But with all the budget battles, their manpower's been cut to the bone. They said they'll get to it."

"*Eventually*, right? But when's eventually?" she shot back. "How many more kids from that block have to die?"

She'd been the caseworker for the family of Agustín Romero, an eight-year-old whose father had carried him into the clinic, blue as death, when he'd stopped breathing. With paramedics en route, Jack had done everything he could to open the boy's airway, but Agustín had been down too long. By the time they reached the hospital, his oxygen-deprived organs were failing one by one.

It had been one of the longest nights of Jack's life, waiting helplessly for that beautiful child to die. Especially after trying to explain to the weeping family why, only days before, another doctor from the clinic had turned them away, saying that the boy's asthma was a chronic and not a communicable or life-threatening condition.

Not life-threatening, my ass. Tell that to the Romero family.

Since then, Jack had treated twelve more kids with breathing troubles at the clinic—and falsified the charts of every one, diagnosing contagious diseases instead of asthma, then slipping their parents drug-company samples for their treatment. And if Agustín's death had hit him hard enough to push him to what might amount to professional suicide, what had it done to Luz Maria, who'd seen only a small fraction of the suffering he had witnessed?

"Maybe we both need to get out of this cesspool," he said bitterly. "We can find some nice, clean jobs in the suburbs, help nice, clean yuppie kids learn to deal with their own sense of entitlement."

Luz Maria's eyes flashed. "Maybe that M.D. after your name cancels out who you are. Maybe it erases what happened to our papa, what's happening to so many of our people still. But it will never, ever be that way with me."

He doubted she remembered their father at all; she'd been only a toddler when he disappeared. And yet she claimed his memory, held it to her like a merit badge of unremembered suffering. Ten years older, Jack bit his tongue to keep himself from reminding her that he still bore scars from those days.

Changing the subject, he said, "You've made a lot of friends since you've been here. Maybe *you* can tell me who hates me enough to send that photocopied file to Darren Winter?"

She shook her head. "You have friends here, too, Jack. And all of them seem really mad about your getting in trouble. It's a stupid law—a travesty—but those idiot reporters are making it sound like you did something terrible. And Winter—the man's a—a complete . . ."

She threw her hands up, clearly at a loss for words.

"What about the clinic?" he asked. "Is there someone here who'd like to see it shut down? Someone, maybe, who's angry over the hours or the lousy pay or the conditions?"

She cracked a smile. "That would be all of us. But it's not like most of the employees couldn't find a job somewhere else. Especially the nurses. Do you know what kind of signing bonuses they're paying at the suburban hospitals these days? Everybody's crying for nurses."

"Ever make you wish you'd gone into medicine instead of social work?"

She shook her head. "You know how blood makes me throw up and I faint when I see needles. But that's okay. I'm better at shaking things up, getting things done for people."

"So I'm hearing—and seeing, too." Since the hospital district had sent her here, she had been a strong and sure advocate for patients, helping them navigate the confusing maze of social services and charitable programs to keep their families fed and housed and clothed. Impressed, the nurses dubbed her "The Piranha," for the fearless way she tore into her clients' problems.

At a rap against the security-glassed panel of the front door, Luz Maria looked up. "There's Sergio. Want to say hi to him? And I do mean 'hi,' Jack, not the third degree. He gets too much of that from Mama as it is."

Jack smiled, imagining that whatever details Mama

hadn't ferreted out through her infamous cross-examinations, she had undoubtedly discovered through her contacts at the *yerbería*, the herb shop she'd owned for sixteen years. No matter whom her son or daughter might date, Mama could be counted on to know someone who knew someone who could provide the lowdown on the man or woman's family, education, and potential earning power.

Jack nodded to his sister. "I'm heading out now, too."

After walking out beside his sister and locking the front doors behind them, Jack shook hands with Sergio Cardenas, a very serious guy in his mid-twenties who wore a lot of black and kept his hair in a neat ponytail almost as long as Luz Maria's braid. Jack had only met him a time or two in passing and didn't really know him, but something about the man disturbed him nonetheless. Maybe it was the depth of his stare, the uncomfortable silences between them, or Jack's own longstanding tendency to overprotect his little sister. Or maybe it was the motorcycle in the parking lot. Sitting beside the damaged Explorer, the thing looked sleek and deadly as a bullet.

The rain had stopped, yet the lot glistened beneath the lone security light, and puddles filled the ruts that pockmarked the asphalt.

"Kind of a wet night to ride, isn't it? Streets are pretty slick." Jack tried to keep the warning casual. Still, Luz Maria crossed her arms to let him know she considered him way out of bounds.

But Jack couldn't help himself. He'd seen far too many victims of motorcycle wrecks during his ER rotation, far too many shattered limbs and fractured skulls, too much flesh abraded so badly by road gravel that it looked like raw hamburger. He glanced at his little sister's pretty face, unmarked by either age or blemish. And unsmiling, at the moment.

Sergio hooked his thumb toward the bike. "See? I brought two helmets. I'll take good care of her, man."

Jack looked him in the eye, meaning to hold him to that vow. The stare Sergio returned was brooding, almost sullen—the kind of look that most men understood meant trouble, but that a lot of women fell for.

"Your truck." Luz Maria's eyes widened as she took note of the damage. "Can you get inside?"

Jack nodded. "Passenger door still works."

Sergio surveyed the dent and gouges with what looked like cool disdain. "Tough break," he finally mumbled.

Jack ignored the annoyance spiking through him and kissed his sister's cheek. "You two be careful out there, all right?"

Sergio nodded, but once the couple had put on helmets and climbed aboard, he revved the engine loudly and roared off, sending a rooster's tail of pebbles flying. The sand and stones popped like hail against the Explorer's freshly gouged hood.

Jack glared after the retreating bike. Next time he saw Sergio, the two of them were going to have a serious talk, no matter how much it upset Luz Maria.

As he fought traffic on his way to his Memorial-area apartment, Jack felt a killer headache building. He was worn out, not only from concern over his sister and the threat to his career and clinic, but from two years of slapping bandages—literally or figuratively—on the various afflictions that plagued the human body. Hurried and perfunctory as it often was, Jack knew his work diminished suffering and—as it had been intended—eased the strain on the county hospital's overcrowded emergency room.

Despite this, he still suffered from what one of his colleagues termed Little Dutch Boy Syndrome. For every finger he stuck into the dike of health care, ten more leaks burst out around him. Women went back to husbands who drank too much and beat them. Parents failed to have their children immunized because they feared deportation far more than disease. Patients stopped taking their prescription drugs as soon as they felt better. Others couldn't afford to fill their prescriptions in the first place, or were too terrified to deal with a potentially life-threatening diagnosis . . .

Reagan Hurley rose wraithlike to haunt him. His ears rang with the harsh rasp her breath had made in his stethoscope.

Deliberately he shoved the memory from his mind. Of all the ailments out there—and he was reminded daily of their endless and terrible variety—asthma was the one he least wanted to dwell on.

He wanted nothing more than to down some aspirin, throw on jeans and a sweatshirt, and enjoy a Rockets game, a beer, and pizza. But before he could sag into the weekend, he was going to call Reagan to demand that she pay for the damages to his vehicle— as soon as he deleted every message from his machine that began with Darren Winter's voice.

Since the overstuffed bastard had charmed or cajoled his private number out of his informant, Jack had been overwhelmed with the man's increasingly insulting "invitations" to respond to his allegations on the air. Come Monday morning, Jack would answer to hospital administrator Dr. Ellen Fowler; until then, he didn't have a thing to say to anyone about the decision he had made.

Though he'd expected messages, Jack hadn't banked on the news van he saw parked around the corner from his usual space. He never would have spotted it if the complex's main electric gate hadn't shorted out in the wet weather, as it was prone to do. But the moment he caught sight of the white van, he realized the TV stations meant to jump on his case, too.

He shouldn't have been surprised, not with the way the media was already speculating what Winter would do with a two-year term as mayor—and bandying about comparisons not only to Schwarzenegger and Ventura, but to Ronald Reagan, who had parlayed his celebrity into the presidency. Jack's part in the story was no more or less than today's fresh angle, a blood offering to feed the ravening machine.

Fear knotted in his belly at the thought of facing some ambush reporter, possibly one holding a stolen facsimile of Jack's own signature on yet another patient record.

"So how do you explain the diagnosis of tuberculosis, Dr. Montoya," the viperlike voice hissed inside his throbbing head, *"when no TB test was given?"*

Despite the chill, hot moisture prickled on his upper lip and brow. It was bad enough to think of losing his job or seeing the clinic shut down, but what about those kids he'd been treating for asthma? How many would grow sicker or maybe even die?

"Damn it all." Jack thumped the steering wheel, his hopes shot for a night of pizza-and-basketball oblivion. He turned out of the entrance and considered driving to his mother's house in the Heights. Then another thought occurred. What if Winter or the other reporters had her address as well? After all, she'd been the emergency contact on Jack's employment forms, and someone, somewhere, had clearly leaked his personal data.

A nightmare image flashed across his vision: reporters confronting him on Mama's lawn, then his mother struggling to defend him, her anguish captured for the evening news. Or Luz Maria coming home, losing her temper, and saying something that would endanger her job, too, and put the last nails in the clinic's coffin.

Once more, Jack changed course, this time heading for the address that lay beside him on the SUV's seat. Though he would have preferred to do it via telephone in case she was even more unstable than he suspected, it looked as if he'd be confronting Reagan Hurley face to face.

Chapter Three

The man in the old green Ford didn't normally stoop to torchings, but he had to hand it to the Firebug. This shit was giving him a primo rush. Not so much the heat and flames, nor even the shrill of the first alarms. It was the getting out so smoothly that really did it for him, then the sitting back to watch the residents scurrying around like roaches, followed shortly by the arrivals of the pumper and the first news van.

The rising smoke was still almost invisible against the dusk-dark sky. But it wouldn't be for long, he reasoned as he heard the sirens of additional fire trucks approaching. The blaze would grow and spread, exactly as his old hero had assured him. Who knew?—It might take out the whole apartment complex, an older place that more than likely had no sprinkler system.

The Ford's driver fought a smile, thinking how they would put it all on TV, the pictures and the interviews with people displaced by his work. They would get a statement from some firefighter, too, who would shake his head and moan that all this trouble had been started by one person.

An unknown arsonist.

He liked it, and he would like it even better when they figured out where the blaze originated, started putting two and two together, and ended up with a freaking stampede of reporters, all here at his bidding.

He'd give his left nut to stay and watch it, but when he saw the dented red Explorer leaving, he reminded himself he still had another job to do.

And as a bonus, he would get to find out if the Firebug had been on the money on another count as well: that apartment buildings were a good start, but a living man burned best of all.

Finding Jack Montoya's home address was child's play, though the information came at a steep price.

Reagan remembered hearing, years ago, about the *yerbería* Jack's mama had bought down off of Shepherd, and as luck would have it, Mrs. Montoya herself answered the telephone when Reagan dialed the number she'd found in the phone book.

When Reagan identified herself and asked how she was doing, Mrs. Montoya rewarded her with a litany of complaints about both Joaquín, as she still called Jack, and the baby, little Luz Maria, who had somehow gone and grown into a woman. Jack, Mrs. Montoya claimed, worked too hard and didn't visit her enough, while who could keep up with Luz Maria and all those *novios* calling the house at every hour, wanting to take her to expensive restaurants?

After Mrs. Montoya described how she had successfully treated her own supposedly deadly gallstones with cactus tea and some kind of spiritual mumbo-jumbo, the woman finally asked, "And how is your mama these days?"

"She's dead," Reagan answered, the way she always did, because the truth was not only harder to explain but far more painful. "It's been five years now."

"*Qué lástima!* Such a shame. Did she live to see your wedding day, at least, or any *nietos* born? You know— grandbabies? My son and daughter, they are waiting until they drive me to my grave to give me *nietos*. But then, in these times, children do not think so much of their mothers, only having fun."

Reagan smiled and sat cross-legged on her living-room rug so she could scratch the greyhound's pink-white belly. His tongue lolling out the side of his mouth, Frank Lee thumped his tail against the floor. On her television, which she kept on low for background noise, Kramer tumbled into Jerry's apartment on a *Seinfeld* rerun.

"I don't have kids, or a husband either," Reagan told her, already uncomfortably aware of where this conversation might be leading. Still, if she wanted to get that signature this weekend, she was going to have to bite the bullet. "Listen, Mrs. Montoya, I called because I was hoping to look up Jack—your Joaquín."

"Really?" A wheedling tone infused the heavy accent. "Did I mention to you, my Joaquín is a *doctor*? And I think he would enjoy hearing from a nice girl. You are still a nice girl, aren't you?"

"Oh, yes, ma'am," Reagan fudged, though she doubted that a female firefighter who sometimes boxed would fit the señora's definition.

"And not too fat, with all the fast food?"

"Oh, no, ma'am—at least, that's what people tell me."

"Modest, too. This is a good thing. Here, I give you

41

his address and the phone numbers," she said. *"Normalmente,* I do not think much of this new way of young women calling men for dates, but since the two of you already know each other and my Joaquín is too busy saving other people's *nietos* to worry that his own mother will drop dead before he gets around to such things, you have my blessing."

In spite of her complaints, Mrs. Montoya's health couldn't be all that bad or she wouldn't have had the breath to finish that sentence. But maybe, Reagan figured, recent events had clouded her judgment when it came to lung power.

After thanking the woman for her help and promising to visit the *yerbería* for some sort of candle that would supposedly improve her love life, Reagan tried to extricate herself from the conversation. When several attempts proved futile, she finally resorted to reaching out her front door and ringing her own bell to make it sound as if company had arrived.

She admitted the deception wasn't very nice, but sometimes a girl had to do what a girl had to do.

And what she had to do was track down Jack Montoya and get that signature before he went out for the evening. His mama might believe he was home thumbing through medical journals, and Darren Winter might think he'd tormented Jack into hiding under a rock somewhere, but Reagan didn't suppose for one minute that any man as good-looking as Montoya was spending his Friday nights at home alone.

Rising from the floor, she grabbed her jacket.

"Later, buddy," she told Frank Lee, who was already eyeing the sofa speculatively. "And stay off the furniture."

Yeah, right, the thirty-five-mile-an-hour couch potato's look said, and Reagan knew she'd be vacuuming white hair off the blue cushions later. Though he'd allegedly chased artificial bunnies with gusto for his first four years of life, Frank was one greyhound who took his retirement seriously.

Conceding defeat on that front, Reagan steeled herself for a far more important battle, one that she could not afford to lose.

And opened her door to find the enemy on her front stoop, his expression stony and his raised fist poised to knock.

When the door swung open and Jack saw Reagan's eyes flare in surprise, he said, "I'm here to see how you'd like to pay for the damage to my vehicle."

"What?"

He'd give her this. She bluffed well, covering her guilt with an upturned palm and an expression of pure bewilderment. Too bad it was bullshit.

"I know you were the one," he said. "I heard what you were saying on the way out of the clinic."

Looking past him, she appeared to focus on the truck, which he had parked across the street. She made a show of wincing, pretending that the sight of the dented door upset her. "A couple of off-color comments and you think I'd do *that?*"

He nodded. "I *know* you did it. You're a hothead, always were."

A large, white dog's head peeked around her at his voice. For a moment, Jack feared he might get bitten, but the animal yawned before turning to disappear into the house.

Though Jack was five or six inches taller than she was, Reagan got right up in his face. "Yeah? Well, trust me, if I wanted to get back at you, I wouldn't stoop to petty vandalism."

He didn't give way, not a fraction of an inch. "There's nothing petty about that. It's sure to cost at least a couple grand to fix."

"Maybe you should bill your buddy Darren Winter. He's the one who's been whipping his 'warriors' into a frenzy over whatever the hell he's so worked up about. Have you been home yet and listened to your answering machine?"

"Don't try to pawn this off on someone else. I have the proof right on my truck."

She stepped out, closing her front door behind her and fisting one hand against her hip. "This I've gotta see. Lead on, McDuff."

As she followed him off the small porch, her confidence ignited the first spark of doubt in his mind. Refusing to acknowledge it, Jack led her across the neatly trimmed lawn to his truck's mashed door and gestured toward the green streak.

"Does this look familiar?" he demanded.

She studied it before asking, "Should it?"

"Your car's green, isn't it?"

She looked right at him and flashed a Cheshire cat's grin. "Why don't you come see?"

After taking him around the side of the house and past a hedge of bushes drooping with moisture, she led him to a small, detached garage, which listed slightly to the right. With a flourish, she pointed out the deep blue Trans Am inside the open door. "I rest my case, Mr. Prosecutor. Oh, excuse me. Make that *Dr.* Prosecutor. But go ahead and check for damage if you want. Sure, she's got some dings and scratches, but you won't find any red paint."

He walked around the vehicle, though by this time he realized he'd been an idiot, coming here and launching into her when common sense should have told him that anyone, from one of Winter's listeners to a run-of-the-mill vandal, could have done the damage. Why had he been so quick to latch onto the conclusion that his former neighbor had gone to such extremes?

Maybe because she'd taken up residence in his mind from the moment he had seen her in the exam room. Had his devious subconscious used suspicion as an excuse to look her up?

"I'm sorry," he said honestly. "Looks like I had it wrong."

She cupped a hand to her ear. "What was that? I don't think I heard you. Could that have been an apology you mumbled?"

"You heard me just fine," he said. "I've—uh—I've had a rotten week, and I—I guess I took it out on—"

She snapped her fingers, as if something had just come to her, and pointed at him. "Green car—old, ragged-out thing. I think I might have seen him. Jackass nearly ran me down as I was leaving."

She coughed into her hand, a grating sound that went on longer than it should have. "Come inside," she said once she recovered, "and I'll tell you what happened—*if* you can refrain from accusing me of anything else."

He hesitated.

"Oh, come on. Frank Lee doesn't bite—or he wouldn't make such a good therapy dog—and I don't either. Call your mama if you don't believe me."

"You've talked to my mother?"

She flashed a stunning smile that affected him far more than he would admit. "Oh, yeah. This afternoon. And she was sure to fill me in on all your failings—at least until she figured out I've never married."

He swore at the thought of enduring a round of questions from his mother about his "relationship" with their old landlord's daughter, but he did follow Reagan toward her front door.

"You really need to get working on that *nieto* thing," Reagan said over her shoulder. "Your mother must be starved for grandbabies if she's willing to settle for a Protestant, blond *gringa* daughter-in-law."

"Don't worry," he shot back. "Once she realizes how obnoxious you've gotten, she'll scratch you off her list of hot prospects."

"Huh. I can be plenty charming when people aren't unreasonable—or accusing me of things I didn't do."

She led him inside a comfortable-looking living room with gleaming yellow pine floors and over-stuffed blue furnishings clustered around an old-fashioned braided oval rug. Near the center of a bank of built-in bookcases, a twenty-one-inch TV was tuned to a local newscast. On the shelf above it, a fire helmet—undoubtedly her late father's—sat in a place of honor beside several framed photographs, one of Patrick Hurley in his department uniform, another of a younger, trimmer version in a boxer's robe, his grin radiant and his gloved fist held high by a referee. Among the pictures sat the snow-white pillar of a partly burned-down candle.

No wonder she's not married. What living man could possibly compete with the memories centered in that shrine?

At her whistle, the skinny white dog jumped down from the sofa, where he'd been lounging upside down.

"Beat it, Frank. We have company," she said, then turned toward Jack. "Would you like to have a seat? Maybe something to drink?"

He wasn't about to get all chummy with her, no matter what she knew. "What I'd like to do," he said, "is find out who wrecked my truck so I can report it to the police."

Yawning, the dog slipped beneath one of her hands and leaned against her leg.

"All right, have it your way," she said as she stroked the narrow white head. "When I finally got out of your clinic—with nothing for my trouble, I might add—this big green car came barreling toward me. I had to jump back out of the way to keep from being hit."

"Did you get his license number?"

She shook her head. "He disappeared too fast. The guy was really moving."

"Did you see him, or notice what kind of car it was?"

She hesitated, looking toward the ceiling as if trying to remember.

"Something American and four-door," she said. "Maybe a Plymouth or a Chrysler, one of those old tanks. And it was painted that ugly avocado color, like they used to make back in the seventies."

"What about the driver?"

She shook her head. "I don't know. A guy, I guess. I don't think he was black, but beyond that, I'm not sure. He had one of those stocking-cap things pulled down low, the way a lot of the gang kids do these days."

Old car, stocking cap—it probably was some kid, slamming into Jack's truck for some imagined slight. Maybe his baby sister had squalled when Jack had given her a vaccination. Wounded machismo so often defied logic. Jack had seen men stabbed for the craziest things, especially on Fridays, when young men flush with weekly paychecks blew a good part of them on liquor.

Over Reagan's shoulder, flames danced on the TV screen and tugged at Jack's attention.

"Could you turn that up?" he asked, realizing it was the building, not the fire, that had hooked him. "That looks like my apartment complex."

Sparks shot angrily into the night sky as a two-story building collapsed upon itself, while above it, the underbelly of a smoke cloud pulsed orange with reflected fire. As the floodlit image faded, a chill ran up Jack's spine. Though there were probably a number of similar complexes around the area, his gut clenched with the certainty that it was not only his building but his apartment burning—along with a number of others.

Reagan turned around and snatched a remote off an end table. The volume climbed as the Asian-American anchorwoman's expression sobered. "Recapping our top local story, about twenty minutes ago, a Houston firefighter was rushed to Memorial Hermann Hospital's Trauma Center in what appeared to be very serious condition. So far, we are unable to release that firefighter's name, but as soon as relatives are notified, we expect to have that information for you."

As the woman's voice-over gave the address—*Jack's* address—the screen flashed on an image of an ambulance pulling away, its lights and siren going full blast. Near the corner of the screen, Reagan pointed out a fire truck.

"That's my station's pumper—and that's *my* crew on the scene."

Her fear and horror sliced through Jack, wrenching his mind from thoughts of his neighbors' safety and his possessions. Turning, she rushed toward a cordless phone—only to have it ring before she reached it.

She grabbed it up, her eyes wild and her body trembling as if someone had injected her with pure adrenaline. "Beau? Is that you, Beau? Who's down? Who is it?"

She went silent, visibly straining with every cell to listen. And crying out in response to something that the caller said.

"I should have been there. This was my shift, *my* shift, damn it."

Jack was overcome with the urge to lay his palm on her shoulder, to offer her whatever comfort human touch could. But she'd started pacing frantically, her body language all but screaming, *Keep your distance.* Clearly sensing her distress, the white dog tried to follow, nervously winding himself around her legs.

"I'm—I'm going to the hospital," she said into the phone, pushing past the greyhound. "And sure, sure— I'll be careful driving over. Get back—get back to work. Stick with Zellers, and get that fire out, Beau. *Kill* the bitch for me, and for him, especially. Kill that fire for the captain."

As soon as she'd hung up, Jack said, "I'll be glad to drive you, Reagan. They took him to Ben Taub, right?"

She turned, staring at him oddly, as if she had forgotten he was there. A moment later, the fog appeared to lift, and she shook her head emphatically. "It's all right, Jack. I'll be fine."

"I know shock when I see it, and besides, that's my apartment complex burning. It could be that all this is related—that car you saw, the damage to my truck, the fire."

She pursed her lips. "Maybe, if it really is your place."

"Don't you think the cops are going to want to talk to both of us?"

Again she shook her head. "I didn't see much—barely got a quick glimpse of the driver. Besides, I don't give a damn what the police want. All I care about is getting to my captain as soon as possible."

"Then quit arguing and let me drive you," he insisted.

She took a deep breath, as if winding up to shout at him. Instead, she nodded and said, "Fine—if you can handle a stick shift. We're going to take my car."

"But why? Mine's running just fine."

"Yeah," she said, her expression darkening, "but *mine* doesn't have a big, fat target painted on the side of it."

Chapter Four

"This has gone too far," Jack was telling her as he drove toward the hospital. "*Damn* Darren Winter—I never cared about the politics, never gave a rat's ass where those kids or their parents came from. All I wanted to do was keep them breathing."

"Hurry up, Jack, please. You drive like my grandmother," Reagan complained, unable to focus on anything but Joe Rozinski. Her father's captain and now hers—a friend to both of them. More than a friend; in her case, he was the man who'd taken her hand at her father's funeral. The man who'd helped her find the strength to say good-bye.

Part of her understood that Captain Rozinski had consoled her in order to help himself get through the guilt and trauma of losing one of his men. But it didn't matter why he'd done it, only that the kindness planted that day had taken root . . . and sustained her through those nightmare years in her mother and stepfather's house.

Though Jack was still talking, saying something

about one of her headlights being out, the strains of bagpipes overrode his words. The bagpipes that had played at her father's memorial service.

Her throat closed around what felt like a pinecone wedged inside it, and approaching headlights turned kaleidoscopic in the prism of her tears. Rozinski couldn't die; he *couldn't*. She couldn't stand to join the parade of dark blue uniforms that marched in silent homage, couldn't bear the memories of watching from the front row while hundreds, perhaps thousands, of firefighters filed into the space in a hush so profound it made her want to scream to shatter it.

Only this time, instead of holding her hand and re-assuring her, he would lie inside the casket while *she* joined the surreally silent cortege. And the specter of their final conversation would forever poison decades of fonder memories.

As Jack turned into the parking garage, Reagan's sense of urgency evaporated into terror. He pulled into a second-level space and shut off the engine, but icy fingers clamped around her throat. She couldn't move—could barely breathe—for fear of whatever news awaited them inside the hospital.

Jack laid a hand on her arm. "Are you all right, Reag?"

The shortening of her name jerked her back to the days when she had tried to tag along with him, an eight-year-old shadow to a thirteen-year-old boy. Most often, he'd yelled at her, "Get on home, Reag. I got things to do with the *vatos*. Us guys can't have no *bebés* followin'."

Especially, his tone had said, the white daughter of the couple who owned the bungalow his family rented. Though the house Reagan's family lived in was barely any bigger, his behavior hammered home the unbridgeable expanse between owner and tenant, white girl and Hispanic boy.

But when no others were around, he would sometimes allow her to help him as he fixed a bike chain, or join in her efforts to rescue a stunned fledgling from a neighbor's tomcat and nurse the little mockingbird to health. On one memorable occasion, he had even helped her with her homework.

But never, ever, would he have touched her, the way he touched her now. And never had he looked at her as he was looking at her this evening, his dark gaze so serious and earnest that it made her fidget. And God knew, she had never been so aware of the masculine squareness of his jaw, the way his throat worked as he swallowed . . . or her own desire to touch the hollow just beneath it, to feel the way it moved.

Jerking her arm away, she told herself she'd been wrong about him earlier. He must be a damned good doctor if he could shunt aside his own horrendous problems to feign interest in hers. That was all it was, she told herself, no matter what else it might feel like.

She sucked in a breath. "I'm fine," she said. "I'll be okay."

Because whatever happened, she'd be damned if she would let him see her fall apart. Once he saw how strong she was, how well steeped in the stoicism of her mostly male department, he'd forget his reservations about signing off on her return to work.

Her mouth dried instantly as guilt knifed through her. Had she sunk so low that she would use her captain's injury to try to thwart the man's own wishes?

Jack climbed out of the car and came around to her side, meaning, she could tell, to open the door as if she were an old lady or an invalid. Or as if, in the twenty years since she had seen him, he'd acquired a polish he hadn't had before.

She beat him to the punch, emerging on her own and hustling toward the ER's entrance, which she remembered from her days riding the ambulance.

Despite her earlier resolve, she nearly lost it in the hospital's family consultation room, where she found Donna Rozinski, Joe's blowsy and big-hearted second wife, slumped on one end of a comfortable-looking sofa across from a muted television. As Donna tugged absently at a long lock of her blond-streaked red hair, her green eyes remained dry. What struck Reagan most, though, was the way the outsized, forty-something woman, always so extravagant with both her laughter and her tears, seemed to have shrunk into herself . . . and how irredeemably alone she looked.

Breaking from Jack's side, Reagan rushed toward her, only to see her crewmember Cal Wilkins heading in the same direction, a cup of coffee in one callused hand, a diet cola in the other. For a moment, his jeans and plain gray sweatshirt jarred her, until she remembered that he was on vacation, supposedly at his brother's Hill Country hunting lease. Maybe the rain had washed out his plans, or maybe some premonition had kept the fifty-year-old veteran home today.

C.W. frowned at her, the brown skin of his forehead crinkled in confusion. "Figured you'd be on today or I'd'a called you, too."

Reagan said, "I'm glad you're here, C.W."

"Same goes," he said before leaning toward Donna. "Why don't you have something cold while we wait for the doctor? You like a Diet Coke, right?"

When she ignored the offered can, Reagan took it

and set it on the narrow table beside the sofa. Unlike the impersonal waiting areas situated around both the trauma and medical sections of the ER, the family room was as cozy and inviting as if it were in someone's home. It was also the spot where the ER staff ensconced the families most likely to be hearing the worst news.

"I'm here, too, Donna" Reagan lowered herself into a crouch and fought off the tickle of a cough. "I'm here for anything you need."

Donna nodded but turned her face so she wouldn't have to make eye contact. Rising, Reagan backed off, thinking of how she'd pulled away from Jack out in the car, how his sympathy had threatened to breach the fragile hull of her composure. Whatever happened to Donna's husband, before this day was over, Donna risked sinking beneath a flood tide of heartfelt offers and kindly meant advice. Reagan remembered that much from her father's death, remembered her mother shrieking, *"I can't stand it anymore. Why can't they just leave me alone?"*

As she and C.W. stepped back into the corridor, she saw Jack out of the corner of her eye as he flagged down one of the nurses. For a moment, Reagan's attention snagged there, painful as a ragged nail when it caught and tore on fabric. Would the small Hispanic woman tell him it was over—that someone was coming to tell Donna Rozinski her husband of two years was gone?

C.W. touched Reagan's elbow. Unlike most days, today the man's age showed in deep grooves beside his brown eyes and a gray cast to his skin. "Nobody's come out yet, but from what I hear, a ceiling came down on Joe, a heavy beam across the back. He wasn't breathing when they pulled him out. Paramedics revived him, but—"

"So he was alive, right? He was breathing on his own by the time they got him here?"

C.W. nodded stiffly. "He was, with oxygen. Took a lot of smoke, though. His mask got knocked off. And they had to dig him out from under a big pile of debris."

"The captain's strong. He'll make it."

Her gaze locked with C.W.'s and dared him to defy her. When she'd first been transferred to the station, he had made no secret of the fact that he had no use for a woman on the crew.

" 'Specially one the captain didn't bother asking me about first," he had told her, "one that's practically a family member to him."

Though C.W. was the only black man on the shift and he had never bothered taking a promotional examination, his courage, work ethic, and long experience made him far more a leader among the men than many who outranked him. So Reagan had set about winning him over, buying off the man in his own coin. If he charged into a burning building, she not only hung with him, she tried to learn from him and make herself useful in the process. If he decided to clean the fire truck when it came back filthy after a 3 A.M. blaze, she was in on that, too—even when she suspected he was only doing it to try to convince her to go back to the ambulance—or at least to transfer to another station. After a few months, he'd put the word out that she would make a decent firefighter, and, as she'd expected, the other guys fell right in line.

His big hand grasped her forearm. "He'll make it. He's too damned stubborn not to. But even if he doesn't, we'll do right by him—and his family, too."

Reagan clasped his arm back and felt something flow between them, a kinship and a calling she would never in a million years be able to explain to the likes of Dr. Jack Montoya.

Not even if it were the price he set upon his signature.

"I'm sorry," Analinda Alvarez told Jack. A tiny woman with short dark curls and huge brown eyes, the trauma nurse looked tired, yet pumped up on the breakneck speed of her work. "I haven't heard anything about him. We have a lot of patients—there was some kind of rush-hour pile-up on the freeway. It's a little early still, but we've already got the makings of another wild Friday night."

Jack nodded at his former coworker. He remembered all too well the accidents and knife wounds, the shootings and the overdoses, people rushing headlong toward mortality in their eagerness to celebrate the end of the workweek.

He thought fleetingly of Luz Maria on the back of that macho asshole's motorcycle. Maybe he'd call her cell phone later, make sure she was all right.

"But you might try asking them." The nurse gestured toward a pair of men who stood talking farther down the hallway.

Jack spotted the blue uniforms of the Houston Fire Department and thought he recognized the older of the two men, a heavyset man with a graying brown comb-over, as Robert Anderson, an official who often made statements on the television news.

As Jack approached, the men's conversation ceased, and he introduced himself.

The younger of the two, a wiry, dark-haired man with a wide gap between his front teeth, jerked to attention at the mention of the name. "You said Montoya. Are you Dr. *Jack* Montoya?"

"Yes. I wanted to talk to you about—"

"Can you show us some ID? Something with your address."

Despite his confusion at the request, Jack pulled out his driver's license.

The younger man whistled through those widely spaced teeth. "Here's our man, Chief."

"We've been searching for your body," said the man with the comb-over. He gestured toward the other firefighter, who was already pulling a walkie-talkie from his belt. "Call dispatch and let 'em know we have him here."

The man stepped aside to carry out the order.

"What the hell is going on?" Jack demanded.

"A few minutes after the first pumper reached the fire at the Newgate Apartments, an anonymous caller tipped off Channel Four news that—this is a quote, sorry—'that fuckin' greaser Jack Montoya's cookin' in there.' The news crew called 911 right away to report it."

Jack flinched, more at the hate implicit than the ethnic slur.

"So the injured firefighter—" Jack began.

"Captain Rozinski and his crew were conducting a search-and-rescue sweep when the structure partially collapsed," said the man with the comb-over as the younger firefighter rejoined them.

"I'm so sorry he was hurt," Jack said. "Have you heard anything about his condition?"

The firefighters' gazes met, and he saw a nod of what looked like approval pass between them.

"We appreciate your concern." The district chief then introduced both himself and the younger firefighter. After they shook hands, he added, "According to the paramedics, Rozinski's injuries appear life-threatening. He was down for ten minutes, his mask knocked off his face, and the hot gases . . ." Breaking off, he shook his head. "This is one of the best trauma centers in the country."

Jack nodded. "If I were seriously injured, this is where I'd want to be."

"You have any idea who the caller could have been, or what this is all about? You have an enemy?"

"Apparently," Jack said. "Someone vandalized my truck this afternoon in the parking lot of the clinic where I work. One of your firefighters, Reagan Hurley, may have seen the man as he was leaving."

"Hurley?" the district chief echoed.

The younger man said, "Patrick Hurley's girl. Remember him? On-duty death in the mid-eighties, that big warehouse fire off of Washington Avenue. She joined the department a few years back. Real gung-ho type, from what I hear."

The district chief nodded, and Jack said, "I've had some trouble lately. It seems that someone at my clinic either gave or sold Darren Winter one of my patient's medical records, and he's called my diagnosis into question."

The younger man whistled through his teeth, and the district chief said, "So you're the guy. The police are going to want to speak to you—to both you and Ms. Hurley, I imagine. But they won't be the only interested parties. You'll have to talk with investigators from Houston PD, arson, the state fire marshals, maybe even the feds, depending on what comes up in the investigation. I'm afraid this is going to be a very long night for everyone involved."

Jack nodded, numb with the thought of how his life had spun out of control. A man lay near death, he and his neighbors had lost their homes, and now, it seemed, every detective in the region would be burrowing into the case, masticating details like a host of strong-jawed beetles chewing a fallen tree to pulp.

If he'd had any chance of keeping his treatment of the other children from the media, it had just gone up in flames . . . along with what was left of his career.

Chapter Five

"We had to call in the feds," Reagan heard an arson investigator say to the HPD detective outside the administrative office where they had left her waiting. In spite of the odious detective's demands that she stay put, she had edged near the open doorway in hopes of slipping out for an update on Rozinski. Instead, she'd found the two men conversing about eight feet down the corridor.

Unlike suppression firefighters and EMTs, the guy from the arson division—she thought she'd heard him called Salinas—wore cowboy boots and a denim shirt with a pair of jeans that fit his long, lean body to perfection. "That joint task force'll be all over this now that BorderFree's faxed a statement to the media."

Could he mean BorderFree-4-All? A sick chill gave Reagan gooseflesh at the thought of the bombing in San Antonio. She remembered the images from the news as if it had happened yesterday and not last spring: survivors screaming, a mosaic of shattered glass glittering on the sidewalk, three bodies being carried out of the Immigration and Naturalization Service District Office under bloodstained sheets, hooded militants sending videotaped demands for open borders to the television stations. Terrorism right here in Texas.

She had to bite her tongue to keep from running through the door and demanding to know what a radical, anti-immigration-law group could possibly have to do with the fire at Jack Montoya's apartment. Could it be, despite the vandalism and Winter's radio attacks, that Jack had never been the target in the first place? After all, what did an East End Clinic doctor have to do with U.S. policy?

"We probably have a half hour before the FBI and ATF get here," the pale and lumpy Detective Norman Worth grumbled to the arson investigator. "I would've rather hauled 'em both downtown for interviews, but we might as well get what we can while the getting's good, 'cause you and I both know the feds won't give us shit once they take over."

"You really think Montoya could be good for it—or at least involved?" the arson guy asked.

Worth gave a sloppy shrug. "Why not? It'll make his pal Winter, who's been rippin' him a new one on the air day after day, look like an irresponsible bigot. Besides, Montoya wouldn't be the first guy who decided to take one for the team."

"You're saying that 'cause he's Hispanic?" Salinas bristled, squaring his shoulders and raising his voice slightly. "You figure we're all in league or something?"

"Here's what I figure," Worth said. "Right now you're wasting time asking the wrong guy questions. As long as the witnesses are cooperating, let's keep at 'em while we can."

As the police detective turned toward her, Reagan slunk back to her seat and picked up the lukewarm Dr. Pepper she'd been nursing for the past hour. A moment later, Worth closed the door behind him and fished a cigarette out of the pocket of a worn and tweedy sports jacket. He took a seat behind the big desk and pressed a button on his microcassette recorder to resume the taping.

"So how long have you been seeing Dr. Montoya?" Ignoring the hospital's rules, he lit up and puffed, closing his eyes with the pleasure of it.

Reagan hoped some kamikaze night-shift clerk would come running at the smell of smoke. She'd enjoy watching this dough-bellied cop, with his pasty face and his snotty attitude, get taken down a peg or two.

Besides, the cigarette smoke was making it difficult to breathe. She coughed, maybe louder than she needed to, but instead of taking the hint, he looked around the desk he had commandeered until he found a coffee mug colorfully decorated with the words "World's Best Mom." Without batting an eye, he flicked the ashes into some kid's gift. Next to his ersatz ashtray, the glowing red numbers on a digital desk clock changed to 1:08 A.M.

"Like I told you before you stepped out, I'm not seeing Jack Montoya, or anybody else," Reagan repeated, pissed that no matter how many times she denied it, the same question kept popping up, as persistent and annoying as fire-ant mounds after rainstorms. "Don't you want to hear about the green car or the driver?"

Waving to dispel a silvery mouthful of smoke, he glanced down at his notes. "Not unless you've come up with something new to add this time."

Come up with. She narrowed her eyes, not liking the

turn of phrase. As a firefighter, she'd worked around enough cops at scenes of accidents, assaults, and murders to know skepticism when she heard it.

"What I want to know," the detective went on, "is how long your *friend* Dr. Montoya has been wrapped up with BorderFree-4-All."

Did he honestly believe Jack was involved? Try as she might, she could not suppress a shudder.

"What makes you think that?" she asked. The idea was so outlandish, so far-fetched, that she couldn't wrap her brain around it.

He blew smoke out of the side of his mouth and looked her over in a way that made her skin crawl. "What do you know about it?"

"Nothing. Why should I?" It was really getting to her, the way this detective was talking to her and staring at her as if she were a suspect.

"Look, I'm trying to be patient," she burst out, "but all I want to do is go back out there with my captain's wife and the guys from my crew."

Several of them had arranged relief so they could come stand vigil. She belonged with them—her family, to all intents and purposes—not cooped up in this makeshift interview room answering the same damned questions all night.

"There's been no change in Captain Rozinski's condition. I checked on my way back from the men's room."

Liar, she wanted to scream. She knew damned well he hadn't gone anywhere except to confer with the arson investigator. But accusing him wasn't going to get her out of here any faster.

"You said Jack Montoya was at your house when the two of you heard about the fire," Detective Worth continued. "Since doctors don't make house calls and you look the way—the way you do, I've gotta figure he had some *other* reason to drop by."

Narrowing her eyes at him, she forced herself to speak slowly and distinctly. "He's an old friend, that's all." Reagan uncrossed her legs after she noticed Worth studying the nervous jiggling of her foot. "My parents owned a rental house, and his folks were our tenants back when we were kids. But that was a long time ago. I haven't even seen him in—I don't know—twenty years or so. Until today."

"And you decided to renew this *acquaintance* because . . ."

She wished she were facing Detective Dough Gut in the boxing ring instead of across a desk. Blood and teeth would be flying, and none of them would be hers. "As I mentioned earlier, I needed a release to return to work signed, so I went by his clinic."

Worth made a show of flipping through his little notepad. "Where you had some sort of altercation?"

"A minor disagreement," she amended. *Altercation* sounded like something a cop would write on an arrest report. "And he came by my place later to get things straightened out. For old time's sake, I suppose."

Detective Worth raised an incredulous eyebrow, and she had to bite her tongue to keep from swearing.

"He ask you out before the news story came up?" he asked.

She snorted a humorless laugh, thinking of how angry Jack had been with her—and how irritated when she'd mentioned his mother's *nieto* plans. "Not hardly."

"Guess he hadn't gotten to that part yet," Worth said. "So you don't know anything about his friends at BorderFree-4-All?"

She thought of what Jack had said on the way here in the car. *I never cared about the politics, never gave a rat's ass where they came from. All I wanted to do was keep some kids alive.*

"No way is Montoya tied up in that stuff," she said. "All he cares about is helping patients, especially the kids."

"But you said you haven't seen him in decades."

One left hook. That's all she'd need to knock this turkey on his ass. It would damn sure be easier than explaining a gut feeling.

"You know I'm with HFD," she reminded him. "Like the cops, we're on the streets all hours, and we meet a lot of citizens, most of them on the worst days of their lives."

He nodded.

"When people are under stress," she said, "they say things and do things that give you a feel for who they are. The defense attorneys of this world would probably say you're making snap decisions, but on the streets you have to, don't you? Otherwise, how do you know the guy who meets your ambulance at the scene of a stabbing isn't about to whip out his knife to finish off the vic? How do you know he isn't gonna take a crack at some bystander—or at you?"

As a detective, he'd undoubtedly once worked in uniform. He knew the score as well as she did, and she saw the agreement in his blue-gray eyes, saw, too, the realization that the two of them had certain experiences in common.

"You do get an instinct for it," he conceded. "You have to, to make it on the streets."

"Well, *my* instinct tells me that Jack Montoya's about the furthest thing you can imagine from a killer.

Even as a kid, he was such a decent sort—but this is about now, and everything I've seen tells me there's no connection."

Worth tapped more ash into the day clerk's mommy mug and shrugged. "Maybe. But what I'd like to know—and what the feds are going to be damned interested in learning—is why BorderFree released a statement praising Montoya's 'acts of defiance against an unjust law' and calling him a 'martyr to the cause.'"

She thought about it for a moment before speaking. "Aren't martyrs usually dead? Why would they think that unless they were the ones trying to kill him—"

"Every possibility will be investigated."

Including that of Jack's collusion in some kind of plot to ruin Winter, Reagan added mentally. She didn't bother arguing the point, though. Otherwise, this detective would undoubtedly jot "hysterical girlfriend" next to her name on his pad.

Standing, she rubbed the small of her back, then twisted until she felt a satisfying pop. "Is the inquisition over? I've been sitting here forever, and I could really use a break."

He shrugged and flipped through his notepad once more. "I think I have all I need for now. But arson wants to speak with you again."

She groaned. She'd talked to those guys twice already, and she had nothing else to add. "Not before I find a ladies'. Unless some of you folks want to follow me there, too."

"Be my guest," he told her.

She hotfooted it out of there before he could change his mind—or some other investigator could jump in. She supposed they were tag teaming, switching off between her and Jack, and she wondered how much more pointed, even accusatory, their questions were to him.

And why, exactly, she should care.

It was only the late hour, she told herself. That and the fact that since the two of them had been together when he'd learned about the fire and she'd heard about Rozinski, she had begun to feel almost as if they were comrades in arms.

But despite what she had told Detective Worth, how could she know for certain that she and Jack were fighting on the same side? As Worth had reminded her, before this afternoon she hadn't seen the guy in twenty years. Who was she to say what he had gotten into? And even if he had nothing to do with BorderFree-4-All, he hadn't denied Winter's charges. By sidestepping the legal guidelines for the treatment of undocumented aliens, hadn't Jack Montoya set in motion everything that followed?

Including, she realized with a sickening jolt, Joe Rozinski's injuries.

Her misgivings intensified when she stepped into the family consultation room. The captain's wife had dozed off, leaning against an older woman who looked as if she might be Donna's mother. But it was the way C.W., Beau LaRouche, and three other uniformed crewmembers looked at her that made Reagan's stomach drop into her shoes.

"Is there . . . has there been any news?" she asked, telling herself she was only imagining the suspicion in their faces.

Beau raked his fingers through wavy, sandy-colored hair that was always an inch or so too long for regulation. Tanned, muscular, and younger looking than his twenty-four years, Beau generally put Reagan more in mind of some rich woman's boy toy than a rookie fire-fighter who'd grown up in a rough north-side neigh-borhood. Tonight, though, his reddened eyes and nervous movements made him seem edgy and unpre-dictable, almost dangerous.

During the nine months he'd been at the station, he and Rozinski had had their run-ins—usually over both his hair and his unauthorized variations on the official uniform. Even so, Beau would follow Rozinski to fight the fires of hell itself, and Reagan was almost sure he'd been with the captain during the building collapse. Knowing Beau as she did, she was certain, too, that if Rozinski died, Beau would blame himself.

After darting a glance toward C.W. and the other firefighters, Beau gestured for her to follow him into the hallway.

Her heart in her throat, she stepped outside and waited until he closed the door behind him. He opened his mouth to speak, but she was faster on the draw.

"Has something happened?" she asked. "What did the doctors say?"

He hesitated, some question in his deep brown eyes. When he finally did speak, toothpaste-commercial-white teeth flashed against his golden skin. "They're monitoring the oxygen levels in his blood. There's damage to his lungs and trachea, and they've put him on a ventilator to keep him from losing any more ground."

She closed her eyes against the burning. "Do they think he'll make it?"

"They're 'cautiously optimistic,' but he's still critical."

Struck mute by disappointment, she swallowed past a painful lump. Maybe it was her exhaustion or the endless interviews, but the situation had taken on the feeling of a nightmare, one she prayed she would wake up from any minute.

"What the hell happened?" she asked.

Beau flinched, a sign that he'd already been asked this question more than once. "The captain, Zellers, and me were making our secondary sweep when part of the roof gave way. All this debris rained down and buried Rozinski. We couldn't even find him 'til his PAS went off."

That would mean Rozinski had been down for thirty seconds, which would have triggered the personal alarm system. How much longer, Reagan wondered, before they'd dug him out and gotten him outside? She didn't ask, though, for she trusted that Beau and Zellers, a seasoned, solid firefighter, had done everything they could—and because they would have to endure more than enough second-guessing as it was.

Beau's gaze flicked up to meet hers.

"Everyone's been wondering—why have they been questioning *you?*" The question tumbled out of him sounding bewildered—and more than slightly hostile. "What could you have to do with this? You weren't even at the fire."

"I don't have anything to do with it," she said, "but I may have seen something earlier. I saw a man who *might* have vandalized Jack Montoya's vehicle and could've set the fire, too. At least, that's what the cops and arson seem to think."

"Montoya? Wasn't he the guy we were looking for inside the apartment?"

She nodded. "Yeah. I happened to be in the neighborhood of his clinic today. He's a doctor on the East End."

She decided to keep to herself the part about her visit to his office.

"Is he the one you showed up with? His picture ran on the news, and C.W. said he saw the two of you come in together. You know him?"

"Not lately. We grew up in the same neighborhood, that's all. But we were talking about the damage to his SUV when you called me about the captain."

"Tell me the two of you aren't dating. From the stuff on TV, the man's trouble. *Huge* trouble."

Once again, Reagan found herself denying a relationship with Jack.

Beau's gaze hardened, and she recognized the same skepticism she had seen from the detective. Why was the simple truth so hard for them to believe? It wasn't as if she had a reputation for sleeping around. Hell, it had been months since she'd even gone on an honest-to-goodness date. She liked men well enough—too well, upon occasion—but her odd hours and her refusal to get involved with coworkers or suffer through another blind date hadn't exactly filled her dance card.

"I'll cover for you," Beau said, "but if I were you, I'd stay as far from Jack Montoya as you can. Because I got a gut feeling that by the time this investigation's over, his ass will be in jail. And maybe on death row, if the cap . . . if the captain doesn't . . ."

Beau pinched the bridge of his nose as his voice hitched, but it didn't matter. She understood what he was trying to tell her. In Texas, an arson leading to the death of an on-duty firefighter was a capital offense.

And if Joe Rozinski died, the union and its members would push hard for an arrest, a conviction, and the execution of whichever parties they deemed responsible.

* * *

"I'm asking you again"—Jack looked Arson Investigator Esteban Salinas directly in the eyes—"am I a suspect here?"

When Jack had first asked whether he should call an attorney, the investigators had told him it was certainly his prerogative, but they'd also assured him that no one was looking to arrest him.

But Jack didn't like the tone of these questions, which had started out innocuously enough but invariably led down the same thorny path.

"How was it you drew the attention of the media?"

"So, Dr. Montoya, can you tell me if there's some personal enmity between you and Darren Winter?"

"Would you mind giving us the address where your vehicle is parked? We'll need to impound it to look for evidence."

And especially troubling: *"Can anyone besides Ms. Hurley and your sister verify your whereabouts throughout the afternoon and early evening?"*

Salinas shook his head and passed Jack one of the two coffees he had brought up from the hospital's cafeteria. "There's no need to get defensive. We're just trying to cross our t's and dot our i's here—in case there are any questions later."

Though the coffee was both tepid and doctored up with cream and artificial sweetener instead of black as he preferred, Jack drank it for the caffeine. He probably should call someone, he thought, if only to keep the investigators from wasting their time trying to catch him in some inconsistency about where he'd been at what time and with whom. Still, he hesitated, thinking that "lawyering up," as he'd heard it described, would mean a long delay and probably a trip to police headquarters for more "voluntary" interviews. Besides, it went against his grain to cloud the basic fact of his innocence by acting anything but eager to answer questions. By stalling and behaving as if he were guilty, wouldn't he slow the arrest of the real culprit?

Arson Investigator Esteban Salinas sipped his coffee. Along with the police detective, Salinas's Anglo partner had disappeared from the borrowed conference room, and Jack couldn't help wondering whether they had decided he would be more comfortable with another Hispanic asking the questions. Not that Salinas looked the part, in spite of his surname. With his fair skin, angular features, and blue eyes, the inspector could as easily have been named Smith or Williams—except that when he returned along with his "good cop" offering, he had greeted Jack in informal border Spanish.

Jack answered in English, and Salinas had quickly taken the hint and dropped the here-we-are, a-couple-of-young-*vatos*-from-the-neighborhood routine. Which was just as well, considering his mention of a Latino radical group that had supposedly lauded Jack as some kind of hero.

"I don't know anything about them other than what I've seen in the papers and on TV," Jack said. "But from what I understand, I sure as hell don't want to be their poster child. How they could blow up a place that served poor immigrants in the name of helping them—I don't see the logic. But then, I've never understood terrorists, no matter what their cause."

"Do you know anyone connected with BorderFree-4-All?"

Jack shook his head. "Not at all, unless one of my patients is a member. It's not exactly the kind of information people volunteer during medical examinations."

Even as he spoke the words, he mentally shuffled through the roster of his regulars. Nearly all of them were mothers, young children, or elderly; most of them struggled to get along from day to day. Jack had a hard time imagining any of them toting guns, building bombs, or donning hoods in their spare time.

"Has anyone from the group ever tried to contact you in any way?" Salinas asked. "Maybe with a solicitation for donations, or an invitation to join?"

Jack rubbed the stubble along his jawline. If someone offered him a hot shower, a good meal, and a quiet corner, he would confess to almost anything. *Anything*, if they would throw in a fresh pot of black coffee.

"I get hit up for every kind of cause you can imagine. I guess the charities all assume that doctors are not only rich—which is pretty damned humorous in my case—but philanthropic. But I would've remembered a request from that group. Hasn't happened."

Salinas typed Jack's response into the laptop computer he had used throughout the evening. Despite the late hour, the arson investigator was fast enough that he didn't miss a beat.

Once he was finished, he passed Jack a business card. "That's all I have for now. If there's anything else, we'll contact you at—you'll still be going to your mother's house, right?" Salinas used the computer's mouse to scroll up, then read off the address and phone number, along with Jack's cell-phone number, from his notes.

Jack confirmed the information and said, "You mean I'm free to go?"

Salinas glanced up from his computer. "Actually, there are some agents on their way to talk to you—FBI and ATF. They're members of something called the Lone Star Terrorism Joint Task Force—along with half a dozen other alphabet agencies."

Jack's heart skipped a beat. This was getting more serious by the moment. He'd been a damned fool not to recognize it from the start, but that didn't mean he had to *stay* an idiot. "I'll need to make some calls first. I think I'm going to want that lawyer after all."

Chapter Six

Cell phones were not only banned in this section of the hospital, they usually didn't work because of all the electronic equipment. Unwilling to risk being overheard at the bank of pay phones, Jack stepped outside into the shadowy margins of the ambulance bay.

A chill wind stole beneath his jacket and blew his hair across his eyes. Raking it back, he saw that even at this hour, the bay remained busy. The Houston Fire Department crews of two advanced life-support units were in the process of unloading patients, while not far away, a pair of EMTs climbed into a third ambulance, apparently to head back out into the streets.

Typical Friday-night mayhem at its finest.

At least the activity would keep anyone from paying Jack much heed. And as long as they kept the sirens off, he ought to be able to hear whomever he called.

Jack stared at the telephone in his hand and wondered, who the hell *should* he call? It was after two A.M., and he didn't exactly have an attorney on his speed dial.

Earlier, he'd phoned his mother to let her know he hadn't been hurt in the fire at his apartment. She had been concerned but surprisingly practical about the whole thing, inviting him to come to her house once he finished talking to investigators, even though he had told her that might not happen until morning. But his mother didn't know the half of it, and he wasn't about to wake her at this hour to frighten her with the details.

He thought next of his sister, but hesitated at the idea of catching her with Sergio and having her bring her boyfriend into this business. Besides, if he reached Luz Maria at the house, their mother would inevitably get sucked into it.

An ambulance attempting to pull out into the street flipped on a siren briefly. Apparently, the driver was trying to get the attention of the news van that had edged into his path as it reversed into a spot along the curb.

Jack shifted to better see around the nearer of the two parked units. At the sight of the line of various news vans, trailers, and floodlights, he stepped back into the shadows.

But not before someone grabbed his elbow and pulled him even farther in.

"Watch it," said a voice behind him. "There's a camera pointed this way, and I'm pretty sure they're watching for you."

In his haste to turn, Jack nearly dropped the phone. "Reagan—I thought you'd be with your captain's family. He hasn't—"

"No, no. He's still alive, thank God. I just . . . I needed some time alone to pull myself together. And after being inside for all these hours, the cold air feels kind of . . . I guess you could call it bracing. At least it's waking me up."

She seemed to be speaking—and probably breathing—more easily tonight. Maybe she would feel better, now that the sky had cleared. Houston's frequent wet spells triggered myriad breathing problems.

"What makes you think those vans are here for me?" Jack spotted the camera set up in a blocked and unused former emergency approach, then put the bulk of an ambulance between himself and the lens. "Don't they always show up when a firefighter or a cop gets hurt?"

"It's not just the local stations. That's the CNN van, the one trying to squeeze into that spot that's too small. And besides, there are way too many of them."

"I wonder if the guy who called Channel Four and told them my body would be in the apartment tipped off other people, too."

"You mean the arsonist brought the media into this?"

"That's why the fire department thought I was inside."

She said nothing in answer, but as a brittle silence took shape between them, Jack knew she must be thinking about her captain, how he might die as a result of that phone call.

"I'm sorry," he said quietly. "I have no idea who the bastard was that did this, but I'll do everything I can to help the authorities figure it out."

In the distance, another siren grew louder as it drew near. Instead of trying to talk over it, Reagan said nothing until the ambulance pulled into the far end of the bay.

When the blare ceased, she said, "I have to know one thing, Jack, and I have to know for sure. Do you have anything to do with BorderFree-4-All? Have you ever?"

A tremor in her voice bespoke her emotion, yet he heard no accusation in her questions. *Thank God*, something in him whispered, though he couldn't say why that absence brought him such relief.

"I don't know anything about that group except that those filthy murderers have smeared my name by using it this evening."

"Do you think they did it for some reason? Set the fire, I mean?"

He shrugged. "I have no idea. I don't know all that much about them, and I can't imagine what good it would do them. But why would anybody want to do it? There were other people living in that building besides me—older couples, families with children. I was told all the residents got out, but—It is true, isn't it?"

He saw her nod, her pale hair gilded by the light streaming through the glass door. For a moment, he wished he could touch it, find out if it was as silky as it looked.

"I've heard the same thing, so I guess so," she said. "But maybe it wasn't that group. Maybe it was Winter. You seem to be pretty near the top of his shit list lately."

"Winter." Jack spat the word out like a curse. "He's been a pain in the ass, but he doesn't strike me as the kind who goes around trying to burn out the people he's criticizing. If that were true, half the country would be in flames."

"I don't mean he did it personally. But this afternoon, that jackass gave out a link to what he implied was your home phone number. What if one of his listeners—some unbalanced head case—typed it into his computer and reverse-searched the phone book? What's to keep this sicko from finding your address and taking matters into his own hands?"

"Do you think that could have happened?"

"It's easy enough to do on the Web, and if *I've* thought of it, you know those news crews have. I'm sure they're drooling all over themselves to be the one to break a new angle on this Winter story. He's big news—people all over the country are watching this election, trying to guess how far he'll go."

"I wish I'd never heard of Darren Winter." Mentally, Jack added, *or better yet, that he'd never heard of* me.

"So who were you calling?" Reagan asked, nodding toward the cell phone he still held. "Do you need a ride or something? I could leave for a few minutes and run you back to your SUV."

Jack shook his head. "The police impounded it for evidence. I take it they're looking for evidence the vandal might have left behind. I hope you don't mind, but I gave them your address so they could get it."

"That's fine."

"Actually," Jack admitted, "I was trying to think of how to get a lawyer. You don't know anybody I could call at this hour?"

"They *aren't* arresting you."

He was gratified by the disbelief in her voice—until she added, "Are they?"

He shook his head. "No, they aren't, but I don't like the way these questions are going. And they're bringing in some task force: the FBI, the ATF, and heaven knows who else. It's sounding really serious."

She crossed her arms in front of her breasts. "You didn't think it was before?"

He caught the incipient anger in her voice and sensed that, like a gas leak, all her temper needed was a stray spark to ignite it.

"Of course I did," he added quickly. "With your captain injured and so many people out of their homes, how the hell could I think anything else? But I never imagined anyone would suspect I was a criminal—or that I might have been the one who did this. Why the hell would I want to burn down my own place and wreck my SUV?"

In the pause that followed, an ambulance's doors slammed. They both looked over as a child, no more than three, was wheeled inside the ER. The tiny dark-skinned body jerked against its bonds in what looked like a grand mal seizure. Despite the cold night air, the toddler was clad in nothing but a diaper.

Jack swallowed hard, hating, as he had always hated, to see a child suffering. For a long time, he had wanted to go into pediatric emergency medicine, but he'd never been able to distance himself sufficiently to tolerate scenes such as this one—or the brutalized bodies of the youngest victims of abuse. One night in this very emergency room, he'd decked a smirking, strutting bastard who had brought in his four-year-old daughter with vaginal bleeding and contusions, along with the lamest cover story Jack had ever heard. Fortunately, the sorry son of a bitch had not pressed charges, but the incident had been enough to make Jack rethink his career plans.

"Wait 'til morning," she advised. "You can tell the investigators you'll call them and come in for an interview after you've had the chance to retain legal services."

"I can do that, make them wait?"

"Since they're not arresting you," she said as she

nodded. "You've been cooperative. We both have. But they have to end the interview as soon as you ask for an attorney, and they'll wait a reasonable amount of time for you to hire one and come in. And even though it'll be Saturday, it's Houston, where we have more lawyers than hydrants. You ought to be able to find somebody decent."

"Are you sure? How do you know all this?"

"I'm a career criminal. I was only kidding about all that firefighter stuff."

When his gaze jerked to meet hers, she laughed. "Had you there for a second, didn't I? Sorry, my morbid sense of humor cranks up after midnight. The truth is, I've been around enough investigations—patching up assault and accident victims and putting out arson fires'll do that for you—that I couldn't help picking up a few things."

He smiled. "I'm quicker on the uptake after a night's sleep."

"Then get some. If the investigators you talked to were the same ones grilling me, you'll need a clear head."

"They're grilling you? Do you get the idea they think you're a suspect?"

"Not me," she said. "Not yet, at any rate."

He winced at the thought that simply being a witness—or a victim—could cause an innocent person so much trouble. "Are they done questioning you?"

"I doubt it," she said. "If they're bringing in the feds, I'd say the fun has just begun. But they can wait for me, too. I'm finished talking to them for tonight."

"I think I'll take your advice. I'll grab a cab at the main entrance, then catch a ride to my mom's house. She's expecting me. I'll start phoning attorneys in the morning." It infuriated him that he would have to foot the bill, but what choice did he have?

She pulled her keys out of her pocket. "If you call a cab, some reporter's bound to spot you. Let me give you a lift to your mom's place."

"You're leaving?" Given her reaction to her captain's injury, he'd figured she would stay.

"I need to stop by my house to let the dog out. Afterwards, I'm coming right back." She took a deep breath, then shuddered out a sigh. "It's just . . . I really need a break, you know? My crew—my friends are looking at me funny since I've been questioned, and I wasn't at that fire tonight, like I . . . like I should've been."

The raw pain in her voice sent an answering jolt through him, and before he could stop himself, his hand settled gently on her shoulder. "The asthma isn't your fault. And even if you'd been there, the same thing could have happened."

She turned away from him. "You don't know that. No one will ever know. But I would have gone in with him. I would have been there when it—"

"Don't do this to yourself, Reag."

"Don't call me that," she lashed back. "You don't even know me anymore."

"I know enough to see you're torturing yourself for no reason. Who's it helping?"

After a pause, she whispered, "No one."

"Come on, then. Let's go for that ride."

She nodded. "Better go tell the detectives or the arson investigator you'll contact them in the morning. Otherwise, they'll be imagining the worst. And don't mention you're going with me, or they'll suppose we're cooking up some kind of story. That jackass Detective Worth is already convinced we're sleeping together."

"I've been suspected of worse things." He smiled at her.

Her answering smile looked strained, but he caught a spark of her old spirit in her eyes.

"Well, *I* haven't," she said, "so hurry up and meet me at my car before I change my mind."

For the sake of his promise to the Firebug, the driver of the green car kept the images alive throughout the night. Not only the smashing glass and the exploding colors—yellow, white, and blue around the spill of fuel—but the tremendous *whoosh* as the flames took hold of not only the wooden framework of the fireplace where the bottle struck, but the carpeting and sofa where the flaming mixture splashed.

In its own way, it had been so fucking beautiful.

Grabbing a handful of fast-food napkins from the dashboard, he wiped his nose, still running from the acrid petroleum odor. While the doctor and his woman were inside the hospital, the driver had risked losing them to run to a nearby burger joint, where he had washed up in the restroom. But no matter how he scrubbed his face and neck, his hands and arms, the smoky stench clung to his hair and clothing, as damning as a freaking set of fingerprints if the cops should pull him over.

And the stinking food had given him a gut ache, too, coating his intestines with a greasy film that left him sweating out the hours he'd spent waiting. But he remained inside the parking garage nonetheless, eager to figure out where the doc would be staying, now that his home was gone.

And planning how to catch the man alone to deal with him.

The girlfriend had come out first, and this time he recognized her. The parking lot, of course, the one over by the clinic.

She had been the one he'd nearly mown down on his way out, a long, lean bitch, and sexy as hell, despite the pale hair cropped closer than he liked it on a woman. He remembered glancing in the rearview and seeing the way she'd stared after him—the only one he knew of who could place him at the scene.

The only one who might connect him to the fire at the apartments . . .

He wondered how it would play if he were to grab her and snatch a piece of ass before he left her somewhere dead. Close that pretty mouth before she started talking to the cops.

His grip tightened on the steering wheel, and his skin seemed to constrict around his body as an internal current raised the coarse hairs along his arms. A strange, hot flutter replaced the queasy ooze inside his belly, and he had a vision of himself as a great, dark, predatory presence—a goddamned stalking tiger bringing down a lithe gazelle.

Then, when he next saw the Firebug, he would bring a far better offering than a pale imitation of the "master's" arson jobs. He'd bring something the burned-up bastard would never top, now that he wasn't much more than stinking bandages over clots of fresh scar tissue.

Yet the driver hesitated, thinking of the carefully constructed plan and the contact who'd helped craft it, who had made the calls from various pay phones and used a digitally altered recording to get across their message. If he changed the plan, would he risk everything—including his reward?

When the woman didn't pass him to leave the garage within the next few minutes, he wondered if she was having trouble with that piece of shit she called a car. Temptation gnawed at him, and he pictured himself walking two rows over and asking her, "You need some help, miss?"

They would both laugh at the way his appearance scared her, at this late hour, and he would pop the hood to take a look, his well-practiced smile convincing her it was a good thing he had come along, and not some criminal. A few minutes later, he would have her leaning toward the engine, overbalancing as she strained to see some part he pointed out.

And utterly helpless when his hand clamped over her mouth and he jerked her back into the last and longest nightmare of her life.

Leaving the hospital with Reagan was not a good idea. Though Jack mentioned it to no one, he wondered what would happen if the two of them were seen together, sneaking around like a pair of teenagers—or criminals. Would Reagan, too, be forced to hire an attorney because their paths had crossed today?

After tracking down the two arson investigators, Jack hesitated near the exit to the parking garage. He lingered there for several minutes, weighing what common sense was telling him against the image of Reagan waiting for him outside, shivering inside her idling car.

"Oh, what the hell," he said before stuffing his hands into the pockets of his black jeans and striding toward the second level.

It wouldn't be the first time of late that his emotions pushed him past his better judgment. But this time, his hurry also propelled him beyond something equally important: a seemingly empty green sedan hidden in the darkest corner of the parking garage.

The driver of the green car gave his head a shake, realizing at the same time that, despite his grandiose plans for the blond bitch, he had been drifting off to sleep. He'd been startled by a shift in shadow—one he now recognized as Jack Montoya trotting past, between him and the red security light.

His heart hammering, he whacked the steering wheel and swore at his own weariness. Another minute or two and he would have been out cold. Would have missed the doctor's departure—and then where would he be?

Less than a minute later, when the couple drove out past him, he was ready. Despite its faded paint and scratches, the worn upholstery and the stolen plates, the old Ford thrummed eagerly to life, its performance a testimony to his automotive talents.

Now it was time to test again his skill as a tail. Time to find out where it was the doctor imagined he'd be safe.

Chapter Seven

Used to working twenty-four-hour shifts, Reagan had punched through the membrane of fatigue into energy reserves fueled in equal parts by nerves, caffeine, and pure determination. She could run for hours on that heady mixture; keyed up as she felt, she couldn't sleep now if she tried.

The traffic had thinned somewhat by this hour, but Houston's Medical Center never really slept. Day or night, one might find the streets jammed with both pedestrians and vehicles carrying medical and support staff, families and friends of patients, emergency crews, and local media. Some Friday and Saturday nights, a visitor might mistake the scene for a street festival.

As Reagan left the parking garage, she pulled up short to let two women, both wearing scrubs beneath their jackets, cross in front of her car. They were smiling, their hands animating what appeared to be a friendly conversation. One of them paused to sip a steaming, overpriced beverage from what must be an all-night coffee shop.

It was the type of scene she had seen a thousand times, ten thousand maybe, and yet tonight, it smacked her as surreal.

"It doesn't seem right," she said to Jack. "How can they go about their lives as if everything's normal, when the captain's inside, maybe dying, and your life's been turned upside down?"

"I know what you mean," he said. "But you and I both see people hurt and suffering, sometimes worse, in our jobs. All the while, we stand at the edges of their nightmares, going about our normal lives."

As they made their way toward the Heights, Reagan wondered what "normal life" would be after today, and whether she had been wrong to slip away from her crew and Donna in the hospital. Perhaps Jack was thinking along equally somber lines, for he didn't speak except to give directions to his mother's house when they reached her neighborhood.

"I really appreciate the lift," he added as they turned the corner. "Damn it all. Look at that!"

Reagan pulled over, her eyes focusing on a half-dozen vans and pickups parked in front of a neat one-story bungalow. Even from half a block away, she could make out the logos of a couple of television stations.

Jack swore again. "I was afraid of this. What I'd give to know who the hell leaked my mother's address to those vultures."

Backing around the corner, Reagan drove past another vehicle and made her way out of eyeshot of the news crews.

"Do you know where you're heading?" he asked. "There's a half-decent motel off of—"

"Stay at my place," she offered. "I have a guest room and an extra bed."

"Do you think that's a good idea, Reagan?"

Something in his tone made her stomach feel as if it had just fallen through the floorboards, especially when she glanced over and noticed the intensity of his regard. Shaking off her misgivings, she said, "Why not? You've just lost everything you own, so you don't need to spend the money on a room you won't be using more than a few hours anyway. I'm going right back to the hospital, so we won't . . . we won't be tripping over each other. And besides, you can feed Frank Lee and take him out in the morning so I won't have to ask Miss Peaches to do it. She usually works late, and she gets a little testy if I call her before noon."

Not only that, but after a long night spent photographing murder scenes, accident sites, and the occasional autopsy for the Harris County medical examiner's office, Peaches was likely to show up needing a shave—of her chest hair, which she invariably left exposed by some sort of low-cut top.

"What kind of name is Miss Peaches?"

Reagan snorted at the thought of Jack picturing an old-fashioned Southern girl. "That information's strictly on a need-to-know basis," she answered, not wanting to get into it. "Let's just say she's a nice neighbor lady who spoils Frank Lee when I'm gone."

"You said before he's a therapy dog of some kind?"

She nodded, momentarily distracted. "Yeah, we make weekly visits to a nursing home nearby. It's the only thing besides a crowbar that'll get the big lummox off my furniture."

Once they reached her house, Reagan took Jack inside through the back door, which led into her kitchen. Gesturing toward the fridge and pantry, she said, "You're probably hungry. Help yourself to anything you see. I'm going to wake up my fabulous watchdog and take him out. Then I'll show you around."

Rousing Frank Lee took some doing, as he was comfortably ensconced atop her bed, snoring with his head on her pillow. Six feet away, the ultimate dog bed, a billowy bag whose advertising promised never-ending comfort, lay unused.

"What am I going to do with you?" she asked the stretching greyhound. "That bed cost more than your therapy certification."

Frank Lee yawned in answer, his long pink tongue curling—which was probably the most exercise he'd had all week.

After walking the dog, she returned to find Jack munching the last of a pack of peanut-butter crackers from the pantry. He washed it down with milk, then rinsed the empty glass and set it in the sink.

"Thanks," he said. "I'm more wiped out than anything, but I needed to eat something."

Nodding, she fought an impulse to brush a few crumbs off his upper lip. An image reared up from the past, of the day the thirteen-year-old came home from school with his glasses broken and a suspicious swelling beneath his left eye, both resulting, she knew, from the stand he'd taken against Paulo Rodriguez and his delinquent brothers at the bayou. To save her, she understood now, from something an eight-year-old could never cope with.

But Jack had long since grown past the brave boy she remembered. She had only to look at the strong shoulders and the rough stubble on his face to see that. She had only to see him looking at her with his man's eyes—with a man's needs reflected in their darkness.

"Let me show you to the bedroom." Against the

quiet backdrop of the ticking kitchen clock, her traitorous words sounded suggestive. Disgusted with herself, she chattered on. "This is the bathroom. There are extra towels beneath the sink, and I think I have a spare toothbrush in that second drawer, probably a pack of disposable razors, too. Here's your room—sorry you'll have to share space with my treadmill and punching bag. But the sheets are clean, and there are blankets in the closet if you need them. The thermostat's out here in the hall. If it's too cold—"

"It's fine," he said as the greyhound trotted up and sniffed his hand. "Don't worry. Uh, do you have an extra key, so I can lock up when I leave?"

She nodded, then went to get him one. "There's a tub of dog food on top of the refrigerator. If you'd give Frank two scoops and take him out back to do his business in the morning, I'd appreciate it. Just put him back inside before you go."

"So Killer here can guard the house, right?" Jack's hand glided over the animal's smooth white head, and he gave the dog an exhausted-looking smile.

Reagan wondered how it would feel to have him look at her with the same easy affection, his eyes bleary after a night spent—

She gave her head a shake to clear it and quickly said good-bye. She needed to get the hell out of this house, before the evening's stress and whatever-the-hell estrogen attack she was suffering conspired to push her into doing something stupid.

Or *more* stupid, she decided, as she'd already crossed that particular line when she'd invited him to stay here at her house.

* * *

It was all Jack could do to keep from reaching out to Reagan as she turned to go. Though his better judgment provided a thousand reasons he should keep his peace, at that moment he would have given almost anything for the perfect pretext to get her to stay here with him.

And not only in her little house, but in his bed and arms as well. He wanted—needed desperately—to lose himself in a woman, to forget the nightmare that his life had become. Between the ebb and flow of memory and what he'd seen today—or yesterday, he supposed—of Reagan's courage and compassion, he saw a thin sliver, no more than a scalpel's edge, that gleamed with possibility.

The possibility of a cut straight to the heart, he warned himself as he listened to her moving through the house and toward the back door. The dog's toenails clicked behind her on first the wood floor, then the tile.

Let it go. Let her go. Act as if you have two working brain cells and the sense to use them.

From the direction of the kitchen, he heard the back door open. His ears strained for the sounds of closing, locking, leaving. Instead, he heard a faint but distinctive riff from AC/DC's "Highway to Hell."

He didn't realize it was her cell phone's ring tone until he heard her say, "Hello. Beau? What's wro—oh—oh, God. That's not right. It *can't* be. He can't be. I won't believe it—I'll be right over. No . . . what do you mean, you don't need . . . you don't need me there?"

Understanding immediately that Captain Rozinski's condition must have worsened, Jack raced down the hall, past the darkened living room, and into the kitchen. There, he found her leaning in the open doorway, her head down and her back against the frame as the cold night air pushed its way inside the house. Her white dog nosed at her free hand, nervously trying to insinuate himself beneath it, as if for reassurance. His thick tail thumped rhythmically against the side of a wooden cabinet, beating out a funereal drumbeat.

The cell phone slipped from Reagan's grasp and struck the tile floor. Something cracked, and a small plastic piece spun sideways before coming to rest several feet away.

She glanced up at Jack, her eyes already red. "This is turning out to be a damned expensive night. That was Beau, and he was saying . . . he was saying that . . . that the captain's—"

Jack folded her into his arms. Pulling her inside the house, he closed the back door. Shutting out the cold wind, but closing in her grief.

Instead of collapsing into his embrace, she remained so rigid he felt as if he'd wrapped himself around a sculpture: something angular, metallic, and utterly unyielding.

"I'm going to flatten Beau next time I see him." Despite the threat, Reagan's voice thinned and rose, like a guitar string tightening as it neared the breaking point. "He might be upset that I was questioned, but what right does that give him to tell me the captain's dead?"

"Reag, please listen," whispered Jack, his mouth pressed not far from her ear, his hand rubbing soothing circles on her back.

"He isn't," she insisted, her head jerking stiffly from side to side. "I told you my crew was looking at me funny—and now they're mad I left. If he had *really* died, I would have been there. I would have been there for Joe Rozinski, the way he always was for me."

Jack pulled back, gripping her shoulders and holding her at arm's length so he could look her in the eyes. "They wouldn't lie about this, Reagan. No one would do that."

"Then they're mistaken. There could've been a mix-up, the doctors might have gone to the wrong room and told the wrong people about some—some other . . ."

He watched her face fall as her denial wound down like a clock. As an EMT, she'd undoubtedly heard patients' loved ones do the same thing on numerous occasions, as their minds scrambled to find purchase on the terrifying slopes of sudden death. For Jack's part, experience had never made it any easier to witness, particularly in someone he knew personally—someone he had thought, only moments earlier, that he would like to get to know a great deal better.

The thought crashed down upon him that she would always link him with her captain's death—as both the media and the authorities would undoubtedly attempt to do as well. Yet when tears broke through the dam of her objections, she collapsed into the refuge of his arms.

"It can't be right." Again and again, she repeated the words, until her voice grew hoarse and her breath strained audibly inside her chest.

He wondered where, if anywhere, she had an inhaler.

"It *isn't* right," he told her as he steered her toward the living room. "It's never right when someone dies, never fair to the people left behind."

He guided her to the sofa and helped her slip out of her leather jacket. Once settled, she folded her knees nearly to her chest and wrapped her arms around them tightly. He sat on the sofa's opposite end, within easy reach of a Tiffany-style lamp. Yet he contented himself with the dim light leaking from the kitchen.

Grabbing a box of tissues, he set it on the cushion between them. "It's especially hard when the death is cruel or senseless . . . when it didn't have to happen."

As she mopped her eyes and blew her nose, he thought of the weeks his father had been missing, the call the Border Patrol made when his body had been found. The disbelief, the hurt, and the fury had set in like a caustic rain, eating away his flesh, leaving almost nothing of the boy who'd lived and loved in innocence. For a long time, he'd hated everyone—the *coyotes* for their murderous greed, the Border Patrol agents for their lack of interest in the crime and their failure to catch the culprits, and even his own mother for allowing Papa to visit his mother—the Mexican grandmother Jack had never known.

Reagan, too, would hate, only she would hate *him*. And there wasn't one damned thing he could do to change it. But he could help her now, for as long as she would let him.

"Is there someone I can call for you? What about your mother?"

"My—my mother doesn't—doesn't give a damn about me," Reagan told him, pausing to breathe between her words. "She m-made her choice—long ago."

"You're going to need some medicine." He hated to bring it up, but there was no sense in letting this episode get out of hand. Though emotional stress didn't cause asthma, it could sure as hell exacerbate an existing problem. "Do you have a rescue inhaler, or better yet, a nebulizer?"

"I don't—I don't want to—"

"Do you want to end up in the ER? That kind of thing stays in your medical records," he reminded her, though instinct told him she'd already had at least a handful of similar episodes. He'd really like to get her to Li Chen, the pulmonologist he'd mentioned earlier.

She looked up into his face, her pupils wells of darkness against the lighter irises.

"I'm not your doctor," he assured her. "I'm only asking as a friend."

She fished an inhaler from the pocket of her jacket and, after a moment's hesitation, used it.

He wondered whether he should count it an act of trust or desperation. He was curious, too, about what had caused her falling-out with her sole surviving parent, but asking was a bad idea, especially tonight.

After she took a second shot from the inhaler, he said, "You really shouldn't be alone."

She moved both the jacket and the box of tissues to the floor and slid close beside him, then shocked him by laying her head on his shoulder.

"I'm not alone," she whispered, her breath warm against the hollow of his throat, bare since he had unbuttoned his shirt. "Not as long as you're with me."

His body reacted instantly, heat surging in his loins, anticipation tingling in every synapse. He didn't move; he didn't dare. Even the breath froze in his lungs.

When she turned her body, her fingers stealing beneath the open shirt and her warm lips pressing against his, he knew damned well that this was a mistake, but it didn't stop his mouth from opening to claim hers in a kiss that rocked him to his core.

The waves of answering sensation offered the oblivion they both yearned for. The kiss went on and on, lengthening as he rolled to pin her against the cushions, their bodies writhing, struggling to silence the pain this night had wrought.

His own need flared so urgently, he nearly took what Reagan offered without stopping to think—or care—that it was wrong. His hands were fumbling to unhook her bra, his mouth sliding to taste the long curve of her pale neck by the time his conscience slipped into gear.

You're one sorry bastard if you take advantage of her.

He palmed a warm breast, squeezed it, heard her gasp in pleasure and surprise. Thumbed the button of her nipple and groaned to feel it peak.

"Yes," she rasped, and he wanted more than anything to make her shout his name.

A man died tonight, his mind screamed, *and you would use that to get inside a woman?*

Groaning with regret, he managed to push himself away. When she moved toward him, he raised his hands. "I can't. *We* can't, not tonight."

He heard her breathing heavily, and much more easily, as she sat up.

"God, Jack. God, I'm—I'm sorry. You must think I . . . you must think I'm some . . . some horrible slut, to do this . . . do this now, when he's dead, when my captain . . . my friend is—"

He wrapped his arms around her, this time out of empathy instead of lust. "It's all right, Reagan. You're in shock still. We've both had an awful night. We're exhausted—anyone would understand. I'm certainly the last one to throw stones. I didn't exactly beat you off with a stick.

"You should go to bed now," he said quietly. "You'll feel better in the morning."

"I just wanted to forget for a little while," she whispered as she stood. She reached down for his hand. "I still want to."

Her invitation was unmistakable, as were her loneliness and vulnerability. He hesitated on the blade's edge, realizing that no matter what decision he made, the outcome he had feared was now inevitable.

One of them was going to feel this cut straight to the heart.

Chapter Eight

Jack Montoya could go straight to hell, thought Reagan as she stepped into the shower.

She couldn't get the water hot enough, couldn't get enough lather from her bar soap or enough water pressure from the showerhead to wash away even the top layers of her fury. She was still shaking with outrage over the way Jack had kissed the top of her head as if she were a child, then quietly told her, "I think it would be best if you went to bed alone."

As if she were not only blind to the desire in his eyes but insensible to his body's reaction to their tangle on the sofa and the raw need building in his kiss. He wanted her—she knew it. He needed an hour of mindless passion as desperately as she did.

Her flesh tingled at the memory of his strong hands cupping her breasts, the way he'd swiftly pinned her to the cushions. She closed her eyes, but behind the lids she could see the act their grinding foretold, could almost *feel* him entering her heat. An instant later, she twisted the faucet far to the right, for suddenly the water felt unbearably warm.

But the icy torrent did nothing to wash away the pain that lurked behind her lust. Instead, the grief she had fought so hard to dampen burst to the forefront, so that she found herself sobbing and shivering, her tears streaming hot against her now cold face.

Maybe Jack *had* done her a favor after all, she thought as she wrapped herself in a towel. Maybe he understood that sex with a near stranger would prove every bit as destructive an impulse as deadening her pain with drugs or alcohol.

That might explain his actions, but it left a more important question: Why didn't Jack Montoya feel like a stranger to her heart?

After drying, she pulled on her oldest, most comfortable sleep shirt, an oversized, long-sleeved tee from the dilapidated gym where she worked out—the same gym her father had trained in years before she was born. But the memory of the day Joe Rozinski had introduced her to boxing broke her down again.

It had been a charity match between a Houston firefighter and a cop, though Joe had told her mother he was taking the ten-year-old to Astroworld. Smart move, considering that the newly remarried Georgina would rather have seen Reagan ride a hundred roller coasters than have anything to do with the Houston Fire Department. Intent on fitting into her well-heeled husband's world of exclusive clubs and cocktail parties, Georgina had packed up the memories of her old life and put them in cold storage—or at least that was the way Reagan saw it.

Even so, her mom had welcomed Joe Rozinski's periodic offers to take her daughter off her hands. Some days, Reagan was almost certain that both her mother and stepfather would have given her to passing strangers to get a break from all the commotion she stirred up in their household.

Served their snooty asses right for trying to pretend her dad had never existed. If she hadn't hauled a few of his things out of the trash, they would have left her nothing to remember him by—not the flag from his coffin, his fire helmet, even a damned photograph. And certainly not the chance to talk about him—something that invariably sent her mother fleeing to her professionally decorated bedroom to lock the door.

Had it not been for Joe Rozinski, Reagan might not have survived what a school counselor once politely termed her mother's "coping strategy."

But as she turned the lights off and blindly groped her way to bed, Reagan thought that for the first time, she might just understand it. Sometimes, for some people, holding on to memory was like holding a live flame in your cupped hands.

A fire far too bright to look at—and far too eager to consume.

More than an hour later, Reagan remained awake, staring at the slowly spinning shadow of a ceiling fan that she habitually kept running, even on the coolest nights that Houston had to offer. She couldn't stop thinking of her family and the part that the captain had played in its undoing so many years before: the day he'd come up their walk, beside the fire-department chaplain, and told them what had happened to her father.

It had been the week before Christmas, and Reagan

had at first thought this strange visit must be part of some surprise her daddy had planned. Until her mother took one look out the picture window and dropped the ornament she'd been hanging on their tree.

The blue bulb exploded when it hit the wood floor. Reagan could still hear the thin glass shattering, could still feel her own quick pulse of anger. That ornament had been her favorite, one she didn't think she could live without.

But she hadn't understood then. Not yet. Not until the captain was standing on their doorstep, his tears washing clean gullies on the soot-stained landscape of his face.

Above Reagan, the fan blades did their death dance, while beside her on the nightstand the clock radio's red digits changed to four A.M.

She reached for the telephone beside the readout. Then, before she could change her mind, she quickly punched the number she had programmed first on her speed dial, despite the fact that it had been years since she'd last called it.

It rang twice, then three times, before someone picked it up.

"Mmm . . . um, hello . . . who is this calling?" The woman's voice was edged in fear as she braced for the worst, in the way of sleepers awakened by a ringing in the stillness of the night.

"It's Reagan," she said softly, as if her tone could blunt the news she had to share. "I thought you'd want to know that Joe . . . that Joe Rozinski died this evening. Of injuries he sustained on duty, at a fire."

Reagan couldn't decipher the next sounds she heard, couldn't say whether they were whispers or the animal-like snuffles of a woman crying. The next thing she was sure of was the soft click of a receiver, followed by the cruelly loud dial tone.

Reagan listened to it for a long time before hanging up her own phone and then falling into a sleep as black and thick as tar.

Jack woke from a sound sleep to a woman's screaming, a shriek worse than anything he'd heard since a member of a mowing crew had been carried into the clinic with a partially severed foot. Jack was on his feet and moving, still wearing yesterday's black jeans, before he took in the basic facts: he was in a strange house at mid-morning, judging from the sunshine streaming through the window.

Reagan Hurley's house, he realized as he burst shirtless from her guest room. Following the noise, he threw open a door along the short hall and saw her struggling on her bed, arms thrashing and her bare legs kicking off the covers. Frank Lee paced the floor, whining and then looking at him pleadingly, clearly no more disposed to guard his mistress than he was to be a watchdog.

"Wake up." Jack kept his distance to avoid her flailing limbs. "Reagan, wake up. You're having a nightmare."

"It burns," she cried out, her breathing sounding strangled as it had last night. "It burns—it burns me. Put the fire out."

Was she dreaming of her captain? Though the house was cool, perspiration filmed her face as her body twisted. Her sleep shirt had crept up, exposing her lower body, but her distress kept Jack from enjoying what would ordinarily be one fine view.

Closing in, he repeated her name, then grabbed her shoulder.

Her right fist shot out and caught him on the chin. Though he stood nearly six feet tall, outweighed her by a long shot, and worked out at the gym four times a week, the blow set him on his ass beside her bed.

"Ow," she murmured, shaking her hand and rubbing the knuckles. "That—that hurt."

"You're telling me," Jack said, his fingertips probing his sore jaw. A little higher, and he might have been searching for his teeth on the room's ivory carpet.

Her blue eyes fluttered open, and she stared down at him. "Jack? What the hell are you doing in my bedroom?"

He thought of pointing out that last night, she'd been eager enough to get him in here. But he decided that getting belted once before coffee was more than enough. "You must have been having a bad dream. You were screaming, scaring poor Frank half to death."

Jack didn't add that he'd been equally alarmed. For one thing, her bare bottom—now at eye level—was proving one hell of a distraction.

To his regret, she pulled the hem of her oversized T-shirt down to cover herself.

"Did I hit you?" She ran her palm over sleep-spiked hair to sleek it back, then once more glanced at her knuckles. "My hand hurts."

"I can tell you, I didn't crawl in on the floor. You have a killer right, you know that? You must use that punching bag for more than decoration."

"I fight in the female lightweight division, strictly amateur."

He managed a smile and rubbed the tender spot on his chin. "That felt pro to me."

Her answering smile fell almost before it started, and he wondered if she was remembering her dream or the worse nightmare of her captain's death. Her breath hitched, but a moment later, her delicate jaw tightened and her shoulders squared, reminding him for all the world of a soldier steeling herself for battle, despite her puffy eyes.

"If you'll give me a minute, I'll throw on some clothes."

He nearly told her not to bother on his account, then thought better of it. But she speared him with a hard look, as if some flicker in his expression had allowed her to read his mind.

"If you're having second thoughts about turning me down last night, you might as well forget it. You were right," she told him. "I was half out of my mind, but I can tell you one thing. I won't repeat the offer."

His gaze smacked up against hers. "If you do, you'd better damned well mean it, because I'm not lobbying for sainthood. And you're one temptation I won't say no to twice."

She opened her mouth as if to shoot back some remark, but before she could get it out, she seemed to change her mind. Climbing out of her bed, she turned her back to him and pulled open a closet. "Okay, then," she finally managed. "Soon as I change, we can grab you some ice for that chin of yours and maybe scrounge up breakfast. Then I'll drop you at your mom's place—provided the coast is clear."

"I don't need ice," he said. "And I'll call my sister and get her to pick me up here. But I wouldn't say no to some toast or cereal—on the condition that you'll have something, too."

She shrugged a shoulder. "I don't feel much like eating."

"Sometimes you just have to go through the motions. You won't be any good to anybody if you don't get some food inside you. Did you have anything last night?"

He could see the argument gathering like a storm behind the lightning flash of her eyes. But to his surprise, she merely shook her head.

"It never crossed my mind," she said. "But I suppose you're right about eating. I feel like I've been run over by a truck."

In a way, they both had. But what Jack wanted to know—what he hoped like hell the investigators would find out soon—was who had been behind the wheel of their misfortune.

By the time Reagan threw on a charcoal-colored, long-sleeved tee, a pair of jeans, and her boots, then ran a brush through her hair and washed her face, the aroma of brewing coffee pulled her, nose first, to the kitchen.

She was thankful Jack had put on the white shirt he'd been wearing yesterday. It might be wrinkled, but at least it covered that well-developed chest of his. Clearly, he wasn't one of those hypocritical MDs who gave lip service to exercise without bothering to make time for it himself.

"And here I thought you doctors didn't deign to make the coffee."

"Are you kidding?" He pulled a carton of eggs out of her refrigerator. "By the time we're through with residency, we're all a bunch of caffeine fiends. I hope I didn't make it too strong for your taste."

"Unless the spoon stands up in the cup, I'm good," she said as she flipped on a small under-cabinet TV to a local news broadcast. "Let's see what they have about the . . . about what happened."

Apprehension gave her lungs a quick squeeze, until the picture on the screen resolved into a chamber-of-commerce weather forecast: warming into the high sixties by midday, with gobs of sunshine, a stark reminder that yesterday's nasty weather had been an aberration.

She wished uselessly that yesterday's fire could blow over as quickly. Swallowing past a knot of pain, she blinked away the threat of tears and pulled out the utensils she would need.

"How do you like your eggs?" asked Jack as he filled the narrow space before the stove.

As if he'd been here all his life. As if he belonged. Annoyance prickled. "Make yourself at home, why don't you?"

If the sarcasm bothered, or even registered with him, he gave no sign. "Scrambled?" he tried. "I know how to do that."

She shrugged her shoulders and plunked down on a barstool at the counter. Her kitchen might be small, but it had been the previous owner's first-class remodeling job that made her fall for the old house in the first place. The warmth of reclaimed brick and Mexican tile set off the amber beauty of the cabinetry and inspired her to fill the hanging racks with chef-grade pots and pans. She was still learning to use them properly, but at least she'd progressed beyond her old canned-soup-and-frozen-dinner habits.

Contrary to her words, she was happy to let Jack cook a simple meal of eggs and toast. Right now, sitting on this stool and holding herself together required all her concentration.

When Darren Winter's long face flashed on the television screen, she used the remote control to nudge the volume higher. The blue sky behind him and the wind ruffling his thin, sandy hair told her that someone had caught him out-of-doors to stick a microphone into his face.

"How do you respond to allegations that your criticism of Dr. Jack Montoya may have led to the death of a Houston firefighter?"

Reagan recognized the voice of a local field reporter well known for his fierce ambition. Did he hope to gain national attention by going after the celebrity mayoral "candidate"?

Jack's head jerked toward the television at the mention of his name.

The camera panned out, revealing that despite Winter's somber expression, he was standing on a sun-drenched patch of golf course.

"First of all," said Winter, replacing a driver in his golf bag, "let me express my heartfelt condolences to the Houston Fire Department and especially to the family of Captain Joe Rozinski, a true hero of our city."

A hero whose death would be overshadowed, Reagan realized, by this link to Darren Winter. Nausea swept away her hunger, and her shoulders tightened. Her glance touched on Jack's for a moment before she looked back to the screen.

The obligatory expression of sympathy behind him, Winter's face hardened, his gray-blue eyes growing flinty. "As for this ridiculous accusation, I am deeply offended by the mayor's self-serving attempts to profit from Captain Rozinski's death. As anyone who has read the Bill of Rights knows, free speech is a cornerstone of this great country, one that would be severely undermined by any ill-conceived attempts to hold journalists accountable for the unfortunate interpretations of sick individuals or the actions of known terrorist factions such as BorderFree-4-All. Now that's all I have to say on the matter—until such time as I accept the mayor's apologies for his cowardly attempts to call my patriotism into question for his own political gain."

Jack might be a family doctor, but he swore with the precision of a surgeon—and the colorful artistry of many of Reagan's fellow firefighters.

"*Carajo,*" he cursed. "Have you ever heard such self-serving bullshit in your life?"

"Only every time that jerk opens his mouth," said Reagan as Sabrina McMillan appeared onscreen.

The short-skirted navy suit the mayor's campaign manager had chosen no better disguised the woman's long legs than her tightly controlled, rich brown mane offset her bedroom eyes. Her bright red lipstick made her moving mouth look like a wound. Revolted by the thought—as well as the memory of one particular fire call to the woman's penthouse—Reagan turned off the television.

"We won't get any facts there," she said, "just another string of sound bites. Joe Rozinski could have put in his twenty and retired years ago. Instead, he gave this city—gave this city and his family and his friends—everything he had, every day of his life. And for what? So his death could become a damned political football? They don't even care who he was."

When she met Jack's stricken expression, Reagan remembered that he, too, had become a sidebar to the story. "I'm sorry," she added. "Did you want to see more?"

Shaking his head, he went back to his cooking, his

handsome face both grim and drawn. "I've seen more than enough," he told her as he scraped the eggs onto the plates she took out.

Neither of them said a word while they shared their somber meal. As they were finishing, someone banged at the back door, and both jumped at the sound.

"That must be my sister," Jack said. "I called while you were dressing."

But Frank Lee was wagging his tail beside the door, as he did whenever a visitor was someone he knew well. Peeking through the curtain that concealed her kitchen window, Reagan closed her eyes and swore.

Why couldn't Luz Maria have come and gone already?

Glancing toward Jack, she said, "This could be a little awkward," then opened the back door to let Beau LaRouche inside.

Beau looked as if he'd had a rough night. His sandy hair was a tangled mess, his faded tan looked sallow, and the stubble of his beard growth made him look more like a north-side vagrant than the pretty boy he usually resembled. Instead of petting Frank Lee, as he usually did, Beau pushed away the narrow head that nudged his hand.

"Hey, Hurley. You get any sleep at all?" His brown eyes looked concerned—until he caught sight of Jack, who crossed the kitchen and offered his hand.

Beau's jaw thrust forward, and a vee engraved itself into the space between his brows. Ignoring the outstretched hand, he rounded on Reagan. "What the hell is this? You're having breakfast with this . . . this goddamned . . . I don't even know what the hell he is. But I know this for damned sure. If it weren't for him making a big name for himself with those BorderFree nuts and

111

pissing off Winter's disciples, I wouldn't be here talking to you about a memorial service."

She'd seen Beau plenty mad before, usually when one of his firehouse pranks backfired. But she had never seen him like this, had never before imagined that someone who would spend hours conning her into trying paintball—which hurt far more than he'd promised—could look so close to violence.

She stepped forward, meaning to put herself between the two men before Beau took a swing at Jack. But Jack sidestepped her neatly, his dark gaze boring into the younger man's.

"I want you to know," Jack said, not looking a bit concerned that Beau was several inches taller and a good twenty-five pounds heavier, "that no matter how the fire started, I'm truly sorry about what happened to your captain. I don't know what's going on, don't know anything except that I go to work and do my job day after day, the best I can. But if someone set that fire to kill me, I will damned well find out who it was."

Something inside Reagan resonated with the raw emotion in his voice. This was no carefully scripted, official "expression of condolences," as Houston firefighters and Donna Rozinski would receive from public officials for weeks to come. Jack Montoya's regret over the loss of life was as genuine as his anger and bewilderment about the circumstances.

Yet Beau surged toward him. "You're a lying sack of shit, Montoya. I'll kick your goddamn ass—"

"No." Adrenaline shooting through her, Reagan grabbed his upper arm. "No way are you punching anybody in my house. You hear me, Beau? Jack's leaving anyway. As soon as his ride gets here, he'll be making arrangements to go see the FBI and arson, the police and all those guys. Do you really want him walking in black and blue and telling how you hit him?"

"If he hits me"—Jack's voice had frosted over—"*I* won't be the one walking around bruised."

Reagan sighed in relief when a knock at the front door interrupted. Luz Maria had come to get her brother.

Ignoring Beau, Jack introduced Reagan to her, saying, "I'm sure you don't remember, but the Hurleys were our landlords for a while. Reagan lived next door before she and her mother moved."

"You weren't much more than a baby then, but it's good to see you again." Though Reagan was keeping half an eye on Beau, she took in Luz Maria's big eyes and thick, dark ponytail. Jack's little sister wore jeans and a tight, cinnamon-colored sweater; her fresh-faced prettiness didn't suffer from her lack of jewelry or makeup.

Luz Maria offered her a smile, but worry darkened her eyes. "Thanks so much for taking care of Jack last night. Mama and I barely slept, we were so upset about what happened."

To Jack, she added, "Uncle Julio brought you some clothes and things from his store to get you started. I hope we guessed your size right."

"Thank you for that. And thanks again, Reagan, for everything."

As he stepped outside, Reagan wondered when she would next see him, and why the suspicion that he was leaving her life weighed so heavily on her mind.

She watched the siblings walking toward a long white Buick wagon, listened to the drift of their receding voices. "So Mama trusted you with her car?"

"Mama finally got to sleep around four. I didn't bother waking her . . ."

The door in front of Reagan slammed shut as Beau reached around her to give it a hard push. She jumped at the unexpected sound and whirled toward him.

Beau glared down at her, caging her against the door with his outstretched arm. "You told me you weren't seeing him, that you weren't involved in this."

She ducked beneath his arms and stalked back toward the kitchen. He might be half crazy with grief, but this was a Beau LaRouche she didn't know—or much like. "I told you the truth. I don't have anything to do with what happened, and I've never dated Jack Montoya."

Beau grabbed her arm with bruising pressure and spun her toward him. Frank Lee whined and tried without success to wedge himself in the narrow space between them.

Beau was so close, his unnaturally white teeth were a blur. "So you slept with him instead?"

Her heart ricocheted around her chest, and she had to struggle to keep the fear out of her voice. "Cut it out, Beau. Now. This isn't you talking. It's the situa—"

She was falling, head snapping backward, before she heard him shout, "Shut up. Just shut up."

She landed hard, banging her elbow on the door frame between the dining room and kitchen. But that didn't hurt half so much as her left cheekbone. He'd hit her, Reagan realized. Beau LaRouche had actually punched her in the face.

Judging from the way he went sheet white, Beau had just realized it himself. He stared down at his right hand as if it were some alien attachment in a plot worthy of a *Star Trek* rerun.

She was so stunned by his action, so blown away that Beau, her buddy and one of the best rookie firemen she had ever seen, had hit her, she couldn't think how to react.

Beau backed into the kitchen, his eyes round with horror. "Reagan, oh, my God," he murmured again and again, reminding her of the stories he had told about his father beating up his mother, about how much Beau had hated it.

His hand reached for the knob of the back door.

"Don't you walk out of this house," she snarled, her arm draping over Frank's back as she used the big dog to get up off the floor.

Taking heed of her words, Beau didn't *walk* out. Instead, the rookie firefighter turned and ran like hell.

A minute later, his souped-up old Camaro revved, and she heard the crunch of gravel as he reversed into the street. Running to the front of the house, Reagan brushed aside a curtain with a trembling hand.

In time to see the silver coupe barreling in the same direction that Luz Maria and her brother had just taken. If Beau caught up with them somehow . . .

Ignoring the throbbing of her cheekbone, Reagan raced to grab the portable phone. Remembering that Jack's mother, in her enthusiasm, had given her his mobile number as well his landline and work numbers, Reagan found the slip of paper in her bedroom and hurriedly punched in the digits.

Only to hear a ringing from her own guest room.

Following the sound, she located Jack's cell phone on the carpeted floor, where it lay half hidden by the quilted comforter of the neatly remade bed.

So what now? By searching for Jack's number, she'd blown the chance to try to follow Beau.

115

She could call Jack's and Luz Maria's mother, but she hated the idea of upsetting the woman over what would probably turn out to be nothing. She thought of calling 911, but that would mean getting Beau in trouble for something she only imagined he might do, not to mention dragging the police into what had taken place between them. It might also end the career that he had worked so hard for, only hours after both of them had lost a man they loved.

Tears hazed her vision, and still her index finger hovered above the lighted keypad. Should she make the 911 call and destroy a good friend unhinged by guilt and grief? Or should she risk allowing him to hurt or maybe even kill another man?

"How stupid can I get?" she asked herself as she hit the speed-dial number she should have punched in in the first place.

"Answer," she whispered repeatedly into her phone. And wondered what to do if Beau did not.

Chapter Nine

His new lawyer's paralegal drove Jack to a Cheap
Wheelz location near Telephone Road just after dark.
As was the case with all the other outlets in the fran-
chise, this one operated out of an old storefront in a
mostly empty strip center in a neighborhood predomi-
nated by small homes and apartments that had seen
better days.

His driver, a pudgy redhead in her late fifties, gazed
at a chain-link fence topped with curls of razor wire.
On the other side, parked in neat rows, sat a ragtag collection of vehicles Paulo regularly rounded up at bank
repo and government seizure auctions. A few were
nice enough, late-model sedans, pickups, or sports
coupes that gleamed beneath the color-muting security
lights. More, however, bore visible dents and scrapes or
mismatched quarter panels.

"People actually *rent* these things?" asked the paralegal before darting a nervous glance toward a pair of
young black men carrying long-neck beer bottles.

As the two passed, Jack nodded toward one and

lifted two fingers from the dash in greeting. He had immunized the man's infant son a couple of days earlier.

"Not everyone has credit cards or auto insurance policies," he explained. "Cheap Wheelz serves a need in low-income neighborhoods."

Defensiveness came naturally when Jack spoke to an outsider, but the realities of Paulo's enterprise were far more complicated. From what Jack had heard, rentals at places like Cheap Wheelz were anything but cheap, and the business's true income, which came in the form of cash, was easily hidden from the IRS. Paulo's chain, which he promoted as a form of civic-minded philanthropy, could as easily be seen as a parasite on the community it served.

After thanking the woman for the ride, Jack walked into the storefront, a clean, beige-tiled space ringed by inexpensive plastic chairs and softened by large tropical plants in painted pots. Framed photographs and news clippings decorated the walls, all of them featuring "Paul" Rodriguez, his successes, and his contributions to various local charities. In every case, the outsized Paulo dwarfed the officials pictured beside him.

When Paulo came around the counter, his jowls were a little heavier than in the photos, and the streak of premature gray in his goatee was more prevalent than the last time Jack had seen him. He looked good, though, with his expensive haircut, huge diamond-stud earring, and a dark gray suit far sharper than anything Jack had ever worn. No tie, though. Paulo's shirt was partially unbuttoned and light green, the color of new money.

Grinning, Paulo pumped Jack's hand energetically. "You get things straightened out?"

Still wondering if he'd been wise to accept his old friend's offer, Jack scrounged around for a halfhearted smile. "Working on it. Thanks for staying open late for me."

"*No problemo.*"

"The other day, I meant to ask you. How's the family?"

"You know, the usual: Carlos and Jaime in the joint again, both of 'em sayin' how they didn't do it." Paulo shook his head over the brothers who had never taken to the straight and narrow. "Mama's takin' care of my boy while I'm working."

The last Jack knew, the woman was bad-mouthing Paulo all over town on account of how her oldest son had somehow cheated the other two out of their share of the business. Maybe Paulo's success had changed her mind, or maybe she'd been won over by the special needs of her grandson—or by whatever she was paid to look after the boy. Senora Rodriguez had always struck Jack as the mercenary sort. But maybe she had to be, since her good-for-nothing husband had drifted out of her life many years before.

"I can't tell you how much I appreciate the use of one of your cars," Jack said. "Otherwise, I'd be walking."

"Don't worry about it, '*mano*.'" Paulo produced a set of keys. "In this neighborhood, we look out for each other, especially when some outsider's gunnin' for us. Now, did you get to talk to Winter?"

Jack accepted the keys but shook his head. "This federal task force kept me busy all day rehashing the same old stuff I told the arson investigator and the cops last night. But from what I understand, Winter's getting a lot of flak for what he's done."

"Yeah. I been keepin' an eye on the TV." Paulo gestured toward a set bracketed—and padlocked—to a shelf high in the corner. "But the bastard's turnin' the

situation all around like it's some big-ass damn conspiracy with BorderFree, the mayor, and the whole
freaking Democratic party."

Something on the screen had attracted Jack's attention. "Could you turn the sound on? Higher—please."

Wearing one of their trademarked desert camo
hoods, the spokesman for BorderFree-4-All stood, fist
raised, before the camera. When he spoke, his deep
voice boomed out an accent more reminiscent of
upper-crust Mexico City than the penniless border-
runners he claimed to represent. "We will never allow
the martyrdom of Dr. Joaquín Montoya to go unher-
alded, nor will we allow the tyranny of bureaucratic
oppression to go . . ."

The words faded as the news show segued into images from last May's INS bombing and the broadcasts
that had made BorderFree-4-All both a despised presence and a household word.

"This is all I need—" Jack's words choked off, and
his eyes widened as he recognized one of the un-
hooded faces in the background of the story.

It was Sergio. His sister's boyfriend.

"Son of a bitch!" Jack swore. "Luz Maria's going out
with that guy, the one in black, with the long ponytail."

Paulo shook his head scornfully. "That punk? Your
sister's got no taste, man. I asked her out a few times,
but she never gave me half a chance to—"

"I have to go talk to her," Jack said, a terrible suspicion overwhelming his surprise that Paulo would hit
on the much-younger Luz Maria. "Which car do I
take?"

After switching off the television and locking up behind himself, Paulo led Jack to the nicest vehicle on his

lot, a jet-black Mustang convertible that couldn't have been more than a year or two old.

Jack shook his hand. "Thanks, Paulo. I promise you, I won't forget this."

"I'm counting on it, *compa*."

Paulo's smile as he spoke was wide and bright and friendly. But as Jack started the car, he couldn't help wondering: Did small fish see that same expression before the shark's jaws split to swallow them alive?

"Joaquín, you did not call me," Jack's mother accused the moment he walked in the front door of the little purple house on Waverly. Just beyond the entry, the dining room was lit with at least thirty Our Lady of Guadalupe candles, which were meant as a plea for miracles—no doubt, on his behalf. In case Guadalupe wasn't up to the challenge, Mama had also dragged out the wrought-iron-framed portrait of Saint Jude, her collection of tiny lucky plastic skeletons found over the years inside loaves baked to commemorate the Day of the Dead, and a lime-green rabbit's foot, which she stroked continuously with her short fingers.

Never let it be said that his mother didn't cover all the bases.

"All day, I cannot go to the *yerbería* because I worry for you. I worry and I worry, so much I am shaking—see?"

When she raised a spastic hand in evidence, Jack decided he had seen less expressive grand mal seizures. "You should get that looked at," he said dryly. "It might fly off any minute."

Both of her hands stopped shaking and fisted at her hips. "What is the use of leaving messages if you never listen to them?"

Jack used two fingers to rub the bridge of his nose. The last thing he needed was one of Candelaria de Vaca Montoya's legendary it's-all-about-me attacks. Yet as much as he wanted to plug his ears and walk past her, he did owe her an explanation—and an apology as well. With her still-black, short curls deflated, her favorite purple pantsuit wrinkled, and her spiky black lashes clumped with moisture, she did look genuinely distraught.

He encircled her with his arms and let her lean into his embrace. Tiny as she was, the top of her head barely reached his chest. "I'm sorry, Mama. The interview ran later than I thought, and I never got your messages. I lost my phone somewhere, maybe at Reagan Hurley's last night."

He should have called Reagan from the station when he had realized it was missing. But this morning's run-in with her coworker had made him hesitate. Whatever her health status, Reagan was a firefighter. And the firefighters were clearly closing ranks against him.

Though he'd used a pay phone to call Paulo about a car, Jack realized he'd only delayed the inevitable. With his home—and home telephone—destroyed, his cell was the only means his answering service had of reaching him if one of his patients needed him. Though he wasn't on call this weekend, he couldn't in good conscience remain out of touch.

His mother pulled away to look at him. "I still cannot understand why you would not come here last night. I could have shooed away all those reporters. Did you see when you drove up? They all went away this morning, after I show them your pictures. Such a sweet baby you were, how could anybody think you would do those bad things they are saying?"

Jack winced and breathed a silent prayer that his bare-bottomed *niño*-on-the-rug shots weren't gracing the airwaves as they spoke. Now that he owned virtually nothing, his last scrap of dignity didn't seem too much to covet. But it didn't surprise him that the media hadn't bothered coming back. Knowing Candelaria, she had lined up everyone from old priests to his kindergarten teacher to legions of her faithful customers to vouch for his good name. Like Luz Maria, their mother had a tendency to bludgeon obstacles until they were bloody pulp beneath her size-four feet.

"You're a wonderful mother," he said, and meant it. Embarrassing and hypercritical as she could be at times, he could at least count on her to defend him to outsiders. And unlike the attorney she had recommended to him—the "genius" son of a favorite customer—his mama wasn't charging him a dime.

She beamed and touched his cheek before a worried look crossed her expression. "Now, about this Reagan Hurley. If you ask me, this young woman is in too much of a hurry to start giving me *nietos,* with this inviting you to spend the night in her house."

Jack rubbed his aching forehead. "I told you this morning, you don't have anything there to worry over. Reagan was just being kind to an old family friend, that's all. Believe me, after the situation with her captain, romance was the last thing on her mind."

But the thought sliced through him that sex had not been, that the pain that put her in his arms could as easily have put her in his bed. Remembering the way she'd kissed him, the way that lean, fit body felt against his, Jack turned sharply from his mother and walked into the kitchen, where he grabbed a can of cola from the fridge. Partly because he needed the sugar-and-caffeine boost, but mostly to get his mind off Reagan's tight curves before his body's reaction to the thoughts disgraced him.

"Is Luz Maria here?" he asked to change the subject.

As eager as he was to confront his sister about Sergio, he realized she was unlikely to be at home. The last time Luz Maria had spent a Saturday evening home alone, she'd been sick with an acute case of strep throat.

But his mother nodded. "She is in her bedroom, doing who-knows-what on that computer. She says she is upset about your problems, but I think she have some kind of fight with that boy, Sergio. I told her he was no good. A man who never speaks of his past, who will say nothing of his family—how could such a person make a husband?"

Under other circumstances, Jack might have figured that Sergio did not enjoy playing Spanish Inquisition with his girlfriend's mother. But the news video pointed to a far darker explanation. "I'll go and speak to her, then."

"You would talk to Luz Maria and not tell me about why these questioning people must keep you all day?"

Tired and stressed as Jack was, he knew his mother well enough to sidestep her landmines in his sleep. "As soon as I finish with Luz Maria, nothing would make me happier than to get your advice about my troubles—unless I could do it while eating some of your good cooking."

His mother beamed, apparently satisfied for the moment. Jack kissed her cheek, then started down the hallway, his soda in hand.

He hadn't made it to Luz Maria's room before the phone rang and his mother called him. Coming down the hall, she cupped her hand around the mouthpiece of the cordless. "A lady for you—and she is Senor Mayor's *personal assistant*. She says it is *muy importante*. And unlike my only son, this busy lady has been calling here all day."

With that, she thrust the receiver toward him. "Here. You talk to her now. Luz Maria can wait, but this lady, she has other important things she must do for her important job."

Her voice dropping to a whisper, his mother added, "She is single, too, this woman—and no boyfriend either. I asked last time she call."

Staring at the telephone, Jack sighed. He didn't care whether this woman represented Mayor Youngblood or the president; he didn't want to take the call.

But his mama had him cornered, and he realized that in less than the time it took to explain his reluctance to her, he could easily brush off one of the mayor's flunkies. At least dealing with Darren Winter's barrage all week had taught him something useful . . .

Accepting the cordless, he said, "I'll take it in your room," mostly because that was the location of the other extension. Otherwise, his mama would most likely hurt herself in her rush to pick it up to eavesdrop. No one was as impressed by titles and the trappings of power as good old Candelaria. She would be telling her customers for weeks, Jack figured, of how she'd spoken to Senor Mayor himself—even though, if pressed, she wouldn't be able to come up with Thomas Youngblood's name.

"Jack Montoya," he told the caller, quietly closing his mother's bedroom door behind him.

"Sabrina McMillan."

A current of sensuality rippled through the syllables, and instantly Jack recalled the woman from her frequent television interviews. No mere assistant, this was the woman the mayor had brought in from her last position in Atlanta to resurrect his faltering campaign—a campaign in which he'd spent far more time shadow-boxing an officially undeclared opponent than his official, and hopelessly outmatched, rival. Sometimes known as "the politician's secret weapon," Sabrina McMillan had worked all around the country, where she had racked up an astounding twelve-year winning streak.

She was a hired shark, pure and simple, but one given to wearing killer heels and form-fitting suits cut to showcase generous curves. When Mayor Thomas Youngblood first hired her, there had been quite a few jokes about the nature of her qualifications for the job, but within weeks of her arrival from Atlanta, Sabrina McMillan had lived up to her reputation as a shrewd political player.

Whatever the stated purpose of her call, Jack knew it had but one goal: to somehow reel in more votes for her boss.

"What can I do for you?" he asked her.

"Oh, it's not what you can do for me, Jack. It's what I—I mean Mayor Youngblood—can do for you."

Her laughter, rich and knowing, sent a frisson of awareness along his nerve endings. But for some reason, the face that popped into his mind was Reagan Hurley's.

"What are you talking about?" He was too intent on confronting his sister—and far too battered by the events that had taken place since yesterday—to want to play Double-or-Nothing Entendre with a strange woman, no matter how sexy her voice.

"We wanted to let you know that Mayor Youngblood has personally ordered both the police and fire chiefs to take an active role in the investigation of any hate crimes perpetrated against members of our Mexican-American community, whether they are legal or illegal residents."

Suppressing a sigh, Jack said, "And you're calling here to tell me this because . . . ?"

"Because Mayor Youngblood believes that no federal investigation should target any Houston citizen because of pressure from certain radio personalities or—"

"Hold it, Ms. McMillan. Are you saying that I'm being targeted by the task force because of Darren Winter's bullshit?"

"I'm saying, Dr. Montoya, that perhaps you and I should meet. It seems to me the two of us might have some common interests."

Jack could see it all now, the mayor trotting him up to some podium like a dog on a leash, then making some long-winded speech that boiled down to *"I'm not Darren Winter. Here, see? I love Mexicans—we're real amigos. So those of you who can vote, vote for me."*

As much as Jack hated Winter, he'd be damned if he would resort to playing the token brown guy on the stage—not even if it was the price he'd have to pay to get clear of suspicion. Besides, Youngblood would drop him faster than a flaming *habañero* if he figured out just how flagrantly Jack had violated the laws limiting the medical treatment of illegal residents. The mayor would have to distance himself to keep from being embroiled in a debate of Darren Winter's choosing: the question of whether public dollars should "reward" his city's uninvited—but economically essential—guests.

Jack rubbed his temples, trying to assuage the

headache building like a bank of storm clouds. "I'm sorry, Ms. McMillan. This isn't about politics."

That suggestive laugh again, then: "Really, Jack. If you'll only open your eyes, you'll see that *everything's* political, in one way or another. I'm sure if we could get together—"

"I'd tell you the same thing. Thanks for calling, though. And you can tell the mayor I appreciate his stance against hate crimes."

"If you change your mind, I can guarantee you'll see—"

"Sorry, have to go now," he said. "I'm getting another call, and it may be my service."

Though this phone line didn't even have call waiting, he broke the connection.

On his way out of the bedroom, he grabbed two over-the-counter, extra-strength migraine tablets from one of the many bottles crowded together on the nightstand. And for the first time he could remember, he thanked his lucky stars that his mother was a hypochondriac.

Downing the pills with a swallow of cola, Jack dealt with one headache and braced himself for what he feared would prove a worse one—the conversation with his sister about the man she had been seeing.

When she didn't respond to either his knocking or her name, Jack cracked open the unlocked door and peeked into the room. "Luz Maria?"

A small dresser-top lamp was on, illuminating a room still decorated with the white furnishings, fuzzy throw rugs, and yellow walls she had favored as a teen. Aside from the addition of a computer sitting atop her student desk, and a couple more colorfully painted Oaxacan wooden animals in her collection, nothing had changed; even the pile of unfolded laundry lying on her rocking chair looked suspiciously familiar.

Though the PC was turned on, Luz Maria wasn't in front of it. Instead, she lay atop her floral comforter, turned away from him. A black wire snaked along the curve of her back and disappeared beneath her wavy, loose, black hair. About the same time he spotted the headphones on her ears, he made out the muted notes of the Tejano ballads she lived for. No wonder she hadn't heard his knock.

"Luz Maria," he repeated, touching her gently. Only to feel her shoulder shake beneath his hand.

"Please, Mama. I said I needed to be alone a while," she complained, scooting away without turning over.

He lifted one side of the headphone off her ear. "I need to talk to you. About Sergio."

Slowly she turned, until he could see that her eyes were wet and her face blotched with crying. Sitting up, she pulled off the headphones and said, "Jack," then threw her arms around his neck.

He pulled her arm away from his throat so he could breathe. "Mama thinks you had an argument. Have you two broken up?"

"They've got it all wrong." She flung a quick gesture toward the screen of her computer.

Following her gaze, he saw that the page was displaying a news site. On closer inspection, he recognized his own picture in the corner. He recognized it as a copy of an employee ID photo from the hospital system, one he'd always thought made him look like some sort of criminal.

But even so, Luz Maria's distress surprised him. All

week, as the reporters bore down on him, she'd expressed anger about the "stupid law" he had ignored, but very little real concern about the likely consequences. This morning, when she had come to pick him up, she had been more practical than emotional about his situation.

He grabbed her desk chair and spun it around. "Let's get back to my question. What's going on with your boyfriend?"

And what the hell do you know about his ties to BorderFree-4-All? Yet he held his tongue for now, convinced she'd clam up if he came on too strong.

When Luz Maria glanced at the open door, Jack walked over and closed it, even though he could plainly hear their mother working in the kitchen.

Before he could sit down again, Luz Maria said, "He didn't tell me anyone would try to kill you. He said . . . he said it would make people pay attention to the cause."

Her words plunged into his gut like a switchblade. The room spun around him, and Jack grabbed at the desk with one hand, trying desperately to keep his seat.

She pulled a wadded tissue out of the pocket of her jeans and blotted puffy eyes. "It wasn't supposed to go like this. They were supposed to talk about the law, but the real issue is getting lost in Winter's campaign. Everything's turned on us—on you."

His little sister was involved. Not so long ago, he'd tied her shoes and read her stories. Proudly watched her first communion. Escorted her to her *quinceañeras*, the rite of passage celebrating a fifteen-year-old girl's ascent to womanhood. And finally, over these last few months, their work situation had helped him get to know his sister as an adult.

Or at least he'd thought he knew her. But how could he, if she could hide something this huge from him?

He turned away, unable to look at her. Yet somehow, he forced words past the razor wire tangled in his throat. "You copied the Elena Suarez file, didn't you? You were the one who passed it on to Winter."

Her silence drove the switchblade deeper. Unconsciously his hand swept across his stomach, some part of him expecting to feel the hot gush of fresh blood.

"Say it, Luz Maria. Tell me what you did." His anger bounced the words around the small room. The mirror above her dresser trembled with the sound, so that in its depths, the house appeared to quiver.

Their mother's footsteps clicked down the hall. A rap at the door followed, and then: "You mustn't fight, you two. I will be finished with the *flautas* soon, and some *borracho* beans, too."

As if they were no more than children, and leftover beans and fried rolled tacos could bring a halt to Armageddon. When Jack heard his mother walk back toward the kitchen, he turned toward Luz Maria. Her face had grown wax-pale, with tears streaming down like the melted droplets dripping down a candle's sides.

But all he could think of was the flame—the fire he'd seen ripping through his apartment building on the news. "You betrayed me, Luz Maria. God damn it, you threw me to the wolves. And somehow, what you did caused a dozen families to lose their homes and a fire-fighter to—"

"The—the cause is bigger than the problems of the individual. Compared to freedom, each of us is nothing, no more than a single ant toiling to build a greater good—"

131

"Don't you hear yourself? Do you actually believe that bullshit you're spouting? Or were you so hot to get Sergio between your legs that you handed him the keys to your brain?"

She reached toward him, but didn't dare to touch. "Please, Jack. I swear, it wasn't like that. What's happening along the Mexican border is nothing short of murder. Our father died because of—"

"You don't even remember him." Jack didn't bother trying to keep the disgust from his voice. "If you did, you'd know that family meant everything to him. Hell, he was killed trying to go and see his mama. And I can tell you, he'd be sickened that his own daughter would sell out her brother. He'd be shamed that a firefighter had to die because—"

She stood and faced him, tears giving way to some fierce passion that made her face flush and her eyes gleam. "BorderFree-4-All didn't set that fire. We only wanted to start a public discourse. We never intended for some loco criminal to hurt people—but don't you understand? Maybe now they'll see it. Maybe now the truth will come out after all."

She gestured toward the monitor, and though the screen saver had replaced the image with a slide show featuring tropical sunsets, he understood she was referring to the media.

"Every struggle," she said, "every cause worth fighting for creates some collateral damage."

"*Collateral damage?*" Jack exploded, certain she was parroting her lover's garbage. "Tell that to Reagan Hurley. Explain that to her captain's family and his friends."

Though the door remained closed, he became aware

of the aromas of his mother's cooking: the cumin and onion from the beans, the frying corn tortillas of the *flautas*. Five minutes earlier, he'd been starving; now the thought of eating made him want to vomit.

His sister was a criminal. Or at the very least, she'd been brainwashed into stealing medical records for a group of terrorists. The authorities had to be told. And there would be no way to spare their mother.

Luz Maria sank into the desk chair, where she held her forehead in one hand and grabbed a fresh tissue with the other. She looked as if her outburst had drained the energy from her. Or as if she, too, had started thinking of the consequences to her own life. "I am sorry for that poor man," she said softly. "And I'm sorry, too, that you've been hurt by what I did. I never meant—"

Jack gave her no quarter. "How long has this been going on?" he asked. "How long have you been involved with BorderFree?"

If Luz Maria's association went no further than copying a medical record and sending it to Winter, she'd lose her job for certain, maybe even her career in social work, but he couldn't see her doing jail time. But if she had had anything to do with last spring's bombing or last night's deadly fire, would that make her an accessory to murder?

At the thought, his stomach lurched. He wanted to take back the questions, but she was already answering.

"I'm not exactly involved with them. I only . . ." She gave a hopeless shrug, bringing to mind the girl she'd been so recently. "I just love Sergio, you know? From the first time I met him a few months ago, he's made me feel . . . he makes me feel I can do something important. I can change things. I don't have to sit there in that clinic day after day, listening to people's problems, patting hands and spouting useless platitudes."

Jack breathed again. "So you haven't met the others?"

She shook her head. "He never let me. But he says those people who blew up the INS office weren't what BorderFree is all about. He says they've been kicked out, they've left the country, and—"

"You're going to have to tell the task force, the ones I spoke with today." Jack plunged on, ignoring the way her face drained of color. Yet he remained her brother, despite the foolishness of her mistakes. "You're going to have to tell them about Sergio, about how he made you take that file—"

"No." Once more, she jumped to her feet. "I'm not about to lie to anyone, and I will never, never give Sergio up."

"Sergio's a criminal. I have no doubt that he's wanted. If you don't want to risk jail—"

"I can't let them do that to me," said Luz Maria, her voice faltering even as her gaze dropped. "And I won't help them catch the father of my child."

It took several moments for her meaning to sink in, for the knife to twist and hollow out his wound. She was pregnant, Luz Maria. The same bastard who'd corrupted her ideals had put his baby in her.

Jack's vision blurred with tears. She looked at him, frozen, waiting to hear what he would say. Scared, too, judging from the way she'd stepped back. Did she imagine he would strike her?

Mama's footsteps preceded her voice in the hallway. "Joaquín y Luz Maria, come and eat some dinner. And whatever you two fight about, I don't want to hear it at my table."

She didn't. For his part, Jack stumbled through the obligatory compliments of their mother's cooking, though every bite went down like a mouthful of ground glass. As promised, he gave a halting, half-coherent summary of the hours he had spent being interviewed by several law enforcement teams. The customer's genius attorney son, he assured her, had acquitted himself admirably, advising Jack of what he should and shouldn't say.

Luz Maria, too, picked at her dinner, occasionally sneaking a glance his way, but looking down whenever their gazes collided. Other than "Pass the salsa," she said nothing until later, when the two of them teamed up to do the dishes while their mother took a call from her sister in Galveston.

Jack kept his voice low. "When did you find out?"

Luz Maria plunged her hands into the hot dishwater. "Two days ago."

Was that why she'd seemed so distracted and upset yesterday? "Did you tell him last night?"

On the kitchen window in front of her, one of the Virgin of Guadalupe candles flickered, shifting the shadows as it moved.

She shook her head. "I wanted to. I meant to, but he was so distracted. And then I got to thinking, what kind of position is he in to be a father?"

"Don't you think you should have thought about that sooner? Didn't you have sense enough to use protection?"

Though she continued washing, Luz Maria nailed him with a look.

"All right, all right," he said, drying a platter. "Forget I asked. Doesn't make much difference anyway now. Do you know how far along you are?"

That shrug again, the one that broke his heart. "Six weeks, maybe. No more."

He took a deep breath. "Have you decided what to do?"

Be the doctor, not the brother, he tried to tell himself, but when he thought of an abortion, Father Renaldo's words set up an ancient echo in his brain: *a mortal sin, amoral sin, immortal sin.*

Yet it was not his right to judge, nor could he tell Luz Maria what to do with the baby if she chose to have it. He could only be there to support her choice. And he would, he realized, for no matter what she'd done to him, she was still his baby sister.

"I won't end the pregnancy, I know that," Luz Maria answered. "I just can't imagine doing it, living with that decision either. But, God, Jack. I don't know . . ."

Her tears splashed into the dishwater, each one setting off a chain of ripples that disappeared into soap bubbles.

"No matter what, you're still going to have to speak to the authorities before they come looking for you. They will, too. From what little I could gather, there's a lot of pressure on this task force. They need to hang someone for BorderFree's crimes. Don't let it be you, Luz Maria. And don't let that baby suffer for it, either."

For several minutes, she said nothing. The house went so still, they could hear their mother in her bedroom speaking rapid-fire Spanish on the telephone, telling all she knew about Jack's situation. What would she say when she learned of her daughter's?

"We'll call my lawyer. 'Genius' or not, he really does seem to know his business," Jack said. "And then we'll go see the investigators from the task force."

When his sister looked up at him, there was panic

in her eyes. "I have to see him first. I have to talk to Sergio."

Jack shook his head. "No way. I know it's hard, but you need to cut your ties now."

Cut your losses, he was thinking, but he had the good sense not to say it.

She shook her head, her expression half disgust, half pity. "You don't know a thing about love, do you? I'll go with you, I swear it—but not until I talk to Sergio about the baby. I don't care what you think of him. He's the father, and he deserves to know."

"He deserves a fist down his damned throat," Jack told her. "for what he did to you, for what he's done to me. For what he's cost a lot of other people. Besides the bombing in San Antonio, I can tell you the authorities are thinking BorderFree's involved with last night's—"

"I told you it wasn't Sergio who set that fire. It wasn't BorderFree at all—" She flung out her hand, splattering him with drops as warm as tears. "Never mind about that. Just lend me your rental, will you?"

He was instantly suspicious. "My rental? Why would you want Paulo's car instead of Mama's?"

"The supertanker needs gas, for one thing, and I don't want to stop."

He pulled the keys from the pocket of his jeans, but he didn't give them to her. "You sure that's the only reason? You aren't planning to take off, are you? Because that would mean big trouble, and not only with the authorities. Paulo . . . well, I don't have to tell you Paulo's reputation. For dealing with people who abuse his trust."

He saw the spark of fear, gave it time to catch, and welcomed it, if it would make her think twice about driving off into the sunset with Sergio Cardenas. She had to understand that his way was the only way. She had to think smart, so they both could survive this. "It's nine now. I'll need you back by midnight—or I'm calling the head of the task force and giving them everything I know about your boyfriend."

The truth was, Jack knew precious little. A name and Sergio's involvement with both BorderFree-4-All and Luz Maria. He had no idea where Sergio lived, what he did for a living. In retrospect, Jack saw that his sister had been vague from the start about the details.

She looked him in the eyes and held his gaze. "I'll come home soon. I promise."

Handing her the keys, he said, "Be sure to keep your phone turned on, too."

She nodded, then stood on tiptoe to kiss him on the cheek. "Thank you for trusting me in this, Jack. I won't forget it. Maybe—maybe while I'm gone, you should call your lawyer. I'll want to talk to him when I get back."

After grabbing only a small purse—no packed travel bag, thank goodness—Luz Maria slipped out the back door. Jack stood at the back window, watching her and fighting the compulsion to run out and stop her.

Later, he would wish to God he had.

Chapter Ten

The Firebug might have his areas of expertise, techniques he'd perfected over a decades-long career, but the driver of the beat-up green Ford was no slouch either. Experience was fine as far as it went, but it took another kind of mind entirely to see the potential in new shit and adapt it to purposes the brainiacs who made it never dreamed of.

Take GPS, for instance. From what he'd seen in a story on the news, he'd learned that fishermen had been using Global Positioning Systems to locate exact spots on the open ocean. As it got cheaper, the new technology spread to regular Joes who considered stopping to ask directions about as manly as sitting down to take a piss. What the story neglected to mention was that you could also use it to find just about anyone, as long as you could get that person to carry a transmitter.

Or as long as you could stick one under the bumper of the target's car. In this case, a year-old black convertible from the Cheap Wheelz lot off Telephone.

Now that the media was barking up the right tree, it was time, he thought, to stop playing with his quarry. Time to finish this shit, tell the Firebug his story, and get ready to enjoy the kind of life he deserved.

A life where he could stop imagining the pungent smell of gas and kerosene . . . and the satisfying crackle of the flames as they devoured a man's corpse.

Standing six-two in stiletto heels, Miss Peaches leaned her heavily made-up face so close that Reagan had to fight the urge to draw back. Whatever her neighbor's surgical and hormonal status (*not yet* and *extra-estrogen-with-cherries-on-top*, respectively), Reagan was never quite sure what to make of her.

But then, even if Peaches had remained James Paul Tarleton of Amarillo, Reagan suspected that knowing her—or him, as the case might be—would remain a unique experience.

"I still can't believe that precious boy did that," said Peaches.

Reagan fingered the bruised swelling on her cheekbone, which she knew had long since peeped through the foundation she'd used to disguise it earlier. No one at the Rozinski home had remarked on it—in fact, no one had said much of anything to her—but it was possible they hadn't noticed. Or if they had, they must have figured that, sick or not, she'd gone back to the gym for a little sparring practice.

Peaches's tone turned naughty. "I may just have to take that young man over my knee and give him nine kinds of what for."

Whatever Reagan's current feelings about Beau, this was not a mental image she liked to contemplate. So she turned back to the task of opening the bottle of merlot Peaches had brought over to share.

Frank Lee's ears pricked toward the sound of the cork popping, and an astringent, grapy scent perfumed the air. Reagan poured a glass for the blonde, but left her own empty.

Her neighbor frowned, sinking onto a barstool and crossing a pair of shapely legs barely hidden beneath the sparkly skirt of an emerald-green dress. While Reagan meant to crawl into bed as soon as she grabbed a late-night snack and called Jack about the phone he'd left here, Miss Peaches was only getting started for the evening. "You aren't going to join me in a glass? The goddess knows you need to wind down, after the day you've had."

Reagan shook her head and pulled a bowl down from the cupboard. "Don't think so. Besides, red doesn't go with P'Nut Crunchies."

When she took a box of the sugary kids' cereal out of the pantry, Peaches splayed the scarlet nails of one hand across her chest dramatically. "No, no, no, Miss Reagan. This will not do—not when I would bet my best push-up bra that you didn't eat a bite all day at Miz Rozinski's."

Reagan didn't argue when Peaches rose from the barstool and snatched away the bowl, then marched to the freezer and dug out a container of frozen vegetable-beef soup from the batch Reagan had put up a few weeks earlier. Peaches popped it into the microwave, then started it defrosting.

Reagan let her. At forty-seven, Miss Peaches might be pushing the envelope of club-hopping vampdom, but she'd always done a creditable, if somewhat mind-boggling, mom act. And like a lot of mothers, Peaches had a knack for reading minds. Between the time Reagan had spent at the FBI field office and the hours she'd spent helping Donna Rozinski take phone calls, coordinate arrangements for Monday's memorial service and Tuesday's private funeral, and act as a buffer when the flow of visitors grew overwhelming, Reagan had had no time to eat anything more substantial than the apple she'd snagged from a fruit basket. Besides, eating a real meal would have meant stopping and sitting, maybe even thinking about the captain, or what Beau had said when she'd reached him on the telephone this morning.

"All these months, we've been hanging out, talking all the time and going places, having a great time—and—and I was just waiting for the perfect moment to take things to the next level. I mean—I know you're a few years older than me, but we're so damned right *together. Can't you see it?"*

She closed her eyes, trying to tune out his words and listen to Peaches chattering about some transsexual she knew who'd gone ahead and had the surgery before an attractive woman convinced him—or her—to become a lesbian.

"Confusing," Reagan murmured, but what really baffled her was how she could have missed both Beau's violent temper and his shifting feelings toward her. At twenty-eight, she really wasn't so much older than he, but to her mind, they were worlds apart. And had he really thought of playing paintball as some kind of a *date*?

"And then to find you were screwing that—that son of a bitch, Montoya—only a few hours after Joe died . . ."

In spite of her denials, Beau had gone on from there, talking about how he'd like to smash Montoya's face in, how he'd kill the guy and anyone else involved with the fire that had cost the captain his life.

"It's all talk," she told herself, repeating what she'd thought when he said it.

The microwave dinged, and Peaches asked, "I know very well you haven't been listening to a word I've said. So what is it that's 'all talk'?"

"Beau, carrying on about what he's going to do to everybody. The big jerk's just running his mouth."

Peaches arched a brow that had been tweezed to within an inch of its life. "You mean, the way he was when he hit you? Did he even apologize for that?"

"Not exactly. Come to think of it, all he did was list his reasons," Reagan said as Peaches set the bowl of soup and a spoon in front of her. The beef, tomato, and oregano aroma smelled far better than stale cereal. She lifted the first bite to her mouth.

"Those are called *excuses*," Peaches told her. "My ex-wife was full of them."

Swallowing hard, Reagan did a double take. This was a revelation, one that, from the sly look in Peaches's brown eyes, had been dropped purposely as a distraction.

Even though Reagan realized that, she couldn't resist the bait. "Your ex-wife?" she echoed.

Peaches favored her with a calculating smile. "Eat your soup, sister. Then we'll talk."

Reagan hurried to comply, as much because the soup's flavor had awakened her appetite as out of curiosity. As she ate, she found she had to focus on the mechanics of raising her spoon, chewing, and swallowing. Otherwise, she could not keep thoughts of Joe Rozinski, Donna, Beau, and Jack Montoya from choking her.

Once the bowl was empty, Peaches poured her a glass of merlot. But before Reagan could take a sip or ask about the mysterious marriage, the cell phone lying on the kitchen counter rang.

Jack's cell phone, which he'd called earlier to ask about.

"That's not mine—" she started, but it was too late. Peaches was already launching into her routine.

"Reagan 'Hellcat' Hurley's line. Manager Peaches Tarleton speaking."

Reagan grimaced, and the room's temperature zoomed up to sweltering in an instant. How many times did she have to tell her neighbor that she despised that sexist nickname and she didn't need a manager?

But behind Peaches's mask of makeup, her skin was going gray. White rimmed her wide eyes, and the hand holding the phone appeared to spasm.

Reagan rushed around the counter, her training convincing her that her neighbor was suffering a heart attack, maybe a stroke.

"Peaches," she said sharply. When there was no response, she tried, "James Tarleton."

"Who—who is this?" Peaches stammered. "What—what can I do?"

Something in her voice made Reagan grab the cell phone and press it to her ear. "This is Reagan Hurley," she said, "are you calling for Jack—"

But her words were interrupted by the caller's sobs, a loud crash, and a shrill, truncated scream.

Halloween wouldn't take place for another week, but the big strawberry blonde who answered Reagan's door looked enough like Ginger from *Gilligan's Island* that Jack wondered if she was on her way to or from a costume party.

She didn't appear to be in a party mood, however. From the way her forehead crinkled and the dampness gathered in her wide-set eyes, she looked as if she was about to burst into tears.

She stood there looking at him with a deer-in-the-headlights expression until Reagan, who was standing in the living room some ten feet behind her, said, "Come in, Jack. I have to talk to you."

She set the cordless telephone on the lamp table by the sofa.

"Do you have my phone?" he asked her.

But as he edged past the tall woman, he got a clear view of Reagan's face. "Jesus, Reag, what happened?"

A purple contusion had bloomed along her cheekbone, the mark standing in stark contrast to the sweaty pallor of her face. She seemed unsteady on her feet, too, as she moved toward him.

The white greyhound pressed close by her side, his ears pinned back and his tail tucked far between his legs.

When she didn't answer, Jack took Reagan's hand. "Did someone hurt you? Was it that guy this morning? Beau?"

He thought that was what she'd called the guy. The firefighter had been furious, but Jack had been certain that by leaving, he could defuse the situation. Had he instead abandoned Reagan to the bastard's fury?

Reagan shook her head. "That's not important, not now. A few minutes ago, someone called your phone here."

With a shaking hand, she gestured toward the open doorway to the kitchen, where he could see it lying on the countertop.

"I think—I'm almost certain—it was Luz Maria."

"What do you mean you're almost sure?" he asked. "She didn't say?"

"She was screaming, Jack, screaming that she was scared. And then there was this horrible noise, a crash and—"

An electric jolt of panic shot through his system. "Did she hang up? Is the connection still good?"

Reagan shook her head. "It cut out. I'm so sorry—"

"I picked up the phone," the Ginger clone said. Her voice was deep, throaty, thickened with emotion. "She was crying and shouting, 'He's right behind me. I can't shake him.'"

"Oh, God," Jack said, running shaking fingers through his hair. "I need to call her. Let me use your phone right now."

"We tried," said Reagan. "It rang and rang, but there was no answer. The number on the screen matched the one stored in memory under 'Luz Maria's cell.' I—I called 911 to report what we heard. I even spoke to a police supervisor, but because there's not a live call, there's no way to pinpoint her location. I'm not even sure if she was at home or in a car."

"Probably, she was driving. I let her take my rental just a few hours ago." He fumbled with the keys to his mother's Buick as he dragged them out of his pocket. "I have to find her."

Reagan grabbed his hands and held on to them tightly. "Listen to me, Jack. The dispatch supervisor and the firefighters in telemetry will be listening for accident reports. If something happens—if they find her, we're going to get a call here."

"But what if they don't find her? She could be any-where."

"You don't have any idea where she was going? If we can narrow down the location—"

"I don't know." Why hadn't he made her tell him? Why had he let her go at all? How could he have been so stupid as to imagine she'd be safe going to Sergio? "I have to find my sister. I—I'll go and check the hospitals."

"You're not thinking straight, Jack. You should stay here. We can contact the hospitals on your phone."

"Not my phone. Luz Maria could call back any minute."

"Then we'll use my cell," she said. "When I dropped it last night, a piece snapped off, but it's still working. That way, we'll leave the landline open in case the dispatcher calls back."

"I can't just wait around," he said. "I'm the one who let her go. I never should have—"

"Your sister's a grown woman," Reagan interrupted. "I doubt she needs or wants your permission to go anywhere."

"She damn well needed my car." Even as he said it, he could almost hear Reagan thinking what an idiot he'd been, after the apparent attempt on his life only yesterday. And she didn't even know the worst, about the kind of man her sister had been on her way to see.

But the father of her baby wouldn't hurt her . . . would he?

"I'll drive over to Memorial Hermann, then to Ben Taub," he said, naming the two big trauma centers. "She could be en route now, in an ambulance, but maybe by the time I get there—"

Before he could react, she snapped the keys out of his hands. "Yesterday you knew enough to keep me from driving. You don't need to be behind the wheel."

"Damn it, Reagan." He reached for the keys, but

she'd stepped back, looking far calmer than she had moments before. She was pulling herself together for his sake, he realized. Either that or drawing on her experience in emergencies.

"If you have to go, I'll take you." Turning to the taller woman, she said, "Peaches, I know you had other plans, but could I get you to stay here? Then if anyone calls, you can either take a message or give them the number to my cell phone."

The woman stepped out of a pair of extra-large stilettos. "After that call, I couldn't go out anyway. Not with that poor girl out there somewhere. Frank and I'll stay here and hold down the fort."

Reagan gave her a hug. "I don't know what I'd do without you."

"Just remember that," Peaches said in a low growl, "the next time you even *think* of calling me James Tarleton."

A few minutes later, Reagan and Jack were gliding in her Trans Am beneath a night sky gone pink and starless with the haze of light pollution. As she made the corner of 18th and Heights, she struggled to tamp down thoughts of their drive to Memorial Hermann Hospital the night before. How she'd never even gotten the chance to see Joe Rozinski. How she'd been pulled into an investigation, then left the hospital without ever telling him what he had meant to her.

The chill that overtook her had nothing to do with the cooling night air. And everything to do with the echo of Beau's words when he'd seen Jack Montoya at her house this morning. *"You told me you weren't seeing him, that you weren't involved in this."*

She'd said that she wasn't, but the thought occurred

to her that she had either lied or been mistaken. That some kind of freak twister had dropped down from the clouds yesterday and sucked both her and Jack into its vortex. The spiral might be whirling them around, ripping their lives to tatters and shredding sanity, but those same winds had also trapped the two of them together.

Or so she told herself, as if she couldn't have let Jack drive off to search for his sister on his own. What was it to her if in his hurry, he ended up smeared across some intersection because he ran a stop light? People wrecked cars all the time in Houston. She'd scraped them up, bandaged and hauled them, even hosed their blood and brain matter off the streets. She'd had to learn to handle it, to stop taking each accident personally—to face such everyday tragedy with the stoicism or gallows humor that enabled emergency workers to survive to do their duties.

Yet certain things still shook her: a grown man in his prime, reduced to crying for his mama; a child in pain, with no living parent to console her; a carload of teenaged victims of alcohol, inexperience, and their own youthful delusions of immortality. Each time one of these slammed up against Reagan's wall of ice, invisible fault lines spread out. But this evening, Luz Maria's phone call had wedged a crowbar in the cracks and brought her defenses tumbling down.

Reagan was used to picking up the pieces for the citizens of Houston after the worst happened, doing the best she could to get people through the first few hours. But Jack's sister had screamed in the moments before the blow fell, in the face of the terrified realization that something horrible was bearing down. Something Luz Maria could not escape, no matter how she tried.

Reagan swallowed hard and glanced at Jack in the passenger seat, saw him staring at his cell phone as if his will alone could make Luz Maria call to say that she was safe.

"Maybe I'm overreacting," Reagan offered. "It could be that her phone broke—or the battery died. She might be looking for a pay phone now."

It was a stupid explanation and Reagan knew it, but she didn't give a damn. If denial could ease Jack's mind for a single moment, let him have it. The truth would be there anyway, lying in wait for the instant he dared to look it in the eye.

And once faced, no matter how hard a person tried, he couldn't look away. Couldn't *un*-know what had been accepted. Couldn't unravel threads woven into the fabric of grief.

Reagan's eyes burned worse than ever, and her lungs—her damned, pathetic lungs—began to shrivel like a pair of empty plastic bags inside her chest.

Don't be a wimp, she told herself. *Fight past it.* There wasn't any smoke here, no hairy cats or dust mites either, and she hadn't run up a flight of stairs with all her gear.

Which makes it mental. Which means that I can stop it if I set my mind to it.

Reagan had played the same game with herself on a number of occasions. Sometimes she won. Other times, the sensation of weight crushing her chest or the panic of not being able to gulp enough oxygen got to her, and as gray spots swarmed her vision, she reached for the inhaler. Or even worse, strapped on her mask and allowed the noisy nebulizer to deliver her a mist that eased the tightness so she could get back to sleep.

That relief proved, she finally admitted to herself,

that she had asthma, for as a previous doctor had informed her, one of the main hallmarks of the disease was that it responded to asthma medications.

"I should—I should call my mother," Jack said. "If—if someone phones the house, she needs to—needs to be prepared. And someone should be with her."

Reagan nodded, seeing the good sense of his suggestion. Though members of the fire department would stay with Donna Rozinski around the clock if need be, it was her mother and sister, who had both flown in from her home state of Alabama, who would get her through the coming days emotionally. "Does your mom have family nearby, or a close friend?"

"There's a sister here in Houston, my tía Rosario. I'll call her, too, but . . ."

Another glance found him still looking at his phone. Reagan fished hers out of her pocket and handed it to him. "Use mine. Peaches will know to leave a message if she can't get through. Go ahead, Jack."

"But what if you're right?" he asked. "What if it does turn out to be nothing? Then I'll have upset my mother for no reason—"

"She'd want to know, Jack."

"I—I guess," he said.

Reagan couldn't help hearing his side of the conversations with his mother and his aunt. How he told both that maybe, just possibly, his sister might have had some sort of mishap, that he was checking on her now and would let them know as soon as possible.

"Please don't cry," he told his mother, who had apparently read between the lines. "I promise, it will be all right. I swear it. Please . . ."

By the time they'd finished, Reagan was pulling into the parking garage at Memorial Hermann. Unsettled by the raw emotion she'd heard in his conversations, she couldn't bring herself to look him in the eye.

Inside, she trailed behind him as he went into the emergency room and found a curly-haired Hispanic nurse who appeared to be in her mid-thirties. Reagan thought she recognized the woman from the previous night.

"I have reason to believe my sister has been involved in a serious car wreck," Jack told her, then gave Luz Maria's name and a brief description.

The nurse's dark eyes were sympathetic, but Reagan recognized the barricade that slid down like a garage door to shield her heart from grief. "Doesn't sound familiar. But let me see what I can find out for you, Dr. Montoya."

She left them waiting in one of the small clusters of chairs that offered the illusion of privacy. Not far away, another grouping—a dark-skinned family whose women dressed in saris—stared blank-eyed at a television tuned to a nature show. Reagan felt a numbness set in, that familiar sense of the waiting room as an island out of time's slipstream.

The woman checked with the other triage nurses, called admissions, and even went so far as to contact the staff of Life Flight, the hospital's helicopter transport service, but she found no record of either Luz Maria Montoya or a Jane Doe coming in this evening.

When she returned with the news, Jack said, "Then we'll go check with Ben Taub."

The nurse's head shook. "I called over there, too. The only MVIs they've had this evening involved an elderly couple and a forty-three-year-old black man. No young females. I'm sorry. But this could be very good news. Probably, she'll either call or show up at home."

Jack nodded numbly and returned to the seats, where he leaned forward, resting his head in his hands. Reagan thanked the nurse, whose name tag read A. Alvarez, before settling beside him, saying nothing, but feeling his anxiety in every cell.

She thought of Beau, how he would doubtless see all this as some sort of half-assed justice, would say the universe was paying Jack Montoya back for his part in Joe Rozinski's death. But Reagan couldn't see it that way, couldn't see how another wrong, another family's grief, would serve to balance anything. Just as she couldn't stop her hand from settling gently on Jack's back.

"Come on, Jack. Let me take you to your mother's."

He didn't look at her, but when he shook his head, his hair fell forward, nearly into his dark eyes.

Once more, her hand moved, seemingly of its own volition. And it seemed to her, she could already feel the bangs beneath her fingertips, coarser than her own hair, but smooth and clean and pleasant to the touch as she swept it back.

At that moment the cell phone tucked inside her leather jacket played a familiar riff from "Highway to Hell." And as it had been the last two times she'd answered it, the song turned out to be a fitting omen of the message she'd receive.

Chapter Eleven

Jack caught only a glimpse of Reagan's face before she turned away from him. But in that split second, a shadow had darkened her blue eyes.

"Wait," she told the caller as she began to walk toward the ambulance bay doors. "I can't talk here."

Something in her voice brought him to his feet, and he followed her outside, into the same area where the two of them had spoken the night before.

"You're sure?" she asked quietly. "Wrong side of town, but yeah, it's possible if they jumped up on the freeway. God, no, Peaches—I can't—he doesn't need to see that. First let's give the ME a chance to ID the body—"

Jack could scarcely keep himself from ripping the phone out of her hand and demanding to know what the hell was going on. Perhaps he would have if his heart weren't slamming so hard into his chest wall that his lungs were squeezed against the cage of ribs.

Yet Reagan had stopped talking and glanced sharply

his way. From the way her head jerked and her eyes flared, she clearly hadn't known he'd been behind her.

"Hang on a minute," she said into the phone before she clamped a palm over the mouthpiece. "Go back inside, Jack. Right now. I need to finish this call, and I can't do it with you—"

"You know something about Luz Maria. I want to hear it, Reagan. No matter what it is, you have to—"

She shook her head. "I don't know anything right now, and I can't find out if you won't let me finish. If you'll go inside, I swear I'll tell you every single thing I know once I get the details."

She'd mentioned the ME, Jack thought as he backed toward the entrance. The medical examiner, who would need to identify a body.

Inside Jack something melted, leaked down through his legs, and cemented his feet to the spot. Reagan glanced in his direction, then walked away from him, talking in hushed tones as she moved. He stared after her, struggling to read meaning in the cant of her hand, the movements of her legs and shoulders, the way she stepped from the light into a band of deeper shadow. He wanted to rush to her, but he remained so firmly rooted he wondered how he would ever move again. So instead, he threw desperate prayers up to the heavens: jumbled snatches of the rosary, half-remembered Latin phrases, insane offers to God, as if the Creator took plea bargains. And through the tangle wove the desperate refrain: *Please, God, no. Don't take Luz Maria. Please.*

Reagan turned and walked toward him, the darkness hiding her expression until she'd nearly reached him. When the light from the glass door at his back finally touched her, he wondered if her grave expression was the same one he slapped on when he had to give a patient bad news.

"This may be nothing," she said. "Probably, it is."

It was the same line he told people when he referred them to oncologists. When he knew, deep in his bones, that it *was* something, something terrible and deadly.

"When she's not snapping shots of kids' soccer teams, Peaches works part-time as a forensic photographer for the medical examiner. She got called in to do an acci—well, I guess you'd call it a crime scene, involving a young female, possibly Hispanic. But there's no ID on the victim, nothing to indicate it's—"

"She's *dead?*"

Reagan hesitated for a moment that stretched out far too long. Jack tried to hold her gaze, but she looked away, seeking out the safer territory of an ambulance backing into the nearest loading area.

"You said you'd tell me everything you knew," he reminded her. "You swore it."

He heard her sigh before she spoke. "The victim's clearly DOA," she said, looking him in the eye now. "But we won't know who she is until they finish—"

"Where is she?" Jack demanded.

"I can't tell you that. You'll have to wait and find—"

"Like hell I will. If it's Luz Maria—if—if it's really . . ." He couldn't force out the words, couldn't even bring himself to think them. She was his little sister. He'd just seen her. She'd told him she was going to have a baby.

And she'd said she was coming back home before midnight.

When he glanced down at his watch, he had to blink away hot moisture before he could make out the dial.

The time was 1:38 A.M., and Mama hadn't called to

say his sister had come home. And Reagan had heard a scream that came from Luz Maria's cell phone.

He pushed past the nausea and wrenched his mind open to the unthinkable.

Laying his palm on Reagan's upper arm, he told her, "Take me there now, to the scene, and I promise, I'll never ask another thing of you again."

"They aren't going to let you see her. You understand that, don't you? For one thing, your sister's not even a missing person at this point. And they can't allow a civilian to compromise the scene."

"We'll cross that bridge later," he said. "Let's just worry about getting there for now."

Reagan shook her head, but she pulled her keys out of her pocket. "I should have my head examined . . . but I have to know, too. That call . . . I keep praying it was only a fender bender, and that she's been too distracted since then to pick the phone up off the floorboard."

Though Jack remembered that Luz Maria had told Reagan's friend someone was following her, he said, "That's probably it."

"Yeah, I'm sure it is," Reagan answered, as the two of them headed back toward the parking garage.

But Jack would bet his last dime she didn't believe it any more than he did.

As they turned onto Binz on their way to Highway 288, Reagan prayed that Peaches would beat them there. If not, the cops would likely send them packing before she could even pull out her fire department ID.

Maybe it would be better if they did. Maybe then Jack could be spared a sight no family member ought to see.

Reagan knew she had to warn him, had to talk him out of attempting to pull strings to get his way.

"They think the woman was pushed out of a speeding car on 288," she told him. "Although that may or may not be what killed her."

For a long time he said nothing as they sat at a red light while an HFD ladder truck raced by in the opposite direction, the wail of its siren at odds with the preternatural silence of the hour. When she resumed driving, he spoke, his voice as flat as the EKG of a cadaver. "She was wearing a light-orange top, with jeans. I think she had her silver watch and maybe silver earrings."

"The body—whose-ever it was—was found nude." Chalk-dry in her throat, her words were barely audible, but when she saw him flinch, she knew he'd heard.

"It isn't Luz Maria," she repeated.

"It can't be."

Once more, they fell silent as the Trans Am drifted over the eerily empty streets.

"I—uh—I've lived here all my life," Jack told her. "But I've never driven through this neighborhood."

Reagan grasped the change of subject as if it were a lifeline. Perhaps, for him, it was.

"It's part of my territory," she said. "I hear it was really something once."

She turned a corner, and they passed huge brick homes that had fallen on hard times. Derelict cars, many missing tires, were parked haphazardly in front of sagging porches, lit only by those streetlights that hadn't been shot out. Beside the doors and windows, bushy oleanders and overgrown azaleas crouched, serving better as cover for criminals than landscaping.

"We get a lot of calls from senior citizens out here," Reagan explained, more to fill the dark void than because she thought he cared. "Most of these houses look good on the outside, but the interiors are falling down around their owners' ears. But the area's getting gentrified along the edges—yuppies buying the properties and fixing them up, driving up the prices. It's happening all over the inner loop."

"Good for the neighborhoods," Jack said absently.

She shrugged. "Good for the yuppies and the houses, but not the original residents. Their taxes shoot up so high they have no choice except to leave. I always wonder where those seniors end up—in nursing homes or some little apartment near a son or daughter out of town. How many of those elderly transplants take root—and how many just wither and die?"

Reagan winced, realizing that the conversation she'd meant as a distraction had plunged back into gloom. For the rest of the drive, she kept her mouth shut and simply left him to his thoughts.

Once they hit the freeway, they ran into more traffic, which had slowed due to rubbernecking near the line of emergency vehicles. A fire truck was parked farthest back, partially in the right lane, its lights flashing to protect the scene from the bleary late-night—or early-morning—drivers crawling by. Reagan passed the cop cars, the ambulance supervisor's SUV, and the ME's van before identifying herself to a black female cop directing traffic. She pulled in front of Peaches' ancient Saab and a second fire truck.

When Jack reached for the door handle, she grabbed his arm.

"Wait for me," she said before picking her purse off the floorboards and digging for her fire department ID. "Let me talk to Peaches or those firefighters and see what I can find out before you go charging in."

She thought she saw him nod, but she must have

been wrong, because by the time she'd introduced herself to a burly bear of a fireman with thick, protruding eyebrows and a woolly red-gray mustache, Jack was standing next to her.

She shot him a warning look before the driver, who had called himself Red McGaughey, asked, "Hurley? Are you Patrick Hurley's daughter?"

At her nod, he explained, "I worked with Pat back when I was a rookie. Damned good firefighter."

It was all the opening she needed. After thanking him, she launched into a brief explanation of why they were there and what they wanted. "Do you know any more than we do?"

The veteran firefighter shot Jack a wary glance.

"I spent a lot of time in Hermann's ER," he said. "I've seen a lot of Friday nights."

Apparently, Red decided Jack was "in" too, because he shook his head and told them, "It's a fucking shame, a goddamn crime, what filth will up and do. God knows if the poor thing was dead when she hit the road, but she by-God was once a couple of cars ran over her. I didn't see much of it—been in this long enough that I don't look any more than I have to, I can tell you. But what I saw was pretty bad. I hope like hell it's not your sister."

Reagan was struck by the shifting of the pronoun, the way a person went from "she" to "it" in death. She'd doubtless made the same transition in her own speech on dozens, maybe hundreds, of occasions, but she wasn't ready to make the transition this time . . . not with Luz Maria's very live scream still echoing through her brain.

"Long black hair?" Jack asked him. "Maybe in a ponytail. Silver watch, and possibly silver earrings,

160

too. And she has a tiny tattoo, a little fairy on her shoulder blade. The left one."

Glancing at Reagan, he flashed a weak smile that did nothing to dim the pain in his dark eyes. "It was World War Three when Mama saw she'd done it."

From the fireman came another head shake, a pursing of the lips, a string of curses about the waste of it. And then: "I don't know. Can't say for sure. Could have had black hair. Might have been a white girl or Hispanic. Might have been a lot of things."

Without another word, Jack started walking toward the floodlit knot of cops and other personnel.

"Hey, wait, Jack. Stop." Reagan trotted up behind him and hooked his bent elbow with one hand.

Tearing his arm away, he turned on her, his eyes reflecting the lurid flash of scarlet lights. "If you think for one damned second that I'm sitting here this close and—"

"You want to get arrested?" she demanded. "You want to add that to everything else the cops and lawyers have to sort out? 'Cause I'm not bailing your ass out tonight, and I doubt your mother can handle it at this point."

His arms dropped to his sides, and he simply stood there, defeated . . . for the moment.

"Let me go in, tell them what we know. Maybe I can talk the investigators into letting us take a look. For one thing, if we can ID the body, it'll make their job easier, and the investigation will go faster. You wait here, and this time I mean stay still. Or I'll tell 'em to arrest you myself."

She wasn't sure how long her threat would hold him, but she hurried away and found a couple of cops and another firefighter. After she explained the circumstances, the firefighter, Dan Berryhill from her class at the academy, was all for letting her and Jack look at the corpse. One of the police officers agreed, but the other was a stiff-necked weasel who insisted upon calling a superior for approval.

When he went to his unit to contact the station, his partner griped, "Tight-assed little shit-wad has to have a signed note every time he takes a dump."

She shrugged and waited, then introduced Jack when—big surprise—he showed up to join them. Finally, the pinch-faced weasel returned and gave them a reluctant go-ahead.

"If you ask me, though," he bitched, "if Lieutenant Scheffield weren't off on vacation, he'd never go for this."

The man's partner and the firefighter escorted them to the spot where Peaches was busy taking pictures of something behind a tarp held by two firefighters to shield the body from the view of passersby. Reagan barely recognized her neighbor, as she'd changed into a pair of jeans and a white blouse, pulled her strawberry-blond hair into a no-nonsense ponytail, and held an outsized digital camera with major-league attachments in front of her face.

After the officer said something to Peaches, she shot Reagan and Jack an agonized look before snapping the lens cover on her camera and turning away.

Reagan took Jack's hand and gave it a squeeze, then told him one more time, "It won't be her."

Jack looked at her so hard she could read the naked fear behind his eyes. And then, without another word, he let go of her hand and walked behind the orange tarp.

Reagan followed, her stomach pulled into a tight

knot, though she tried to tell herself she'd doubtless seen worse.

But the bearlike fireman, Red McGaughey, had been right. This was bad. No one, no matter how young or vibrant or attractive, left a pretty corpse once struck by multiple cars cruising at freeway speeds. It was hard to look past the damage, the limbs twisted at impossible angles, the flattened sack of abdomen, the split flesh and the leaking fluids. And nearly impossible to compare this corpse to the beautiful woman she had met that morning, especially when moisture kept blurring Reagan's vision, no matter how many times she wiped her eyes.

Jack turned his back to the poor, broken thing, pinched the bridge of his nose between his fingers, and let his head fall forward. Within the shifting flicker of passing headlights, Reagan saw tears streaming down his face.

"Oh, God," she cried, and threw her arms around him.

He grabbed onto her, his arms tightening until she could barely breathe.

"It—it isn't her."

His words felt warm against her scalp, but Reagan wasn't sure she'd understood him, his voice was so thick with emotion. Pulling back, she looked into his face.

"It's not—it's not Luz Maria," he said. "Thank God, it isn't her."

They fell together, both of them now weeping against the onslaught of relief. But not only relief, for mingled with it was the horror of the ending they had witnessed, spread across that length of pavement, and the stark realization that for one family, the morning would bring no miraculous reprieve.

163

Chapter Twelve

While Jack retreated to the Trans Am, Reagan forced herself to take another look at the woman's corpse. This time, she squatted down—carefully avoiding a viscous, stinking puddle—and really made herself look into the woman's face. She wasn't a masochist, but she had to reassure herself that Jack hadn't spoken out of shock, that he hadn't denied the body was his sister's because he didn't wish to admit it to himself.

But this wasn't Luz Maria. Reagan saw it easily enough now. The body was too heavy, the facial features too coarse, and the hair too short and frizzy. Her hands, too, were all wrong, the fingers stubby and the nails far shorter than Luz Maria's coral-painted ones.

Satisfied, Reagan whispered to the dead woman, "I don't know who you are, but I hope like hell they catch whatever bastard did this to you. And I pray you'll rest in peace."

She rose and turned away, her face heating at the sight of the firefighter she'd known from the academy behind her, clearly listening. Tall and muscular, Berryhill had removed both his bunker coat and helmet, the latter of which exposed a freshly shaven—and somewhat pointed—head.

But her embarrassment died when she focused on his badge, which had been shrouded in black tape, as HFD badges always were when a firefighter died in the line of duty. For a moment, Joe Rozinski's face superimposed itself over Berryhill's. Scowling at her, the way he had when she'd refused to listen to his arguments about her transfer.

The keys slipped from her grip, jingling as they struck the pavement.

Berryhill picked them up and dropped them into her hand, but her expression must have told him that there was something more than clumsiness in play. Touching the badge, he asked her, "Did you know him?"

Reagan nodded. "My shift, my captain . . . my friend."

"Sorry to hear it. You've had a hell of a couple of days, haven't you? But at least this wasn't your boyfriend's sister. By the way, I didn't catch his name."

"He's not my boyfriend, just an—an old acquaintance," Reagan told him, though by now the denial rang false, even to her ears. What they'd been through hadn't made them lovers, but it had forever pushed them beyond mere acquaintances.

After stammering her thanks for Berryhill's help, Reagan left without mentioning Jack's name. Because the last thing she needed was the rumor circulating that she'd been seen again with Jack Montoya. The same man so many firefighters believed was at the root of Captain Joe Rozinski's death.

.

"I fucked it up, oh, God. I really screwed this thing up."

The man sitting in the green Ford couldn't stop rocking. He didn't feel much like the predatory presence he'd imagined last night. In fact, he wished like hell that he could call the Firebug to ask him what to do.

The Firebug would know. The Firebug would have ideas, the way he always had. But what the pathetic bastard *didn't* have these days were ears, or working hands to hold a phone up to the holes that he now heard through.

So instead the driver called his contact. What else could he do? After he'd discovered his mistake, after he realized it had been a woman in the sleek black Mustang instead of Jack Montoya, he had taken her impulsively—thrown her in the backseat and started driving aimlessly.

But what the hell to do with her? What to say if she came to?

This was not the way he'd planned it. She was not the one he'd meant to punish, not the one whose death would net him the life he deserved. And try as he might, he could not take pride in her moaning, nor in the stench of gasoline from the backseat.

"What the fuck now?" he asked as the contact's telephone rang and rang. When an answering machine came on, he hung up and started rocking in his seat even harder.

"What would the 'bug do if he'd screwed things up this way?" he thought aloud, as he was prone to do when the whole world went to shit. "He'd make a new plan, hash out angles. Figure out some way to make it look like he meant to do it all along."

The driver gulped deep breath after deep breath and released them one by one. It cleared his head enough to fight back panic.

And he smiled at the realization that he'd had the answer all along.

He could do this. He'd watched and listened for so many years that he could think this thing out—he could further the contact's goals and fix this—with the same skill as the man he had both hated and admired all his life.

As he waited in the car, Jack watched Reagan talking to her photographer neighbor, the strawberry blonde whose telltale Adam's apple and huge feet had brought Jack to the conclusion she must have begun life as a man.

Not that Jack gave a damn about such trivia, especially after what he'd been through tonight. Though he couldn't remember the last time he'd broken down and wept, he didn't give a shit about that either—didn't care about anything but finding Luz Maria, hugging her—and then possibly strangling her with his own hands.

It occurred to him that she might have set up this whole thing at Sergio's prompting. That the terrifying phone call and "crash" had been a put-on to clear the way for Luz Maria to run off with the father of her child.

Was it possible his sister could have done something so hurtful? He could barely credit the idea, but up until this evening, he would have bet a year's salary that she would never get mixed up with a violent radical group, either. Or risk his career by passing on one of his patient's records.

Some part of him whispered that it was easier to be furious with Luz Maria than to imagine she'd ended up like the poor, broken creature lying on the asphalt not fifty yards behind him. A person could get past rage, but that kind of grief—the sort of suffering the murder victim's family would endure—would forever blight the lives of the survivors.

And no matter how angry he was, how frustrated at the way she had allowed Sergio to brainwash her, Jack would always love his sister enough to hope that she remained both safe and happy. And to imagine some point in the future when the two of them might resolve their differences and heal.

Reagan opened the driver's-side door and climbed in. "I'll take you home now, Jack. You need to wait there with your mother."

"But I thought we would go look—"

"I'm sorry, Jack." She shook her head. "But running all over the city isn't going to help. Checking out more bodies won't help, either. I'm worried about Luz Maria, too—that phone call really shook me. But tomorrow, if they'll still have me, I'm going to help with the arrangements for my captain, a man I know for sure is dead."

If they'll still have me . . .

Swallowing hard, Jack wondered what he could not bring himself to ask: Had one of the firefighters on the scene recognized him and accused her, much as her friend Beau had this morning? Or was her conscience warring with her empathy? Either way, something had made her draw back from him in the minutes since the two of them had comforted each other.

Yet the reason didn't matter half so much as the painful suspicion that she was about to disappear from his life, to barricade herself behind the fire department's unyielding wall of blue. "You'll call me if you hear anything?"

The car coughed and sputtered as she tried to start it. She pumped the gas pedal, then popped the dashboard with the bottom of her fist. "I've flooded the damned thing. It'll take a minute before it wants to start up."

"About my sister," he repeated. "If you find out anything, you won't make me wait for an official phone call. Will you?"

The look she shot him was decidedly annoyed. "You really think I'd do that? Then you don't know me at all."

"Maybe I'd like to," he said, so softly that the words faded into the sounds of the old engine turning over. "Maybe I've caught a glimpse of something under that tough-girl act of yours. Something I think might be worth the effort to uncover."

He thought he heard her swallow, but she wouldn't meet his gaze. Instead, Reagan flicked on her turn signal and waited until the officer directing traffic waved her out into the lane.

"Under other circumstances," she said as the car picked up speed, "I might—I might see something in you, too, and some possibility for—"

She shook her head and seemed to fight to force her next words free. "But these aren't other circumstances, Jack. They're about the worst that you can get."

"I won't argue with that."

"Good thing. But that doesn't mean I don't care about you, or about what's happened to your sister. I'll want to hear, too, no matter what the hour."

He nodded. "I promise I'll let you know as soon as I do." Heaven only knew, Reagan deserved that much consideration.

"You sure Luz Maria didn't give you any idea where she was going?" Reagan asked.

He hesitated, weighing the instinct to protect his sister against his need to talk through the situation. It occurred to him that Reagan would almost certainly run to the authorities with anything he said, especially if she thought it had something to do with her captain's death.

Jack took his time in speaking, choosing his words as carefully as if the wrong combination might explode. "There's a man she's been seeing lately. His name is Sergio. I've never known much about him, but what I do know, I don't like. Dresses in black to go with his cycle, sports a hard-ass attitude. You probably know the type."

Reagan made a face. "The dangerous bad boy. I dated a few of them myself—before I figured out they're a lot more trouble than they're worth."

Irritation spiked through him at the thought of Reagan running around with such losers, but he roughly shoved aside the thought.

"Unfortunately, I think Luz Maria's a few years away from that conclusion." *If she lives long enough.*

"Are you worried that this Sergio might have been the one following her?" Reagan asked. "Were they having any trouble that you know of?"

He hesitated, then decided to come clean. Whether she'd run to the FBI or the police or even the media, Reagan had earned the truth. And it was bound to come out anyway. "Big trouble, I'm afraid. This evening, I saw Luz Maria's boyfriend on the news, in a background story to do with BorderFree. He's—he's one of them."

Reagan sucked in her breath sharply. "You *lied* to me? You told me last night you didn't have a thing to do with those murdering sons of—"

"I was telling you the truth. I don't and never have. But my sister admitted tonight that she knew of Sergio's involvement. Not only that . . ."

He hesitated, every instinct warning him against implicating Luz Maria in the theft of medical records—and the chain of events that had led to Joe Rozinski's death. Suspecting that Reagan would be out for his sister's blood if she heard that now, he instead settled on the news that had rocked him earlier. "Right before she asked for my car keys, she told me she's pregnant. She begged me for the chance to at least tell Sergio before she ended things, even if she wasn't sure how he'd take the news. She swore she'd go with me to talk to my attorney in the morning."

"Sergio wouldn't be the first scumbag to run out on a pregnant girlfriend," Reagan said as she turned toward the Heights. "But if Luz Maria has information on him, and if she let it slip that she was thinking of going to the authorities . . ."

"I know," Jack said miserably. "I know what an idiot I was to let her go, but if you'd heard her promise . . . She said she'd come right back."

"I don't doubt for a minute that you did what you thought was best." As they passed a working streetlight, panes of dim illumination swung through the moving car. "But on the other hand, did you ever consider that your little sister could have lied to you? Maybe she was just saying what you wanted to hear, looking for an out."

He nodded, somehow both offended and relieved to hear Reagan voice the same suspicion that had occurred to him. "I can't completely rule out that possibility," he admitted. "Especially after listening to her spout that bullshit dogma the way she did last night.

She might as well have been quoting from their manifesto—as if those nutcases from BorderFree-4-All had brainwashed her."

For some time, Reagan drove in silence. When she finally did speak, her voice had grown harsh.

"I'm sure it's easier for you to think your sister's some kind of victim—or a sweet little innocent who's been led astray by big, bad Sergio," Reagan told him, "but if she faked that call tonight, nothing can excuse her actions. And if she had some part in that arson, any part at all in what amounted to the murder of my captain, Luz Maria had better damned well stay missing. Otherwise, I promise you, I'll haul her ass straight to the task force on my own."

Chapter Thirteen

As the Trans Am reached the Heights, it slipped past a hodgepodge of beautifully restored Victorians, newer town homes, humble one-stories not unlike her own house, and the occasional down-at-the-heels bungalow poised for some investor to snap up. But the familiar landmarks barely registered—only the fact that she remained inside this car with Jack Montoya.

The same Jack Montoya who'd been lauded as a hero by BorderFree-4-All.

During the past two days, her interviews had strung out endlessly. Every agency in North America seemed hell-bent on hearing her story about the man in the green car and questioning the nature of her relationship with Jack. Time and again, she'd gotten her back up at the tone of the investigators' questions and the clear suspicion of Jack that more than one had voiced. She'd thought the task force had fallen into the blame-the-victim routine, the lazy route to finding some poor scapegoat for the arson—and maybe for the higher-profile San Antonio bombing, too.

But Jack's revelation about Luz Maria's lover cast a new light on the subject. Reagan thought about her passenger's insistence that he'd only learned the truth this very evening, and thought, too, of how Detective Dough Gut would scoff at the claim.

Sure is awfully convenient, how you just happened to hear it for the first time tonight, the cop sneered inside her head as he tapped out another cigarette inside the mommy mug. *Or did you just decide that selling out your little sister might buy your own freedom?*

Reagan slid a glance Jack's way, only to see his head canted forward, his lips moving as if in silent prayer. Prayer for Luz Maria's safety, she was certain—not his own.

Instead of selling her out, was he covering for his little sister, even risking his own future to keep her out of danger? Though her own mother hadn't set much of an example, Reagan knew that plenty of families held together, no matter what the cost.

But even without blood ties to blind her, Reagan could not escape the memory of the clipped scream she'd heard on Jack's cell phone—or the suspicion that Luz Maria had already paid the ultimate price for her involvement with murderous radicals.

As Reagan turned onto the street where Jack and Luz Maria's mother lived, the echo of that frantic cry conjured up the horribly mutilated body she and Jack had gone to see. The darkest corners of her imagination manufactured the poor woman's last moments— with a soundtrack of the phone call that Peaches and Reagan had received.

"I'll pick up my mom's car in the morning," Jack told her as they approached the purple bungalow.

Before she could respond, her car's single working

headlight caught a movement, a silhouette passing in front of a lit window along the house's side. She stopped short, pointing at it. "What's that?" she asked Jack.

Instead of answering, Jack jumped out of the car and shouted, "Sergio? I need to talk to you, man."

"No, Jack," Reagan called after him. "What if he has some kind of wea—"

It was no use. Jack was gone already, disappearing around the back of the house, hot on the heels of the stranger, who had turned and run.

Jumping from her idling car to get a better look, she could tell the direction they had taken by the outraged barking of several neighborhood dogs. As she shut the passenger-side door, Reagan considered following, but only for a moment. She might be in good shape otherwise, but her lungs were in no condition for a footrace—even if she were dumb enough to tear off into the darkness after two larger, stronger men.

Instead, she climbed back behind the Trans Am's wheel and jammed it into gear. For once, the heap didn't disappoint her but instead put its big V-8 at her disposal, squealing around the corner ahead, then slowing only enough to make the next one without fishtailing. Despite her fear for Jack, Reagan grinned with the pleasure of the big engine's response and her body's answering surge of pure adrenaline.

There—she saw a man break out of the bushes between two houses and hop over a chain-link fence. Before she could react, he disappeared into the band of shadow between a detached garage and the far higher security fence surrounding the parking lot of a boarded-up old corner grocery store. She raced toward the driveway and slammed on the brakes, blocking his exit.

As she looked around for Jack, she realized that if Sergio wanted to escape, she'd left him little choice but to go through her.

A second man—Jack—clambered over the chain-link fence and looked wildly up and down the street. She wanted to shout at him, to warn him where she'd seen the runner disappear, but like so many other things, the passenger-side electric window wasn't working.

A fraction of a second later, she saw Jack's head whip toward the sound of an engine revving. Before she realized what she was hearing, a motorcycle buzzed out of the narrow opening, swerved around the hood of her car, and took off down the street.

Seconds later, Jack climbed in the car. "Go, go, go!" he shouted. "Catch him."

Reagan floored the accelerator, blowing through the same stop sign the motorcycle's rider had ignored.

"Was it really Sergio?" she asked over the deep roar of the engine.

"It's—him." Jack was struggling for breath. "But—but he took off before I could ask him anything."

"You're lucky he didn't kill you first and ask questions later." Reagan was gaining on the motorcycle and its rider, but she had no idea what she'd do if she caught up to him. The man was probably a terrorist, wanted by the FBI and half a dozen other agencies. And if he'd really hurt or killed Jack's sister, chances were that he'd do anything to keep from getting caught.

"I can't let him go without finding out if he's seen Luz Maria, if she's broken up with him, or if they're running off together," Jack said. "If we let him shake us off, I might lose my last link to her."

Though she knew that pushing seventy through the black tangle of mostly residential streets was dangerous, she couldn't bring herself to refuse Jack. For one thing, Reagan suspected that Sergio was the key, too, to finding out who had set the fire that killed her captain. And even more importantly, she wanted to catch Sergio for Jack. Not only for Luz Maria's sake, but because in spite of Reagan's efforts to keep her distance from Jack, she'd begun to think of the two of them as partners . . . and maybe even something more.

She slowed briefly, rolling through another intersection, then into an area dominated by warehouses, salvage yards, and an abandoned body shop. Most glowed with security lighting, which apparently served as a convenience to the gang-bangers who regularly painted every exposed surface with their signs.

In the instant before they splashed into the first pot hole, she recognized the emblem of the West Side Kings. Their seat belts jerked them backward, and Reagan fought to keep the wheel from tearing from her grip. Gritting her teeth, she swerved around a rutted stretch of road that she recalled hearing had suffered a water-main break a few days earlier. The narrow street remained wet, its pot-holes hidden by deep puddles.

Recovering from the jolt, she watched the more agile cycle widen the distance between them.

"We're never going to catch him if he hits an open lane," she said. "The car's fast, but that bike's faster. We've got to catch him before he reaches Washington Avenue."

The engine raced as she pushed down the accelerator. A scrawny cat chose that moment to launch itself into her path, and she swerved to miss the little sucker by a whisker.

The motorcyclist gained more speed—too much more. As he passed another security light, the bike suddenly lurched sideways. Another pothole, Reagan guessed, as the rider wobbled, over-corrected, and lost the battle to stay upright. Tires sliding out from underneath him, he went down, bumping, skidding, and spinning along the rutted asphalt until he finally came to rest.

The accident could have torn his leg off. Should have, at the very least, put the guy out of commission. But as the Trans Am slid to a stop beside the cycle, Sergio pulled himself out from beneath it and half ran, half staggered toward the gap between a recycling center and a leaning, boarded-up old house nearly hidden behind a swath of weeds.

Before Reagan could say anything, Jack leapt from the car. She threw the car in park, then followed, shouting at him, "Wait!"

Behind the high security fence surrounding the recycling center, a pair of huge rottweilers barked savagely, their thick toenails tearing at the metal links.

Sergio lurched to the left, to head around the back side of the abandoned house. Jack was gaining on him, but Reagan's lungs were already burning, screaming in protest. She would never catch the two, so instead she circled around the front of the old house, hoping—as well as dreading—that she would intercept the injured man.

Almost there.

Jack was closing the gap quickly, leaving only yards between him and his sister's lover.

A security light—perhaps tripped by a motion

detector—flooded the space between the old house and the snarling, leaping dogs. Colors splashed before him: the faded yellow-green of thigh-high, tangled weeds, the glistening, dark crimson that soaked the leg of Sergio's jeans.

Despite the blood and his awkward gait, Sergio reached down to pick up a dented, rusting metal trash can, which he knocked into Jack's path.

Too close to avoid it, Jack flew over the overturned can, his knee smashing into something hard and hidden in a tangle of sharp thorns.

Swearing, he struggled to his feet, then shouted at Sergio's retreating figure. "Damn you, stop! I only want to ask you about Luz Maria."

Instead of slowing, Sergio disappeared around the old house's corner. Heading for the street, Jack guessed, and freedom.

At Jack's first step, his right knee collapsed, and he noticed for the first time his torn and bloody jeans. Gritting his teeth, he pushed past pain to rise again and lumbered off, now nearly as clumsy as the man he pursued.

A wild, clearly female shriek hastened his footsteps and launched his heart into his throat.

"Reagan!"

He found them struggling on the ground between the boarded house and a bank of metal storage units. Sergio was on top of her, trying to pin her face-down while Reagan bucked frantically and fought to flip over.

"Get the hell off of her!" Jack roared as he lunged forward.

The next moment splintered into shards that impaled his heart. Sergio's hand darted into the inner pocket of his jacket and emerged holding something that gleamed coldly beneath the security light. The distant shrilling of a siren, Jack sensed, could never come in time.

With his free hand, Sergio grabbed the hair at the back of Reagan's head, pulling it backward and bringing the handgun—some kind of big-ass automatic—to her throat, angling the weapon so a bullet would rip through her brain.

Jack wanted to vomit, but instead he stumbled in his haste to stop.

"Not . . . one . . . more step." Sergio was breathing so hard, he could barely make himself heard. "I'm not going with you. Don't you understand? Those fascist bastards would rather kill me than let us get a word out about the cause."

Reagan's eyes had gone huge with terror, but dark determination flickered in their depths. Slowly her fists tightened, and the fear shafted through Jack that she might try to fight her way free.

"Jesus, Sergio," he said. "Let her go, please. I don't— *we* don't want to take you anywhere. It's just—I have to know. About my sister, that's all. Then you can go—go anywhere, goddamn you. I don't care about that. I only want to know that Luz Maria's safe."

From inside the boarded house there came the sound of clattering, maybe something falling over. As if the derelict hulk wasn't so abandoned as it appeared.

"Luz—Luz Maria?" Sergio huffed. "I haven't seen . . . I came to look for her. The feds and cops— they're getting too close. They're all around my place. It's time to cut out while we can."

"The police . . ." said Jack. Could they have been chasing Luz Maria when she tried to phone him? Had they arrested her? Maybe that explained why she hadn't called back.

"I'm out of here." Lowering the gun, Sergio released Reagan and began to rise.

Still kneeling, she turned toward her captor. Too quickly, for he raised the muzzle until it trembled only inches from her face.

"No—please, no." She raised her hands in surrender and stared past the gun into his face. "I—I only—I have to ask you. About the fire that killed my captain. I need to understand *why*. You have to tell me. Please."

"Reagan, let him leave," Jack told her. Was she trying to get herself killed?

"Keep still, both of you," said Sergio. "I don't want to hurt anyone, but I'll do what I have to."

"Like you did with Luz Maria?" Reagan whispered, her question barely audible.

Sergio shook his head emphatically. "No. Not to Luz Maria. Never. I told you, I went looking for her. I have no idea where she's gone."

Jack wondered if Sergio had any inkling that Luz Maria was carrying his child, but a glance at Reagan convinced him not to risk pouring more fuel on the fire.

"What about my captain?" Reagan repeated, her words full of pain.

And love as well, thought Jack. A love so powerful that she would risk anything—even a bullet—for answers.

Sergio frowned at her. "You mean that fireman? We didn't do that—didn't have a thing to do with those apartments. Why should BorderFree want to burn out friends?"

"*Friends?*" Her voice was clearer this time. Looking up, she stared at Jack, her eyes widening in horror.

"The cause needs more of his kind," Sergio added. "Those brave enough to risk their careers, even their lives, for our people."

"I don't want to be your martyr," Jack protested. "I don't want any part of BorderFree. Except for Luz Maria. I need to know she's okay, that's all. Then I don't give a damn where you go, as long as it's away."

Sergio nodded. "When I find her, I'll see that she calls you. You have my word on that."

The word of a terrorist. The word of a man who held a gun on Reagan.

Sergio backed away slowly, the pistol shaking harder than ever.

"Wait," said Reagan. "You have to tell me. If it wasn't BorderFree, then who? Who set that fire, damn it?"

Jack's heartbeat thundered, and his nerve endings stretched painfully, dreading the crack of gunfire and the smoke-sharp scent of burning powder. Dreading the torrent of blood, bone, and brain matter that he was sure must follow.

But instead of firing, Sergio sneered at her. "You want to know who torched that building? Then follow the money. At the end of the trail, I'll bet you'll find a can of gasoline."

He took another step back before he turned and ran, his injured leg slowing—but not stopping—his escape. Even as Sergio disappeared into the darkness, Jack grew aware that the sirens he'd heard had come no nearer, but faded out instead.

Probably, no one had ever called for help. In this area at this hour, who was there to see or hear them?

Not caring, he hurried to Reagan. But before he could drop beside her, she was struggling to her feet.

"Don't try to get up," he warned, remembering her struggle with Sergio. "You might be seriously injured."

Though she grunted as she rose, she didn't let pain slow her. "Come on," she said, "or he's going to get away."

Jack gripped her upper arm hard enough to make her cry out. "Are you insane? He has a gun."

"Let go of me, Jack. We don't have to *catch* him. But if we can see which way he goes, we'll tell the cops."

Still he didn't turn her loose. He couldn't—not until he was sure that Sergio had enough of a head start that he wouldn't try to slow them down with bullets.

Because even if it cost him his last chance to find his sister, Jack couldn't bear the thought of risking Reagan's life again.

Chapter Fourteen

Though Reagan strained to hear the sounds of a motorcycle starting, she heard nothing past the renewed barking of the monster dogs behind the fence. Had Sergio abandoned his wrecked cycle and taken off on foot?

Or would he choose a faster exit: the car she had left running?

"Let me go, before he disappears." Tearing loose from Jack's grip, she vented her frustration on him. "Don't you *want* him caught? Don't you want to find your sister?"

"I'm not giving him an excuse to shoot at us. God, Reagan. You were nearly killed here. Don't you get it?"

"Here's what I get. My heap's out there idling, and Sergio may need a ride now."

Leaving Jack behind, she took off toward the street. The motorcycle still lay where it had come to rest beside a wide puddle—and Reagan released the breath she had been holding at the sight of the Blue Beast parked beside it, its door open and its engine silent. Apparently, the thing had stalled.

She ventured a smile toward Jack as he came up behind her. "Houston may have a car-theft problem, but it's nice to know that at least some of our criminals have standards."

But even as her words died, her smile disintegrated into trembling—a full-blown bodyquake—as Jack's words belatedly sank in: *You were nearly killed here. Don't you get it?*

She could still feel Sergio yanking her head back by the hair, could feel the gun jammed into her neck. Could smell his sweat and blood and desperation—or had that been her own?

And since he was on foot, he might still be somewhere close. Somewhere hidden in the darkness, where he could change his mind about leaving the two of them as witnesses.

Her lungs constricted at the thought, and she heard the wheezing start anew. And hated herself for it—knowing that *real* firefighters, men like Joe Rozinski and her father, would never allow themselves to go to pieces this way.

Jack took her arm again, to guide her toward the passenger-side door. "You don't look good, Reag. You could be going into shock. Come on; get in. I'm taking you to the ER."

"The hell you are," she hissed, yanking herself free again and stiffening her shoulders. "It's a case of nerves, that's all. Mine—mine are just a little louder than most people's."

"Listen to me," he said. "We can't hang around here. I heard something in that old house. There may be gang-bangers inside, or—"

"Probably just some junkies wishing we'd leave so those dogs'll shut up." She slid into the passenger's seat with enough deliberation to make it seem like her idea.

He shut her door, then circled around and climbed behind the wheel, where he peered out through the windows. "Looks like Sergio's long gone. But right now, I'm more concerned about you. You really need to see a physician."

"Must be . . . my lucky day. I can see you just fine. Now take . . . just take me home, please. I'm only a little banged up, and I've got . . . I've got my inhaler in my pocket. Besides, do you really want to spend the next eight hours talking to the authorities again after someone at the hospital files a report?"

Maybe he was thinking of his own hours spent in interview rooms, or maybe the incident with Sergio had shaken him up more than he'd admitted. Whichever was the case, he restarted the engine—despite its coughs of protest—and drove toward Reagan's house.

"Go ahead and take a couple puffs," he told her, gesturing toward her pocket.

"I'll be fi—"

"If you don't, I'm driving you straight to the hospital, where they can put it in your records."

"Don't try to blackmail me again," she said, "and stop trying to push me around. You may be a doctor, but you sure as hell aren't mine."

Nonetheless, she ripped the inhaler from her pocket and, turning away from him, took one puff and then a second. She leaned her head against the cool glass of the window, allowing the shame to seep through her even as the medication relaxed the swollen tissues of her lungs.

"It's not so bad," Jack told her. He laid a hand on her shoulder and gave it a squeeze. "Plenty of people deal with worse things. You ever think that maybe you're

186

too hard on yourself? And on everyone who cares about you?"

She didn't speak until her breathing eased. "You know what my last conversation with my captain was about? He was telling me how I was dragging the crew down, how I was useless to them. He would have made me transfer back to the ambulance, for my own good—and for theirs."

Jack turned onto Washington Avenue, where a number of empty businesses and parking lots were lit up despite the hour. A handful of motorists drifted in the lanes behind them or passed from the opposite direction. But to Reagan, their lights all seemed as distant and indistinct as the hidden stars above them. As if each glow were a separate galaxy and this all-too-quiet car a universe unto itself.

"And the h-hell of it," she whispered, her voice breaking, "is that Joe was right. And I—I couldn't even tell him. I couldn't even thank him for standing up to me when I was wrong."

She was crying now in earnest, and inside her, she felt a door slam shut. A door she'd been wedging open for far too long.

God, how it hurt to hear it close for the last time. . . .

"I'm sorry," Jack said simply, wise enough not to offer platitudes.

"I didn't tell you this before," she said, "but Joe Rozinski and his wife—not Donna, but a sweet lady named Flo, who died of cancer—took me in when my mother kicked me out, back when I was sixteen."

"Your mother . . . ?"

"Mom wanted to forget she'd ever had another husband." She shrugged. "I was a reminder—and I didn't

187

exactly go out of my way to make things easier on anyone."

"That I can believe." Despite his words, she heard the flicker of a smile in his voice. "Still, I can't understand how she could kick you out."

"We all make choices." Reagan could hardly believe she had brought up this old garbage at a time like this. Maybe she really was drifting into shock. Even so, the words floated from her mouth, as light as puffs of seed from white dandelions. "She chose Matthias Wooten over me."

"Matthias what?"

"Wooten," she repeated. "My stepfather, Mr. Got Rocks. A real charmer—with some interesting notions on how to keep a teenaged girl in line."

"He didn't . . . didn't . . . hurt you, did he?"

For a long while, she let the question hang while the old arguments played out in her head. Arguments fostered by Wooten's need for control along with her instinct to lash out at the pain caused by her mother's indifference.

Or at least Reagan had believed it was indifference at the time. Shaking her head, she sensed a thick fog lifting from the past, leaving everything so painfully crystalline that the memories' edges sliced like broken glass. "All of us—we hurt each other. Maybe . . . well, there's no maybe about it. I was as wrong as either of them. But at the time, I couldn't see it."

She wondered at the suddenness of the revelation, after all these years. Was it the captain's death, Jack's clear love for his family, or the act of staring down a gun barrel that had somehow altered her perception?

"So what are you going to do about it?" asked Jack.

She shrugged. "What's to do? It's all water under the

bridge now. And hey, we do exchange cards sometimes. Christmas, anyhow."

She'd been going for a note of levity, but the effort fell flat. Instead, she changed the subject as they turned into her neighborhood. "So how are you holding up, Jack?" Glancing toward him, she saw something she hadn't noticed earlier. "Is that—is that blood on your knee?"

Though he didn't make eye contact, she caught his fleeting grimace.

"Let's worry about you right now. Your breathing sounds much better."

She waited until they pulled into her detached garage, where she noticed the overhead light must have burned out. Stepping out of the car, she nearly bumped into Jack, then realized he'd been coming to open the door for her.

"You have to stop that." Though she stood less than two feet from him, she couldn't make out his face in the weak light.

"Stop what? Don't tell me you're one of those women who's insulted by a little courtesy."

She shook her head. "Not that. I'm talking about the way you changed the subject when I asked how you're doing. Is that how it always is with you? Do you bury your own pain by tending to someone else's?"

"So now you're analyzing me? I didn't think they taught head-shrinking at the academy."

His voice was a rough rumble, reminding Reagan of the sound of Sergio's motorcycle engine. Clearly, she'd offended him.

But it wasn't as if she hadn't pissed people off in the past. So why should it bother her so much that she'd hurt him?

"Come on inside," she told him. "I may only be a lowly EMT, but I can squirt Bactine and slap on Band-Aids with the best of 'em."

"I don't need—"

She couldn't suppress a smirk. "Shoe's on the other foot now, right? Better set a good example, show me how to be a decent patient."

She figured it was an indicator of his stress level that he didn't put up more of a fight. With Jack two steps behind her, she walked up the steps, unlocked the back door, and flipped on the kitchen light switch.

Except it didn't work.

Remembering the dark bulb in the garage, she stopped dead in the doorway.

"Frank?" she called. "Frank Lee."

But the greyhound didn't come. She figured he must be sound asleep—probably on her bed.

"What is it?" asked Jack, yet he kept his voice low, as if he, too, sensed something wrong.

Her gaze swept the kitchen. "The power's out, I guess. The lights aren't working, and I don't see the digital display on the microwave, either."

Taking a step back, she looked toward Peaches' window, only to see the bluish flicker of the television's light.

"The circuit breaker must've flipped. The wiring's pretty old, and maybe Peaches was playing with my appliances again. She forgets you can't run the microwave, the dishwasher, and the garbage disposal all at the same time."

"So where's the fuse box?" he asked.

She tried to slip past him. "It's behind the house—hey."

"You aren't going back there by yourself."

She rolled her eyes, though she knew he couldn't see her. "Is this some kind of macho Mexican thing, or are all you docs so obnoxiously pushy?"

"My sister's missing, my place has been torched, and someone's just held a gun on you. So tell me, Reagan, is it just a blond thing, or are all you firefighters so idiotically reckless?"

She couldn't help herself. She laughed, surprised to hear that Jack could still give as good as he got. "And here I thought they'd gone and laid the polish on at med school with a trowel. You're all right, Montoya. Let's go together, then."

When they did, Reagan was surprised to find Frank Lee in the fenced portion of her small back yard, hiding beneath one plant in a thick row of bushy oleanders. Peaches must have been more shaken up by Luz Maria's phone call than she'd let on. She'd never forgotten the dog outside before.

"Hey, boy," Reagan called softly, bending as she reached toward the greyhound.

Though he allowed her to approach, he slipped out of range of her touch, whining and sidling away from her like a spooked horse.

"Frank?" she called again, edging nearer to him. "C'm'ere. It's all right, boy. We'll give Miss Peaches a talking to for leaving you out—ahh!"

She jerked her hand away from the big dog, turning it over to look at the wetness she had felt. At that moment, Jack must have flipped the circuit breaker, for light came streaming from the back window of the kitchen.

Light that highlighted the thick, red substance on her palm.

The dog's white coat, she saw, was splattered with it, and she heard Jack behind her, sucking in his breath.

"That's blood," he said while she knelt down to check her pet for cuts.

"I realize that," Reagan told him as her hands glided over head and body, legs and tail. She looked up at Jack from over the greyhound's trembling back. "The question is, whose is it? Because it's certainly not Frank's."

Chapter Fifteen

His heart pumping like a piston, Jack's gaze slid along the back of the house, from the kitchen window to two others, all of which were now lit up. Remembering the layout of the small house from his earlier visit, he thought that one window belonged to the bathroom, while if he looked through the other, he would see the guest bedroom where he'd slept. But with all the windows set well above the sloping yard, there was no way to peek in through any of them.

Reagan let herself out of the fence and started around the side of the house opposite the garage and kitchen door. When he followed her into the narrow gap between her house and her nearest neighbor's vine-covered fence, Jack could see that these windows, too, were glowing—and one of them was open.

Beneath it, someone had set a wooden crate upside down. Several of the slats were bent, as if someone heavy had stood on them. Or pushed off the box to slide through the open window.

Careful not to break the crate, Jack stepped onto its

193

edges. Still, it creaked in protest as he peered into the house.

Climbing down, he whispered, "There's no one in the living room, at least. And both the TV and the stereo are still there."

But instead of looking at him, Reagan was frowning at her hand. "This isn't blood at all," she said. "Here, smell it."

"What?" But before the word was fairly out, he caught the oily odor. "Is that—?"

"It's paint. But how could—? I had a couple of cans stored in the garage in this old crate. I was going to try an accent wall in the . . . but never mind the Martha Stewart stuff. How could Frank Lee get in it?"

"I don't like this," Jack said and reached for his pocket. "One of the police detectives gave me his card. He said I should call him if—"

"For what?" she asked. "Because of an electrical malfunction and a dog that got into a can of paint? For all we know, some delinquent's been snooping around, getting his jollies."

"It doesn't feel right."

She shrugged. "I'll admit it's kind of weird, but we've been through a lot the last few days. We're probably extra jumpy.

"I see so much of that at work," she continued. "People with problems freaking out over a squirrel running in the attic or tree limbs tapping windows in a storm. I can't tell you how many calls we get after every summer thunderstorm, when the clouds part and the sun hits all that moisture. People see steam rising from the streets and rooftops, and they dial 911 reporting smoke. I'm not making one of those calls. I won't have the cops smirking over us, or worse yet, bringing in those task-force guys and making us explain what we've been up to."

Jack couldn't care less who laughed at them, but she had a point about the task force. If he was questioned about his sister, what the hell would he say?

"If it makes you feel any better," Reagan added, "we'll peek in a few more windows before we go inside."

Nodding his agreement, Jack carried the box to the next window and started to climb up on it. This time, nails squealed as they pulled loose.

Reagan grabbed his elbow. "Here, let me, before the box breaks. I'm lighter."

He backed off, allowing her to take his place. But no sooner had she stepped up and looked through the window than Reagan cried out and jumped back down.

"Oh, God," she cried, her hand flying to her mouth and her body shaking spasmodically. "I . . . I saw . . . I saw—"

"What is it?" he demanded. "Did you see someone in there? Or has someone robbed your place?"

Her head jerked from side to side, and her legs buckled so suddenly, he had to grab her to prevent her from collapsing.

"It's not . . . it's not thieves," Reagan blurted, struggling not only to stand, but to drag him toward the open back door. "And it's not teenagers either. It's . . . it's Luz Maria, Jack. Luz Maria's *here*."

Chapter Sixteen

Reagan staggered after Jack as he pounded toward the back door.

"Wait," she called after him, thinking about the possibility that someone else remained inside the house. Someone who had come into her bedroom, who had left Luz Maria.

But it was no use. Jack was already up the steps and flying through the kitchen. And even if he heard her, Reagan knew he wouldn't care.

Breathing hard, she followed, though she was already tearing her cell phone from her pocket and dialing 911.

"I need an ambulance." She stopped running to shout at the dispatcher. "I need an ambulance right now—and cops. There's been a stabbing—and I think the guy's still here."

Reagan had no idea if what she said was true, or if the mess she'd seen through the window had been more paint instead of blood. She only knew that her words would bring a swift and sure response—which was exactly what they needed . . .

Even if the woman inside was dead already.

"Reagan. Reag, get in here. I need you," Jack called.

Something in his voice sent panic sparking along her spinal column, prompting her to hang up on the dispatcher's questions as soon as she gave the address.

Bracing herself for what she'd glimpsed from outside, Reagan rushed inside her bedroom. And into a scene so terrifying that it took every fiber of her training and experience to keep herself under control.

Damp crimson dripped from every surface: words whose every brush stroke looked like a slashed and bloody wound. Everything on her walls and dressers had been smashed to pieces. Broken glass from framed pictures, lamps, and a mirror's bright shards sparkled beneath the overhead light and the slowly turning, scarlet-spattered fan blades.

And in the middle of it all lay Luz Maria, arranged carefully atop the now-speckled, white bedspread, where she looked absurdly peaceful in her funereal pose, with her slender hands clasped on her chest and her loose hair arranged in a smooth coil that crossed her neck. A light, multicolored throw had been placed over her and tucked beneath her folded arms, as if whoever left her here had wished to keep her warm. Or had wanted to hide whatever outrage lay beneath the cloth.

Yet the covering did nothing to disguise the fumes of paint and gasoline.

"Luz Maria, wake up. Luz Maria, can you hear me?" Jack was bent over his sister's face as he spoke, his trembling hand pressed to her throat. Feeling for her carotid pulse, Reagan realized.

Even before he nodded, she saw the shallow rise and fall of Luz Maria's chest. Still, she made no response to Jack's voice. Definitely unconscious.

"She's breathing, but it looks quick and shallow," Reagan told him. "We have paramedics en route."

As Jack peeled back one of Luz Maria's eyelids, Reagan saw the dark bruising across her swollen brow. Moving closer, she saw, too, the abrasions on her otherwise-pale face: abrasions that Reagan recognized from her years of working accidents.

But why would Luz Maria have an air-bag injury? Though the fine white powder clinging to her skin seemed to confirm it, Reagan had to put her question on hold for now.

"Pulse is weak and rapid; skin cool and clammy to the touch," Jack said. "But the pupils are equal and reactive."

Reagan carefully lifted Luz Maria's hands—noting what felt like a fractured forearm as she did so—then peeled back the cover to check her chest for any injury that might impede her breathing. The clinging, pale apricot T-shirt showed neither blood nor a deformity.

With the stench burning in her nostrils, Reagan glanced at Jack, saw him pushing aside his sister's hair to observe her neck before running his hands along it. As he proceeded, Reagan pushed the throw aside, exposing the whole of Luz Maria's body.

Including the bloodstain between her legs.

"We've got some bleeding," Reagan coughed out. "Heavy spotting anyway, soaking through the jeans."

"Neck looks and feels all right. But where the hell's that ambulance?" Jack reached for Luz Maria's left hand.

"Try the other one," said Reagan. "I think she's got a broken forearm on that side."

Jack did as she suggested, pressing down on the

base of his sister's thumbnail to watch for capillary re-
fill. Reagan looked on as the nail bed slowly returned
from white to pink.

Shocky, yes, but not advanced shock. At least not yet.

And still Luz Maria made no response whatsoever
as Jack repeated her name.

When Reagan could no longer stand the fumes, she
stepped over the contents of several emptied drawers
and threw open both windows. To her immense relief,
she heard sirens approaching from the street.

"I'll go let them in," she said.

As she turned to leave the room, her gaze landed on
the wall beside the door, on the still-dripping words
that screamed: AMERICA FOR AMERICANS—
BORDERS FREE 4 DEATH.

Dear God.

Dragging her gaze from the blood-red slogans, Reagan bolted for the door, her mind overloading with her
own shock, worry over the injured woman, and a
swarm of unvoiced questions.

Who could have done this? How and why? Despite
the inflammatory message, had Sergio somehow been
responsible—the same Sergio they had chased and
cornered? The same Sergio who had held a gun
pressed to her throat as he swore he knew nothing
about Luz Maria?

Reagan wracked her brain, struggling to remember
whether he had smelled of paint fumes, as this room
did; whether he'd been wearing blood-red smears.
He'd been dirty, yes, and bleeding from his fall on the
motorcycle, but aside from that his black clothing
showed no—

Flashing red lights distracted her. Stepping out the
front door, she flagged down an advanced life support

squad unit—the type sent to the most serious emergencies. They pulled in front of her house and flipped off their sirens, but she heard more wailing drawing near.

Both the police and a transport ambulance would soon be here, but for right now, she was happiest to see the first paramedic that climbed out of the emergency-equipped Suburban. As usual, half of Vickie Carson's frizzy chocolate curls had escaped her hair clip to swirl around her round face like Medusa's hissing locks. Although she looked a few pounds heavier, Vickie moved with the same brisk confidence and purpose Reagan remembered from the days the two of them had ridden together.

Reagan felt better knowing she was here, for Vickie was an expert in assessing and stabilizing patients on the fly. And unlike Jack, she didn't have to deal with the emotional fallout of treating a family member.

Vickie, her fellow paramedic, and their EMT/driver began pulling their equipment out of one of the ambulance's compartment doors.

"What's up, Hurley?" Vickie asked her. "Dispatch says the assailant may be on site. Do we need to wait for the cops to clear the scene?"

"The scene's safe—and they won't need to send a pumper crew for manpower, so you can have them turn around," Reagan answered.

"The patient's a Hispanic female," she continued, "early twenties. Breathing but unconscious. Looks like a trauma case, possible MVA. Here, let me grab that stretcher for you."

"But it came in as a stabbing," the EMT said, his narrow face a study in confusion.

Which was understandable, considering that car-accident victims weren't often found indoors.

Vickie's fellow paramedic, a light-skinned black man in his mid-thirties, slammed shut a compartment door and frowned at Reagan, his expression just as puzzled.

"At first glance, it looked like it could be a stabbing, but it's definitely not that," Reagan said, shaking her head. "Her brother's a physician. He's in with her now. We did a head-to-toe and found no sign of penetrating trauma. There's some facial bruising and abrasions, what looks like vaginal bleeding and apparent fractures of the distal radius and ulna. And this is definitely a crime scene. You'll see when you get in there."

"A motor-vehicle accident? At a crime scene?" the EMT asked, the creases in his forehead digging deeper.

"Injuries seem consistent. Besides the facial abrasions, she has some kind of white powder all over her," Reagan answered. Ignoring the curious stares of a couple of neighbors who had come outside in bathrobes, she pushed the wheeled stretcher toward the front door.

Vickie asked, "This your house?" as she and her partner followed Reagan up the walkway.

Reagan nodded. "We found her like this when we got here, maybe seven or eight minutes ago. We were running all over, looking everywhere for her, and she ended up back here."

Vickie cut her a sharp and curious look, but she asked no personal questions, not even when Reagan led them to her bedroom, and the second paramedic muttered, "Holy shit."

Jack looked up from Luz Maria. "Oxygen," he told them. "We'll need to get her on O_2 right away."

"I understand you're a physician, sir," Vickie responded. "Is this your patient?"

"She's my sister, damn it. Just get a mask on her. And we'll need a C-collar, in case there's—"

Vickie didn't move. "Are you taking responsibility for the patient and the scene?"

Reagan placed a restraining hand on Jack's arm. "Let them do their job, Jack. They know what they're doing."

"She's my little sister," he repeated, while the EMT stepped outside to radio a cancellation on the pumper call.

"Then help her by explaining what we know already. And back off. Back off so we can get her to the ER fast."

He stared at Reagan, pain welling in his eyes like blood from a fresh wound. For several beats, she didn't move, didn't even blink, as she waited for Jack's common sense and training to overcome emotion. He must know as well as she did that his interference would only slow the process, and that his attachment to his sister could overwhelm his judgment.

His shoulders sagging, Jack nodded and took a step back. As the paramedics and the EMT worked, he gave them the details, as calmly and thoroughly as if he were discussing a total stranger . . . and not the sister he'd helped raise.

The sister some sick bastard must have left here after running her car off the road.

Things changed when the first cops showed up. The two of them took one look at the slurs splashed across the bedroom walls, looked at each other, and said, "Roll call."

"This is the address the lieutenant mentioned, right?"

"I'll radio it in, Mike," said the older of the two, a thickly built specimen with an ill-fitting uniform and an accent that sounded more like Philly than East Texas. "The feds from that task force'll be all over this."

Apprehension coiled in Jack's gut, distracting him from the paramedics as they taped Luz Maria securely to the backboard. The sight of her, with a C-collar underscoring her facial injuries, sent fresh anxiety spiking through him.

Would the investigators try to take him away from her, to question him again for hours at the FBI field office?

"I'm riding with them in the ambulance." His voice was firm and his gaze unyielding as he zeroed in on the remaining officer. "We'll be at Ben Taub's ER."

The younger cop was young indeed, a skinny white kid with an Adam's apple that jerked like a fishing bobber in a stocked pond. "I—uh—I don't know if I can let you go to the hospital. We'll need to question you, sir."

"Then you know where to find me."

The female paramedic said, "On three," then counted off until the crew moved his sister to the stretcher.

"Are you the homeowner?" the officer asked him.

Reagan had been lifting the paramedics' jump kit and monitor to return them to the ambulance, but she looked up at the question. "That would be me. I'm the one who called this in."

The Adam's apple twitched, but the young officer held his ground. "We'll need to interview you."

"But I was going with the—"

"Someone has to explain to us what happened."

She glanced down at Luz Maria, then nodded to Jack. "You go on with her then. I'll talk to these guys and meet you at the ER when I can."

"You don't have to come—" Jack began.

She silenced him by pursing her lips in obvious annoyance. "I'll be there," she repeated, her gesture sweeping the trashed room. "I have a stake in this, Jack—and I have a heart."

So far, his attention had been fixed solely on his sister. But now, he saw that all around the room, angry red slashes formed letters. His gaze lit on the set that read, NO MORE GRAVY TRAIN—FUCK THE WETBACKS!

The words rocked him like a body blow, sending his breath hissing through his teeth and jerking his attention back to Luz Maria. And riveting his thoughts to the splotch of bright red blood that he had seen between her legs.

Rage roared through him, shuddering along his limbs and drawing both his hands into painfully tight fists. A rage so all-consuming that he knew that if he found those responsible, nothing would prevent him from killing whoever had laid hands on his sister.

Chapter Seventeen

Reagan counted herself lucky that the young officer allowed her out of his sight long enough to help the squad's crew pack up their equipment. Not that she had any intention of taking off, but she wanted a last word with Jack before he left.

She caught him behind the ambulance as the EMT and paramedics loaded Luz Maria. The flashing light bar pulsed a lurid intermittent glow.

Leaning close to him, she said, "I want whoever did this caught. For your sister, and for Joe Rozinski, because you can't tell me all this stuff is not related."

He looked her in the face, his dark eyes narrowing. "And you think I don't want the bastard caught? How the hell can you imagine I—"

"I think you're conflicted. You've been protecting Luz Maria your whole life; we both know it. You'll think long and hard before you implicate her, even to put the man who did this behind bars."

He said nothing, but she could feel words warring within him: arguments he didn't dare raise with so many ears around them. Yet the heat of his regard seared her flesh like a hell-hot August sun.

"Just so you know," she told him, "the decision's out of your hands. I'm going to give a full and accurate accounting. I have to, to be able to look myself in the mirror—and to stand up at Joe's services with my head high."

He nodded slowly, then turned away, leaving her to shiver in the absence of his gaze.

As he climbed inside the ambulance, she noticed a figure standing across the street, a tall man wearing dark sweats, who stared at her with single-minded purpose, his arms folded across his chest as if he were either chilled or angry.

"Beau?" she called out, walking toward him. "Beau LaRouche, is that you?"

As she stepped into the street, a rust-spotted station wagon hit its brakes. She stopped short, then waited for the driver to finish cursing her in Spanish and ease past the emergency vehicles.

By the time she looked up again, Beau had vanished. Leaving a sick feeling in her stomach and a question roaring through her mind.

Who was she to pass judgment on Jack for wanting to protect his sister? She had only worked with LaRouche for the past nine months, yet she'd failed to report what had happened at her house yesterday morning. And even now, with his earlier threats toward Jack ripping through her brain, she mentally balked at the idea of telling the police about his presence here tonight.

Because he's not the guilty party, her conscience supplied. *There's no way he hurt Luz Maria or set the fire he was working to put out.*

Yet she doubted that Luz Maria had set ablaze her own brother's apartment, either. But that still didn't prove her innocence any more than Reagan's rationale did Beau's.

Her first lie was the hardest, Reagan realized. Her heart pounded out a quick tattoo, but she forced herself to look the older cop straight in the eye.

"Where'd you get that bruise?" he repeated, his voice deceptively casual as he pointed to her cheekbone.

She touched her face reflexively. "I guess it's from that guy we chased, the one we saw hanging around Jack's sister's window."

After that, the slope grew steadily slicker, making it increasingly difficult for the truth to keep its footing. But that was the way of lies, thought Reagan. Once even the smallest was uttered, that cosmic mote of falsehood took on weight and gravity until, before one knew it, it was spinning on its own. After the first, she had to tell more, leading the officers away from Beau to focus on tonight's ordeal with Sergio and Luz Maria.

So much for the self-righteous bull she'd thrown at Jack about her "full and accurate accounting."

Though the younger of the two cops didn't seem to notice, the thick-necked veteran honed in on her nervousness as the night wore on. He must have passed word to the head of the task force on his arrival, too; either that or the FBI's special agent in charge had some sort of sixth sense. Whichever was the case, the man's questions grew increasingly more pointed, until the sharp-faced, sharp-eyed man sat across from her at her kitchen table and demanded to know why she had told them earlier that she was not involved with Jack Montoya.

"I *wasn't*," she insisted as she watched yet another

gloved technician leave her bedroom. "I did tell you, though, that I'd known him a long time ago, when both of us were kids. And since all of this started, it's gotten weird, you know?"

The agent's skin was so white it nearly glowed in the room's dimness, so white that though his card read R.J. Lambert, she had long since mentally renamed him Casper. "Has it gotten so 'weird' that you've forgotten that the man might be involved in a terrorist organization, to say nothing of your own captain's death? I'm not just pulling this idea out of thin air, Miss Hurley. We've subpoenaed Montoya's records, bank and credit-card statements, phone bills, all of that—and I can tell you, this is very real, and if you don't cooperate fully, you could be making one hell of a mistake."

With every syllable he banged a big gold class ring on the table, as if he were attempting to subliminally telegraph his authority to her. Her dislike deepening with each tap, Reagan decided he was even worse than Detective Dough Gut.

Bluffing, she decided. The jerk was bluffing about his "evidence," piling on intimidation, figuring he could scare her into breaking down.

"Jack stopped by to express his condolences and see how I was doing." It was none of their business that she'd invited him to stay the night—and she didn't even want to *think* about the humiliating way she'd thrown herself at him after hearing of Joe's death. "When he left, he forgot his cell phone. And then tonight—or last night, I should say—I get this call on it, and it's a woman screaming. I heard how frightened she was. You think I should ignore that? You think you could tell me how?"

Though he never got around to answering her question, Casper and his cohorts strung her out for hours, leading her back over the rough terrain of her account whenever another of the team arrived. Trying to trip her up, she figured. The investigators seemed especially interested in what she could tell them about Sergio: what he looked like, what he'd said—especially the part about following the money—and whether he had given any indication that he and Jack were well acquainted. And not a one of them would give her any news on Luz Maria's condition, no matter how often Reagan asked.

Though the sun was by now peeking through the windows, and Peaches had long since come and gone—taking poor Frank with her for some warm milk and a bath—the interviews dragged on. Finally, Reagan's patience reached its end.

"We're finished now," she told an ATF guy whose prematurely white hair put her in mind of the actor Peter Graves.

"Says who?" he asked as he glanced at his partners. "I thought we were going back over the events leading to your finding Miss Montoya in your bedroom."

With her hand rubbing at the stiffness in her neck, she looked longingly at the now-empty coffeepot. "You'll have to get it from your colleagues, because unless you're arresting me, I'm out of here. I'm going to the hospital to find out about Luz Maria."

The man threw up his hands in a pretense of surrender. "Look, I'll tell you what. We'll call there, check on her ourselves, and let you know how things are going."

"I guess you misunderstood me. You've collected your evidence, gotten your pictures, and picked my brain until it's bleeding. Now I want every one of you out of my house."

"You don't want to get this cleared up now?" Casper interrupted, banging once more with his ring.

Reagan felt her temper spike past reason. "Knock on that freaking table once more and you *are* going to arrest me—for disorderly conduct when I cuss your lily-white ass into traction."

That got a laugh out of the ATF guy and a frazzled-looking older woman from the state fire marshal's office. Reagan got the feeling that neither was a big fan of the ring-banging routine.

For whatever happy reason, their reaction seemed to take a little of the wind from Casper's sails. After the obligatory spiel warning her about the gravity of the case, the importance of giving complete and accurate statements to agents of the government, and how now might be a super time to upgrade locks on her doors and windows, they finally packed their things and vanished.

Leaving her alone in an all-too-silent house.

She didn't see them out. Didn't even get up from her kitchen table. Instead, she laid her head down on her crossed arms and closed her eyes against the staccato images that stuttered through her mind.

The apartment building blazing on the television news; the fire truck as she imagined it, heading out without her; the grill of the green car racing toward her; the dead woman on the freeway, her twisted limbs contrasting sharply with Luz Maria's carefully arranged, blanketed form.

Carefully arranged, mused Reagan. As if the one who'd brought her here had cared about his victim.

The next thing she knew, an alarm was ringing and she was coughing—choking on air thick and bitter with hot ash. Her lungs seized as moisture streamed from both her nose and eyes.

She flailed her limbs—or tried to—in an attempt to get away. But something was confining her, preventing her escape, even as the wall of smoke pulsed orange with the fast-approaching flames.

She couldn't drag in breath enough to scream. Couldn't move or call for help or—

Heart thudding wildly, Reagan woke up blinking in a warm, yellow streak of sunlight shining through her kitchen window. The telephone was ringing, as she realized that it had been, off and on, for quite some time. That must have been what she'd heard as she'd slept.

Still shaking from the dream, she jerked her head toward the microwave. But the digital display was flashing 12:00, so she focused on her watch instead and saw that it read 10:37. *Damn it.* She had meant to drive straight to the hospital, to check on Luz Maria.

Was that Jack calling? God, she should already be there with him, as she'd promised. How could she have allowed herself to drift off to sleep?

She rose too quickly, knocking over her chair as she reached for the wall-mounted cordless telephone.

As soon as she said hello, the caller said, "Rea—Reagan, is that you?"

She nearly dropped the receiver as her pulse pounded in her ears. All traces of fatigue were swept away on a fresh surge of adrenaline. "Matthias? Matthias, oh my God, is Mom—? Has something happened to my mother?"

"No, Reagan."

At least her stepfather didn't bristle over her calling him by his first name, the way he always had. Maybe after all these years, he'd decided it didn't matter. Or maybe he was too upset to care.

"Your mother . . . your mother's healthy enough," he said, then cleared his throat. "It's just . . . she hasn't been herself since you called the other night. Why would you? After all these years—it was after four A.M., you know that? You might have given her a stroke."

"I thought she'd want to know." Reagan felt her own blood pressure rising at the censure in his voice. Why had she imagined that he might have changed? "Or would you rather she found out on the news or in the papers?"

"What was it you said to her? What was it that couldn't wait 'til morning?"

"You mean she didn't tell you?" asked Reagan, thinking that Matthias Wooten wasn't the only one who hadn't changed. She'd thought that by this time her mother would have gotten therapy or something, maybe even learned to cope with the past all on her own. "Joe Rozinski died on duty, at a fire."

"I think I read about it—he was that friend, wasn't he? That one you went to stay with?"

"He was my captain," she answered, her anger boiling over. "And my father's. He was the one who broke the news to Mom and me. And the one who finished raising me when the two of you couldn't get the job done."

Her stepfather swore softly, as though he didn't want someone in the house to hear. "Why'd you have to go and dredge up all that old stuff for her? We were all set to go on this three-week cruise, everything first-class and—"

"Didn't you hear me? I said the man was dead, not

212

fucking playing possum to screw up your vacation."
Reagan tried hard never to let her language degenerate
to this point, but she was so far beyond incensed that
hot tears coursed down her cheeks and the warm brick
of her kitchen had just dissolved in a red haze. "For
some reason, I thought that maybe you and my mother
had gotten past thinking the whole world revolves
around you and your damned money—"

"Don't you understand?" he interrupted. "Whenever the phone rings at night, whenever a strange car
pulls up at the curb, your mother starts shaking, thinking it's about you. That it's *you* who's died on duty. *You*
whose funeral she'll have to live through."

Her mother thought about her, even worried? The
same mother who hadn't bothered calling after the attacks on 9/11, when so many firefighters had been
killed?

"But I imagine you've always known that she would
suffer," Matthias went on, the rising emotion in his
words threatening to blister her ears if not her heart.
"You knew it from the day you told us you meant to
become a firefighter like your father. You knew it, but
you simply didn't give a damn."

He slammed the phone down hard. The second time
she'd been hung up on in as many days.

But on this occasion, she asked herself, had both her
mother and her stepfather had some reason for their
anger? Was it possible that Reagan's decision to throw
herself into suppression firefighting had been less
about honoring her father than about punishing her
mother? Or were Matthias and Georgina Wooten simply another pair of self-absorbed, pretentious boomers,
caught up in the world of who-owned-what?

For a lot of years, that had been the easy answer,

but Reagan was no longer quite so sure it was the right one.

After letting out a deep breath, she picked up the chair she'd knocked down, then found some clean clothes she'd left folded on the dryer—a small mercy, since there was no way she was going back into her room to face that mess. She made time to shower quickly, brush her teeth, and dry her hair, then added a little makeup to counteract the walking-dead look of the pathetic stranger in the mirror.

But lipstick couldn't cover her unanswered questions, no more than a few haphazard swipes with her mascara could disguise the haunted look in her blue eyes.

Or her own uneasy thoughts about her family . . . and the sad, misshapen forms that love could take.

Chapter Eighteen

Though fatigue had long-since blurred his vision, Jack stared hard at the doctor. "You're sure about this? I'd rather hear the whole truth than the sugar-coated version."

Back when veteran obstetrician/gynecologist Danielle Fischer had worked out of Hermann Memorial, the med students had christened her "The Hummingbird" for her habit of rushing in for ER consultations at lightning speed, then tossing off dead-on diagnoses in the wake of her retreat. But this morning, outside the private waiting room where Jack's mother and aunt were ensconced, Dr. Fischer's plump body had gone dead still, and her blue-eyed gaze remained unflinching, even if she did frown at Jack's suggestion.

"I don't have time to deal in half-truths, Dr. Montoya. The pregnancy your sister mentioned to you—I'm afraid she's suffered a miscarriage. But there was no bruising or abrasions to indicate a sexual assault. No semen was collected either. It's possible the pregnancy's loss was triggered by your sister's accident, but that's not necessarily the case. I'm afraid we'll never know for certain."

Jack freed the breath he had been holding. As bad as things were, at least Luz Maria hadn't been raped. "Was it . . . was it a complete miscarriage, or will you need to—"

Dr. Fischer shook her head, and her wiry iron-gray bob flipped back and forth. "Nature's taken its course. I—I'm sorry for your family's loss, especially under these circumstances. I was told your sister was awake a little earlier, while the neurologist examined her. Were you able to speak with her?"

Jack shook his head, gritting his teeth. "By the time I was *allowed* to go in, she was asleep again."

The very fact that she'd awakened was a good sign, especially since she'd responded appropriately to simple questions and commands. But he wouldn't feel right until he talked to her himself, and he was still pissed that the special agent in charge had refused to allow a nurse to interrupt the interview to tell Jack of his sister's change in status.

Fortunately, Dr. Fischer didn't ask him to explain his comment. She had already begun rattling off the items printed on the photocopied list of aftercare instructions that she had foisted on him. Once finished, she zipped off—in typical Hummingbird fashion—to another patient upstairs.

Still standing outside the private waiting room, Jack rubbed his gritty eyes and thought of walking to the cafeteria for more coffee. He hesitated, not only because his nerves felt raw from all he'd drunk already, but because he knew he was avoiding going back inside the little room where his mother and Tía Rosario waited. Or more specifically, because he didn't know what to say about his sister's pregnancy.

Now that it was over, was there any point in telling them? Tempted as he was to avoid the whole difficult conversation, Jack couldn't make himself believe that silence was the right thing. During his years of practice, he had seen all too many of his patients' toxic secrets explode out of the past, with devastating consequences. He'd gradually come to the conclusion that when the truth was locked away in darkness, it put out malignant roots.

Why not come clean now, while his mother was still thanking God that her daughter would most likely make a full recovery? Then, after he broke the news of her miscarriage to his sister, she wouldn't face the added burden of hiding her emotions from their family. Wouldn't that be best for Luz Maria?

But something about the idea gnawed at him. For one thing, though his mother and her sister had always supported each other, they were fierce competitors as well, with each worshiping at the altar of her family's respectability. Would the childless and incurably old-fashioned Tía Rosario lord it over his mother to the end of time that her daughter had gotten pregnant out of wedlock? Whether or not she did, his mother would likely be furious that he had "disgraced" her by sharing the information with his aunt. Jack wished he had a sounding board to tell him whether his sleep-deprived, stressed-out brain had thought through all the implications.

And not just any sounding board, he realized. He wanted Reagan Hurley, who would be as quick to tell him he was dead wrong as she would be to stick up for what she saw as right.

Damn straight, her voice muttered in his head.

Despite the situation, he couldn't help smiling.

It was funny, how quickly he had gotten used to having her around, had grown to appreciate her fierce loyalties and her outspoken frankness, even the stubbornness that had originally thrown them into conflict. Funny, too, how in the two days since her offer he had so often regretted throwing away the chance to lose himself in her arms for a while.

Not that he truly believed Reagan was capable of something so fleeting as a one-night stand, any more than he was. He sensed they were alike in that: people who made few commitments, but took each one as seriously as the most sacred of vows.

But whether she was still tied up in giving a statement, or had gone to help her captain's family, or had simply decided to crash for a few hours, Reagan hadn't shown up. Instead, another woman hurried toward him, her swaying gait grabbing his attention even before the click of her high-heeled pumps on the tiled corridor.

"Sabrina McMillan," she told him, thrusting her hand out.

As they shook, he saw that her nails were painted crimson, to match her lipstick. The contrast of the red, against the blazing royal blue of the woman's skirted suit hurt his tired eyes.

"I recognized you from TV." He wondered what Greater Houston male would not. With its body-hugging fit and deep V, her outfit looked as if she'd ordered it out of the Victoria's Secret catalog.

"I recognized you, too, although I must say, Jack, you're *much* better looking than that photo on the news." She looked up at him through lowered lashes, evidently trying the demure routine.

He didn't buy it for a moment. "I'm afraid you've caught me at a difficult time," he told her as he reached for the closed door. "I need to speak with my family about my sister's condition."

"How *is* your sister?" She pushed a loose tendril of rich brown hair back into her upsweep, then caressed the arrangement with her fingertips. "When we heard about the . . . incident this morning, the mayor and I were terribly concerned."

Concerned with how they'd use it, Jack thought, his exhausted mind forming an image of Luz Maria in a wheelchair, being pushed onto a campaign platform. Then unceremoniously dumped once Mayor Young-blood heard about her involvement with BorderFree-4-All.

"She's had a tough time of it, but it looks as if she'll eventually recover. Thanks for asking," he said. "Now, if you'll excuse me . . ."

"But wait. Please, Jack. I understand the car she was driving was found wrecked this morning, in a ditch off a rural road in Galveston County."

"Galveston County?" Jack repeated. What would she be doing there? But only Luz Maria could tell him the answer to that question. And possibly Sergio as well.

But there was one thing Jack was sure of: He'd be hearing from Paulo Rodriguez before the day was out. With one of his best cars wrecked, someone would have to pay. Jack figured it would most likely be him, and something told him Paulo wouldn't be content to stand in line behind Jack's medical-school loans or his need to rent a new apartment.

It was sure to be a difficult encounter.

"Was the car . . . was it vandalized?" he asked. "Like the room where we found Luz Maria?"

"I don't believe so." Sabrina opened an expensive-looking purse and pulled out a business card.

"There's a foundation Mayor Youngblood's put me in touch with," she said. "You may not have heard of the Trust for Compassionate Service—they like to keep a low profile. But one of the things they do is aid the victims of hate crimes."

She handed him the card, which listed the name and contact information of a man named Isaac Mailer, along with the trust she had described. "Mr. Mailer is very interested in your case, and your sister's."

Jack was certainly no expert on the finer things, but the raised brown print and thick, parchmentlike card stock all but shouted money. "Why? Why would some high-dollar trust care about my family? What's their angle on this?"

Sabrina gave him the sort of smile people bestowed on the less fortunate. Or the simple. Beneath her flawless makeup, her eyes crinkled at the corners, hinting that Sabrina was considerably older than she looked.

"They do a lot of good work in the Valley, too, helping the uninsured and such. From what I understand, the trust was built on an endowment left by the heiress to some cattle ranch about the size of Delaware. Some soap-opera tale of woe's behind it, how she never married because her family kept her from a young Mexican cowboy she loved. I think they had him killed or castrated or some such. I can't quite remember."

With a wave of her hand, she dismissed the tragedy.

"Anyway, the trust's pockets are deep enough that they don't have to worry about state funding—or their patients' immigration status. You really need to call this number."

Jack frowned down at the card. "And you're giving me all this—the heads-up about the car and this contact—in exchange for what?"

Slyness edged her smile and a suggestion laced her words. "Really, Jack. We need to work on that suspicious nature. It's a gesture of goodwill, that's all, not tit for tat. If you feel moved to make a similar gesture, simply call me. That's all there is to it."

With that, she handed over her own business card. He saw that at the bottom she had added her personal cell-phone number in pen, along with *day or night!*

When he'd seen her on the news, he had first gotten the impression of a shark. But now that he'd actually met Sabrina McMillan, Jack amended his impression. This woman was the serpent in the garden, a demon in the flesh, and he had absolutely no doubt about what kind of tit she offered for his tat.

Despite the fact that the mayor's strikingly attractive and immediately recognizable campaign manager was all but draping herself around Jack, Reagan thought he looked relieved to see her. Which, in her opinion, spoke well of the man's taste.

"You look like hell, Montoya," she said by way of a greeting. "How're you holding up?"

"I'm fine," he said before introducing her to Sabrina McMillan.

"So you're a fireman?" asked Power Suit Girl, her lip curling in palpable distaste.

"Nooo, I'm a fire*fighter*," Reagan corrected, shaking

the fembot's hand a little longer and harder than necessary. "You know, one of those poor mugs who trots
up to your penthouse when you light up your curtains
with the flambé?"

Watching Sabrina redden was the most fun Reagan
had had in days, mainly because she knew the woman
was thinking of the paraphernalia the crew had seen in
her apartment. Shackles, whips, and a truly amazing
assortment of spray cheeses and feather dusters. Just
thinking about that night made Reagan's lips pull into
what was undoubtedly a wicked smirk.

"For the record," she told Sabrina in a confidential
tone, "my vote's with Mayor Youngblood. Seems to
me the man's in a position to remember with gratitude
the fire department's hard work and discretion."

Especially since he'd been in Sabrina's penthouse
at the time of the incident in question. Working on
their campaign positions, they'd both claimed all too
loudly.

Reagan didn't care—or care to imagine—*what* positions they'd been practicing, so long as the city dodged
the bullet of the Darren Winter write-in.

Abruptly Sabrina McMillan remembered another ap-
pointment. Without meeting Reagan's gaze, she zeroed
in on Jack. "Don't forget, you have my number."

Her heels click-clicked as she swayed down the hall.

Jack looked at Reagan, confusion written on his features. "What the hell was that about?"

"You don't want to know," she said. "But if you ever
decide to call her, I hope you're not lactose intolerant."

"All I can say is, you must have gotten a few hours'
sleep. You're as full of piss and vinegar as ever."

Reagan thanked him for the compliment before

saying, "Tell me about Luz Maria. What did the doctors say?"

She followed him down the hall, where the two of them sat in an otherwise unoccupied bank of chairs in a waiting area. Outside a nearby window, brilliant October sunshine burnished the still-green leaves of the park across the street.

"She woke up earlier," Jack said, "and she responded pretty well to the neurologist's screening questions. They did some testing, too, and the results look encouraging. But that bleeding you saw—she's had a miscarriage."

Reagan nodded slowly, not sure how to respond. On the one hand, the miscarriage solved some problems, but still, it was a sad event. "I'm glad the head injury doesn't seem serious," she said.

"It's still too soon to say that. With that long a period of unconsciousness, there could be all kinds of residual damage, even changes to her personality. They'll be observing her for another day at least, waking her every hour for a neuro check, and she'll have some follow-up visits as well."

"I see. So have you spoken to her yet?"

Jack's head shook. "By the time I found out she was awake, she'd gone back to sleep again. I want to talk to her—about what happened, and about the miscarriage, too."

"Does she know yet?"

"I don't think so. And neither does my mother. I was thinking I should tell her and my aunt, get it all out in the open."

"Don't you dare, Jack. That's not your decision." Sometimes he was such a control freak it made her crazy.

He chewed his lip in thought. And then, when he looked up at her, she saw in his brown eyes the boy she'd worshiped. Only this time, she looked past the hero who'd saved her from Paulo, and she also looked beyond the half-grown child who had so angrily accused her mother and her of moving to the suburbs to get away from people like him. This time, she saw all the way down to the fear inside his heart. Fear that he would be helpless to ease his sister's pain. Fear of the consequences of what had once seemed like a simple and compassionate decision to help a child draw breath freely.

Reagan ached with the bone-deep realization that she was *gone*, utterly gone on this man, and that she would go to hell and back to help him through this.

"I thought . . . I just figured," he said as he leaned forward to rest his forehead in his hands, "it would be better for her to have the truth all out at once."

"You're exhausted, Jack, and God knows you've got every reason to be stressed out. But this isn't a tooth you're pulling. It's your sister's business," she said gently, though she would have liked to swat the side of his head with a rolled-up newspaper. Why did men always feel the need—in fact, the responsibility—to charge ahead, fixing everybody's lives? Or maybe that was just a doctor thing, the result of having people come to him all day for solutions.

Still, she had to give him points for good intentions, so she kept her voice low and more or less free of exasperation. "You're going to have to get past the fact that you helped raise her. She's a grown woman now, one who's made her own mistakes. You can still support her, be there for her if she'll let you. But Luz Maria will have to figure things out herself, the same as the rest of us."

Aside from the questions of her miscarriage and relationship with Sergio, Jack's sister was going to have to sort through some other issues, too. Reagan might have left out the incidents with Beau, but she had seen no way around telling members of the task force what she knew about Sergio, including the fact that he had been involved with Luz Maria. Reagan had been quick to add that Jack had seemed both shocked and appalled to learn that his sister's boyfriend had ties to BorderFree.

But now wasn't the time to bring up the legal situation. Not when Reagan couldn't keep herself from leaning over and putting her arm around Jack's shoulder. "Come on, champ. Let's get you to bed."

He looked up, a tired grin warming his handsome features and the devil playing in his dark eyes. "And here I thought you weren't going to repeat the offer."

She shook her head and stood, then helped hoist him to his feet. "If I ever do, I can assure you, you're gonna need a full night's sleep. Now, let's go. I've learned a few things bringing patients here when I was on the ambulance. I know a place they'll let you crash for a few hours."

Trying to move him was like trying to tow an anchored barge.

"But what about my mother and my aunt? And what if there's some change in Luz Maria?"

"Don't sweat it. I'll go talk to your family—I'll even take them home to rest and clean up if they'll let me. And I'll come and get you if there's any news."

"I thought you had to help out the Rozinskis."

"I called over there a while ago. Donna's already got more help than she can stand." Reagan didn't add that Beau had been there, and there was no way she wanted a scene with him to disrupt the preparations for their captain's services.

Reagan's words finally loosened Jack's feet, and she had him moving him toward a room where she knew that bone-tired residents sometimes grabbed an hour's shut-eye.

"And if the cops or the task-force guys come for me?" he asked.

She flashed him a quick smile. "Then I have absolutely no idea where you've gone."

In spite of Jack's exhaustion, not even the black chasm of sleep provided respite. At least it didn't seem that way when someone shook him roughly after what felt like only seconds of sleep.

He looked up to see a huge figure looming over him in the dimness.

Jack shot out of the bed in record time. And felt his face heat at the realization that his "attacker" was one of the ER nurses, the heavyset black woman who had tried so hard to let him know his sister had woken up.

"Didn't mean to scare you, sugar." She flipped the lights on and dished up an apologetic smile to go with her deep Georgia accent. "Thought you'd best get up, though."

"Is something wrong with Luz Maria?" He dragged his fingers quickly through his hair to push it out of his eyes.

"Not that I know of," she told him. "But 'less I miss my guess, you got other trouble brewing. Your girlfriend out there, she's got herself some temper. And I do believe she's fixin' to let it fly sufficient to get herself hauled out of here."

It took Jack several moments to realize the nurse must be talking about Reagan. Had she finally lost patience with R.J. Lambert, Detective Worth, or one of the other investigators?

After thanking his informant, Jack hurried out of the room that residents had dubbed Motel 666. Glancing at his watch, he swore as he realized that instead of sleeping merely minutes, he'd been down for nearly four hours.

What had happened in that time?

His heart sank when he spotted the answer near the waiting area in the form of Paulo Rodriguez, who was nearly chest-to-chest with Reagan. And shouting down at her as if she were a puppy that had piddled on his carpet.

"You got handed your free ticket out, so why don't you take that tight white ass of yours back up to the suburbs where the little blond *chicas* belong," he told her.

Reagan didn't back off, not a hairbreadth. Instead, she balled her fists and snarled up at him, "Because this particular little *chica's* about to kick your flabby ass."

Hustling toward them, Jack was quick to interrupt. "How about the two of you tone this discussion down a little? Unless you want security to throw you out."

Both gazes jerked toward him, then blinked in apparent surprise, not only at Jack, but at the number of people in the waiting area who were staring in their direction.

"Come on," Jack told them. "Let's take a walk out-side and cool off. There's a little park across the street where we can talk."

Getting outside had been an excellent idea, Jack de-cided, not only for the two combatants but for him as well. There was something about the fluorescent glow and antiseptic odors of hospitals that drained away his spirit, something that only nature had the power to counteract.

The sun had descended behind a nearby building, and the day's warmth was slowly ebbing from both the side-walks and the air. Yet he was comfortable in his shirt-sleeves, and his spirits lifted at the sensation of a light breeze against his skin and the sight of a live oak's branches stirring with the progress of a squirrel.

Both Paulo and Reagan appeared calmer, too, Paulo looking at a mother walking twin toddlers on a pair of leashes while a tiny puffball dog ran loose at her side. Reagan, for her part, was staring at the pale disk of the rising moon.

"You two shouldn't be allowed in the same zip code," Jack told them. "This isn't the first time I've had to step between you."

The illusion of peace evaporated as Reagan turned to glare at Paulo. "Yeah, well, he's still a bush-league bully."

Paulo grabbed the lapel of his expensive suit and snarled back, "You better watch who you call bush league. I never got a goddamn break my whole life, but I could buy and sell your ass three times over."

"Sorry to disappoint you, Paulo. But unlike your girlfriends' asses, mine's not for sale."

Jack felt a stab of irritation. "Why don't you knock it off, both of you? We aren't kids anymore, for God's sake. Now, either tell me what's going on, or take this little lovefest somewhere else. Because, frankly, I have plenty of other things to worry about."

"My Mustang, *por ejemplo*," Paulo tossed back at him.

"I'm really sorry about that," Jack told him. "If I hadn't let Luz Maria borrow it, she never would have been hurt, and your car wouldn't have been—"

"I was sad to hear about your sister, *compa*," Paulo told him, though he darted a glance at Reagan as he spoke. "I'm glad she's gonna make it."

Reagan nodded almost imperceptibly, and Jack suddenly got it. The two of them must have argued after Paulo strolled in demanding to know who was going to pay for the damage to his car. No doubt, without a word concerning Luz Maria.

"Who did it, man?" asked Paulo. "That's all I want to know. Who messed with what was mine and what was yours? I heard about that racist shit they found all over the walls around your sister. If that bastard Winter had something to do with it—"

There was a promise of violence in the words that detonated cold shocks in Jack's gut. Much as he hated Darren Winter, the sort of retribution he'd grown up calling "street justice" wasn't going to fix this mess.

"I'll take responsibility," Jack offered. "I may not have much else, but I have some insurance." With all the disasters, both physical and financial, that wandered into his clinic day after day, insurance had seemed a necessity, one he hadn't fully appreciated until he'd called his agent earlier.

Triggered by the dusk, the park's automatic lights kicked on, and the diamond stud at Paulo's ear winked brightly.

Paulo shook his head and pinned Jack with a hard look, then thumped an index finger against his chest. "I tell you this straight up, *amigo*. Somebody's gonna pay. And it fuckin' won't be you or me."

Chapter Nineteen

Reagan stared after Paulo as he stalked off toward the parking garage. She'd seen his ugly face plastered in the papers often enough to know he'd built himself a business and glad-handed the right people, but she'd never trust the jackass as far as she could throw him. To her way of thinking, kids who took pleasure in tormenting anyone younger or smaller didn't magically grow into sainthood, no matter how much time they spent polishing the halos they fashioned out of stolen hubcaps.

"Friends like him will make your enemies obsolete," she mused.

Jack pulled a face. "Someone should tell that to the crowd gunning for me. It would be a hell of a lot more convenient if I could consolidate my troubles into one man. But at least Paulo's popped out of the woodwork with offers of support. It's more than any of my other friends have done."

"Last I noticed, *I'm* here." She felt peevish saying it,

but being unfavorably compared to Paulo brought out the worst in her.

To her utter astonishment, Jack took both her hands in his and looked her in the eyes. Something in his dark gaze made her stomach flutter, just the way it had when they were kids. Only now, she understood that the feeling was attraction. It was dead stupid, ill-timed, and probably disastrous as well, but that realization did nothing to diminish the reality.

"You certainly are," he said, "and it means more to me than I can tell you."

He was going to kiss her; she saw it in his face, heard it in his voice.

Desperate to throw a damp towel on this lunacy, she started babbling. "Your sister was awake again. Your mama and your aunt saw her. They didn't get much out of her. She didn't want to talk, they said."

"She'll speak to me," he murmured, but his face still hadn't lost that look, and his hands still held hers firmly.

The contact felt so warm and safe, it was almost impossible to focus on the downside, or even to remember that there was one. The fine hairs on her neck rose, and a hot tingling started in her lips, only to spread to places she had no business thinking of in public. She sucked in a deep breath in the hope that some of the oxygen would make it to her brain.

"I took your family home," she said, "to get a little rest and eat. Your mama's car's still here, though— she told me you picked it up from my place earlier. She thought you could drive it to the house if you'd like—but if anything more happens, you're to call her *instantáneamente*."

"Hey, that's pretty good for a blond *chica*."

"One of my many talents." Apparently, the deep breath hadn't helped, for her voice had gone all raspy, a surefire sign of estrogen impairment.

Wise up, screamed her better judgment.

His thumb caressed her knuckle, and she felt her willpower ebb away. In a last-ditch effort, she warned, "Those cops are probably watching, and the FBI."

"Let 'em watch *this*, then." Rebellion crackled in his words as he let go of her hands and dragged her into his arms with the desperation a drowning man usually reserved for a life ring.

For a split second, she thought the two of them had been struck by lightning, despite the fact that she hadn't seen a single cloud. What she did see was the electric flash of blue-white arcing at the outer edges of her vision. And she could swear she felt the soles of her shoes melting to the sidewalk.

But as the current running through her strengthened, it came to Reagan that Jack Montoya was *kissing* her, kissing her for all he was worth. Which to her way of thinking was about a million bucks . . . and climbing steadily.

Just as she was really settling in and beginning to enjoy herself, the rational part of her mind got the upper hand. Pushing herself away from him, she felt an almost painful jolt as his lips left hers.

"You—you want to commit suicide, you leave me out of it," she stammered.

He drew back to look at her as if she'd landed a right cross to his heart.

"Think about it," she said. "You know, WWYLD?"

"*What?*"

"What Would Your Lawyer Do? Or *say*, in this case?"

Jack smiled ruefully. "He'd probably say he wished

233

he had a bighearted, beautiful, brilliant woman of his own to kiss."

She hooted. "If I'm so smart, what am I doing kissing you back?"

Raising his brows, he ventured, "You just can't help yourself?"

Before she could come up with a suitable retort, something in Jack's pocket beeped. He pulled out his cell phone and flipped it open, then shook his head, his expression sobering. "Sorry, Reagan, but I'm going to have to get this voicemail."

She meandered toward one of the benches and told herself she should be grateful for the interruption. So why, then, did a rush of disappointment overwhelm her?

Before she could begin to order her thoughts, Jack rejoined her. Whatever he'd heard had swept the last fragments of lust—or lunacy—from his expression.

"I've got to get away from here," he said. "I'll check in on my sister, and then—"

"What is it, Jack?"

He hesitated, the wind ruffling his dark hair, tugging wisps of it in front of his eyes. She longed to brush it off his forehead, but she didn't dare touch him. Not if she wanted common sense to rule the day.

"I have to leave for a while," he told her. "It's about—one of my patients."

One of his illegal *patients,* she decided.

A thought occurred to her, so dangerous and ugly that she had to warn him. "Have you stopped to think that someone could be setting you up? I caught some of the news in the waiting room, and I can tell you, the media's all over this, right down to the so-called 'hate crime' committed at my house. They couldn't be more thrilled if someone had burned a cross. Just think of the fun they'd have if they could catch you doing something shady. Or what about the authorities? From what I hear, there's a hell of a lot of heat on that task force. This could be a sting, right?"

Jack didn't deny anything. "The party that called—I know this person, Reagan. She would never trust the authorities, or the media either. She can't afford to."

So his patient was definitely a foreign national. Was it a mother calling for her child? Or did Jack's illegal acts of compassion extend to adults as well?

She decided it would be better not to ask, better not to know any more than she did already. WWYLD, she reminded herself, even though, so far, she hadn't bothered to consult an attorney.

Considering the tightrope she was walking whenever she spoke to investigators, it might be time to change that. Even if she already could guess—but didn't want to hear—what any first-year law student would almost certainly tell her.

Stay as far away from Doctor Jack Montoya as you can.

As Jack walked back inside the hospital, he was already working through the logistics, his mind running through the precautions he would take as he moved pharmaceutical samples from the clinic to his mama's car, then took the new inhalers to the mother who had called about her little girl. It wasn't strictly an emergency—the child wasn't currently in distress—but she needed more medication to keep her wheezing under control. Since the girl's asthma tended to peak in the hours before dawn, Jack wanted to get the inhalers to her this evening.

But Reagan walked beside him, her presence pulling

at his attention with the gentle insistence of the sea tugging at a wader's legs. Turning toward her, he noticed the smudges of fatigue beneath her eyes. "You should go now, Reagan. Grab something to eat and get a good night's sleep."

He struggled to steady his voice, though he wanted more than anything to take her home, to lay her down and kiss her until the dam broke and all their grief and tension could spill free. . . .

No, that wasn't right, he realized. He'd been lying to himself to think he wanted Reagan as some anonymous release from stress. He simply *wanted* her, as he had from that first moment she had set foot in his office.

She nodded. "Home sounds really good now—even if I can't sleep in my own bed."

"Are you allowed to get it cleaned up?"

She nodded. "I'm going to call a company that does that sort of thing. Insurance ought to cover most of the work.

"But I can't worry about that now," she added. "All I can think about is getting through the services tomorrow. I still . . . I still can't believe Joe's gone. I don't know how I'm going to make it through the services."

Her grief cast a pall over his thoughts. How could he have thought of making love to her while she was in such pain? "I wish I could go with you. I'd like to pay my respects, for one thing."

"Bad idea," she said. "Really terrible right now. Just pray for Donna, will you? And pray the task force finds the bastards who caused her husband's death."

"I plan to do more than that. I mean to get them to stop wasting their time on me and put everything they've got into finding Sergio—or whoever set that fire."

Her blue eyes glistened. "I hope to God you can."

Fighting the impulse to gather her in his arms again, Jack quickly changed the subject. "I know you're eager to get home, but I'd feel a whole lot better if you stayed somewhere else until you've had new locks installed and an alarm put in. I'd like to pay for—"

She shook her head. "Forget about paying, Jack. You've lost everything you own, and I can handle my deductible. Besides, I've been meaning to put in an alarm ever since I moved into the house."

She'd lost so much because of him: her captain and close friend, as well as her sense of security. Jack's mind replayed the gut-freezing moment when Sergio had pressed his gun against her head—and he thought of how she still had more to lose.

Such as her life, which he had come to feel was more important than his own.

"The best one you can buy," he told her. "I'm telling you, it's on me."

"We can argue about that later," she said in a tone that told him it wouldn't do him any good. "And I'll be fine tonight. Peaches has offered me her guest room as long as I need it, and she's already defrosting one of her supposedly world-famous chicken jalapeno casseroles."

"That sounds like a great idea." Whatever the state of Peaches's gender, she—or was it really *he?*—seemed to be a true friend. The casserole sounded good, too, especially since Jack was likely to grab a fast-food saturated-fat bomb on his way to the clinic.

"You want Peaches's number?" Reagan asked. "I'd like to hear if there's any change in Luz Maria."

She gave him the phone number, and Jack started programming it into his cell phone's memory. Halfway through, he paused, his finger hovering over the keypad. "About what happened across the street before," he said, "I'm sorry, Reagan. I have no business dragging you into this any deeper."

Ever so gently, she took the phone from his hands and punched in the remaining digits. Passing it back, she nailed him with an unflinching storm-blue gaze. "Nobody drags me anywhere, Montoya. I'm here because I want to be. For you."

It took everything he had not to pull her back in his embrace. He wanted—needed, really—to believe what she was saying and to believe in what he'd felt between them as they'd touched. But there was something else, too, something hard and cold that glittered in those eyes of hers.

The hunger to find Joe Rozinski's killer.

Jack couldn't stop wondering, did that explain the rest? Was Reagan's interest in staying close to him motivated by her need for revenge?

And would that revenge destroy his sister, who had already suffered so much for her errors? His mouth went dry at the thought that he might have to be the one to tell Luz Maria. About her lost pregnancy. And perhaps about Sergio as well, for Jack knew that, with her head injury, Luz Maria might very well not recall the events that had led up to her accident.

Including who had run her off the road.

But at the moment, Reagan was looking at him, her declaration still hanging in the air.

"Thank you," he said simply as he pushed the button for the elevator. "If you don't hear from me before then, I'll call you after the services tomorrow."

"That would be fi—"

"Montoya," someone called from behind them. "Dr. Montoya, may I have a word with you?"

Jack stiffened at the voice, which he'd been hearing in his nightmares—as well as on his answering machine—for the past two weeks.

As Winter stalked toward him, the first thing Jack noticed was the permanent set of scowl lines engraved in his long face. Which made sense, considering the man was perpetually pissed off about the sorry state of the country—or the fact he didn't run it, at least for the time being.

The radio commentator's frown deepened, and he loosened the knot of his red tie as if the thing was choking back his anger. "I just wanted to *thank* you, Dr. Montoya"—venom dripped from every syllable—"for robbing this city of its best shot at a decent mayor—"

"You mean Thomas Youngblood's dropped out of the race?" Reagan interjected. She might be playing dumb, but malicious glee shone in her eyes.

Winter's face flushed, the red contrasting with his sandy hair and sun-bleached brows. But he spared Reagan no more than a dismissive sneer before returning his attention to Jack. "I don't know how you orchestrated these . . . these *stunts* of yours with those murdering radicals, but I swear to you I'll find out, and I *will* clear my name. And see you in prison—or better yet, deported, you filthy, connivi—"

"I hate to interrupt you mid-tirade," Jack said dryly, "but they don't deport Americans."

"Whose idea was it to paint quotes you'd heard on my show on those walls?" Winter demanded. "You knew damn well the media would be chomping at the bit to link me with this bullshit—"

"It's hell, isn't it?" asked Jack. "Having irresponsible broadcasters tell lies about you on the air."

"If they *are* lies," Reagan added.

Winter glared at her. "Who the hell are you? Another of those goddamned radicals? Or just one of their whores?"

Jack knew the man was upset, but the insult to Reagan stunned him—and sent his temper rocketing past the boiling point.

Reagan was one step ahead of him. "Listen, you pompous, horse-faced windbag of a—"

Jack brushed past her. "I . . . have had . . . just about enough of your shit, Winter."

Alarm flashed over the man's expression. He took two steps backward, until he smacked into the wall opposite the elevator doors.

Jack didn't relent. He was up in Winter's face now, so close he could smell the man's sweat. "You want to come after me, I'll take that, but you don't talk your trash to women. And especially not this one."

A tone sounded, and Jack heard the whoosh of the elevator doors behind him. He heard voices as people stepped out, but he was well past caring what they witnessed.

"I want an apology," he demanded, borrowing a page from Paulo's book and thumping a finger against Winter's chest. "Not for me, but for her—and for my sister, too. For taking up my time with stupid accusations about how we orchestrated these *stunts* just to make you look bad."

Winter's blue eyes locked on Reagan, and his upper lip curled. "I see she's not just any whore, she's yours."

Reagan might have been the boxer, but Jack didn't have such a bad right cross himself. He put it to good use, punching Winter's face so hard that he heard bone crack.

Fortunately, it wasn't his, as evidenced by the blood

leaking between the broadcaster's fingers, which formed a protective bridge over his almost certainly broken nose. The man might have a horse face, but he bleated like a goat.

For about half a second, Jack felt exultant—until a security officer jerked him backward and wrenched his arms behind his back. Then he felt exactly like the idiot he'd been. The last thing in the world he needed was to add an assault charge to his current problems.

What would your lawyer say? Reagan's voice teased in his head, while the real version somewhat less wisely told the sniveling Winter he was lucky Jack had decked him before she did.

"I'm fine, I'm fine," Jack told the guard, a small but tough-looking Hispanic with a jagged, livid scar across his throat. "I shouldn't have hit him, but he called my lady friend a *puta*."

"You gonna hit him any more?" the guard asked, talking over the sound of Winter's cries.

"I'm done, I guess," Jack said, his embarrassment rising as one of the nurses stopped and stared at him. It was bad enough that he'd backslid to his days as an adolescent troublemaker, but this incident would be all over the hospital district in no time. And all over the news, too, where Winter would be sure to transform this particular molehill into Mount Everest.

"No, no," Winter was telling a second security officer while dabbing at his nose with a handkerchief. "I won't be pressing charges, and I won't need medical treatment either. This is a private matter, and it's over now."

Amazed, Jack jerked his gaze toward the speaker, who caught his eye and asked, "Isn't it, Dr. Montoya?"

Winter pasted on a let's-be-reasonable-adults look and extended his free hand toward Jack. "I'm terribly sorry about your sister, and about anything I said in the—uh—the heat of the moment that may have offended your lovely friend here. Please, let's put all this unpleasantness behind us."

Bowled over by the suddenness of the man's change of attitude, Jack glanced at Reagan, who tipped her head in the direction of the gathering crowd of onlookers. In a flash, Jack understood completely.

If this incident reached the ears of reporters—as it was almost certain to—Winter would rather project a magnanimous persona than allow the public to see him as the self-serving, trash-talking crybaby he was. And Winter was a man who knew exactly how to play the media. Unless Jack shook his hand and mumbled some sort of apology himself, he was bound to look like a hot-tempered thug, the poster boy for every negative stereotype about Hispanic males and their machismo.

Yet Jack found that his pride was the bitterest pill he'd had to swallow in some time.

Such a bitter pill that he almost choked on his words as he got out the apology. But rather than taking Winter's hand, Jack clenched his own into a rock-hard fist and quickly turned away.

Chapter Twenty

At the sight of Luz Maria, looking so small and fragile in her hospital gown, Jack shoved aside his fury and frustration.

Backing down and telling Winter he was sorry had been as painful as spitting out a mouthful of blood and broken teeth, but it was nothing—absolutely nothing—compared to seeing the way bruises and abrasions had blossomed on his little sister's face. Her eyes were closed, but he couldn't be certain whether her air-bag-abraded eyelids had swollen shut or she was sleeping.

Unable to bring himself to speak, he studied the bandaged arm that had been elevated on a mound of pillows to reduce the swelling. He'd been told the bones would need setting before a cast could be put on, but the doctors wouldn't risk putting Luz Maria under until they felt more certain about the extent of her head injuries. For the same reason, she'd been given only the mildest of over-the-counter pain relievers.

No question about it, when she did wake, she'd be hurting. And in spite of the terrible consequences of the mistakes she'd made, Jack wanted more than anything to soothe her, to fold his little sister into his arms the way he had when she'd awakened with night terrors as a child. He needed to rock her and murmur to her, "Shhh . . . hush now, *mi princesa*. I've scared off all the monsters, so you're safe now, I promise."

His eyes burned and his vision blurred with the realization that the monsters had come back, fiercer and more ravenous than ever. And this time, he'd been powerless to banish them. *But I will see them punished*, he swore. *I'll make sure they pay.*

A nurse came in, a woman with short dark hair and turquoise contacts that made her eyes look bright as jewels. "I'll be waking her for a neuro check," she told him. "Then you can let her know you're here."

As Luz Maria muttered a complaint about being awakened, Jack released a breath he hadn't realized he'd been holding. As she answered the nurse's questions, his sister sounded tired and grumpy—the way she always did when someone roused her after she'd been out late. Though quieter than usual, she seemed like the Luz Maria he knew—until she slitted her eyes wide enough to see him watching.

"How are you feeling?" he asked.

She turned her head to look away, wincing as though the effort cost her.

The nurse took her vitals, then flashed Jack a tight smile before leaving the two of them alone.

"I'm tired," Luz Maria said. "I have to sleep now . . ."

"Do you know why you're here?" he asked.

"So tired."

Jack decided to press, at least a little. "Do you re-member the accident at all? Luz Maria?"

She frowned, but her lips trembled as if she were fighting back tears. "I know about the baby, Jack. They told me the baby's gone."

Bending over her, he softly kissed her forehead. "I'm sorry."

She shrank away from him. "Are you, really? Or do you just feel relieved?"

"What do you want me to say?" he asked. *"Madre de dios,* I've been worried sick about you."

"I need sleep, Jack. I can't . . . I don't want to feel—"

"Who did this to you?" he demanded. "Do you know who caused the accident? Who moved you to Reagan's house?"

Her eyes closed, and she remained quiet for a long while, so long Jack was certain she had fled him in the only way left to her.

He touched her temple gingerly and whispered, "Sleep well, *mi princesa.*"

But before he could reach the door, she muttered, "Sergio . . ."

Sergio *what?* Had that bastard been the one, despite his claims of innocence? Though he was shaking with rage, Jack swallowed back his questions. With her eyes still closed, he couldn't know whether his sister was sleeping or awake, yet either way, he feared that a single word might break the fragile spell of her cooperation.

Luz Maria was murmuring again, so quietly that he leaned close to hear the words.

"He said you wouldn't be hurt. He promised me— he swore it," she murmured.

Jack wanted to ask, was Luz Maria referring to the fire, the damage to his career, or was BorderFree planning something else—something even worse? And why would the pro-immigration group be involved with faking hate crimes against him?

Or was it something else entirely? He remembered what Sergio had told Reagan last night, before the man had fled.

"You want to know who torched that building? Then follow the money. At the end of the trail, I'll bet you'll find a can of gasoline."

As his sister's breaths deepened into those of true sleep, Jack thought about it. Who would profit from the arson, the bizarre tableau in which Luz Maria had been found, maybe even his own death?

Figure that out, he told himself, *and you've got yourself a murderer. Fail to—and you may be the next one killed.*

Jack was already on his way when Paloma del Valle called a second time. *"Apure, por favor,"* she pleaded, begging him to hurry.

Though her daughter, Cristina, had started wheezing, Paloma wanted no part of his suggestion to call an ambulance. "No, no," she'd insisted before switching to her thickly accented English. "You fix. You fix quick now."

He thought of calling for an ambulance himself, but since he was no more than ten minutes away, he decided he could get there just as quickly.

By the time Jack reached the Las Casitas Village apartment complex, darkness had descended over Houston. But nowhere he had ever driven seemed as dark as these anonymous, two-story rows of tan-brick apartments built back in the early eighties.

In another age, they would have been called tenements. In any period, they would be termed dangerous, with pockets of addicts, criminals, and far too many un-supervised, half-grown kids living among families struggling to work their way out to a safer neighbor-hood. In addition, the lower floors were as prone to flooding as was the adjacent, long-abandoned Plaza del Sol. As Jack searched for a parking space near one of the few working security lights, he could still smell the fetid dampness that lingered from last spring's record-setting deluge. Moisture remained evident in the weedy low spots—quagmires, really—that surrounded the com-plex and doubtless provided cover for both rodents and snakes.

It was a damned shame to see the area this way. When Jack was a kid, the Plaza del Sol, with its mostly Hispanic-owned businesses, featured not only indige-nous Central and South American crafts, but a variety of stylish restaurants and shops selling merchandise ranging from fashionable clothing to designer kitchen-ware. Its reputation as a fun and funky alternative to homogenous malls drew a variety of customers from all over Greater Houston, and its growing success had become a tremendous source of pride to the commu-nity. The once-blighted area underwent a boom, with numerous apartments, grocery stores, and strip centers crowding around the plaza.

That boom ultimately destroyed it, for as the area was built up, developers covered so much of it with concrete and asphalt that Southeast Texas's frequent heavy rainfalls had no place to run off. Coupled with a severe economic downturn, three floods within two years had sealed the plaza's fate.

As Jack climbed out of his mother's station wagon, he wondered if the rising waters were taking the same toll on the area's residents. Luz Maria had been the one to point out to him that many children he'd diagnosed with respiratory problems lived in this neighborhood, and one look at the water-stained, graffiti-laden exterior walls made him wonder if the problem was related to something inside the buildings instead of the general environment.

He'd driven here before, on two occasions when Paloma, a single mother, had convinced him her daughter was too sick for the bus ride to the clinic. The last time, he'd even let her talk him into treating a toddler whose parents feared deportation if they set foot in a health-care facility. But for all of that, he'd never seriously considered the building where his patients lived as the possible source of the children's lung ailments. Like most doctors, he had succumbed to the temptation to treat the afflicted organ, or the disease, instead of the whole patient—a shortcoming his social-worker sister had been quick to point out.

"Seeing the whole person is only the first step to solving the problem." Her words floated through his mind, but only now did he realize what she had meant.

Near the open, lighted doorway of a laundry room, Jack passed a trio of teenaged boys, two of whom wore hard looks and black T-shirts that appeared to be hand-painted with a silver insignia of some sort. Gang logo, he decided, and he felt his body go on high alert for some kind of shakedown. Years ago, he'd been jumped and robbed at knifepoint in a parking lot outside of med school, and the tension and watchfulness came back to him like a recurrent nightmare.

Yet when he came close enough to make out what the boys were studying so intently, he felt heat rush to his face. It was a physics book, he realized, and the "gang logo" was the silver panther of the very high school from which Jack had graduated.

"How'd you do it?" the curly-haired one asked another in perfectly unaccented English as he planted a finger halfway down the page. "Come on, *'mano*. Give it up and show me how to do the problem. If my grades don't come up, I'm off the team for three more weeks."

Once Jack passed the trio, he shook his head, disgusted that he'd leapt to the conclusion that a bad neighborhood necessarily spawned bad kids. He'd seen enough gang logos among the graffiti to know the criminal element was here, but even in the worst spots, hope glimmered like a shiny penny at the bottom of a swamp.

Before he could knock, Senora del Valle opened her door and ushered him into an apartment with a stained pink carpet and walls with peeling paint. The furniture looked both worn and inexpensive, and a houseplant atop the TV had turned yellow, but despite the scattered toys, the ratty carpet had been freshly vacuumed and he didn't spot a speck of dust.

"Dónde está Cristina?" he asked needlessly, as her wheezing gave away her location. Following the sound, he went to the kitchen and found the big-eyed nine-year-old sitting at a chipped Formica table, her neck muscles straining with her efforts to breathe. A list of spelling words was laid out in front of her, along with half-completed homework. On her lap sat a worn, stuffed toy owl, which watched over the proceedings.

Though she didn't bother with her usual perky greeting, Jack was relieved to see her color still looked good. He'd been dreading finding blue lips—a replay of Agustín Romero in the hours before his death.

"How was school today? Did you see any cute boys?" he asked, hoping to gauge the severity of her attack by the length of her response. When she was well, the brown-haired little cutie could talk his ears off. According to her mama, she had never known a stranger and was always getting notes home from *la maestra* complaining that Cristina was chattering away in class.

So when she merely wrinkled her nose and said, "Boys . . . are gross," he knew, before he even pulled out his stethoscope or the peak air-flow meter he'd packed, that she wasn't getting sufficient oxygen.

"Where's the nebulizer?" he asked the child's mother as he pulled open the bag containing the premixed solution for the machine.

Paloma del Valle ducked her head, casting her gaze toward the floor. From a bedroom, her younger daughter started crying, and she rushed off to tend the toddler.

"Don't have it," said Cristina, and she, too, looked away. "Not anymore."

Jack bit back a curse, realizing that Cristina's mother must have either sold the nebulizer or given it away—despite the fact her daughter needed it so much that Jack had bought her a used machine with his own money.

It wasn't the first time he'd been burned in such a way, and it probably wouldn't be the last. He wasted a moment wondering if things like this ever happened to suburban doctors, who spoke to their patients across gleaming desks while in covered spaces outside, their sleek black Jaguars waited smugly.

You could do it still, he told himself. If his current situation didn't cost him his license to practice in the state of Texas, Dr. Rick Aldrich had made it clear that his offer to come work in his Galleria-area practice still stood.

But the thought didn't appeal to Jack, even if he would get the opportunity to work with his old mentor. And even if he could go the rest of his career without making another house call or buying some piece of medical equipment for a patient.

As he plastered on a smile for the girl's sake, he dug deeper in his bag. "Since you don't have it anymore," he told her, "we'll just have to go with Plan B."

"Is that . . . is Plan B a shot?" she asked, her wheezing growing louder.

"Ta-da," he said as he whipped out an inhaler. "No shot this time, Cristina. Just a couple of puffs."

And if that doesn't work, he added mentally, *you'll get to take a nice ride in an ambulance—with the lights and sirens going.*

They watched him leave the squalid apartment on the East End, watched the little girl with the stuffed owl run after him and hug the doc good-bye.

"Some people never learn their lesson," said the first man.

The second shrugged broad shoulders. "It's like they just can't help themselves."

"Maybe this kind of thing's addictive, bad as any other jones. Crack cocaine, video poker, and sticking it to the system to help out little kids: they'll probably have support groups for all three soon."

His partner shook his head. "You've been in this job too damned long."

Dr. Montoya stopped to chat with three delinquents, and within moments, the whole damned crew was pointing and talking over something in a book. When a curly-topped reprobate reached for something in his pocket, both of the watchers instinctively bent their knees and gripped their guns' butts, their wildly beating hearts pumping adrenaline throughout their bodies.

Instead of the weapon they expected, a pencil emerged from the kid's pocket. Both men chuckled nervously, sweat breaking out with the speed and severity of a virulent pox.

"Jesus Christ," one muttered. "Now I've seen everything."

"I can see it now," the other told him, "the front-page headlines saying, *'Promising Youth Gunned Down for Doing Homework.'* We'd be the ones who ended up doing time."

"Maybe not the only ones," said his partner as he watched the doctor walking toward his car.

"I think you're wrong on that," the other answered. "I don't figure Jack Montoya's ever going to serve a day. Even if you could get a jury to convict him—which would be one hell of a trick—you can't put a guy like that in prison."

"Why the hell not? He wouldn't be the first doctor to do time."

"A doctor can, for certain, but how're you going to put a dead man behind bars?"

Chapter Twenty-one

The following morning, before the memorial service started, Reagan drove to the transfer office and put in for an EMT position at one of the busiest stations in Houston. The ambulance job, located in a dilapidated East End station not far from the bungalow where she'd once lived, came open periodically, as soon as whatever unfortunate rookie assigned to it was able to transfer to a better position.

The station was the kind of place that was either a firefighter/EMT's first stop or the last, the kind of place where the shift captain—a half-derelict old slacker cruising toward retirement—wouldn't ask too many questions about where she'd come from or why. He'd simply be grateful to have a warm body filling the position instead of a succession of fill-ins, all of whom most likely griped nonstop about being sent to what was popularly known as Hell's Rat-Hole.

Reagan had driven through the old neighborhood before she'd visited Jack's clinic Friday, so she understood how far down the area had slid since the days she and her family had lived there, just as she knew that her patchwork of high-school and street Spanish would be pressed into daily use. But she couldn't care less, as long as the move took her away from the station where she'd worked with Captain Joe Rozinski, Beau LaRouche, and her old crew. By changing shifts, she'd upped the odds of avoiding them almost indefinitely.

Yet until the memorial service, Reagan didn't fully comprehend how necessary such a transfer would turn out to be. As she cut through the sea of uniforms gathering at the head of the march route to the church, she ran into a number of people she knew from her days at the fire academy, along with men and women she had worked with during her time on the ambulance, and those she'd trained with for the annual competition with the cops. As these firefighters, EMTs, and paramedics offered quiet words of comfort, shook her hand or embraced her, Reagan for a time regained the feeling of belonging to something larger and far nobler than herself, a huge family that accepted her, for all her failings, because she was one of them.

But when she reached the vanguard of the assemblage, the coldness of her current crew permeated the warm, late-October Monday morning. From Beau to Zellers to C.W., not a man among them spoke a word to her; instead, they let their expressions do the talking for them. Beau looked as if he would like to punch her in the face again. Several others accused her with furious glares. For his part, C.W. seemed confused and sad, although she thought she read concern in his dark face as well.

But it was the district chief who took her behind a ladder truck and lowered the boom on her.

"I don't exactly know what your involvement is," he

told her, "but at times like these, feelings run hot. Since you're still on sick leave, I think that under the circumstances it would be best if you went home."

"You can't do that," she protested, pinching the tender skin inside her wrist to keep herself from dissolving into tears. "I'm just a witness, that's all, and I have to be here. Nobody was closer to the captain."

District Chief Anderson fidgeted, readjusting his hat to hide his gray-brown comb-over. He appeared to struggle to look her in the eye. "Mrs. Rozinski doesn't want to see you. And she doesn't want you at the funeral tomorrow either."

"What?" Reagan's shoulders drooped, and she grew conscious that she was sweating within the confines of her blue dress uniform. This was even worse than the nightmares she'd been having about being trapped while a noose of flame tightened all around her. Had Beau poisoned Donna Rozinki's mind, too, instead of just their crew's?

She twisted the skin within her fingers, not caring if she left a mark. She'd be damned if she would cry in front of the district chief—or anyplace where that traitor LaRouche might spot her.

Anderson frowned at her wrist before offering, "If you insist on attending, at least go to the back and march with the other firefighters instead of remaining with your crew. We don't want harsh words taking the focus of the service from the man we're here to honor. And we certainly don't want anything adding more pain to the family's burden."

Reagan dropped her gaze. "Yes, sir."

"And Ms. Hurley, if I may be frank . . ."

She shrugged, too beaten down to care if he found the gesture disrespectful.

"I'd suggest you transfer to another station," he said, "to another district—and another shift."

She nodded in answer, unable to tell him she had taken care of it already. And barely noticing that her fingernails had bitten deeper, deep enough to draw blood from that delicate, pale skin.

The thin crescents of pain didn't bother her, nor did the rust-colored swatches she found later on her sleeve. All that mattered was tamping down her despair throughout the long, long service.

And keeping her tears from leaking through the cell-thin barrier of her self-control.

"What makes you think she don't know?" the Firebug demanded. Or tried to, anyway, but what came out was a harsh crow's squawk overlaid by the rasping of his breath.

Fuck it anyway, he thought, and forced himself to repeat the question, for the answer was important to him, more important than anything had been in months and months.

"I told you, she doesn't," said his visitor, his words rough with annoyance. "If she'd recognized me from the car, I would have seen it in her face. If she'd put things together, I would have heard it, too. Hell, you woulda heard the goddamn screaming all the way from here."

Though his outer ears were gone, the Firebug had gotten good at judging voices. He'd had to, since his goddamn eyes had melted in the sockets and even his stinking nose had peeled off like a scab. Yet a man could learn a lot by listening, and what the hell did he have but hours and hours to dissect every word thrown his way like scraps tossed to a half-dead dog?

But nose or no nose, this dog was on the scent. His visitor wasn't near as sure as he was letting on.

"Sometimes," hissed the Firebug, "sometime they put the shit together later. It co—co—"

He began to cough, silently cursing his charred lungs. A cup was pressed into his hands, and he sipped noisily from his straw, wishing for something more than water, something to take the edge off of the ever-present pain. But the one time his visitor had humored him that way, that bitch of a nurse had taken it away before he'd gotten his first taste. Then she'd carried on for half an hour in that high-pitched, insect whine of hers, about how alcohol and his pain medication would form a lethal combination.

Like he gave a flying fuck.

"It could come to her all of a sudden," he finally managed. "When somethin' happens to remind her. And then she's gonna think, where'd I see that guy before? Besides, there's gonna be a lot of heat on this, the stiff being a fireman and all."

"And that's not all," said the visitor. "There's some federal task force on it, too. I heard it on the news."

The Firebug paid no attention. "I goddamn *hate* firemen. They know what kind of job they're takin', know what kinda risks they draw. And then they act all surprised when one gets killed, act like no matter what you *meant* to burn, you set out to charbroil one of their own."

"I never meant to kill him, just that goddamned doctor."

But the 'bug was floating now, drifting on a raft of bitter memories. "I killed one once, in some pissant warehouse fire. An insurance job, for Christ's sake. But they turned the heat so damned high, I had to leave town for six years."

"I know," his visitor told him. "I remember how you didn't send us money."

The Firebug attempted a shrug, but his skin, still healing from the last graft, sent agony streaking up his arm. "I got picked up on some other deal then. Twenty months on some chickenshit little deal where I lit up this—"

"I don't want to hear it. Not now, not when I just told you everything I did, just the way you asked, and all you can do is talk about what you did a freaking hundred years ago."

He sounded sulky, thought the Firebug, the way he had as a snot-nosed kid. That voice used to mean he was about to get kicked out of school again, or the cops were gonna drive by for another threat-laced chat. Something told the Firebug his visitor had made even more mistakes than he'd let on, and the thought of it made his heart pick up speed, as if his crippled body could outrun his fear.

The fear that unless the woman died, too, his last remaining hope would be joining his brothers in the pen. Only this son, unlike the others, would be doing his time on death row.

Chapter Twenty-two

Since Joe Rozinski's funeral last week, Reagan had given Jack excuse after excuse as to why she couldn't see him. She had to see a doctor—a *reasonable* doctor, she'd stressed—about her release to return to work. She had to talk to the head of the task force to find out when she could get her house back into order. She was expecting a call back from her insurance agent, or she had to see somebody regarding her transfer.

She was unfailingly polite, asking after Luz Maria, who was recovering at home while claiming to remember nothing about her accident and little more than that about Sergio Cardenas. Reagan inquired, too, about Jack's mother, and she had expressed the appropriate concern when he told her he'd been placed on administrative leave from the clinic until his supervisors completed their own investigation. But whenever he asked how she was or tried to arrange to see her, she dodged each attempt with the grace and deftness of a *matadora* spinning away from the bull's horns.

But not tonight, Jack told himself. Tonight, Peaches—

who had inexplicably taken up his cause—informed him that Reagan was moving back into her own house. Jack had decided on the spot to drop by unannounced and find out, once and for all, if he'd only imagined the connection he'd felt to her in the park that evening a week earlier.

But first he needed wheels, as he still couldn't get anyone to tell him when the task force would release his Explorer.

With Reagan on his mind, Jack took the keys to the second rental Paulo had pressed on him, then followed the larger man to a lot outside of the dilapidated garage he used to squeeze every last mile from his junkers. Back in the farthest corner, they found a funky yellow compact, its sheet metal pitted beneath a layer of road grime. In the dusky light, it looked more like a hail-damaged kumquat than a car.

"Thanks, man," Jack managed over the barking of the pair of pit bulls temporarily locked in one of the closed bays. "I really appreciate the loan."

He did, too, even though it might have been the sorriest-looking heap in Harris County.

"You don't think I'm crazy enough to loan you another sweet ride after last time?" Standing in the murky glow beneath a security light, Paulo shook his head. "You're already into me for over twenty grand."

Jack's mouth went dry. When he had called earlier with the news that his insurance company was refusing to cover the damage to the Mustang, Paulo hadn't said word one about money. Jack wondered, had he been an idiot to come to this isolated garage to meet his old friend after hours?

Yet Paulo's serious expression broke into a grin, and

he jabbed Jack's shoulder playfully with his fist. At least, Jack *supposed* the blow was meant to be playful—even if the force of it had sent him back a step.

"Just kidding, *compa*. Can't you take a joke?" asked Paulo.

"If you ever say something funny, we'll see about that."

"Don't worry about the Mustang. When it comes to my good vehicles, I got insurance policies up the ass."

Jack dredged up a grin. "Wouldn't it be more comfortable to keep 'em in a file cabinet like everybody else?"

Above his white-streaked goatee, Paulo floated a half smile. But his eyes looked deadly serious. "Just do me this one thing," he said, his voice taking on a rumble as ominous as an approaching thunderstorm. "Now that you got Winter's nuts in a wringer, you make him sing real pretty—when it comes to the neighborhood, at least."

"*Chingado*," Jack cursed. "You still don't get it, do you? The feds don't think Winter or even one of his disciples did the crimes. From what I get, they're focused on tracking down those guys from BorderFree-4-All. They feel like the whole thing's some kind of scheme to discredit Winter, which is the story he's using with his listeners, from what I understand. Those people *love* a good conspiracy."

"The reporters ain't buying it, though, are they? They're still all over Darren Winter, shining laser beams up his ass and lookin' for dirt on him with a freakin' microscope. And you're coming out the good guy, Saint Do-Gooder getting picked on because the guy hates Mexicans. It's spreading through our people, too. Mamas are taping your picture up between the Pope and Jesus, *vatos* are talkin' you up out front of the cantinas. You're their goddamn hero, man. They'd do anything for you."

"You and I must not be listening to the same stations. And neither are my bosses." It was easier to deny Paulo's words than to live with them. Jack didn't want to be a dividing line in the community, didn't want anything except to do his work in peace.

Paulo shook off the idea with a wave of his huge hand. "Nah. You've got Winter where we want him. So why not milk it, get him to talk up the area—you know, to pay us back for the harm he did before?"

"You're kidding, right? This is the same unofficial candidate who's going to be our mayor if the polls are right, the same guy whose nose I broke, remember? The one who came out smelling like a rose when he didn't press charges against the 'emotionally over-wrought Dr. Montoya.' *'You know those Latins and their famous fiery tempers'*—that's what the jackass said—right before he ripped me on the air again."

Carlota Sanchez, the young nurse from the clinic, had called to report Winter's latest bullshit and offer sympathy. Otherwise, Jack wouldn't have had a clue, since he sure as hell didn't care to listen to anything Winter had to say.

Carlota had seemed disappointed when Jack turned down her offer of a warm shoulder to cry on. But this past week, the only woman he had thought of—outside of his mother and his sister—had been the one who was avoiding him.

"Things are . . . this week's a delicate time." Apprehension flickered in Paulo's dark brown eyes. "We can't afford more bad press for the neighborhood, not if we're gonna get the Plaza del Sol reopened. And I don't mind telling you, I've staked everything there. Every fucking favor, every good deed, every dime. I need this, Joaquín. Goddamn therapists and private programs and nurses are eatin' me alive."

His son, thought Jack, but Paulo wasn't finished.

"So you need to come through for me," he continued, his face gleaming beneath a heavy dew of sweat. "I'm asking you as *un amigo*."

Jack felt for him, despite the pressure he was exerting. Paulo clearly had his back against the wall. "I've heard a little about your boy, and I wanted to say how sorry—"

Though Paulo's expression froze over, his voice trembled with emotion. "You think it's me, don't you? That the apple didn't fall far from the dumb-ass tree, seeing how I couldn't even get through school."

"That's not the way it works, man. I've known brilliant men with mentally challenged kids, college professors and doctors—"

"You can have your goddamn MD—and all your goddamn education. But don't you dare feel sorry for my son. And don't you *ever* pity me. You got that?"

"Loud and clear," Jack told him.

But as he drove the sputtering yellow car out of the parking lot, Jack did feel compassion. Not so much for Paulo, but for the son he clearly wanted to pretend did not exist.

Reagan wouldn't have bothered going to her front door if she hadn't been hoping that the overdue repairman might be putting in a late appearance. Earlier today, Beau LaRouche had stopped by, knocking politely and shouting through the locked door that he was ready to forgive her. After she told him to drop dead, the jerkwad had thrown down a bouquet of red roses, called her a bitch, and kicked her door, which had rattled the reinforced steel in its frame and scared her more than a little.

As Reagan peered out through her peephole, her hand hesitated near the heavy-duty chain Peaches had helped her install a few days earlier. What good would it be, spending all that money on deadbolts and alarm systems, if she still insisted on opening her door to trouble? And this *was* trouble, dressed in dark blue denim and carrying a bunch of irises.

"If you're not here to fix my disposal, I can't talk now," she called.

"It's the plumber," Jack replied.

Through the fish-eye lens, she made out his grin. But it was the wickedness in his eyes that made her toes curl and her pulse pound like a war drum.

"I don't see any tools," she managed.

"You let me in there, and I'll show you my tool."

Behind the safety of her door, she rolled her eyes.

He knocked again and called out, "Candygram."

Laughing, she took off the chain, unlocked the deadbolt, and opened the door to him. "You're that clever landshark, aren't you?" she quoted from her favorite *Saturday Night Live* reruns.

When she spotted the hideous thing parked beneath the streetlight, she laughed harder.

"You—you're driving that?" She pointed at something that looked like more like a cat-mauled canary than a compact car.

Leaning against her porch railing, he gave a self-deprecating shrug. "Thought it might jazz up my love life."

"So what're you planning? To cruise Richmond Avenue with the rest of the hotshots, then circle back and scoop up all the hot chicks who laugh themselves unconscious?"

He pretended to hunt around for a pen in his shirt pocket. "Hold it, will you? I need to write that down."

"You can come in for a minute," she invited, brushing her bangs out of her eyes. She was a mess, wearing a paint-spattered T-shirt and a pair of stained gray leggings, and not a speck of makeup. But it was just as well. "I'm ready for a break, and I want to hear about your family."

And tell you why I can't see you again, she added mentally. As wonderful, as freeing, as it had felt to laugh, she couldn't for a moment lose sight of her decision to make a clean break. As he stepped inside, he touched her elbow and leaned close to whisper, "I didn't come to talk about them."

The warm puffs of his breath made the fine hairs on her neck rise, and she was tempted to ward him off with a coating of the Canyon Dawn from her paint brush. But she couldn't force herself to speak or even move, not with his soft words fanning embers that turned her blood to liquid fire.

"I want to know how you are," he said, "how you're getting through this week."

"I'm keeping busy, that's how. I—I'm painting," she said, despite the fact that she'd just finished.

He pulled back to smile at her, then wiped his finger across the bridge of her nose. It came away a cinnamon hue.

"I see that," he said. "Nice color."

"It's water-based so the fumes don't get to me, and it covers up the red," she explained. Her brain was thrumming—along with less lofty body parts—in response to his touch.

Idiot, she told herself. *Get him out of here this minute.*

Instead, she offered him a glass of Shiraz. "I guess I can take that breather while I wait for the repairman. But let me wash my face."

She lingered, washing up and throwing on some clean jeans and a light sweater, hoping he would be gone by the time she came back. Instead, he'd found her corkscrew and was opening a bottle of red wine from the rack on her counter. Near his elbow, the flowers he'd brought sat in a vase, not arranged as artfully as Peaches would have done it, but pretty enough anyway, with their deep blue-violet petals and vibrant yellow throats.

"Every time I turn my back on you, you take over my kitchen." She meant it as a complaint that he was overstepping boundaries, but the words lacked heat. Unlike the traitorous fantasies running through her head.

"I couldn't find the right glasses," he said, looking as relaxed as if he'd just come home.

She pulled out a couple of wine stems and watched him as he poured. "I can't do this," she told him, sinking onto one of her barstools.

"Can't do what?" From across the countertop, he handed her a glass.

"Sit around here talking to you, drinking with you—as if nothing happened last week."

Pain flickered in his dark eyes. "You think I'm asking you to pretend that nothing did? How could I do that, Reag? How could I forget your captain's death and all my neighbors losing their homes? How could I put out of my mind my sister lying in your bed, with all that red hate screaming on your walls?"

He came around the counter and took the barstool beside hers, then swiveled so he could look her in the eye. "I didn't come by to see if we could forget it. God knows, I never will, not even if they catch whoever did it and lock the son of a bitch up for a century. I came to find out if there's a chance—even the smallest—for the two of us to move past this together, or to at least keep that door open."

She spun her seat away from him and placed her elbows on the counter, her eyes staring at the middle distance of the dining room. "Things have changed. They hate me, Jack. All of them. Donna Rozinski, my old crew—the people I thought of as my family."

She felt his palm settle on her back, felt him rub a soothing figure eight. Willed herself not to let him see how it affected her, how her body ached to lean into his strength and warmth the way a stunted sapling yearned for the sun's light.

"Why, Reagan? Those people know you. How could they—how could *anyone*— believe you would have anything to do with hurting your own captain?"

She couldn't force herself to look at him. "Guess—I guess it must be the company I keep. At least that's what C.W. told me when I called him at the station. He said . . . he said word is from arson there was something on your phone bill. Something that suggested a link to BorderFree—"

"I'm sure there was," Jack told her. "My sister stayed at my apartment a couple of days last month when she and Mama were fussing over something. I'm sure Luz Maria used my phone to call Sergio—and as soon as I found out about him, I told arson, the cops, the task force—the whole damned bunch of them. I didn't know before, Reagan. I swear it on my life."

She did look up then, staring into his eyes, seeing the pain and sorrow written in them. She swallowed hard, then said, "I figured it had to be something like that. I believe you, Jack. So why can't my friends believe in me?"

"I'd give anything to change their minds." Jack's voice shook with anger and frustration. "I'll speak to them if you'd like, tell them anything you want—"

She shook her head. "No offense, but your word won't help matters. The only thing that will is time—and an arrest. I'm going back to work tomorrow, at a station a couple of blocks over from your clinic."

"I hear sirens all the time there," he said. "That crew runs constantly."

She shrugged. "They needed someone fast, and I needed a place to let things cool down for a while."

"But your lungs—did your doctor check to see if—"

The question shafted through her, striking a well of fury and resentment. Part of her was still angry about his refusal to sign her form—but mostly, she hated her own weakness.

"Sure, he signed the release. For one thing, I'll be riding the meat-box," she said, calling the ambulance by its department nickname. "My lungs won't matter much there, at least not as much as my back and bedside manner. And the fact that I can speak a little Spanish."

"You're good at it, aren't you?" he asked. "The EMT work, I mean. You did great when we found Luz Maria. Maybe you ought to think about going further with your medical training."

She couldn't answer, couldn't force the words past the lump rising in her throat. Throughout the week, she hadn't talked to anyone, not even Peaches, about returning to an ambulance, about giving up her dream. She'd been hoping that if she didn't say the words, the reality would somehow fade away.

Besides, she had always kept her problems private, reasoning that she was strong enough to handle them herself. *Strong enough once, maybe,* she told herself resentfully. *Or maybe I've been kidding myself all along.*

"I need to ask you something," Jack said. "How'd you get that dent in your front door? And the rose petals lying on the porch?"

She was finished with covering for Beau, finished with allowing the pain of his betrayal to fester like an open wound. Still, it surprised her when she found herself reluctantly telling Jack all of it, from how she had befriended the slightly off-center younger man to how Beau had stunned her by announcing his romantic interest. And how he had hit her on the morning he'd found Jack at her house.

"Why didn't you say something?" Jack asked her. "I would never let that asshole get away with slugging y—"

"Don't you see?" asked Reagan. "He was really suffering that morning. Beau was in there, in the fire that killed the captain. Maybe he had to latch on to someone—anyone—to blame besides himself. I couldn't see destroying his career for that. He's still on probation, as a rookie."

"First of all, there's never any right time for a man to strike a woman. Never. And secondly, that happened the day after the fire. Those rose petals looked much fresher."

She nodded. "He came bearing flowers. Can you believe it? But I wouldn't let him in."

"Smart woman," Jack said.

"I might have forgiven him for hitting me, but Beau's been telling everyone he knows how I've been 'whoring with the guy who got Joe killed.' At least that's how he put it. He's the one who turned Donna and my crew against me."

"I still can't believe they'd take his word over yours."

"A fire crew's a tight group, Jack, and they're hurting—we're all hurting so bad, maybe it's a natural thing to start turning on each other." She sipped her wine, but tonight, it tasted bitter on her tongue. "At least it hasn't spread through the whole department—not yet anyway. Some of my old friends have called. They don't buy that I'd have anything to do with this, and one or two who know Beau suggested he's been running his mouth out of jealousy. I didn't know this, but he had some trouble before over a woman, a female recruit at the academy. She ended up quitting over it, I heard. And then there's the deal with his dad."

"His father?"

She nodded. "I'm pretty sure the man's done time for beating up Beau's mom, among other things. There are a couple of brothers, too—neither of them strangers to the Texas prison system."

"Have you tried to tell your crew this?"

She shook her head. "If you could have been there at the service, if you had heard the disappointment in C.W.'s voice, you'd know. They've bought Beau's bullshit, all of them." Her eyes burned, and her nose dripped moisture. Putting down her wineglass, she reached for tissues from the box on the counter.

Jack pushed the box closer to her and waited for her to blow her nose. He had put down his own glass as well, and sorrow underscored the pain in his expression.

"They didn't even want me there," she told him as hot tears overflowed. "I managed to hang out near the back, b-but Donna wouldn't have me at his funeral."

It seemed so right, so natural, when she found herself standing and wrapped within the circle of his arms. Allowing him to stroke her back, to whisper soothing words. When was the last time she had allowed herself to take whatever comfort another person offered? As close as she had grown to Peaches, as often as she'd allowed her neighbor to spill her heart about the terrible price she'd paid to live life as she saw fit, Reagan had never opened the locked cabinet of her own secrets. She had even told her best friends that her mother was long dead.

But Jack Montoya was no friend. She pulled away just far enough to look into his eyes, to fall headlong into depths as dark as the inky blackness of a moonless night.

One arm still draped around her waist, he raised his free hand to slide his fingertips along the hot, slick pathways of her tears. From her cheek, caresses flowed beneath the curve of her jawbone and down her neck.

He never took his gaze from her eyes, yet those sensitive healer's fingers read her pain the way a blind man read Braille poems. When he touched her lips, she kissed away the salty dampness and watched, transfixed, as hunger etched itself into his face.

Beneath her stomach, an answering need fluttered to life, a quickening within her, and desire seared her from the inside out. Until there was nothing she could do except to close her eyes and quench it, her mouth rising to meet his in the same moment that he moved.

Heaven help her, she thought. Jack Montoya *is* no

friend. Yet if she followed her heart's lead, she would have him as a lover.

Jack had told himself when he had come here that he would consider his trip worthwhile if she would speak to him through her closed door. He had hoped for more, of course—polite conversation on her sofa, a tentative discussion of the possibility that she might see him in six months or a year, when she'd had time to heal and he'd had time to put the fragments of his broken life together.

Her kiss, so warm and unrestrained, washed over him like a startling benediction, a blessing he'd done nothing to deserve.

Nothing but seduce her at her most vulnerable.

In spite of Reagan's repeated attempts to prove her toughness to him, Jack knew damned well how vulnerable she was to kindness. Especially now, only a week after the day her world had gone to pieces.

Had he been the saint that Paulo termed him, Jack would have pulled away. Had he been the best of men, he would have at least reminded her of how many questions hung over his future. Would he lose his job, his license? Would he be forced to flee the state?

But as he'd warned her after the first time she'd kissed him, Reagan Hurley was one temptation he couldn't bring himself to say no to twice. Not with her mouth opening to his tongue and her fingers kneading into his back, with her body pressing against his, her thigh moving over his suddenly hard length, and her breasts flattening against his chest.

He wanted so badly to touch them once more, to cradle their soft roundness, to suckle hardened nipples.

To drive himself into her over and over, kissing her until she screamed his name.

Those were his last coherent thoughts before his mind spiraled from the rational to the primal. Before he gave himself up to an attraction that had lain dormant and half-formed since childhood, only to spring to life full-bodied the first time he set eyes on her as an adult.

An animal could be forgiven for falling back on instinct. An animal knew no better, for it lacked the capacity for moral judgment.

But there were times when circumstance could push a person beyond reason, to a place where painful knowledge was suspended for a while. Reagan wanted to believe that she had come to such a point and that what she did with Jack was mindless, no more than a reflex in answer to a certain look that passed between them or the clean musk scent she smelled as her lips grazed the base of his neck, just below his throat.

She wanted to believe it, yet she couldn't. Not with all of her awareness focused on the hand that stole beneath her sweater and deftly unhooked her bra. Not with the way she melted as his clever fingers cupped and caressed, teased and tormented, until she was peeling off her sweater and arching her back, offering up her throbbing breasts, then gasping in relief when he finally, finally lowered his head and used his lips and tongue to send her spiraling toward heaven. . . .

But the relief she felt was short-lived, for with each caress, the aching pulse between her legs grew stronger, the hot moisture more unbearable. Until she knew she had to stop this, stop *him*, before she gave way to a need that threatened to consume her.

Yet instead of pushing him away, her hand knocked over her wineglass on the counter. She felt the liquid splatter, then soak into the denim covering her thighs.

Pausing to set the glass back on its base, Jack smiled wickedly down at her jeans. "That red wine's sure to stain. We'd better get you out of those."

When he scooped her into his arms, she offered no resistance but only kicked off both her shoes. When he carried her to the guest bedroom, she kissed his neck and flicked her tongue into his ear.

"Oh, my God," he whispered, and she felt him shudder. Just before he laid her down and unfastened her jeans.

He knelt beside the bed before peeling them off her, his face such a heart-stopping mix of lust and awe that simply looking at him made her moan and quiver with anticipation.

"Oh, Reag, you're so damned beautiful," he told her as he removed his shirt. "So absolutely perfect, except . . . some of this wine's gone straight through to your skin."

Leaning forward, he parted her legs to kiss the inside of a knee, laving the tender flesh with his tongue, his hands settling tenderly on either side of her hips, pulling down her lace-trimmed panties one languid millimeter at a time.

"Jack," she cried. She couldn't stand this torture, couldn't wait much longer.

His look told her she wouldn't have to.

"The wine is good," he said, "but something tells me you'll taste even better."

Her world burst into flame. She wanted it to last, but her body might as well have been built of dried kindling. Kindling that exploded as his mouth pressed to her core.

Afterward, she helped him finish his undressing. Then guided him as he came over her, his body reigniting her as his hardness plunged inside.

Moving together, they pushed past her misgivings, pushed beyond all thought of the price she might pay for such pleasure. Pushed and pushed until she neared obliteration once again. But suddenly he paused, balanced on his hands, and stared down into her eyes.

The emotion in his face was so stark it was almost painful, so true that it shimmered in the air between them, making words redundant.

Yet he said them anyway.

"Reagan, I'm in love with you. So much that it scares me."

She met his mouth in a feral kiss, desperate to prevent the words running through her head from tumbling from her lips as well.

Love you. Love you. Love you twice as much, Jack.

When even the kiss was powerless to bank the torrent, she pulled him down to impale her with a powerful thrust. A few more and she cried out, her whole world splintering into white-hot pleasure.

And her blind eyes never saw how the jagged pieces could fall back to slice off bloody slivers of her heart.

Chapter Twenty-three

Time reshuffled the chronology of Reagan's memories, the way it so often does in dreams.

One moment, it was the day after Papa's funeral, and the Hurleys' Mexican tenants—Jack, little Luz Maria, and their mother—were bringing over a candle in a tall glass cylinder decorated with a prayerful Virgin Mary.

The next moment, her father, in his uniform, was leaning over the lit candle, blowing it out, and telling Reagan, "Fire's dangerous. It burns."

Relief burst its banks and flooded through her, but when she cried out, "You're not dead," and tried to hug him, his figure dissipated, along with the wick's smoke.

Yet she smelled him in her nostrils, the scent of woodsy aftershave gone bitter with the ash.

Then, as if he'd never been there in the first place, she and Jack were in her old back yard, and she was chattering away at the handsome boy from next door. "Mama told Aunt Lilly we're moving soon as the insurance money comes. We'll rent this house out, too, and go away."

"Where to?" asked Jack.

She shrugged, feeling absurdly happy that he had spoken to her, that he had laid his warm palm on her shoulder because she felt so bad about her papa. "I dunno exactly. Somewhere boys won't call me 'blond bitch' when I play in the front yard. Someplace more of the kids will look like me."

Jack let his hand slide off her back. "She wants to take you someplace with no brown people—except for maids and lawn boys who don't speak 'til they're spoke to. That's the kind of neighborhood your mama has in mind."

The anger flashing in his eyes told Reagan she'd said something wrong, something bad and ugly. She stiffened, her hands knotted in small, determined fists. "She never meant a thing like that! My mama's a good lady. She just worries, that's all."

Reagan remembered hearing Mama tell Daddy, *"Look at all these beer cans in the ditches—and last week I found a needle. This neighborhood is going downhill fast. Pretty soon we'll be the only decent people left."*

But decent didn't mean *white*, did it? It meant good and kind. Like a big boy who'd helped her with her homework, even though he'd complained she was a pest.

With that day in mind, she said, "I think *you're* nice." And meant it.

"Glad to hear it." His chin rose and his lip curled in a look that made a lie out of the words. "Maybe you can hire me to mow your lawn or pick your trash up. My mama, she can scrub your toilets, too."

When the gate banged shut, she had wanted to run

after him. But before she could take a step, Joe Rozinski—the older version, not the younger man who had been her daddy's captain—threw his arms around her and said, "He's not for you."

And the burning smell grew stronger, until she realized Captain Rozinski was on fire. She struggled, pleading with him—but he wouldn't let her go.

As the flames began to taste her, she knew a pain unlike any she had ever felt before. As her limbs began to glow red, then crumble like the burned tips of Mama's cigarettes, Reagan started screaming.

Screaming until she could no long draw breath.

Reagan's thrashing woke Jack from a sound sleep, but it was the wheezing that made him bolt upright in bed.

Her bed, he realized with a start, and it all came back to him, the way their passion had sparked, bursting into an emotion more powerful than anything he'd known before.

"Wake up, Reag." He shook her shoulder and saw, when lightning flashed, that her eyes were wide already. In that split second he saw, too, that she looked both frightened and disoriented. Was it the asthma that upset her, or waking up with him?

He felt around, his clumsy movement tipping over the small lamp on the guest room's nightstand. After catching and righting it, he switched it on, flooding the small room with warm, yellow light. Reagan was sitting up against the headboard, the sheet pulled up to hide her breasts. One long, lean leg was exposed, however, reminding him of the things they'd done—and bringing his body to attention.

But her wheezing had worsened, and she avoided

meeting his gaze . . . as if the thought of what they'd shared embarrassed her.

"Sounds like you need your nebulizer," he said, turning away to pull on his jeans. "Come on; I'll help you set it up."

She didn't try to argue but crossed to the closet and took out an oversized fire-department T-shirt to hide her nakedness.

Something was wrong, he realized, and it wasn't just her breathing. He wanted to ask about it, but first he needed to address the immediate problem of her wheezing.

Once more, lightning flickered, and he heard the first grumble of thunder closing in.

Fifteen minutes later, she was sitting on a barstool by the pass-through counter that looked into her kitchen. The nebulizer purred beside her, its medicated vapor curling from the plastic mask that fit over her nose and mouth.

Reagan lifted the mask to say, "I told you—you don't have to fix that."

Jack turned from the sink. Still shirtless, he held an Allen wrench in one hand and a pen-sized flashlight in the other. "Put that back on—right now."

She'd frightened him at first, the way she couldn't speak. Or simply didn't for some reason, he thought uneasily.

"Damn bossy doctors," she murmured and tugged the hem of her T-shirt to cover her bare leg.

He frowned, disconcerted by her newfound shyness, so at odds with their lovemaking only hours earlier. Though he wracked his memory, he could come up with no hint that something had been wrong. On the contrary, he broke out in a feverish sweat, remembering her body pulsing around his, not once but time after time, and her throaty murmur rising to a cry of what could only be pure pleasure.

Hellfire. His jeans were feeling far too tight.

He consoled himself with the thought that at least he knew she was now breathing well enough to speak. Still, she avoided his gaze, fidgeting with a ragged nail instead.

"What's wrong, Reagan?" he burst out, though he knew he shouldn't speak to her until she finished her treatment. "Having second thoughts about what happened? Is that it?"

She flinched, then gave her head a barely perceptible shake. Lifting the mask again, she said, "I had a nightmare, that's all."

Replacing the mask, she quickly returned to fiddling with her thumbnail. He thought he saw her shudder, as if with an unpleasant memory.

Did she always have so many bad dreams? Or did they only trouble her when he was staying over?

Unsure he wanted to know the answer, Jack turned back to the chore he'd taken on. Earlier, he had recalled what she'd said about the disposal being broken, and he'd gotten her to point out the drawer where she kept tools. Despite her protests, he'd started poking around in her sink, mainly to keep himself busy so he wouldn't hover over her. Besides, he was fairly handy. Maybe he could save her the cost of a repairman, as well as another day wasted waiting for one to show up.

In the darkness outside, rain pattered against both the roof and the kitchen window, behind its row of potted herbs. Nearby, on the counter, two cups of herbal tea brewed and the sweet fragrance of chamomile perfumed the air. Maybe it was the afterglow of sex—a connection that had stunned him with its power—or maybe it was the warmth and light of the small kitchen against night's overarching presence, the sight of the sleeping dog sprawled near his feet, and the feel of the worn old wood-handled tool he held, but he was overwhelmed with the sensation that he belonged here: not necessarily here, in this old house, but beside Reagan Hurley.

The same woman you've been giving nightmares.

The next peal of thunder was louder and closer than the ones before it. The sound curled around the small house with the sinuous menace of a huge snake strangling a rabbit.

Unhappy with the direction of his thoughts, Jack scrounged around for a new subject.

"You know, it's possible the rain's set off the mold spores," he commented as he peered down the drain and used the Allen wrench to try to start the disposal spinning. "And they're heavier at night anyway. If you're allergic to them—"

"I thought you said you weren't my doctor." She must have lifted the mask again, because her voice was clearer.

Something was stuck down the disposal, he realized. Maneuvering the flashlight, he said, "That doesn't mean I stop being *a* doctor when I'm with you. I was just thinking that if you get testing and find out mold's the problem, maybe you can get things under control."

There. He saw something sticking up, something that looked a hell of a lot like the corner of a Manila folder. But who in his right mind would shove cardboard down a drain?

He went back to the tool drawer and started digging. "Do you have a pair of tongs?"

When she didn't answer, he glanced toward her, only to find her eyes glazed over as if she were lost in thought. Too late, he sensed he'd given her the idea that she could resume a career in firefighting. He thought of telling her it was a long shot. He could be wrong about the allergy, for one thing, or it might be one of many factors.

Yet he couldn't bring himself to take away her hope, so instead, he repeated his question.

She gestured toward another drawer, where he found a pair of ice tongs. Sliding them into the drain, he grasped a corner of the folder, only to have it tear when he attempted to pull loose the wedged item.

The torn bit that came free told him he was wrong about the Manila folder. It was instead a heavy ivory paper, the sort of high-quality stock people used to print their resumes or formal invitations. Where was it he had last seen something similar?

He remembered. It had been the business card Sabrina McMillan had given him, not her own but the one belonging to the administrator of a trust. The Trust for Compassionate Service, that was it.

But the next scrap he worked loose from the disposal was no card. For one thing, it was too big. For another, some of the lettering was clearly visible.

Reagan cut off the nebulizer when a change in its hum signaled it was empty. "What'd you find?" she asked.

Though Jack strained his ears, he caught no sign of wheezing. Thank God, she was responsive to the medication.

"I'm pretty sure it's your high-school diploma," he

said. "What's left of it, at any rate. Why would any-one . . . you didn't shove it down there, did you?"

"Of course not."

The look she shot him was insulted. But at least she *was* looking at him again. Maybe it had been a simple nightmare troubling her and nothing at all to do with him.

He wanted to believe it so badly that he grasped on to the thought with all his might.

"I thought the authorities went over this place with a fine-tooth comb," he said.

"Mostly they concentrated on the bedroom and the window where the—uh—the intruder climbed inside. I haven't been home much, so I didn't know the disposal was jammed until this morning. And I never figured it had anything to do with the break in. It's not the first time I've had trouble with it."

"Maybe we should call the cops or Special Agent What's-His-Name—the FBI guy?"

"You mean Casper the Unfriendly Ghost? The ring-banger."

Jack snapped his fingers, thinking of the pale man in the dark suit. "Lambert—that's the one. And come to think of it, he does have a thing going with that damned ring."

She shook her head. "I'm not letting them tear up the rest of my house. And besides . . ."

She paused, looking strained and thoughtful.

"Besides, what?" he prompted.

"Besides, I have an idea—about my diploma, that is. Think about it. Why would anyone care enough about that diploma—that one thing—to destroy it, especially like this?"

Surely there were more efficient ways, Jack thought.

The culprit could have shredded it, burned it, or better yet, simply taken it if he had wanted to be certain it was ruined. But this . . .

"It's almost like it was something personal against you," Jack said. "Seems to me, whoever did this had to be someone local. Someone who knows you, more than likely. What we need to come up with is some kind of link, someone who would . . . What are you thinking, Reagan? Do you know?"

"I'm not—I'm not sure, but there is one connection. One I can't quite dismiss."

"Connection to what?" he asked.

"To . . ."

She clamped down on whatever she had been about to say so abruptly that he wondered if she was protecting someone.

"Are you thinking about *Peaches?*" he asked, his mind spinning back to the day Reagan had said something about her neighbor tripping circuit breakers by using too many of her appliances at once. Still, he couldn't begin to imagine any reason the neighborly transsexual would destroy an easily replaced diploma, especially considering how friendly and helpful she'd appeared.

But Reagan's head was shaking. "No way would Peaches do something so bizarre. I'm afraid I was thinking about Beau."

"Beau? What possible connection could he have to your—"

"We graduated from the same high school. Joe Rozinski lived near there, and I was staying with him and his first wife then. Beau and I didn't go at the same time—he's a few years younger—but we used to talk about the things we both remembered. Teachers we'd had in common, classes we'd both hated, how it had felt to be on the outside. We had that in common, too. I came in as a junior and never really found my niche. And Beau might be a lot of women's concept of eye candy, but he's never really understood how to connect with people."

Jack let the thought sink in for a few moments before saying, "I guess that makes sense, him destroying something that represented what the two of you shared. But when could he have done it? Are you—are you thinking he could have been the one—the one who broke in last week? The one who hurt my sister?"

The idea rolled over him with the force and fury of an eighteen-wheeler. Beau LaRouche had been enraged the morning after his captain's death. Angry enough to threaten him, then use his fists on Reagan. And Beau had been here when Luz Maria came to get him.

"That son of a bitch," he breathed. "I'll kick his big, dumb ass all the way to—"

"We don't know Beau did that," Reagan said. "He could have broken in the next day, before I had the locks changed and the security system set up. There's no way Beau could have been the one to—to hurt your sister."

"Why not? He sure as hell showed no compunction when it came to hitting you."

"Jack, Beau's a firefi—"

"Beau's in deep shit, that's what he is, if I find him before the cops." Jack thought of Paulo's offer, how he had friends who could doubtless rearrange LaRouche's pretty face. It would serve him right, too, a man who would beat up on women, who would set the walls ablaze with a bloody wash of hatred.

But in the back of his mind, Jack knew that calling

in that kind of favor from Paulo would cost him dearly. Besides, as badly as Jack wanted vengeance at the moment, he knew that justice was the goal he should pursue.

"So which is it going to be?" he asked Reagan grimly. "Are we going to the authorities with this, or am I taking care of Beau myself?"

Chapter Twenty-four

Reagan had never taken well to ultimatums. At least, that was what she told herself when she asked Jack to leave.

"I'll be sure and talk to Beau, though. Face to face." As Reagan spoke, she avoided Jack's eyes, which reminded her all too clearly of an evening in the boxing ring last winter. She still recalled the crowd's gasp when she'd clocked Darcy Gordon with a left jab followed by a crushing uppercut. In the split second before she went down, Darcy had worn an expression of utter astonishment, even hurt, that a lesser boxer had popped off a lucky shot.

But surprised or not, Jack Montoya didn't hit the mat. Instead, he put down the tool he'd used to repair her disposal and repeated, "You want me to go?"

She nodded, keeping her eyes on his instead of allowing her gaze to drop to his broad chest, with its sprinkling of coarse, dark hair. A memory of his muscles beneath her fingertips nearly stole her breath away. She wondered if he'd been an athlete, or if he spent a lot of his time off in a gym. Where else would he come by such a set of fine, hard muscles?

Ruthlessly she dragged her mind back on track by turning and stalking to the guest room to retrieve his shirt. But the damned bed was still rumpled, and the air was heavy with the unmistakable scent of sex.

Great sex. Sex that had touched her on levels so deep it scared her.

Swallowing hard, she hurried from the room and tossed him the T-shirt. She breathed a sigh of relief when he took the hint and pulled it on as he followed her into the living room.

"You need some time to calm down," she said, "and think through all this stuff about Beau and your sister."

"This guy tried to kick down your door today," Jack argued. "And now you want to see him? No."

Irritation made her close in on him, even though it put her far too close to his lips—and the memory of the things he knew how to do with them. "Did you just tell me *no*?"

"Seems to me I just told you I loved you, not two hours ago. I really meant it, Reag, and I'm not going to stand back and let you get hurt, or worse—"

"So you think you *own* me now? Is that what all this means? First you try to make your sister's decisions for her, and now you want to make mine? Because if that's the way it works when you love someone, then you can count me out."

The pain flashing over his face made her realize she had hit below the belt. But before she could think of some way to backtrack, or at least soften what she'd said, Jack was heading toward the door.

Pausing, he glared back at her over his shoulder. "I'm starting to wonder, Reagan. Are you protecting

Beau because he's another firefighter? Or is there some reason he's been jealous? Were you really sleeping with him first?"

"Do you honestly believe that?" she demanded. "Because if that's what you think, you can—"

"No." As he slowly turned back toward her, his gaze lingered on the photos on her bookcase.

"No, *what*?" she asked.

"No, I really don't believe you've slept with Beau," Jack said, "just the way I don't believe your kicking me out has anything to do with what I said about him. You know what I really think? I think you're frightened. Not so much about the break-in as about what's happening between us."

She tensed, feeling a stab of apprehension, perhaps a prescient warning of the blow to come.

"I think you've barricaded yourself behind a memory," Jack continued, "and you're scared to death to let anyone get past it—because you don't want them to find out how sad and stunted a soul can be when it grows in the shadow of a tombstone."

He was gone before she could recover, leaving her to realize that she might have gotten in a couple of bruising shots, but it was Jack Montoya who had scored the TKO.

It took days for Reagan to make herself call Beau, days before she could do much of anything except survive the reverberations of her last conversation with Jack.

Oh, she went through the motions well enough. She took Frank Lee to the nursing home, where she passed out Halloween treats, and then to the dog park, where he disgraced his heritage by wallowing in a mudhole instead of running. She also returned to work after learning that her transfer had been expedited by the district chief. She even allowed a couple of old friends to talk her into a lunch date at their favorite little Guatemalan restaurant. But she was lousy company— lousy at everything but fantasizing about making love with Jack—and then kicking herself at the memory of how he'd wounded her.

But none of that lessened her need to confront Beau on the diploma issue, so after getting home from work one brilliantly sunny morning, she gave him a call. Though it was not yet seven A.M., she didn't care if she woke him.

He picked up on the second ring, and she didn't waste a second on false pleasantries. "I need to talk to you."

He hesitated, but only for a moment. "I'm on my way."

"No, Beau. We can talk about it on the . . ." Reagan let the words trail off. He had already hung up.

Great. Now she'd get to piss him off in person.

She grabbed a pair of jeans and a T-shirt from her closet, then decided to hold off on changing out of her uniform. If nothing else, it would serve to remind Beau that she might have moved back to an ambulance, but she was still very much a part of the department. A part of the department that could have his ass fired for hitting her.

She was having a cup of coffee on the bench in her back yard when his souped-up old Camaro pulled into the driveway. As soon as he climbed out of the silver coupe, she called for him to join her. Better that than going with him back inside the house.

From the branches of a live oak, a mockingbird sang a medley of greatest hits from other species, while high above, an airplane painted vapor trails across the sky. Sitting in a warm patch of sunshine and watching

Beau walk toward her, smiling and dressed for a visit to the gym, Reagan could almost pretend the events of the past two weeks hadn't happened.

Almost.

"This bullshit's going to stop," she told him.

The smile curdled, and he stopped in his tracks.

While she had him at a loss, she decided to make sure he was clear that she was no one's doormat. "If you want me to hold my tongue about what you've been up to, I'll expect you to quit running me down around the department. And I mean it, Beau. People are calling me and ratting you out. I've had enough of it."

He glanced up at the bird and then at the neighbor's yellow cat, which was watching from its habitual perch atop a long-unused doghouse. He looked everywhere except at Reagan as he sat down on the far end of the bench.

Noisily he cleared his throat. "I—uh—I was sort of hoping you'd called to say you missed seeing me around. We had some good times, Reagan."

He sounded pathetic, but she didn't waste a moment feeling sorry for him. "You'll be paying for the door you dented. I've decided I want a new one. And you're damned lucky I don't bill you for another garbage disposal while I'm at it."

He looked up at her. "The door I get, and yeah, I'll take care of it. But you're blaming me for breaking your disposal?"

"That's what happens when you shove papers down one. A diploma, for example. Beau, you broke into my house." Try as she might over the past few days, she hadn't been able to come up with any other possibility. But she still couldn't wrap her brain around the idea of him going after Luz Maria.

His expression shifted from hangdog to sullen at warp speed. "Look, I told you I was sorry that I knocked you on your ass. But if you think I'm some sicko who breaks into women's houses and paws through panties and—"

"Ugh. You went through my underwear drawer, too?"

He shot to his feet, his fists clenching. "Ever since you've been screwing that Montoya, you've been acting like a goddamned bit—"

"Why, Beau LaRouche. You bad, *bad* boy." Peaches let herself and Frank Lee inside the gate, then unclipped the white greyhound from his leash.

Instead of bounding to the rookie firefighter as he usually did, the dog hid behind Peaches's legs, which were currently shrink-wrapped in violet-colored aerobics tights.

As Beau's glare turned on Peaches, Reagan latched onto the interruption. "You're up awfully early," she said to her neighbor.

"Had to shoot a crime scene last night. Afterwards, I wasn't in the mood to party. Frank and I had popcorn and watched an old Bette Davis weepie on the sofa," Peaches explained, but the towering strawberry blonde still hadn't taken her eyes off Beau.

Marching toward him, she thumped the center of his chest with an index finger, then punctuated each word with another poke. "You . . . don't ever again . . . mess with . . . my friend. Or any woman."

Beau shoved her hand away and sneered into her face. "Well, I guess that leaves you out, you fucking freak-show reject."

"Hey." Reagan leapt up from her seat and grabbed Peaches's arm just in time to keep her from throwing a very unladylike punch. "Don't worry about this jackass. He was just leaving."

And he was, for, exactly as he had before, Beau turned on his heel and stalked back toward his Camaro. But this time, he hesitated at the car's door long enough to tell her, "You're making a big mistake, Reagan. You have *no* idea how big."

A moment later, the engine roared to life, and the gleaming car lurched backward to the street.

Which would have made for an impressive exit, had it not been for the crunching impact of a blue pickup truck striking the Camaro's left rear bumper.

When Peaches broke up laughing at the fender bender, Reagan smiled and shook her head.

"Serves the jackass right," she said. But she couldn't properly enjoy Beau's bad luck. Not with the memory of his last statement clouding her mood like a portent of a mighty storm to come.

"A person spends the best years of her life putting two children through college," complained Candelaria Esmeralda de Vaca Montoya from the kitchen while she chopped onions—probably in the hopes of coaxing forth more guilt-inducing tears, "and the least—the very least—she should expect is to have them support her in her old age. And what do *I* have to show for all my hard work? Two good-for-nothings fired for bad choices, and not even a single *nieto* as consolation."

Sitting cross-legged on her own bed, Luz Maria flinched at her mother's mention of a grandchild. Though she hadn't spoken of the miscarriage since that day in the hospital nearly two weeks earlier, Jack was almost certain she hadn't gotten over it.

Quietly he closed her bedroom door so the two of them could finish their conversation in peace. Their mother's fiesta of self-pity continued unabated, a maudlin murmur from the kitchen as she worked on her tortilla soup. But now, at least, her children could not make out the words.

"You should explain to her that you weren't fired," Luz Maria told him. Perched on her bed, she put away the book she had been reading and looked directly at him, her reddened eyes wells of regret. Her left forearm, in its hot-pink cast, served as a vibrant reminder of the night he'd thought he'd lost her.

He shrugged. "It's just a matter of semantics. 'Encouraged to resign' is pretty much the same thing."

"God, Jack, I'm so sorry. *So* sorry about stirring all this up. I was such an idiot. I really thought he loved me, and I was so caught up in the idea of doing something noble that I totally lost sight of—"

"Hey, it's all right, Luz Maria. We've been over this before." She'd apologized about a hundred times, though she still stuck to her claims that she remembered almost nothing about her former lover or the organization he had convinced her to support. The feds had leaned hard on her, dangling the carrot of immunity for testimony. Their mutual lawyer advised them, however, that the authorities had little chance of getting an indictment against Luz Maria, especially considering the macabre nature of the assault against her—and the publicity that had followed.

Shaking her head, she grabbed more tissues from the nearly empty box beside her. Next to it sat an empty pint container of Blue Bell vanilla ice cream and a spoon. She'd emptied one a day since coming home. As far as Jack knew, the ice cream was the only thing she was eating, in spite of their mother's efforts to tempt her appetite with healthy and delicious meals.

"It'll never be all right," said Luz Maria. "But at least

you've had another offer. I suppose you'll be taking it and moving to the Valley."

Jack stifled a sigh. "I don't know. It's a hell of an opportunity, but I'm not sure about it."

Isaac Mailer, the director of the Trust for Compassionate Service, had called Jack personally to say the organization had been looking for someone to run a new clinic. It was to be built in one of the poorest pockets of the country, an overwhelmingly Hispanic section of the Lower Rio Grande Valley almost devoid of medical facilities. Though rich in wildlife and tropical beauty, the southern tip of Texas had recently gained notoriety for its obscenely high numbers of birth defects and cases of cervical cancer and malnutrition.

"We're looking to make a difference by educating the community," Mailer had told him, "and to do that we need a bilingual doctor who cares about the people—not the politics."

"What's not to be sure of?" Luz Maria asked. "They're even going to pay off your student loans if you stay at least three years. And think of all the good you could do there, totally unfettered by the strings attached to government funding. This job sounds like it's tailor-made for you."

"As if somebody knew exactly what it would take to get me out of town—or earn my gratitude." Jack hadn't yet mentioned that there was a social worker's position for Luz Maria there, too. He didn't want to get her hopes up until he met this evening with Sabrina McMillan, who had clearly orchestrated the offer, and determined exactly what Sabrina expected in return.

But that wasn't the only reason he was ambivalent about moving. Somehow his sister seemed to tune in on his thoughts.

"It's that firefighter, isn't it? Tell me you aren't waiting for a woman who won't return your calls. Tell me you haven't gone and picked up Rubia Fever." This was Luz Maria's expression for the "disease" of Hispanic men who chased Anglo blondes. "God, Jack. I would expect more sense from you."

Anger heated his words. "Forgive me if I don't think you're the best person to offer me advice on romance."

He felt like the planet's lowest life form when her good hand reached for another handful of tissues. Though he'd saved his sanity by learning to ignore his mother's crocodile tears, he'd never been able to inure himself to any woman's real pain. And even if he someday built an impenetrable fortress around the territory of his heart, he had long ago turned over its keys to Luz Maria.

Sitting down beside her, he hugged her to him and stroked her wavy hair, the way he had when she was a child.

Your sister's a grown woman, he heard Reagan's voice remind him. It had been a sore point between them, the way he tried to both protect and make the best decisions for Luz Maria.

Maybe it was past time that he stopped. Drawing away from his sister, he moved back to the computer chair where he'd been sitting.

"I'm sorry I snapped at you. I'll tell you what, let's make a deal. I won't bring up Sergio if you don't mention Reagan."

Nodding, Luz Maria wiped her eyes. Tears had clumped her lashes, and the edges of her nostrils were chapped and reddened. "Truce," she promised.

"All right. But I need to talk to you about that job in

the Valley. I didn't mention this before, but you've got a stake in this decision, too."

She crumpled the tissue and tossed it in her trash can. "How's that?"

Handing Isaac Mailer's card to her, he recounted the details of their conversation—along with his misgivings about the mayor's campaign manager.

"That seems really strange," she said. "I've been praying for some good to come of my mistakes, but this—it sounds almost *too* good. And pretty conveniently timed, too, since the election's in—what—is it two days?"

"Three. Today's Saturday."

For the first time since her injury, the fire returned to Luz Maria's dark eyes. Distracted from her guilt, she quizzed him about details of both Isaac Mailer's offer and his conversations with Sabrina McMillan.

Afterward, she frowned. "I want this, Jack, for both of us. But not without understanding what the price is. Call the woman. Go meet with her if that's what it takes. While you're doing that, I'll check out this foundation on the Internet."

As Jack rose, she took a seat at the computer, the air around her fairly crackling with impatience. He smiled at the sight, relieved that she was moving toward recovery—and equally pleased that "The Piranha" would tear into this research with the same stubborn intensity she'd used to tackle problems in the past.

Kissing her crown as a good-bye, he said, "Some good *has* come of your mistakes already. For one thing, I'm realizing how much I've underestimated you."

Luz Maria smiled at him. "All I can say," she told him, "is it's about damned time."

Laughing, he left his sister—and prepared to beard the mayor's lioness in her den.

As she sat alone in the darkness of the watch office, Reagan could hear men's laughter from the station's kitchen. She smiled and idly wondered what prank she was missing, but although her new coworkers had done nothing to make her feel unwelcome, she didn't go out and join in the fun.

She had a call to make and, for once, the privacy to do it. Picking up the telephone, she dialed, her fingers hurried by the knowledge that at any moment she could be interrupted by a series of tones and one of the dispatch computer system's nearly unintelligible, but almost always urgent, summons.

Her heart pounded within her rib cage, thumping out the message, *Maybe you should be calling Jack instead.*

At least his messages had left her certain that, unlike the person she was calling, Jack wouldn't hang up on her. In a way, she'd like to talk to him, to get his take on Beau's denial about breaking into her place. But he could call until the end of time before she'd forgive him for what he had said about her father.

"Sad and stunted soul, my ass," she muttered as her mother's line rang once, twice, and then a third time.

They're off on that cruise after all.

With a grateful sigh, Reagan moved to return the receiver to its cradle. Then froze at the sound of someone picking up, followed by a warm and feminine "Hello?"

Her mother sounded cheerful and mildly expectant, as if she anticipated a pleasant social call. Obviously, thought Reagan, she hadn't checked her caller ID unit, if she even had one on her phone.

For half a beat, Reagan considered hanging up, but instead she plunged ahead with the words she'd been rehearsing. "Mother—Mom, it's me, Reagan. I—I've been thinking, it's been too long, way too long, since we've talked."

She didn't count the brief call after Joe Rozinski's death. Certainly, it hadn't qualified as conversation.

"Is everything all right?" Her mother's voice had lost its carefree innocence of a moment earlier. She sounded guarded now and worried, as if she feared more bad news—or an attack.

"I'm fine," said Reagan, though she really didn't feel it. She'd been so damned confused of late, shaken and sleepless with so many doubts. But she thought she'd figured out this one thing, and she meant to say the words before she lost her nerve. "I just wanted to tell you that I . . . that I finally understand. Why you got rid of Dad's things. Why you couldn't stand to listen to me talk about him and make plans to follow in his footsteps. I was so focused on the way your reaction hurt me, I never saw the bigger picture. I never really tried to put myself in your shoes."

Her mother whispered, "For-forgive me, Reagan. I was so weak . . . and so wrong."

In the background, Reagan heard her stepfather asking, "What's going on? Who *is* that, Georgina?"

But instead of breaking the connection, her mother told him, "It's all right, Matthias. I want . . . I need . . . to talk to her."

Gratitude welled up in Reagan. That, and the desire to prove Jack Montoya wrong. She'd faced fires, fought boxing opponents far more talented than she; hell, she'd even challenged a man who'd held a gun on her. What were a few mundane emotions compared to that?

Though her heart was pounding, she forced herself to say the words she'd kept locked up. "I love you. I love you and I realize now, you've always loved me, too. And Matthias . . . he helped me. He helped me understand. I—I appreciate that."

Even for her mother's sake, Reagan couldn't say she loved the man, but she figured that she owed him thanks, at least.

"Oh, God." Her mother was crying now, but something in her voice had lifted, a darkness that had weighted it for all too many years. "You don't know how long I've waited—oh, Reagan. I should have been the one to reach out first. But—but I've been so afraid, and so certain you were lost forever to me. And I was sure it was no more than I deserved."

Reagan wiped away her own tears, but she was smiling, too—and breathing more easily than she had in a long time. "If we can both forgive each other, maybe—maybe it's possible we can forgive ourselves while we're at it. I'm really sorry—sorry for all the things I did to hurt you and to make your life more difficult."

"Then it's true, what I heard?" asked her mother. "You're leaving the department?"

"What?" Reagan felt as if someone had hit her across the back with a lead pipe. "Who would say a thing like that?"

"I—I've kept tabs on you. I still know a couple of the wives. Women whose husbands worked with your father. P-Patrick."

"Well, they're wrong," said Reagan, rising to her feet. "I don't know where they got such an idea, but I'll never—"

Then it happened. The alarm sounded, and a call

came—a 911 hang-up with an address near the old Plaza del Sol.

"Gotta catch this run," said Reagan before she dropped the phone into its cradle.

Rushing toward the ambulance, she struggled to shift her focus to the call—which would more than likely prove to be some kid playing with the telephone—and away from the bile-bitter questions pushing themselves into her throat.

Had her mother's love and forgiveness stemmed from Reagan's phone call?

Or were they contingent on the hope, the same one that Reagan had just dashed, that she was putting not only firefighting, but the department, behind her once and for all?

Chapter Twenty-five

Ignoring the ache in her left forearm, Luz Maria pulled a pair of reading glasses from her desk drawer. Ordinarily, she wouldn't be caught dead in the things, but her eyes felt raw and sore from days of crying. Not so much for Sergio—she'd been stunned by how quickly the mirage of their love faded in his absence—but out of shame at how caught up she'd been in the delusion that the justness of a cause excused every act done in its name, even those that harmed the innocent. She had been so firmly snared by the sticky webs of that false logic that she had been willing to sacrifice her own brother to the lie.

Though the events surrounding her accident remained a great, gaping hole within her memory, she had no doubt that somehow her own sins had set it in motion—and led directly to the loss of the most innocent life of all.

At the thought of her miscarriage, she shoved aside the soup bowl her mother had brought in. Luz Maria was surprised to see she'd finished all of it, though the broth had tasted as salty as her tears.

Once more, she felt grief's sticky fingers, but this time, she shook them off and continued her one-handed typing. So far, her search for information on the Trust for Compassionate Service had proved frustrating. She had found no website and only a scant handful of mentions in a couple of articles from a Brownsville paper, where the trust was listed as a contributor to a childhood immunization program and to a grass-roots group teaching English to parents of school-age children.

As a social worker, Luz Maria had dealt with dozens of charities. Most relied on positive press to help them garner donations, improve the images of their corporate sponsors, and publicize the organizations' goals to those who would benefit from their help. It seemed strange to find so little information on this trust, as if it operated in an otherworldly vacuum, separate from the desperate struggles most groups faced.

Or as if the organization were some kind of facade, with little substance of its own.

Luz Maria's pulse quickened. Hadn't she seen something about that on a television news show not long ago? Though the report had focused on radical groups that raised funds under innocuous-sounding aliases, wasn't it possible that such organizations might use the same ruse to disguise their giving?

Another look at the programs the fund had bankrolled sparked a new idea. Returning to her Internet search engine, Luz Maria typed *El Fondo de Servicio Compasivo,* a translation of the trust's name.

As she skimmed through hits, she tapped her chipped nails on the desk's edge restlessly. *Nada.* She hadn't found a single thing that looked like—

"Wait a minute," Luz Maria muttered to herself. Her fingers popped along the keyboard as she tried various substitutions—the Spanish word for "foundation" instead of "trust," "caring" as opposed to "compassionate."

She tried perhaps a dozen variations before she finally struck pay dirt with *El Instituto de Servicio Humanitario.* The name instantly popped up, not in articles lauding its generosity, but on a website known as Bucktracker, which sifted through public records to trace the funding of what it considered subversive or even criminal groups.

A disclaimer page insisted that many otherwise-reputable individuals and foundations were duped into contributing to questionable causes. Clicking past the legalese, she accessed a link to *El Instituto . . .*

And absorbed the shocking contents, her heart sinking with each word—and her right hand already groping for the cordless phone, along with the ivory business card that Jack had left her.

"Recognize that address?" asked Reagan's partner and driver, Ernie "Magoo" Flores.

Reagan had heard he'd come by the nickname after a late-night accident two years earlier, when he had driven the ambulance into the path of a waste disposal truck that he claimed he hadn't seen. Though investigators later concluded the truck had been running without lights, Flores would doubtless take the appellation—inspired by a blind cartoon character—to his grave. Not that it seemed to bother the easygoing veteran.

"Sure, I know it," Reagan answered. "It didn't take me two shifts to figure we'd be seeing a hell of a lot of the stately manses at Las Casitas."

Magoo slurped from a cup of Dr. Pepper as expansive as his waistline before nodding his approval. "That's what I like about you, Hurley. Quick on the uptake. Plus, you don't stink up the cab half as much as Townsend."

Eager to prevent him from winding up again on the subject of Townsend's gastrointestinal excesses, she opted on a change of subject. Glancing at a decaying row of abandoned shotgun houses, she asked, "You think this area will ever come back? I mean, look at all the building going on. Some of the worst neighborhoods in the city are breaking out in high-class town homes."

"Shit, no," said Magoo. "Not unless they get that bazillion-dollar flood abatement project. But what are the odds of city council putting that ahead of another new sports venue? Ask yourself who has more clout, a bunch of crackheads, illegals, and poor minorities or the fat cats who show up dripping with diamonds and donations at political fund-raisers? 'Cause that's exactly who's lobbying for the new arena."

They pulled into the complex's parking lot, and a group of young men scattered as the ambulance's headlights touched them. Where they had been assembled, a late-model Accord sat with its doors flung open, its body listing, since its driver-side tires had been removed.

"Should I call that in to HPD?" asked Reagan.

Magoo shook his head. "Let's see what we have inside first."

As Reagan gathered her equipment, she wondered if the reluctance she heard in her partner's voice had less to do with getting to their patient quickly than with some unspoken truce he had developed with these thugs. Uncomfortable with the idea, she made a mental note to talk with him about it later.

Reagan hated trying to find apartments in this hellhole. As they took the crumbling sidewalk that wound between the buildings, she saw that at least half of the numbers on the apartment doors were missing. To make matters worse, many of the security lights were either broken or burned out, and the stretcher she was wheeling kept jarring her shoulder as its wheels caught in the breaks in the concrete. A movement in the shadows caught her attention, and someone unseen made vulgar kissing noises.

"Ditch the fat dude, baby, and we'll show you how to spend a Saturday night," one hissed before a beer bottle exploded near Reagan's feet.

Ignoring the rough laughter that followed, Reagan followed Magoo. Thank God he seemed to know where he was going.

"Pain-in-the-ass kids," he said of the catcallers. "You aren't cut, are you?"

"I'm fine." Heaven only knew, she'd heard worse upon occasion. What was a Saturday night on the meat box without a few drunken assholes?

Magoo looked from side to side, orienting himself before he began to pound on an unmarked apartment door.

From inside, Reagan heard a torrent of frantic-sounding Spanish, far too fast for comprehension. Fortunately, Magoo didn't miss a beat.

"*Son los bomberos*," he called, identifying them as firefighters. "*Abra la puerta, por favor.*"

Reagan was relieved when the woman complied

with his request, opening the door and beckoning them inside.

A girl of eight or nine was hunched forward on a threadbare sofa, her skinny arm maintaining a death grip on a stuffed owl. Despite her mother's rapid-fire—and unintelligible—explanation to Magoo and a tiny girl who whined as she clutched the woman's knees, Reagan could hear a harsh rasp that made her own lungs squeeze in sympathy.

Kneeling beside the older child, Reagan let Magoo handle the mother while she began primary patient assessment.

The girl looked up, her brown eyes nearly as wide as the stuffed owl's. "Who—who are you?" she asked in English.

Reagan introduced herself and then added, "I'm here to help you feel better. Can you tell me your name?"

"Cri-Cristina. Del—del Valle. I—I used my *medicina*—for the asthma." She paused to catch her breath. "Just like Doctor Jack said when he came."

Reagan's attention ratcheted up a notch. "Doctor Jack?" she asked, even as she checked the child's pulse.

Cristina's expression brightened. "Dr. Montoya—he lets—lets me call him that. He—he brings me my 'halers. He—he brung that ma-ma-machine once, too, but . . . but we don't have it no more."

Noting that her pauses were lengthening, Reagan used her stethoscope to listen to the girl's breathing. In addition to the wheezes she expected, Reagan detected the light crackling known as rales, which indicated possible fluid in the lungs. Though her lips and nail beds weren't yet blue and she was still alert and oriented, little Cristina wasn't getting nearly enough air.

A nebulizer treatment was indicated, but their ambulance lacked the required paramedic to administer a dose. If the girl went further downhill, they could be in trouble. "Do you . . . do you have your inhaler here now?" Reagan asked, hoping to keep the patient stable until they could get a squad here.

She tried to ignore the tightness building in her own chest, something she had noticed during several of the calls she'd made to Las Casitas. She told herself it was all in her mind, a result of running across patients with respiratory symptoms.

"Mama?" called the child before asking haltingly, in Spanish, where her mother had put the *medicina*.

"We need to call a squad with a paramedic," Reagan told her partner after asking the child a few more questions about her history, "but in the meantime, I think we'd better prepare to load and go." Their term for a quick transport to an ER, a necessity if a paramedic couldn't respond quickly.

While Cristina's mother left the room to search for the girl's inhaler, Magoo gave his walkie-talkie a sharp rap. "It's cut out on me. I think the batteries are dead, or maybe the thing's broken."

When he started toward the door, Reagan said, "Why don't—why don't you let me radio it in? I—I can't understand—a word—Ms.—Ms. del Valle's—say—saying anyway."

Magoo squinted at her. "You all right?"

Reagan had begun taking daily medications to help control her asthma, but Magoo had nonetheless caught her with her rescue inhaler earlier this week, after they'd made a run to a house infested with about a million half-wild cats. Instead of making a big deal of it, he'd only rubbed his reddened eyes and said,

"I'm allergic to the damned things, too. That old lady needs an exterminator, not an ambulance."

Reagan said, "I'm okay," then gave Magoo a run-down on Cristina's condition and suggested he start her on humidified oxygen. By this time, Reagan knew she needed to get out of this apartment—before Magoo had to summon an additional ambulance for her.

So great was her hurry to leave that she stepped on one of the younger child's toys—a ball or something—and began to fall hard, her ankle twisting. With a sharp cry, she stuck out her hand, meaning to catch herself against the wall.

But her hand punched through the rotten wallboard, and she ended up falling anyway—and landing face-down on the pink carpet, which smelled so musty that she began to choke.

"Jesus—you okay, Grace?" asked Magoo—and Reagan had a premonition that she'd just acquired a nickname of her own.

"Yeah—yeah," she said between coughs, though she could no longer disguise her breathing problem.

Magoo reached to help her up, but in her embarrassment, Reagan ignored his outstretched hand and stood without assistance.

"Look at this," he told her, his gaze locked on the hole her hand had made in the wall.

"I—I know. I'm a—real klutz—" Reagan started, until she saw the mold.

Blackish-green and slimy, it looked like an oil slick inside the broken Sheetrock. Magoo gave the section below the break a light kick, and more plaster crumbled, revealing sludge-thick layers. Grabbing a loose corner of the carpet, he peeled it back to expose a stained and stinking pad.

"From the flood—the flood last spring," rasped Reagan. "The—complex never made—never made repairs."

Nodding, Magoo said, "You go on out—right now. Call for backup. Use your inhaler. I'll get the patient's medicine and get her out of here. The whole family, too, if I can talk the senora into it."

"Thanks," said Reagan. She hobbled in the direction of the ambulance, pausing only long enough to take a puff from the inhaler in her pocket.

As she retraced her earlier path, it seemed even darker and the rutted sidewalk more determined to bring her to her knees. She stepped carefully, some paranoid corner of her mind hissing a warning that if she went down here, the lowlifes who'd thrown the bottle would appear from nowhere to swarm over her like vermin. Shuddering at the thought, she picked up her pace.

It was just after ten-thirty on a moonlit Saturday evening, yet she saw no one about. She heard plenty, though, from inside the apartments: snatches of raucous Mexican music, the blaring of a TV, and the unmistakable sounds of a couple arguing, although they shouted in a language that might be Vietnamese. Speaking more familiar Spanish, one woman warned another, "*Ojo, es el carro del patrón. Él está aquí para su dinero.*"

Look out, Reagan mentally translated, her high-school Spanish kicking in. *That car belongs to el patrón*—whoever that might be. *He's here for his money.*

By the time Reagan reached the parking lot, her breathing had eased somewhat, and she had no difficulty calling for support. As she opened the back of the ambulance, she reached into her pocket to pull out the inhaler for one more hit, but a car parked nearby attracted her attention. Not the half-stripped Honda, which sat abandoned with all four doors flung open, but a larger sedan two spaces down.

Forgetting the inhaler, she limped toward the dented Ford, an ancient beater that was in worse shape than her Trans Am. After first checking to be sure the car was empty, she pulled a slim flashlight from her breast pocket, then shone its thin beam along the crumpled fender.

With that spot of light, she saw that the car was the avocado green she had expected, the exact shade of the sedan she'd spotted leaving Jack Montoya's clinic two weeks earlier. Moving around to the front, she ignored the Oklahoma plates—probably stolen—and stared at the same grill that had come so close to running her down in the clinic lot. She repositioned her light to find several spots on the chrome bumper that were scarred with bright red paint.

Paint from Jack's Explorer, unless she missed her guess.

Her breath hissing, she took a step back—a step directly into something huge and solid that exploded into motion, wrapping a thick arm around her throat.

Adrenaline surged through her like a jolt from a defibrillator. Unable to scream, she fought like the hellcat Peaches had once named her, striking backward with her elbow, bringing her booted foot down hard on his, and biting the bastard's forearm until she heard him scream.

"You *bitch!*" With that, he slammed her forward with such force that her body folded over the sedan's hood and her forehead slammed against the windshield. She must have hit her mouth, too, for it flooded with a wash that tasted like hot metal. Spitting blood, she struggled to push herself upright.

Run now. Scream, her brain ordered her aching body, but before she could do anything, her attacker's big hand gripped the back of her neck, and her legs went loose as ribbons.

"He was fucking right," the man screamed in her ear. "Fucking right I shoulda killed you."

Deep and booming, the voice reverberated around the inside of her skull. The sound made Reagan want to vomit. There was a terrible groan, like metal twisting or an animal dying. *She* was the source, she realized, hurting so badly that it barely registered when he grabbed her around the waist and lifted her as if she were a sack of grapefruit. As her body drooped forward at the waist, Reagan's vision grayed out.

"He goddamned *always* has to be right," he muttered as he half carried and half dragged her. "I never should've let myself feel sorry for the bastard."

A second wave of panic overwhelmed her. Now that she'd stopped screaming, the voice sounded familiar— and the suspicion that she knew her attacker convinced her she was in even worse trouble than she'd feared. Was he putting her in his car, taking her away to—? God, he would have no choice now but to kill her.

Would Magoo come out and save her? Or maybe the pumper and the paramedics she had called? Or someone, anyone who might help—even her earlier tormentors with their lewd suggestions and their bottles.

Her attacker stopped abruptly, and Reagan felt huge hands all over her body. With a cry of protest, she jerked toward full awareness and began to struggle. He clamped down on her throat again, cutting off her air, as his free hand finished emptying her pockets, taking her wallet, keys, inhaler, and God only knew what else.

But her hopes that this was merely a robbery faded when he hurled her things into the tall weeds beyond the parking lot.

An instant later, she felt herself tumbling forward. She held on to consciousness by a hairbreadth as the gray haze darkened to an inky blackness. Reagan groaned more loudly and lifted her arms in the hope of attracting someone's attention as the brute lifted her and threw her into the car.

Her hands struck something solid. Nails tore as she scratched the metal over her head—along with the surface of the horrifying truth.

Her attacker hadn't simply thrown her inside the old Ford. He had dumped and locked her in the trunk, she realized—a split second before she heard the rumble of the engine turning over . . .

And the crackling pop of tires as the car began to move.

Chapter Twenty-six

"When I didn't hear from you before," Sabrina McMillan told Jack from across the candlelit table of her beautifully appointed high-rise condo, "I was afraid that perhaps your little friend had been spreading nasty gossip."

It took him several beats to realize the mayor's campaign manager was talking about Reagan. She was many things to him: beautiful, good-hearted, vulnerable, and stubborn, but his *little friend*? Laughing at the notion, he shook his head at Sabrina. "Why would she do that?"

Sabrina smiled seductively over the rim of her crystal wineglass. Waterford, she'd told Jack, apparently hoping he'd be bowled over by her good taste, as well as the condo's panoramic view of the treetops of Hermann Park by moonlight. Jack tried to imagine Reagan in Sabrina's place, her full lips painted the same crimson, her more toned and slender body hugged by the same form-fitting, sapphire-blue halter dress.

Dream on, Montoya, the fantasy-blonde told him as she donned a pair of boxing gloves. Probably to pop him.

"I was afraid she was a little jealous," said Sabrina. "I sometimes have that effect on women. They rarely seem to like me."

Well, duh, Reagan's disembodied voice said from the sidelines.

Ignoring it, Jack told Sabrina, "Poor you."

If she wanted to take it as flirting, he could live with that. The truth was, he wouldn't touch the woman with asbestos gloves.

This time, her smile was as knowing as it was naughty. But this time, despite the candlelight, the expression clued him in that she was perhaps a decade older than she looked. Probably around forty, maybe even older, but still a gorgeous specimen in anybody's book.

She said, "I'm really glad you took me up on my invitation, Jack. I've been saving this Chianti for a very special occasion."

The tip of her tongue darted out to flick away a stray drop, but the action reminded Jack of a snake tasting the air.

He put down his wineglass. "I hardly expected to catch you at home, what with the election coming up on Tuesday."

Gesturing toward a doorway down the hall, she whispered conspiratorially, "Oh, I do most of my work right here, from that room. You wouldn't believe what I have in those files . . . secrets that could bring down a dozen politicians all across this country, stuff so juicy you'd give a testicle to see it."

Jack didn't know about the testicle part, but the teasing note in her voice gave him the distinct impression that at least one of those secrets involved him. Was she offering to share it in exchange for his cooperation?

"As good as it is to see you," he said carefully, "I really came here to talk business. This business with the Trust for Compassionate Service, mainly."

She blinked three times in quick succession. "What's that?"

Playing along with her supposed ignorance, he related an account of his call from Isaac Mailer before adding, "It's a fantastic opportunity. Practically tailor-made for both my sister and me. I suppose I have you to thank for that."

"And you were wondering," Sabrina asked in a breathy whisper, "how you could make it up to me?"

God help him, the way she was leaning forward, he could see right down the front of her dress. For one insane moment he wondered what it would be like to fondle those lush breasts and bed this seductive woman who had clearly been with so many of the country's rich and powerful.

Sure, but how many of them has she ruined? his better judgment chimed in.

Averting his gaze, Jack killed his body's unconscious response by picturing his mama in her bathrobe waxing her upper lip.

Worked every time. Except with Reagan, but with her, his attraction went so far beyond the physical that his willpower had never stood a chance.

He cleared his throat in an attempt to give himself a moment to regroup. Intuition warned him that it might prove disastrous to insult Sabrina with a blatant rejection. If she had half as much influence—and a third as few scruples—as he suspected, she could destroy him and his sister as easily as she had convinced Isaac Mailer to toss them a life ring.

"I'd love to make it up to you," he told her. "But I

told you before, I'm uncomfortable with the idea of getting involved in the mayor's race."

"Maybe you'd change your mind if I could help you understand what a good man, what an honorable man, our mayor is, and how *very* much there is at stake."

He knew exactly what was at stake for those he had been helping. Using his influence as the city's mayor, Darren Winter could see to it that the children of Las Casitas Village were denied medical treatment. How could he stack his personal discomfort over the idea of being used against the health—and perhaps even the lives—of innocents?

Before he could capitulate, however, Sabrina wrinkled her nose and wriggled so provocatively that he had to look away in self-defense.

"I'm terribly sorry," she said, "but this corset's killing me. It's such a distraction to the conversation. Would you mind if I go take it off?"

"Uh, sure," he said and wondered exactly how the hell he was going to escape this sin pit without swapping DNA strands with this woman.

"You know, sometimes it's really hard to get myself out of these things. If you'd like to . . . you know, help, I'm sure we could get it off much faster."

How did she say things like that with a straight face? But something else lurked behind the feigned look of innocence in Sabrina's eyes. Instead of the wicked glint that Jack expected, was that fear he saw?

Why? What could possibly be at stake if she couldn't bribe or seduce her way to getting his cooperation? He knew the election was too close to call, but could the mayor and his secret weapon really believe that Dr. Jack Montoya's endorsement would sway the vote?

Did they make the mistake of believing, as so many white politicians seemed to, that Hispanics all voted as one block?

And even if Mayor Youngblood lost to the windbag from hell, surely Sabrina McMillan's past successes would earn her a new position in another major campaign. Instinct warned Jack that more than the obvious hung in the balance.

Was the secret hidden in the files in Sabrina's office?

Still hesitant to directly reject her, Jack said, "You know, I've never been any good with that kind of stuff. I think I'll just wait out here for you."

"Since you don't want to help, this could take a while." Her pouty look turned inviting. "If you get tired of waiting, you know where to find me."

She swayed off to her bedroom and closed the door behind her. Predictably, Jack didn't hear it lock.

He made a beeline to her office and breathed a silent prayer that she would light some candles and lounge around her bed awhile, waiting for a complete hormonal meltdown to reel him in. Closing the door quietly behind him, he scanned the room and realized that compared to the sparkling perfection of the other rooms, her working area looked like the aftermath of a twister in a mobile-home park. Half-empty, lipstick-stained coffee cups littered the disastrously disheveled surface of her sprawling mahogany desk. Papers were everywhere, some tucked untidily in files while others were fanned out around an overflowing ashtray. Several of the file-cabinet drawers had been left open, and the bookshelves bowed beneath the weight of haphazardly arranged books on politics and campaign theory. Many of the volumes had loose papers sticking out which had been tucked between the pages.

His heart sank. He could search this haystack for hours without ever finding the needle he suspected. He started shuffling through the desktop jumble with wild abandon, praying that the mess would hide his actions and that some relevant phrase would jump out at him.

He ran through endorsements, accountings of entertainment expenses that seemed outrageous at first glance, and several marked-up drafts of what must be a political ad. His hands trembled as he worked, and his mind screamed, *Get the hell back out there before she comes looking for you.*

And then he found it, in a dog-eared single sheet stamped in red letters *Confidential:* a memo reminding Mayor Youngblood of the agreement for flood remediation for the area surrounding the Plaza del Sol and Las Casitas Village apartments.

"The Plaza del Sol flood project . . ." Jack whispered, and in the back of his mind, he could feel a lock's dial spinning toward the memory of a recent conversation—one that clicked into place as his gaze caught the name of the apartment complex's owner.

He began rereading the memo more carefully, but his ringing cell phone interrupted. Praying that Sabrina wouldn't hear it, he jerked it from his pocket and put his thumb over the power switch to shut it off. But a glance at the screen quickly changed his mind.

He answered, speaking in a low voice. "I can't talk now, Luz Maria. I'm—"

"It's a setup," his sister interrupted. "The Trust for Compassionate Service is nothing but a front for BorderFree."

His world reversed course, spinning backward on its axis. *"What?"*

"I tried the number on that business card you left me. The man who answered said he was Isaac Mailer, but that wasn't who it was. It was Sergio, Jack. I'd know his voice anywhere."

"Sergio Cardenas?" Jack struggled to recall how Mailer had sounded, but he couldn't resurrect the voice, nor any suspicion that it sounded familiar. Still, Luz Maria would know, wouldn't she? After all, they had been lovers. Which might mean Sergio had recognized her, too. "Did he know it was you?"

"I don't think so. I hung up—and as soon as we're through talking, I'm calling Special Agent Lambert to give him what I know. I can't let this go any farther—can't risk more people getting hurt, and BorderFree's willing to do whatever it takes to keep Darren Winter out of office."

Despite his situation, Jack felt something in him unclench at the realization that his sister had truly broken free of Sergio's influence. "But what could Mayor Youngblood's campaign have to do with Sergio and BorderFree-4-All?" he asked her. "And how the hell does any of this relate to Las Casitas—"

At the sound of a metallic click behind him, Jack looked over his shoulder—and stared at a totally nude Sabrina McMillan. Though most men would have been mesmerized by the gravity-defying nature of her surgically enhanced breasts, what dried the spit in Jack's mouth was the cocked revolver she held in her right hand.

Chapter Twenty-seven

As her own soft wheezing brought her back to consciousness, Reagan decided she'd give Darcy Gordon this: When that killer right of hers got through, there was no headache in the world to match it. It was simply *sayonara*, sister. Lights out for a while.

But when Reagan cracked her eyelids open, no ref was standing over her and shouting down the count. And when she tried to push herself off the mat, she smacked her head against something hard, less than a foot above her.

She fell back onto a shuddering, uneven surface, where she realized she wasn't in the ring fighting Darcy Gordon. Instead, she had succumbed to a far more dangerous opponent—one who didn't give a damn about the rules.

And one who had locked her in a darkness so complete, she had lost all sense of whether her eyes were closed or open.

Remembering what had happened in the parking lot at Las Casitas Village, Reagan fought the overpowering urge to scream. As long as the car remained in motion, she reasoned that her attacker was the only person who would hear her. If he did, he'd likely pull over and beat the hell out of her or worse.

There's no maybe about it. From the moment that bastard locked you in this trunk, you've been a dead woman. He's only taking you to a more private place to close the deal.

It surprised her, how calmly she was able to envision the likely outcome, as if she were watching a reenactment on one of those crime shows on TV. Suspect pulls into a dark and densely wooded area. Opens the trunk and drags his victim out. Shoots her or caves her skull in with a length of pipe, or maybe he strangles her instead if he's the hands-on type. Could be he rapes her, too, before or even after. If he feels like it.

Recognizing the onset of shock, Reagan then bit down on her lip so hard, she tasted blood.

The spike of fresh pain catapulted her toward panic. She struggled for air, gasping at the thought that she was going to die once this car stopped—unless this cramped, foul-smelling space got her first.

You're going to die if you don't figure something out, said a rational corner of her brain, one steeped in years of training and experience at the scenes of crimes and accidents.

Once she forced herself to breathe at a more normal rate, the tightness in her chest eased slightly. Soon the flow of oxygen clarified her thinking.

You aren't some generic, made-for-TV "victim," she told herself. *And this is not some faceless bogeyman you can turn off with your remote.*

Since she'd been tossed into his car, she was almost certain this was the *patrón* she had heard mentioned at the complex. Belatedly, her subconscious came up with the translation, and she realized he was Las Casitas Village's own landlord.

And someone she knew. Reagan remembered having that realization when she had heard the voice, but for the life of her, she couldn't take the memory one step further. He'd slipped up on her so fast, and her boxing skills had been no match for—

Stop. Right now, it doesn't matter who he is or what you did or didn't do.

All that mattered at this moment was escaping. But how?

First off, try the obvious. Using her hands and then her feet and legs—thank God he hadn't tied her— Reagan pushed as hard as she could against the trunk lid, only to find it firmly locked. She felt around next, long enough to confirm her suspicion that a car this old wouldn't have a trunk release.

Now what? She thought of prying the trunk open or dismantling the lock somehow, but she'd need tools for that, and illumination.

So take an inventory. See if he missed anything when he went through your pockets.

She reached for her breast pocket first, her hopes centering on her little flashlight. It was gone. Either her attacker had taken it or it had slipped out when he scooped her up. There would be no light.

The darkness around her took on weight, like the crushing pressure of the blackness deep within an ocean chasm. Squeezing the air out of her lungs, the thoughts out of her brain, the—

"Don't," she told herself, imagining how disgusted her old crew would be if she fell to pieces.

But what the hell else would you expect out of a woman?

she heard Beau tell them. Chuckles followed, building to a chorus, then a deafening crescendo of guffaws.

Forget those idiots, Joe Rozinski's voice said. *And forget what you don't have. Just figure out what's left.*

With the flesh prickling behind her neck, Reagan wondered if she was dead already—or so deeply unconscious she could hear communications from a corpse. Shuddering, she thrust aside the thought to search the bottom of the trunk, her hands groping first for whatever hard and painful shape was jammed beneath her shoulder.

A jack, maybe? It felt too big and cumbersome to use as either a pick or a pry bar.

She didn't stop, pawing through a couple of bags that stank of rancid grease—and made her swear off fast food—some empty cans that smelled like beer, a sack of nails, and what felt like a half-empty box of lightbulbs.

What else could there be?

As she groped around the trunk's edges, the car turned sharply, then powered up to speed. Her body rolled to one side, jamming against what felt like the spare tire. That wasn't so bad, but her hip banged against something painfully unyielding. *Please, God, let it be a hammer or a screwdriver or a—*

She fished it out from under her, her hope plummeting at the discovery that it was nothing but a can, probably a quart-size paint container, judging from its ridged rim and its weight.

After pushing it aside, she found a pen, which she gripped for all she was worth. It wouldn't help her get out, but if her attacker popped the trunk, maybe she could stab him.

A pen against a mountain, she thought disconsolately. *Or even worse, a pen against a gun.*

* * *

"You have to go," Sabrina told Jack softly, reminding him that, in his shock, he hadn't broken the cell-phone connection.

On the other end, Luz Maria said, "Jack, are you still there?"

Sabrina made a circular motion with the gun barrel, which Jack took to mean he was to excuse himself and hurry up about it.

"I'll call you later, Reagan," he said lightly. "I can't talk about it anymore right now."

"Reagan? Is something wrong there?" Luz Maria asked him. "Jack, what's going on—"

He cut her off, hoping she would understand he was in trouble. Sabrina held out her free hand to him. Though it trembled, a vein of iron ran through her words. "Give me that. Right now."

Jack winced, but he knew better than to contradict a naked woman with a gun. Handing over his cell phone, he tried diplomacy. "Sabrina, you should know I really *don't* believe it. About the mayor being linked to BorderFree-4-All. Thomas Youngblood's too smart and too experienced to get caught up in anything so dangerous. So you don't have to worry about me."

Sabrina's expression darkened, her lip curling in a way that all but shouted *Liar*.

Realizing he'd insulted her intelligence, he tried another tack. "Not that I'd give a damn if he was. What business is it of mine? I'm going to be running a clinic down in the Valley—a place so far from Houston, it might as well be in another state."

He saw her waver and realized that Sabrina expected his self-interest. Praying he was guessing right,

Jack pressed his case. "But I have no intention of going down there and living like my dirt-poor patients. I'll need to take along a generous nest egg, say a hundred thousand dollars?"

To him, it sounded like an outrageous amount of money, but she didn't even blink. Instead, the handgun's muzzle lowered. Now he was speaking the language she was used to: greed.

"The money could be problematic," she said, "if we lose the election . . ."

"So you'd still like my endorsement?"

"Only if it's heartfelt. We'll need to work together to come up with something especially persuasive, something to help your people understand what Winter means to do to them if he's elected."

"It would probably be more heartfelt if you'd put that gun away." He'd never been much of an actor, but he put everything he had into sounding lecherous as he edged closer to the desk that stood between them. His gaze dipping, he channeled every old James Bond movie he'd seen as a kid to say, "For one thing, it's blocking an exceptional view."

A slow smile spread over Sabrina's painted lips, and all at once, her gaze grew languid, heavy-lidded. This was a woman at least as well acquainted with lust as with greed—and far more comfortable with those weapons than with a pistol.

She set the gun down on the desk, but close enough that she could beat him to it if he were inclined to try. She leaned toward him, balancing on her palms on the desk's surface and bringing her shoulders forward to accentuate her breasts.

Jack couldn't help noticing the hardness of the nipples. Either she was a gifted pretender, or she was really as turned on as she looked.

"You know," she said, her voice a velvety whisper, "you're selling yourself short. If we win this election, two hundred thousand wouldn't be too much to ask. I can get it for you—as long as you keep your little friend from making trouble for us."

Reagan. Sabrina thought she knew, because he'd foolishly used her name on the telephone to warn Luz Maria there was trouble.

"I can handle her." The irony of his claim struck him, considering how badly he'd mishandled their last conversation.

"That's good," said Sabrina, her eyes turning cold as flint, "because this city doesn't need two firefighter funerals within a single month."

The threat took Jack's breath away, along with the realization that it had been Sabrina all along, preserving her winning record by any means possible, from bribery to seduction to flat-out murder. Whether or not the mayor knew about it, she must have been responsible for the fire at the apartment complex—and for Joe Rozinski's death. As the task force had suspected, the crime had been about discrediting Winter, making him look like an inflammatory bigot, all along. Only they'd been barking up the wrong tree. Sabrina might have allied herself with BorderFree, but she'd been calling all the shots.

But she hadn't set the fire herself. She would have surely bribed or extorted someone else to do her bidding. And Jack had a damned good idea who it was.

Someone who knew both him and Reagan. Someone who took others' education, even a mere high-school diploma, as a personal affront. And most importantly, someone who had a huge stake in the flood-control project that would make the Plaza del Sol neighborhood viable once more.

Words rang through Jack's memory like hammers striking metal: *"I don't mind telling you, I've staked everything there. Every fucking favor, every good deed, every dime. I need this, Joaquín. Goddamn therapists and private programs and nurses are eatin' me alive."*

His old *compadre*, Paulo, who had tried so hard to convince Jack that he was still a friend. And who would doubtless be the person to kill him if Sabrina said the word.

As the implications detonated inside him, Jack fought back the impulse to launch himself at Sabrina's gun.

Bad idea, instinct warned him. Her hand was so close, all she'd have to do was reach out and grab the small revolver. And she would get away with killing him. If her connections weren't enough to excuse her, the wineglasses at the table, her nudity, and whatever tale she spun about his mistaking her intentions and trying to rape her would surely do the trick.

Leaving her free to rid herself of one last risk.

Reagan.

How could he have been such an idiot, using her name to alert Luz Maria that something had gone wrong?

"Consider Reagan a problem solved," Jack said, thinking on his feet now that his initial panic had subsided, "because I'm *sure* there'll be a place for a bright young EMT with me down in the Valley."

"I'll be certain that there is." Ever so slowly, Sabrina stepped around the desk, her gaze locked on his face with a predator's intensity. "Hmmm. How shall we seal the deal?"

Unbelievable, how swiftly she moved from death threats to seduction. He took the hand she offered, his grip so firm he saw pain—and not a little fear—flash over her expression.

Before she panicked and reached for the gun with her free hand, he said, "I like it rough, Sabrina. It makes things so much more . . . elemental."

She shivered lightly, but both relief and pleasure sparked in her hazel eyes. She apparently understood dark appetites quite well.

Smiling knowingly, she whispered, "Just how rough can you handle? I have . . . I have some things I think you might like . . . in my bedroom."

Jack had the feeling that whatever he found in there would haunt his nightmares for years to come. He breathed a silent prayer that the contents would also offer up the tools to get him out of here alive.

"Well, then, what are we waiting for?" he asked.

Sabrina brought the pistol with her, but she laid it on the dresser when she led him into her bedroom. Perhaps she felt confident that she already had him. Or perhaps her interest in rough sex was more genuine than feigned.

Though the condo's other rooms bespoke elegant sophistication, it was clear that she had paid particular attention to decorating this space. Jack knew nothing about interior decor, but even he recognized the lavish splendor of the darkly massive furnishings, the tasseled nest of pillows atop a gold-embroidered comforter, and the hand-painted erotic caperings that decorated the domed ceiling above the big four-poster bed.

When she paused expectantly, he told her that he liked it.

She preened in response and said, "From the first moment I set eyes on you, Jack, I sensed that you had better taste than you were letting on."

It was a not-so-subtle dig at Reagan, but Jack didn't give a damn. Because at that very moment, Sabrina McMillan opened the door to her armoire—and showed Jack the answer to his prayers.

Chapter Twenty-eight

Within twenty minutes of Reagan Hurley's disappearance, fire apparatus lined the streets around Las Casitas Village, and every man within range of the "firefighter assist" call had joined the search. After one of her coworkers found Reagan's personal items and ID in the weeds, HPD was called in to question every tenant that could be rounded up.

Based on Magoo Flores's description of the incident with the catcalls and the hurled beer bottle, the working theory was that several young males had snatched her for the purpose of sexual assault. Both the firefighters and the cops moved fast, their urgency prompted by the thought that if their sister-in-uniform wasn't dead already, she sure as hell would be if they didn't find her soon.

Fortunately, they caught a break, in the person of one Emilia Ochoa. After being assured that no one had any interest in contacting Immigration, she was quick to tell them how she'd been standing at her window folding laundry when she'd seen the landlord toss the woman into the trunk of his big green car. Senora Ochoa didn't know his name, but it was obvious she feared him. He was a big man who once threatened her when she complained that conditions in her apartment had made her husband sick.

She didn't know the license-plate number of the old car, either. But her account quickly brought investigators to an important—and demoralizing—realization.

They were searching in the wrong place. By this time, the landlord and his victim could be miles away.

Had she thought about the taillights earlier, things might have turned out differently for Reagan. Had she been a little faster to pull away the disintegrating trunk liner and bash through one of the lights with the tire iron she'd found beneath the spare tire, she might have been able to shove her hand through the opening to flag down help in time.

But at the very moment the taillight finally shattered, the car was coming to a stop. Though the engine continued idling, she heard a door open and felt the car wobble as if her attacker had climbed out.

Reagan shifted her grip on the tire iron, her heart leaping like a wild thing in her chest. *This is it*, she told herself. *He heard me break the light, and he's coming back to kill me.*

She braced herself, waiting for the trunk lid to fly open, as well as for the ridiculously slim chance that she could somehow jump up and hit him with the iron. Sweat rolled off her in hot sheets, stinging her eyes and making her body feel as if it would spontaneously combust.

But he didn't come back to the trunk at all. Instead, she heard him slam first one door, then another—as if he'd either put something inside the car or invited another person to join him. Did he need help killing her—or disposing of her body?

As the car started moving again, she wormed around and started beating at the trunk's lock with the round end of the tire iron. From the front, she heard muffled but unmistakably angry shouts before the old Ford accelerated rapidly, its engine roaring.

The driver slammed the brakes, and Reagan's body rolled backward, her head slamming hard against the jack. She groaned and lay still until the urgent need to vomit passed and the car once more began to move.

Gritting her teeth against the pain, she turned the iron around and slipped the angled handle up underneath the lock. It was clear that she couldn't get away with pounding, but maybe, just maybe, she could pry the trunk lid free. During her time in the department, she'd helped to open vehicles at the scenes of wrecks or car fires. Although she'd never had the occasion to escape from a trunk, she at least had a basic understanding of what sort of force and mechanism might do the trick. With the tire iron, she'd get out of here—if given enough time.

In spite of her best efforts to focus on her plan of action, this last thought echoed darkly.

If given enough time . . .

Jack drove with exaggerated care, praying he could get to the FBI field office without a Houston cop arresting him for the way he'd left Sabrina.

Naked as a jaybird and handcuffed to the bed, she had screamed the full gamut of threats and insults—until he returned to her bedroom doorway with a stack of files in his arms.

"No. My God, you . . . you can't take those." Her eyes went wide and her face drained of color as terror replaced raw rage. "They're my . . . they're my ticket out . . . the only way I'll ever break free. Please, Jack. I'll give you anything, do anything you want. You don't know what it's like, being passed around like a damned whore, having to pretend I'm enjoying the sickest . . . oh, please. You can't do this to me. I have to find a way out. I'm getting too . . . I can't keep it up much longer, not even with the surgeries and Botox."

Tears streamed down her face, but he reminded himself that this was the same woman who had threatened to emasculate him with a dull spoon when she'd realized that his interest in her handcuffs had nothing to do with sex. If he made the mistake of feeling sorry for her, she would destroy him in a second.

Patting the files, he assured her, "I have everything I need here—namely, good insurance. If anything happens to me, my family, or Ms. Hurley, I'll make arrangements for the contents to be made public." He hesitated long enough for his words to sink in. He'd found not only damning records of financial shenanigans involving at least a half-dozen well-known politicians, but photos of a few as well, involved in the kinkiest of sex acts with Sabrina. Obviously, she'd been keeping this blackmail evidence as a part of her retirement plan, but if those photos got out, she'd be ruined, too—and none the richer for her humiliation.

He'd left a glass of water and a blanket within her reach, but he shoved her handgun into the pocket of his sports coat, then took all of her phones and threw them into the trunk of the junker Paulo had loaned him.

The same Paulo who, according to the file he'd unearthed on Sabrina's desk, owned Las Casitas Village.

The same Paulo, Jack realized, who must have run down his own Mustang and injured Luz Maria.

Had the bastard meant to kill him, then decided to make a point when he realized that Jack's sister was behind the wheel instead? Or had he purposely gone after Luz Maria, then used the bizarre tableau and scrawled slurs at Reagan's house to put the media on the scent of Darren Winter?

Beginning with the fire and the phoned-in racial epithets, the whole plot must have hinged on rousing the sleeping giant of the city's Hispanic vote. Why else would Sabrina go to such extremes to court Jack's endorsement?

From the years that he had known the man, Jack seriously doubted Paulo had the slightest interest in politics. Had he gotten involved not only to raise money to pay for his son's needs but to increase his status in the community? God only knew the high-school dropout loved lording his success over those around him.

Jack tried not to think about the child—Paulo's supposedly autistic son—who would be left without a parent if his father went to jail. Jack tried, too, to put out of his mind the way the combination of love, pride, and ruinous expenses must have pushed his former friend over the line.

Jack punched the ON button of the car's tinny little radio and turned up the volume on his favorite call-in sports show in the hope that it would drown out the turmoil in his mind.

But the top-of-the-hour news he heard was so upsetting that Jack found himself pulling off the road to listen—then taking Sabrina's gun out of his pocket and placing it beside him on the seat.

Chapter Twenty-nine

From inside the trunk, Reagan heard the crunch of leaves and snap of sticks as the old sedan rolled over them. The big sedan rocked over uneven ground before nosing sharply downhill.

The hole she had smashed through the taillight had made a gift of fresher air. But now it brought her something different—a heavy, marshy scent that told her they were coming close to water.

Did he mean to save himself the trouble—and the risk—of killing her directly by driving the car into some pond or bayou? A panicked cry caught in her throat as images played through her mind of the old Ford sinking, its trunk filling with water and no way to escape.

With a fresh surge of adrenaline blasting through her system, Reagan gritted her teeth and bore down on the tire iron's handle. Her back was screaming from her contortions in the cramped space, but it hardly mattered. Unless she broke free within the next few minutes, she knew she would be dead.

Once the car came to a stop, doors opened—first one and then the other. But the breaking glass she heard next was not the splash that she'd expected.

And the fumes that reached her moments later made her gasp with the realization that he didn't mean to drown her. Instead, he had settled on the fate that fueled her nightmares . . .

The death she could not bear to name—not even in her thoughts.

Instinct had warned Jack that even with his 911 call, the police would never locate Reagan in time. The dispatcher had patched him through to an officer who'd advised him to come in and make a statement, but Jack couldn't bring himself to do it—not when there was some chance that he could think of where Paulo might have gone.

Not his house, Jack had figured. No way would Paulo go there with his mama and his kid at home. His Cheap Wheelz outlets didn't seem like such a good bet, either, as all of them were located on highly visible street fronts.

Jack could think of only one other place to try—the garage where he'd picked up the kumquat, the same one Paulo used to keep his rentals on the road. Unlike the storefront locations, the shop was tucked between a warehouse and a high-fenced lot where out-of-service taxis parked. This time of night it was unlikely that anyone would be about—except the black-and-brown-striped pit bulls Paulo kept to guard the place in his mechanics' absence.

Remembering their maniacal barking, Jack had figured only a fool would set foot on Paulo's property alone. Or one seriously desperate man.

Though thoughts of Reagan in that bastard's hands had left Jack plenty desperate, he didn't end up braving the dogs' teeth. Namely because he listened once more to his instinct—the instinct that told him to follow the single taillight that he'd spotted near the garage—the same one that had led him here to this deserted stretch of bayou.

"First, you gotta find the perfect bottle," the Firebug rasped inside Paulo's mind. *"Too hard, and it won't bust when it hits the floor. Too thin, and it explodes on impact with the window, splashing you with fuel mix and burning you to hell."*

Paulo had chosen wisely, proving that he wasn't going to end up like the scarred horror who was his father. Proving that for him, the fire was just another tool, not an addiction that would eventually destroy him.

Yet something had gone wrong—the impact must have killed the wick's flame. So, pulling out his lighter, he moved closer to the car.

Close enough to hear Reagan Hurley's screams from the locked trunk.

"Let me out," she pleaded. "You son of . . . son of a bitch . . . let me . . . out now. *Please.*"

He thought about the way he'd last seen her, how snotty she had been to him . . . and how goddamned beautiful. Still nearly as blond as she had been when they were children.

It occurred to him that out here, in the dark isolation near the bayou, he could find out if the bitch had wheat-gold hair on both ends.

But it was the thought of how her hair would burn that made him harden—and the thought of how her pleas would turn to shrill screams that made him toss the flaming lighter into the backseat of his car.

Chapter Thirty

Even before she felt the heat, Reagan knew the car was burning. Before the first fumes swamped her lungs, she heard the tremendous, deep-voiced *whoosh.*

Dropping the tire iron, she drew her knees toward her chest and felt her soul pull itself into the same fetal position—not so much with the knowledge she was dying, but with the bone-deep understanding that she had squandered the short time she had been given.

Wasted her life in the futile attempt to live out her father's dreams. For years, she had blown off her supervisors' suggestions to enroll in paramedic classes, her obsession with fighting fires blinding her to the fact that she truly enjoyed the medical aspects of her job. She'd shunted aside her own tastes—clinging to a rattletrap heap because Pat Hurley had once admired that year's model, struggling to best more talented opponents in the ring—even buying an old house because it reminded her of the one where her father had been raised. She had pushed away her mother . . .

And turned her back on the only man who had ever seen through her defenses and loved her for herself.

As the temperature surged upward, Reagan's body began its final struggle, her breaths coming noisily in tight, constricted gulps. But though her lungs refused, her mind filled, not with air but with Jack's presence, and she imagined she could speak to him if she tried hard enough.

"You—you were right," she whispered, her vocal cords impossibly tight against the vapors.

She needed him to know it, that he'd been right to tell her what no one else would dare, and right to recognize the secrets she'd been hiding, even from herself. Right to understand that she was more than the tough scrapper she let on.

"I know you're more than just a fighter," he said as she felt his strong arms wrap around her, *"but you can't afford to be less—especially right now."*

The mirage lifted like a flight of doves, and she found herself alone in the suffocating darkness, save for the crackling of the flame and the deep groan of warping metal and—

Was that Jack—the real Jack—she was hearing?

"Reagan!"

Real or not, the sound of her name sent a jolt of pure energy shooting up her spine. What the hell was she doing, waiting for the fire to eat its way into the trunk?

Coughing too hard to call out, she fumbled desperately to find the tire iron she had dropped. Maybe she'd been hallucinating in her terror, but the Jack who'd hugged her to him had been dead right. So she had a softer side? It didn't have to make her any less of a competitor—a warrior when it counted.

If she was going to die here, she was damned well going to go down swinging.

Jack should have known the driver had not simply disappeared so quickly. He should have known that Paulo must be nearby, watching from the trees.

But the sight of flames burned everything from Jack's mind except Reagan. It was all he could do to fumble through the dialing of three digits, then shout the location to the emergency operator as he pulled his rental as close as he dared to the burning vehicle.

Leaping out of his car, he saw that the initial flare had died back. Though a column of black smoke rose, the fire had settled back to feasting on the car's interior. But the heat was still intense enough to drive him back, forcing him to raise his arm to shield his face as he cried out Reagan's name.

Every fiber of his being, every atom, blazed the message that Reagan was still in there—maybe burned to death already.

Get back from it, his better judgment warned him. *Get back or you'll be killed, too, when it blows.*

Yet when the trunk lid suddenly sprang open, he raced toward the inferno, tossing aside self-preservation for that one chance in ten thousand that the woman who owned his heart was still alive.

In the end, it was Reagan's lungs that failed her. Not her courage, not her grit, but the simple lack of oxygen that left her powerless to climb free of the trunk she had forced open.

Her awareness constricted, shrinking to the primal struggle to draw another breath. Her world turned to swirling grayness, maybe from the thick smoke, or perhaps her eyes were going. And mercifully, she felt nothing at all.

Her brain was shutting down now—failing. Resorting to hallucinations of a rescue, of Jack rushing in, his head ducked, of powerful arms lifting her free, strong legs pumping, running. The scene played out like a movie, as if she were looking through a camera from the treetops.

She watched Jack lay her body flat before a pair of shining headlights, watched him tilt her head back and pour his breath into her body.

Stared down as his head pressed to her chest—and traced the progress of a tear trail cutting through the soot that covered his face. And as her vantage spiraled skyward, she saw the figure, too, coming up behind Jack, clutching a branch as thick and solid as a major leaguer's bat.

No!

At the sight of it, her lungs seized, and Reagan felt herself falling. Plunging like a hawk out of the treetops, then tumbling back into herself.

Where she lay coughing. Hurting. Weeping. And fighting to get out the words, as Paulo's arms drew back in preparation for what would surely be a crushing blow to Jack's skull.

"Ja-Jack," she moaned.

"Reagan," Jack cried, pulling her to his chest in an embrace so tight it threatened to choke off her air again. "Oh, God—Reagan, you're alive."

"Behind you!" she barely managed to choke out.

Later, Jack would be called upon a score of times to tell what happened. But he would never find the right words to describe the way knowledge passed between him and Reagan in that instant.

However it happened—whether it was the panic in her voice or a more mysterious force at work— Reagan's warning arced straight to his muscles, so that he let go of her and spun around, his hand already darting for the pocket of his jacket.

His eyes already seeing Paulo's silhouetted form as the branch swung toward his head.

The crack echoed in the clearing, louder than the flames, louder than the approaching sirens and the sounds of Reagan's weeping. But loudest of all, to Jack's ears, came the sound of Paulo Rodriguez crashing to the ground.

And the sound of his death rattle only moments later.

Chapter Thirty-one

Jack raised his voice to speak over Reagan's choked and intermittent wheezing—the most terrifying thing he had ever heard.

"I can wait for treatment, and I'm riding along with her," he told the paramedic, a small man, thin as a whippet and at least as high-strung.

Moving at double-espresso speed, the paramedic ripped open the packaging for a plastic air mask. The assembled police cars, fire trucks, and two other ambulances strobe-lit him in red. "Hurley's one of our own, Doctor. We're doing everything we can. Now if you'll step aside and let an EMT see to your burn . . ."

Though she'd been drifting in and out of consciousness, Reagan raised a shaking, bloody hand and clamped down on the paramedic's forearm. "Please," was all she managed, but it proved sufficient to melt the man's resistance.

"All right," he said. "If that's what you want."

Jack's knuckles were as blistered as Reagan's arm, but he let her hold his hand when all three were settled inside the ambulance. With a mask strapped to her face and a breathing treatment humming, Reagan's eyes closed and her tight grip eased.

Jack shot a worried look at the paramedic, who said, "We're giving her some good meds, and we'll get her to the hospital in no time flat."

As if to underscore the point, the ambulance started, sirens blaring, and the driver called back, "Hold on. It could get a little bumpy until we're back on pavement—and we're not slowing down for anything."

In spite of the crew's haste, Jack knew things could go south quickly if Reagan's airway swelled shut and cut off her oxygen completely. By the time they reached the closest hospital, she could be gone forever, lost to either death or a brain injury so severe it would amount to virtually the same thing.

"You *can't* go," he told her, hot tears scalding his eyes. "Reag, you can't die on me. Because I love you. Because I want to marry you and make a life with you."

The paramedic, who was rechecking her blood pressure, faded from Jack's consciousness. With his attention focused on Reagan's wheezing, he felt a hot tear course down, then drip onto her cheek.

Her eyes fluttered, and she looked up into his face.

"We'll give my mother those *nietos*," Jack swore; "a little boy with your chin and my cowlick, a tiny girl with dark hair and a stubborn streak a mile wide. Can't you see them, Reagan? Can't you see our children in your mind?"

Her eyes flared, and he heard her sharp gasp. Her hand squeezed his hard enough to send pain shooting up his arm.

Was this it? Was she dying?

"She's sounding better," said the paramedic, and

that was when Jack realized that her breathing had quieted, falling below the level of the ambulance's siren.

"Vitals are improving, too," the paramedic added.

Reagan's eyes closed once more, and her tight grip loosened.

Jack gusted out a sigh, his entire body trembling with relief. "Thank God," he said. "The medications must be working."

"I don't know." The paramedic shot a grin his way. "It could just be that bedside manner you've got goin'. If she doesn't marry you, I figure maybe I will."

Jack laughed—when only moments earlier he couldn't imagine ever smiling again.

Though the day had grown cool and Reagan's hospital room felt chilly, Jack's face was sheened with perspiration when he came in the door, as if he'd been rushing to get to her.

Still drowsy from her long nap, she smiled up at him. "Hey, stranger. I was afraid they might have changed their minds about keeping you at police headquarters."

Her throat hurt, and her voice remained hoarse from the combined assaults of smoke and the breathing tube she'd had removed the day before. But she was determined not to fall asleep on him again.

Jack shook his head. "No chance of that. I won't be charged in Paulo's death, and since Sabrina's run off with all that money from the mayor's campaign fund, she's not exactly in a position to file a complaint against me."

Bending down to kiss her cheek, he asked, "How're you feeling?"

"Better. The doctor said my tests look good. There shouldn't be any permanent damage to my airway, and the other injuries are superficial."

"That's wonderful," he told her, and gently squeezed her wrist above the burned spot.

She noticed that like her hands, which had been scraped raw in her efforts to escape, his right hand was bandaged.

"You're hurt," she said. "I didn't notice it yesterday when you were here."

"You didn't notice much of anything. You were still out of it from the medicine they gave you when they scoped your lungs. I wanted to come back later, but the police—"

"That's all right." She was still focused on his bandage. "Did you get that saving me, Jack?"

He smiled. "It's just a little burn, not much of a war wound."

She looked into his dark eyes. "It's everything to me. I love you, Jack. And never again will I hesitate to say it."

The moment stretched between them like a strand of spider's silk.

"Ah, Reag, you had me so damned scared."

"I know. I remember the ambulance, that ride with you."

A slow smile warmed his handsome features. "You heard me? You remember?"

A tap came at the door, and a nurse stuck her head inside. "I have another delivery for you."

"You can bring it in," said Reagan, "but I'm not sure where you'll put it."

Already, her room was packed with fruit baskets and balloon bouquets, even a box of gourmet cookies from the mayor—who was claiming to be as shocked as anyone about his campaign manager's crimes. Not that it much mattered, in terms of tomorrow's election. Since the latest polls were indicating a large-scale—and surprisingly well-organized—Latino voter backlash against Darren Winter's on-air rhetoric, it looked as if Thomas Youngblood was a shoo-in for a second term.

"Oh, I think I can find room," the red-haired woman told her as she carried in a stand-up cardboard cutout of a huge bouquet of flowers. By way of explanation, she said, "When I told him respiratory patients can't have flowers, he left and came back with this instead."

Laughing, Reagan asked, "Who brought it?"

"Here's a note. He made me promise to give it to you personally. I'd love to stay, but I have meds to pass out."

Reagan thanked the woman and opened the sealed note. As she read, tears welled in her eyes, "Oh, Jack. It's from C.W. and the rest of my old crew. Even—even that jackass Beau. Telling me how sorry they are for making me into a scapegoat after Joe's death, for blaming me so they wouldn't have to blame themselves. And asking if I would consider . . . coming back to help them put out fires. C.W. wrote here—"

She had to stop to wipe her eyes. "He's written, 'Even at half speed, you're a damn sight better than most firemen.' *C.W.*" He said that. About me.

Jack shifted in his seat. "So. Will you try to go back?"

Shaking her head, Reagan explained, "I'm putting in for paramedic's training, Jack. It's what I want now, more than anything."

She searched her feelings, but she found no trace of bitterness, only a newfound optimism and a bright, fresh set of dreams. "Or I should say, more than anything but one thing."

"What would that be?" he asked.

"What you said inside that ambulance," she told him. "The future you described. Unless you just felt safe proposing because you figured I'd kick off."

He moved to sit on the bed's edge and wrapped his arms around her. "You're saying you mean to hold me to that?"

Leaning back in his embrace, she smiled into his eyes, "Every last word, Jack Montoya. Every syllable."

Epilogue

Seven months later . . .

Jack pulled on the sunglasses Reagan had bought him this past Christmas, turned up the volume on his favorite CD, and opened the red Explorer's sunroof in homage to the coming weekend and the glorious June day.

He didn't mind the thirty-minute commute home from Fort Bend County. For one thing, he rarely bogged down in traffic, since most drivers were leaving town this time of day and not coming home to Houston. For another, the drive gave him time to unwind from his workday. Though his new position was in a better-funded, less politically vulnerable clinic, he was still confronted with many of the challenges that he had faced in Houston: long hours, uninsured patients—many of whom spoke English as a second language—and poverty, which limited far too many lives. But here, he felt he was making a real difference. After months of meetings with area medical administrators, doctors, and pharmaceutical representatives, he had set up a program to get more drug samples to patients in the greatest need. So far, they were concentrating on making sure that children, especially, received needed medications, regardless of the legal status of their parents.

But this particular Friday evening, Jack wasn't thinking of his job, but of Reagan's new one, which was to start next week. Tonight, he thought, he would take her out for a nice dinner to celebrate the completion of her paramedic's training. Maybe he would even whisk his gorgeous wife to Galveston for a spur-of-the-moment overnight, if Peaches could be talked into dog-sitting.

At a red light, he pulled his cell phone from his pocket, with the intention of calling his and Reagan's neighbor. But before he could start dialing, the phone quacked, a sure sign that Reagan had once again been playing with his ring tones.

Laughing, he answered without glancing at the ID, "Hey, Reag."

"You can save the phone sex. It's me," Luz Maria said excitedly. "I had to tell you—they finally bulldozed it. And I was right there, whistling and cheering."

"They tore down the apartments? That's terrific." Months ago, Las Casitas Village had been condemned due to toxic mold. Working in her new role in a private charity, Luz Maria had been instrumental in relocating the tenants to new and healthier housing over the past months. She had also worked behind the scenes to make sure the buildings would be demolished so crackheads and dangerous criminals would not move into them.

"So what's your next project, now that you've gotten that accomplished?"

"Badgering the mayor and the city council until they

finally make good on their promises to do something about the flooding in the East End."

"If they weren't politicians, I'd almost feel sorry for them, having a professional pest on their case." The phone gave a warning beep and he asked, "Can I call you back? My battery's running down, and I don't have my charger."

"Don't worry about it. I have a hot date tonight."

"Another one?" If he'd ever needed proof his sister had recovered from her ordeal, her burgeoning social life provided it. Though both Sabrina McMillan and many of the principal players in BorderFree-4-All had at last been apprehended, Luz Maria seemed too immersed in her personal whirlwind of activity to care whether her former lover was ever caught.

They wrapped up their conversation just before the phone went dead.

By the time he arrived home, Reagan, dressed in a silver robe, was sitting back with her feet propped on an ottoman and her eyes closed. At the sight of Jack, Frank Lee raised his head from the blue sofa and yawned prodigiously.

"That's quite the welcome home," Jack said. "Rough day with your mother?"

Reagan smiled and stretched. "The woman dragged me from one end of the Galleria to the other. She's still hell-bent on making up for lost time by teaching me the womanly art of combat shopping. And no matter what I do, I can't convince her she doesn't need to pay for all my purchases."

"So other than that battle, how are the lessons coming?"

Rising from her chair, Reagan allowed the robe to slip off one shoulder and flashed him a knowing smile.

"You tell me," she said, her voice as whispery as silk sheets. "I picked this up today at one of those froufrou, girly shops. What do you think? Is it me?"

Grinning, Jack made a show of unbuttoning his shirtsleeves. "Honey, if it's lingerie, you can bet it's you—until it's *off* you, which won't take me five min— What *is* that?"

She had removed the robe, revealing what she wore beneath. In a pale shade of turquoise, the dress would have been quite pretty—except it hung on Reagan like a sack.

"I'm—I'm very sorry," he said carefully, mindful of how sensitive she had been these past few weeks. "But it looks almost like a maternity dress. It really doesn't fit you."

When her eyes lit up, he guessed her news, even before she told him, "But it will, Jack. In just a few months, according to the obstetrician."

"Oh, baby," he said as he took her into his arms and swung her into his embrace.

"Great diagnosis, Doctor," Reagan answered. "Now how about we move on to the bedroom so I can show off that other little number I picked up?"

Coming in May 2006,
more taut romantic suspense from

COLLEEN THOMPSON

THE
DEADLIEST
DENIAL

a special preview

Chapter One

Hardly a day goes by that we don't hear it. On the news and in the papers or from stories passed along by friends or family members. How someone, usually a woman, has been destroyed by a man she loved and trusted. Beaten sometimes. Humiliated, violated, ripped off, and betrayed.

And then there are the times it comes to murder.

But as we chew these stories over, we think of all the ways it might have been, could have been, probably was her fault. Overwhelmed by the sheer volume of examples, we make ourselves feel safer by pointing out the signs the woman missed—or stubbornly refused to recognize. Telling ourselves we would know better and we would be bold enough to face the truth, unlike the foolish creature whose sad fate made the news.

Afterward, we turn back to our own lives, to the same bad habits, poor decisions, and fractured resolutions that we stumble over almost daily. But that's all right, we tell ourselves, feeling superior in the knowledge that we may have our human foibles, but we didn't fall victim to the worst.

As of this day, this moment, we have not yet partaken of the deadliest denial.

The worst day in Claire Winslow's life started early, with a banging at the front door that began at five A.M.

Predictably, the three-legged sheltie Spence had brought home last year barked her fool head off, so Claire's first impulse was to chase the brown-and-white hairball to the condo's living room and stop the noise before it woke the neighbors.

Her second was to stare in horror at the door as a wave of dizziness broke over her and her body trembled like the most damaged of her patients at the rehabilitation center.

Spence was due home from his shift this morning. But her husband would never bother knocking. Instead, he would try to steal in silently—a real feat, considering Pogo's joyful histrionics whenever she spotted her master returning to the fold. On those occasions when he managed to slip past their sleeping pet, he would remove his badge and holster, then rouse his wife of four years with kisses . . . and often something more. Or at least he'd done that up until his friend Dave Creighton's death back in October.

When the hammering was repeated, she let go of the wriggling sheltie and switched on the nearest lamp. Bursting into motion, Claire trotted back into her bedroom and grabbed her robe, her mind stumbling through the thought: If Spence's dead, I'm not letting them tell me while I stand here in one of his old T-shirts.

If Spence's dead . . . God, no.

She pulled the robe around her tighter and told Pogo, "If your dad's just forgotten his keys, I'm going to chew his ears off."

It would serve her husband right, too, for scaring her to death. Every cop knew his wife worried, even if it was the proverbial elephant in the living room they both tiptoed around, the big dread neither dared to speak of.

And now it's gone and happened anyway, she thought as her feet, seemingly detached from her free will, carried her to the door and her traitorous hand fingered the deadbolt.

Pogo quieted, then crouched expectantly on her single foreleg, her body quivering with the need to either bark or wag, depending on who stood behind the still-closed door.

A memory tumbled through Claire's mind: her husband's reminder only last week that this was San Antonio and not her damned wide-spot-in-the-road-of-a-hometown and she'd end up dead as Dave if she didn't watch herself. He'd been furious at the moment, but it was the absolute terror shining in his blue eyes that made her hesitate now, leaning forward to peer through the peephole, her lips moving in a silent prayer: *Be Spence, be Spence, be Spence.*

It wasn't. With a cry, she fumbled through unlatching the chain and releasing the locks, then threw open the door and asked the two uniformed men, "Is he dead? Or in the hospital? Has someone shot my husband? Why are you here? Tell me."

Pogo lowered her crouch and whined plaintively at the pair. Though mismatched both in terms of uniform and appearance, the men stood shoulder to shoulder, their backs as straight as steel spikes and their hats held in their hands.

Claire's gaze bored into the smaller and darker of the two, the newly divorced sergeant she and Spence had had over for dinner just last Sunday. Claire had invited him out of sympathy, but she'd gotten the impression he had accepted to see how Spence was behaving around her. To make sure what was happening at work hadn't leached into their home life.

Now, Raul Contreras shook his head before releasing a long breath through his nose. He looked hard at her, his deep-set brown gaze so sorrowful that she was reminded of the doctor who had told her, years before, that her sister Karen's cancer had spread to the brain.

Claire's pulse thumped wildly. She was going to die, she thought. Her heart was exploding in her chest.

"No," Sergeant Contreras told her. "Spencer hasn't been killed, and he's not hurt either."

At first, she simply stared, unable to move or speak or draw breath. Had she heard him right, or had her mind manufactured the words that she most needed?

Hoping for some clue, she looked to the taller man, whose tan uniform stood out in contrast to the dark blue of the San Antonio PD. His hair was thick and golden brown and long for law enforcement; his features were strong, his shoulders wide and heavily muscled, as if he'd spent his youth alternating between football fields and weight rooms.

But he hadn't. Claire knew that because she knew him—a fact that shocked her. What was Joel Shepherd from her hometown doing here, at her front door?

"Spence isn't dead?" she asked both men. She needed

that confirmation more than she needed answers—or even air to breathe.

"He's not dead," Joel answered, his voice deeper than she remembered, his eyes a golder shade of green. But his expression remained as grim as the day they'd buried Karen—the girl he should have married instead of Lori Beth Walters, one of her sister's classmates. "I swear it."

Closing her eyes, Claire whispered, "Thank God. Thank God. Thank God."

Anything else she could handle. Anything else she could survive.

But she didn't understand that there were worse things. Possibilities too dark to fathom. Possibilities she first heard in the raw emotion of Sergeant Contreras's and Joel Shepherd's questions.

"May—may we come in?" her husband's supervisor asked.

"Can we call someone to be with you?" Joel added, and for the first time she noticed he wore a sheriff's badge, not a deputy's. "How 'bout your daddy, maybe, or a friend?"

He was laying on the good old boy a little thicker, playing up the country lawman comfort in a way that jolted forks of fear through her midsection.

Shaking her head, Claire backed up, pausing only to snatch up the fifteen-pound dog and press her lower face into the thick warmth of Pogo's fur.

All the better not to scream, Claire thought as the two men entered her living room. Joel closed the door softly, but he didn't lock it. Perhaps he felt safe with his gun in its holster, or perhaps he realized, as Claire was beginning to, that the worst had come already.

"Why don't you sit down?" Contreras asked her.

Lifting her chin from the dog's warmth, Claire felt her temper boil to the surface. "And why don't you quit patronizing me and tell me right out—where the hell is Spencer? Why are you two here instead of him?"

The sergeant took another deep breath. "Last night, your husband was arrested."

"He's bein' held in Little Bee Creek, in the Buck County Jail," Joel added. "My jail."

Claire's knees loosened, and the miniature collie yelped in surprise as she was dropped, then tucked her tail between her legs and hop-bounced to escape into the bedroom. Before Claire understood what was happening, the two men grabbed her arms and steered her to an armchair, where they planted her.

Shrugging off their hands, she cried, "That's a lie. Why would you say such—such—Spence can't be in Little BC. He was on patrol last night down on the River Walk. Right here in San Antonio."

She saw the two men's glances meet, saw how troubled both looked. When neither answered, she said, "Damn you. Damn you both—did my husband put you up to this? If this is some sick joke, it's not funny."

Joel sat on the sofa's edge and angled his long legs in her direction. Those green-gold eyes skewered her, reminding her of the cougars rumored to have come back to Buck County. "This is serious, Claire, and so am I. You're going to need somebody with you. Tell me now so I can call. And then we'll explain it to you."

She flipped her red-brown hair free of her robe's collar. "All of it?"

When both men nodded solemnly, Claire relented. "Call my father. Please. He's number two on my speed dial."

Number one was the entry she really wanted.

Spence's number. If she could talk to him, he'd clear up this mistake in no time.

But Joel got up to call her father, then took the telephone into her bedroom and closed the door behind him. She tried to listen, but a buzzing in her ears overwhelmed the distant murmur of his voice.

"My dad's a criminal attorney, and he lives in Little BC," she told Sergeant Contreras. "He'll know how to fix this. He'll probably drive over to the jail and call us right back, tell us it's not Spence in there. Spence is a really good cop—you've told me so yourself. He wouldn't be arrested."

The sergeant took the spot where Joel had been seated and looked at her from beneath the shaggy overhang of his brows. Like his hair and his thick mustache, they were salted with white strands, the only clue the man had recently celebrated his fiftieth birthday.

"I know this is hard," he said. "It's damned hard for me, too, first losing Dave and now. . . . The truth is, Claire, Spencer hasn't been himself lately. You know that as well as I do."

"He saw a twelve-year-old shoot down a fellow cop." Claire heard the strain in her own voice, the bitterness that bubbled through her words—but there was nothing she could do to stop the torrent. "My husband watched his best friend die over a forty-nine-dollar video game."

Mall security, who had called the police once they caught the shoplifter, had brought him to their office, but they hadn't searched his clothes for weapons. When the two uniforms came in, the kid had panicked, whipping a little .38 out from under his untucked shirt, killing Dave and wounding the store detective before Spence shot the boy dead.

"How can you expect him to snap right back like it was nothing?" Claire demanded. "Aside from losing a close friend, Spence loves kids. And now he's killed one."

There had been knee-jerk outrage in the Hispanic community, since the boy was Mexican and Dave, Spence, and the store detective all white, but the store's video surveillance tape had cleared her husband of wrongdoing. Still, he'd asked Claire over and over—sometimes waking her up in the middle of the night—if there was anything, anything, he could have done to save either his friend or the kid. Every time, she'd told him no, then wrapped her arms around a body made unfamiliar by its tension.

"Spencer said he'd had enough time off, enough of counseling," Contreras told her. "And I was keeping a careful eye on him, believe me."

"Not careful enough, it sounds like. Not if he really did leave his patrol to drive over an hour to Buck County last night. I still don't buy it." She expected her husband's big frame to fill the doorway any moment, expected to hear Pogo's cheerful barking to see her master—the man who had once lifted her from a busy street, where he had found her matted and bone thin, with one front leg mangled from a run-in with a car.

"He didn't work last night, Claire. He called in sick before his shift."

The shock of it went through her, and she wanted to scream, *impossible*. Would have screamed, if she could speak. Because she'd kissed Spence good-bye last night and watched him leave wearing his uniform, his badge . . . his gun.

His gun.

"What did he do, Sergeant?" she asked in a small voice.

"We believe he killed a man in Little BC."

She blinked in surprise at Joel Shepherd, who was standing in the bedroom doorway. Sheriff Shepherd. She hadn't noticed him come back from calling her dad. But it was his words and not his presence that made her mouth go dry.

"No," she told him, shaking her head. "Of course he didn't do that. Why would Spence kill anyone up there? I mean, that's where we have our—"

She clamped down on the thought. This couldn't have anything to do with the Little BC property she and Spence had just purchased and the horse therapy center she had been planning, organizing, and raising funds for over the past two years. This had nothing to do with her dream—

The dream that Spence had asked her to put on hold in the days following Dave's shooting.

She'd told him no, she couldn't. She'd tried to make him understand that it was then or never, that if they didn't close on the acreage before Mrs. Hajek moved into the nursing home, her heir would be sure to stop the sale. Already, her realtor nephew—one who hadn't bothered visiting his aunt in years—had accused Claire of taking advantage of a dying woman. If Mrs. Hajek herself hadn't rallied and threatened to disinherit the grasping little snot, Claire was sure the whole thing would have ended up in court. And if the woman's missing daughter, Gloria, had finally turned up . . .

"We aren't sure what this is about," Joel said as he crossed the room to stand beside her. "But we do know this. Adam Strickland wasn't the only person—"

"Adam—Adam who?" The name struck her as familiar, but Claire couldn't seem to place it.

"Adam Strickland," Joel answered, pausing only to clear his throat, "wasn't the only person your husband wanted dead. There was someone else, too."

"Someone else?" She was still trying to make sense of this—or find the key that would unlock this awful nightmare and let her wake up in her bed.

From the bedroom, she heard her alarm clock go off, an alarm meant to begin her last day at the rehabilitation center, where she had worked for the past five years as an occupational therapist.

This is no dream, she told herself as Joel Shepherd knelt before her. No dream, the thought echoed as he took her ice-cold hand in his.

"It was you," Joel told her. "Your husband, Spencer Winslow, was planning to kill you."

FATAL ERROR

COLLEEN THOMPSON

West Texas gossip paints every story a more interesting shade, especially when a married man goes missing with a small-town banker's wife and a fortune in fraudulent loans. Susan Maddox is tired of feeling like an abandoned woman, and even angrier when the neighbors act as if she's the one getting away with murder. Maybe her handsome-as-sin, bad-boy brother-in-law wasn't the smartest choice of ally, but who else could she trust to recover damning information from her husband's crashed hard drive? Who else is there to pick up the pieces when intruders set fire to her home, a truck runs her off the road, and a trail of dead men stops her cold? Who else can help her uncover a . . . FATAL ERROR.

- -

JUDITH E. FRENCH

AT RISK

He has a memento from each of them. Just little things to bring back memories of the shrieks, the blood. What will he take from the Professor, he wonders? She will be best of all, isolated in her old farmhouse by the edge of the swamp. She has no idea which of the men pursuing her she can trust—the handsome grad student, the bad-boy ex-boyfriend, the wheelchair-bound former police officer. She has no idea that while she fantasizes about sultry nights and twisted sheets, very different plans are being made and studied in intimate detail. She has no idea she is at risk. But all that is about to change.

KATHLEEN NANCE

Jigsaw

A car following too close, too fast, left Bella Quintera wrecked by the side of the road. The identity of her rescuer confirms Bella's fears. Years before, Daniel Champlain had been her lover, but the relationship was one she strove to forget. The NSA agent's rugged good looks still haunt her—as does his betrayal.

Now Daniel demands Bella listen. She is in danger. He wants to know about her new creation, about its implications for national security. What she's designed is worth killing for; but is a master criminal truly after her—or is Daniel again pursuing his ambition, thoughtlessly flipping her life upside down? The peril is real, no game like the jigsaw puzzles she makes in her spare time. And this puzzle has missing pieces: the ones that show whom she can trust.

KATHLEEN NANCE

THE WARRIOR

Callie Gabriel, a fiercely independent vegetarian chef, manages her own restaurant and stars in a cooking show with a devoted following. Though she knows men only lead to heartache, she can't help wanting to break through Armond Marceux's veneer of casual elegance to the primal desires that lurk beneath.

Armond returns from an undercover FBI assignment a broken man, his memories stolen by the criminal he sought to bring in. His mind can't remember Callie or their night of wild lovemaking, but his body can never forget the feel of her curves against him. And even though Callie insists she doesn't need him, Armond needs her—for she is the key to stirring not only his memories, but also his passions.

___52417-1 $5.99 US/$6.99 CAN

TIGER EYE

MARJORIE M. LIU

He looks completely out of place in Dela Reese's Beijing
hotel room—like the tragic hero of some epic tale, exotic
and poignant. He is like nothing from her world, neither his
variegated hair nor his feline yellow eyes. Yet Dela has
danced through the echo of his soul, and she knows this
warrior would obey.

Hari has been used and abused for millennia; he is jaded,
dull, tired. But upon his release from the riddle box, Hari
sees his new mistress is different. In Dela's eyes he sees a
hidden power. This woman is the key. If only he dares
protect, where before he has savaged; love, where before
he's known hate. For Dela, he will dare all.

EVELYN ROGERS
More Than You Know

Toni Cavender was the toast of Hollywood. But when a sleazy producer is found brutally murdered, the paparazzi who once worshipped Toni are calling her the prime suspect. As a high-profile trial gets under way, Toni herself finds it hard to separate fact from fiction.

When an unmarked car tries to force Toni off a cliffside road on a black, wet night, the desperate movie star hires detective Damon Bradley to find the truth. Someone is out to destroy her. Someone who knows the lies she's told . . . even the startling reality that lying in Damon's arms, she feels like the woman she was destined to be. Yet Toni can trust no one. For she has learned that hidden in the heart of every man and woman is . . . *More Than You Know.*
